VAST STORMS OF UNPRECEDENTED
SAVAGERY AND IMMENSE SNOWFALLS
ENGULF THE UNITED STATES IN

THE SIXTH WINTER

The evacuation of Chicago was a gamble—a gamble
that had been undertaken only because the scale of
death in some areas had become disastrously high.
In icy, unheated apartments, families literally froze
to death, and the very young and old suffered from
growing hunger. The supermarkets held food, but
the difficulty of getting to them often outweighed the
advantage.

Medical teams, in cleared spaces in the snow, fought
to save those who were lucky enough to reach them
or be brought to them. But there could not be enough
medical teams for a road packed with hundreds of
thousands of refugees heading west in a blizzard.
Things were going wrong. By the second day, many
of the groups of people beside the road were no
longer waving. They were indistinguishable heaps in
the snow, already dead.

Also by Douglas Orgill
Published by Ballantine Books:

ARMORED ONSLAUGHT

LAWRENCE OF ARABIA

THE
Sixth
Winter

—————

DOUGLAS ORGILL
AND JOHN GRIBBIN

BALLANTINE BOOKS • NEW YORK

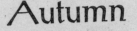

All characters in this book are imaginary, except those whose names are already celebrated in the chronicles, past and present, of science.

Library of Congress Catalog Card Number: 79-19297

ISBN 0-345-29242-1

This edition published by arrangement with
Simon and Schuster

Manufactured in the United States of America

First Ballantine Books Edition: March 1981

PROLOGUE

The watcher crouched in the stony outcrop above the lake, shifted his 120 pounds of weight, and braced his clawed feet against the rocks, staring intently before him. Half a mile away, alternately swelling and receding against the sparse yellow scrub of the tundra, a brown cloud of animals drifted slowly nearer. From over to the east, where a glittering blue tongue of water ended in a wilderness of stunted alder and ash, the watcher on the rocks could hear the bellowing of beasts and a steady thumping and splashing as the first caribou plunged into the shallow water, half walking, half wading, and made for the southern bank. The caribou were much nearer now, and the watcher flicked his long tongue over his black lips as the leaders of the herd struggled out of the mud of the inlet and trotted away down the gully in front of him. There were hinds among them and very young fawns, some of them barely able to keep up with the steady thrust of the herd. These he observed closely.

The wolf was at the very edge of his territory. He had marked it with his strong yellow urine ten weeks before, and no other had yet presumed to cross it. But what was happening in front of him was something completely new in his experience, and he sought to take advantage of it. Turning abruptly, he moved off at an easy lope, five or six miles an hour, keeping parallel with the herd, making no attempt at concealment. Ahead was a long shallow defile, cut deep into the permafrost of the tundra of the Canadian Northwest Territories by the grinding of a glacier long ago. The leaders of the caribou were already pouring into it in a heaving forest of antlers, followed by the hinds and the stumbling fawns, when the wolf stopped in a patch of high scree, threw back his head, and howled.

Almost two miles away, the wolf-howl came as a whisper, the merest thread of sound, to the man who was carefully dismantling and cleaning his binoculars on the table in a little hut set in a meandering belt of green

3

spruce beside one of the small streams that fed Lake Ennadai. He crossed to the dusty window and looked up the long bare hill, whistling in surprise. A man was slithering down the muddy slope in front of him. He wore a faded tartan lumber jacket over a red shirt and thick tweed trousers. His face was broad and flat, his hair lank, black. He carried a hunting rifle, and the pack of a radio transmitter was humped on his back. The white man in the hut went to the doorway as he approached.

"What the hell!" he said. "You're back early, Atahoo. I didn't expect . . ."

"Radio no good," said the Eskimo briefly. "I came to tell."

"Tell what?"

"*Tuktu*," said Atahoo, pointing beyond the swell of the far ridge. "*Tuktu-mie*—the caribou Host."

"What, the Host?" said the white man incredulously. He jerked his thumb at the cloudless blue of the sky. "Migrating now? Never . . ."

"*Tuktu-mie*. Soon you will see."

"How many?"

"Here . . . twenty score, perhaps thirty score. Beyond them, I think, many."

"Only 500? Well, that's not the Host, is it? Just a bit of it that's gone crazy, I guess."

"It is the beginning," said Atahoo. He crossed to the cupboard at the end of the little living room and took out a belt of cartridges. "There was a wolf . . ."

"I heard him," said the other thoughtfully. "But . . ."

"And you have heard that before?" asked Atahoo, his voice heavy with irony. "You have heard a wolf give the caribou-call when the Host is not moving?"

"But, damn it, it's so early," said the white man. "You must be wrong."

From beyond the ridge came once more that long stretched thread of sound.

"The wolf is not wrong," said Atahoo.

4

CHAPTER 1

William Stovin walked down in the warm sunshine through the campus, along the smooth paths between lawns that the sprinklers fought to keep green, across the traffic of Roma, across Lomax, past the brown bulk of the Physics-Astronomy Department, past the outdoor tables where the students sat and read and argued and drank Cokes, and then out to the bus stop beside the Journalism Building.

He'd timed it correctly, as he always did, and the Rio Grande bus came down the wide boulevard a few seconds after he reached the stop. He climbed up onto the step, bought his ticket, and absently watched the untidy sprawl of hotels and motels and gas stations, superstores and dusty trees of downtown Albuquerque roll past his window.

He left the bus beside a vast concrete superstore and walked into the tourist-thronged shadows of the Old Town. There was a Spanish cannon in the square opposite the Church of San Felipe, which he always gave a surreptitious, superstitious pat. He did it again today and then crossed the square to his usual restaurant for lunch. He sat in a ladder-backed Spanish chair at the table they kept for him on this day of the week, opposite the big wallpainting of Don Juan de Onate, who'd been the first colonizer of New Mexico in 1598. He looked at his watch. Diane wasn't here yet. Well, no surprise in that, although he wished she were. She often mocked him, that he was a creature of habit. Maybe, maybe. He liked routine, he thought to himself, half ruefully. Routine gave his mind a chance to get on with something more important. When the waitress came, dark, shining haired, peasant faced and plump in her white blouse and gold-belted red skirt, he smiled at her and said he'd wait.

He pulled from his briefcase the Lithman Report, although he already knew it almost by heart. It backs up

Eddy, he said to himself for the hundredth time. And by God, it backs up me. It was all there, double-checked, amplified even—the Sporer Minimum, the Maunder Minimum. And now, what? The Stovin Minimum. Just take a look at Lithman's tree rings alone. We're getting to the point, he thought, when we can't any longer go on adding two and two and still make three and a half.

Supposing the Maunder Minimum and the Sporer Minimum and the Stovin Minimum weren't anomalies at all? Supposing that the last 15,000 years—with odd deceiving Maxima, like that period in the thirteenth century, for instance, when the English grew wine in Kent—supposing the interglacial of the last 15,000 years was the anomaly? Fifteen thousand years was no more than an eyeblink in geological time. Yet practically the whole of human civilization had taken place in that eyeblink. He pushed his left fist into his right palm and stared moodily at Don Juan de Onate. If only they'd had enough sense to . . .

"Hi, Stovin."

Diane Hilder was standing behind his chair, smiling down at him, a short, chunky square-shouldered girl in old corduroy jeans and a pink shirt under a scuffed leather waistcoat, her platinum-streaked blonde hair in its usual disarray. He felt a stab of pleasure as he got awkwardly to his feet and pulled out her chair.

"I thought you'd stood me up."

"Never stand up a good lunch, Stovin. That's what Mom always told me."

"Sensible woman."

The waitress came and they ordered—for him, the meal he invariably ate: chicken enchiladas, rice, red sauce, half a liter of white wine; for her, cheese and a salad. She poured herself half a glass of his wine and stared critically at his plate.

"Don't you ever get tired of that stuff? Heaven knows what it does to your stomach."

He shrugged. "I've told you before, Diane, it doesn't bother me. It saves a lot of hassle. Thursday is enchilada day. I don't have to waste time thinking about it. And what you've got there"—he nodded toward her salad—"wouldn't feed a chipmunk."

"Well, I have to think about *my* stomach," she said, laughing, and patting it briskly. "I put on two pounds last month."

6

"Horrifying," he said, grinning. She looked at him under her lashes as he carefully cut into his enchilada. He wasn't the kind to put on weight, anyway; that kind of ageless, compact Englishman never did. Oh, yes, he was American now, of course, but he was still English in everything but his citizenship papers. How old was he? It was somewhere in the campus records, she supposed, but she'd never looked it up. Forty? Forty-five? With Stovin, it was hard to tell. And why did she call him Stovin, anyway? Everybody else called him Sto. He disliked "William" almost as much as she did. But it was nice, the way he . . .

"How's *canis latrans?*"

"Thriving," she said. "Still plenty around. I came down from the Pecos this morning—I've been up there above Chico for the last three days—and there was a big one, dead by the road. Hit by a truck last night, I guess. It's in the back of the pickup."

She nodded toward the car parked on the edge of the square.

"You loaded the corpse of a full-grown coyote into the back of your pickup? He must have weighed forty pounds."

"She," said the girl. "*It* was a female. No, I guess I was lucky. A State trooper came by and he helped."

She imitated a deep Texas drawl. " 'Say, ma'am, you know what you can get from these things. Fleas, ma'am, fleas. You understand that, ma'am?' You should have seen his face when I told him fleas were exactly what I wanted."

"Why don't you just shoot a coyote or two?" asked Stovin impatiently. "God knows, it isn't exactly an endangered species."

"Not yet, it isn't," she said flatly. "But, my goodness, we're working on it, aren't we? No, Stovin, I don't kill unless I have to."

"Have it your own way," he said indifferently. Absently, his hand stroked the pink cover of the Lithman Report. She did not miss the movement.

"What do you have there?"

"Lithman."

His voice was too expressionless to be truly casual, she thought. She looked at him curiously. "And you're all het up about it, aren't you? What's he say?"

7

Stovin shrugged. "Pretty much what I say. What I've been saying for the last three years."

She whistled. "Lithman . . . ? He's the man who . . ."

"That's right," he said tonelessly. "He was wrong about the volcano cycle. He exaggerated the dust factor. He's been wrong before. Like I have. Like Einstein was. Like Copernicus was. And they'll say he's wrong again. . . ."

"And is he?"

"No."

"It's a pity," she said reflectively, "that Lithman's so old. People don't listen to old men anymore."

Stovin laughed and sipped his wine. "Well, he isn't going to get any older."

"What do you mean?"

"Lithman's dead . . . heard it on the nine o'clock newscast this morning. He was eighty-seven—just about the most original climatologist in the world. That's what they'll call him, anyway. It's a sort of put-down. A guy who's as original as that must be wrong."

She looked at him, troubled. "Where does that leave you?"

"Oh," he said, more cheerfully, "I'll carry the banner. Though I'm not a young man, exactly."

"Nobody," she said, "thinks of you as old or young or even middle-aged." And that's the truth, she thought.

Stovin called for the bill. She watched him fish in his pocket for a pile of crumpled dollars. Why in hell didn't he use a credit card like everybody else?

"Stick to coyotes," he said as they walked to the door. She offered her cheek. Briefly, he brushed his lips against her. It felt like being kissed by a tortoise.

"You know where you are with coyotes," he said. "Mind you . . ."

"Mind you what?"

"Well," he said, smiling, "if Lithman's right, it's a whole new future for coyotes."

He watched her stride off across the Plaza. She smelled nice, he thought irrelevantly. He always liked that little kiss. But he mustn't, mustn't get to like it too much.

He walked across the square, past the brass cannon, and into the cool shade of the Church of San Felipe. It was quiet there—one of the few places down here where he could think. Outside in the little walled garden, doves cooed. Candles flickered; the altar was piled high with flowers. Only two lamps were lit, and he sat in a light brown wooden pew in the half-darkness and looked around him. Superstitious nonsense, all of it, of course. It could all be demolished with three or four unanswerable questions. And the chief one was: If God existed, what the hell was He playing at? But San Felipe was a healing sort of place, nevertheless. It was a quarter of an hour before he went out again.

Back in his room at the University, he took the Lithman Report from his briefcase. He read it through again swiftly, economically. Then he crossed to his desk, took the black plastic cover off the portable typewriter and, with two fingers, began to type.

CHAPTER 2

Like a gigantic dragonfly, its four stubby opaque wings outspread, Big Bird cruised along the line of the 64th parallel, high above the great Ob River of northwestern Siberia. Three minutes ago, it had reached the bottom point of its periodic low-orbital pass. A relay closed. The hoods over the lenses of the still cameras below the cylindrical twelve-ton fuselage drew back, and Big Bird began—in obedience to the preprogrammed order of those who had dispatched it from a launchpad at Point Arguello on the Californian coast—to photograph the Soviet oilfield installations sprouting out of the Siberian *taiga* wilderness between Igrim and Berezovo, ninety miles below.

In a few seconds, the task was done. Three more relays closed. The long winged tube of Big Bird adjusted its flying angle and moved out to the end point of its orbit, 198 miles above the earth. Forty-eight hours later, the films it had exposed above the River Ob, snug now in six heatproof canisters, shot from an ejection hatch, entered the earth's atmosphere, opened their parachutes and drifted steadily down through a dawn sky to the blue Pacific north of Hawaii. They were the most significant photographs any satellite had ever taken. They brought the evidence of a new age.

9

A copper-colored butterfly beat vainly at the window above Yevgeny Soldatov's desk, as he watched it for a few moments. *Hippothoe,* he thought absently. What was the local name for it? The Farewell Butterfly. Some Siberians called it the Farewell because it lingered on until the end of the brief Siberian summer. And who'd told him that? Valentina, of course. She'd probably be interested. He'd tell her when he went home at lunchtime.

He looked out through the silver birches and larch trees of Akademgorodok. The pink brickwork of the other wing of the Katukov Complex glowed through the trees. A couple of student-researchers, a young man and woman, walked hand in hand through the dappled shadows. With a sigh, Soldatov turned back to his desk. He picked up the paper he had been reading when the butterfly arrived. Now if indeed the dust in the cores from Krasnogorsk could be related to the Ostashkov climax 23,000 years ago, surely there must be . . .

The telephone on the side of his desk emitted a single brief peal. He picked it up and spoke, "This is Soldatov."

The voice at the other end sounded hurried, breathless. It was a voice he knew—that of Andrei Bulavin, a senior climatologist at Yakutsk.

"Yevgeny—I'm glad you're there. Listen . . . it's happened again."

"Where?"

"A place called Ziba. Up in the northeast—a little place nobody's ever heard of. It's got some sort of fish processing plant—part of the local Plan. A population of about 800—900 perhaps."

"What happened."

"Exactly the same as at Kal'ya."

"And were there any . . . ?"

"Yes, there were, Yevgeny. It wasn't nice. It hit a school bus. They haven't got any of them out yet. Apparently the school is by a lake, about three miles out of Ziba. Luckily they've got a bit of an influenza outbreak there, and the bus was only half-full. So it could have been worse. . . ."

"You say it was exactly the same?"

"As far as we can make out. There was a man who saw it—he was on the very edge, but he doesn't make much sense. He was badly shocked."

10

"And it was quite local—I mean, it didn't affect the whole area?"

"Well, we don't have much information yet. I rang you immediately because those were the instructions. But certainly, we've still got normal communications with Ziba. So it can't be too widespread."

"Where are you now?"

"At Yakutsk—at the Institute."

"I think I'd better come up and have a look. Expect me tomorrow. I'll ring you later as soon as I can arrange a flight. . . ."

Carefully, thoughtfully, Yevgeny Soldatov put into a large blue folder all the papers from his desk. He crossed to the wall safe and locked them away.

Then he went out of the Complex, shivering a little as a sudden breath of icy air trembled the sunlit branches of the birches. It's early for winter, he thought ruefully. A glint of copper caught his eye on the hard brown ground. It was the butterfly, and it was dead. He went on down to the car park and drove home to Valentina.

Eight-and-a-half-thousand miles from Akademgorodok, Frank Rhind drove steadily along Highway US 16. He had left Rapid City two hours ago and was now well into the long climb to the Black Hills of South Dakota. It was snowing hard—they'd be skiing early in the Black Hills this year. The crisp brush of his wheel-chains on the patchy surface of the road had a curiously sleep-inducing effect. There was little other traffic—an occasional big long-distance truck, moving east on the other lanes toward Rapid City and Pierre, but hardly anything on his side of US 16. To keep himself awake, he began to work out his possible arrival time. He was now about eighteen miles from the Wyoming State Line. From there it was around 100 miles on to Gillette, and a bowl of Cathy's special soup, and the evening TV. He might even get to see the kids. Say, three more hours, because he couldn't make more than about thirty-five miles to the hour in these conditions.

An emergency diversion sign came up just after the Pringle slip road. He would barely have seen it through the snow, but there was a State police car parked beside it, red warning lights flashing, and the huddled trooper in the driver's seat raised a gloved hand as Frank Rhind went by.

11

He glanced down at the map on the front passenger seat. With luck, this diversion shouldn't be more than a mile or two. Probably just some temporary trouble—a jackknifed truck, maybe—on US 16. There was a tiny place ahead called—he picked up the map and stared at the small print under the glow of the dash—Hays. Hays, that was it. He didn't know it, and he guessed it wouldn't be more than a few houses and a gas station, but there *was* another little road from it, going back to US 16. So that might well be the end of the diversion. He drove on.

It was becoming colder. Even in the car, with the heater full on, he could feel a deepening chill. The snow was packing more and more heavily against the windshield, coming steadily out of a white-yellow sky. A few miles later, the scattered half-dozen lights that were presumably Hays could be glimpsed through the swirling flakes in the late afternoon gloom. Goddammit, if this got worse, he wasn't going to see Cathy or the kids tonight. Was there a motel in Hays? It seemed a mighty long bet, but he might have . . .

Something came over the long dark ridge behind Hays, like nothing he had ever seen, nothing he had remotely imagined. It was a white twisting column, towering into the sky, apparently solid against the driving snow through which he saw it, and moving at tremendous speed toward the scattered lights barely a mile away. Even through the closed windows of the car, Rhind could hear its dull unceasing roar. The lights of Hays vanished as though extinguished by a master switch. Whirling, the white column reared above the place where they had been and then moved steadily away, vanishing over the ridge toward the Black Hills.

In his stupefaction at the sight, Rhind had stopped the car. Suddenly he became aware that he was deadly cold, and that the engine was silent. He pressed the starter. It was twenty minutes before he could start the engine again, although the snow had now ceased. The diversion road was narrow, and he didn't risk the turn. He drove on, alone, to Hays. Or rather, to where Hays had been half an hour before. There was a bridge outside Hays and beyond it a wall of snow. It must be, he thought desperately, fifty feet high. Maybe more. And there was no Hays. The road ended beyond the bridge cut off by the snow wall. Terrified of sliding off the road, he managed

12

to turn the car and then saw something else. At the edge of the snow wall, an extraordinary ice formation like an upward-thrusting icicle sprouted from the ground. He drove to the side of it and opened the car window.

It was a woman. At least, he thought it was a woman. She seemed to be entombed in the column of ice, standing upright on the road. The refraction of the ice made it impossible to see her face clearly, but it seemed to be turning toward Hays. Frank Rhind wanted to drive on and away from the snow wall, but he did not lack courage. Hunching his shoulders against the piercing cold, he went around to the trunk of the car and took out his biggest spanner. With it, he beat and beat and beat again at the ice enclosing that still figure. It was like hammering at granite. At last, with a sob, he got back into the car and drove carefully back to US 16.

The State trooper was still there, huddled in his seat. He looked up as Frank drew alongside. It was a long time before he could make sense of what he was told, but there was one phrase that Frank Rhind used which he was to remember and repeat for the rest of his life.

"But what was it like?" he had asked Rhind. "What did it look like? Listen, I'll have to make a radio call. I'll have to know exactly what it looked like . . ."

And Rhind had looked up at him for a moment without speaking.

"I guess," he said at last, "it was like God. Only it wasn't any God that I've ever learned about."

RECIPIENT: *President of the United States (one)*

COPIES FOR INFORMATION: *Members, National Science Council (five); Dr. William F. Stovin, Visiting Professor (Climatology) University of New Mexico (one)*

AUTHOR: *Melvin H. Brookman*

AFFILIATION: *Chairman, National Science Council: Director, Connecticut Institute of Technology*

PRESENTATION: *Extract from Technical Report 66/ 10/8, from the Office of the Chairman of the National Science Council to the President of the United States*

TITLE: *Recurrence of Blocking High Conditions in Climatic Fluctuations*

ONE   *With reference to your Minute 88, the attached interpretative outline may be of some use to you.*

TWO   *Since the 1940s, the globe has been cooling down, with a fall in average temperatures now reaching more than one-half degree Centigrade.*

THREE   *This change is not of great concern in itself, since yearly, seasonal, and even daily fluctuations cover a bigger range in temperature than this.*

FOUR   *However, there are now noticeable increases in snow and ice cover at high latitudes in the northern hemisphere. These, combined with the cooling, are producing a recurrence of so-called "blocking high" conditions, which cause extreme weather conditions to persist for months at a time in many parts of the northern hemisphere.*

FIVE   *Weather at the latitudes of North America, Europe, and the U.S.S.R. is dominated by the guiding hand of the jet stream, circling the globe from west to east at high altitude. In warm decades, such as those prior to 1950, this jet follows an almost perfect*

14

circle around the globe. At the same time, it pushes with it a succession of weather systems: rain, followed by a dry spell, more rain, and so on. But when the atmosphere cools, the jet stream becomes more erratic, swinging in zigzags, first north and then south, and becoming very weak and susceptible to disturbance caused by sea temperature and by snow and ice on land and sea.

SIX. Recent severe weather conditions in North America and elsewhere are a result of this weaker, more erratic pattern of windflow. High pressure building over the southwestern United States seaboard, aided by ocean temperature conditions, zigzags the jet stream so that it is too weak to push the "blocking high" system away. A dominant flow from northwest to southeast is established across the whole of the United States east of the Rockies, encouraging the southward flow of the jet stream and cooling a great area of ocean south of Newfoundland. The severe United States winters of 1977 and 1978 marked the return of this pattern as a common feature after more than 100 years of relatively equable weather.

SEVEN This fall in sea temperature helps to produce a new bend in the jet stream, allowing a "blocking high" system to become established in the region of the British Isles.

EIGHT In winter, this can produce severe snowfalls and extreme frosts over the whole of Britain. In summer, the same "blocking high" will produce severe droughts. The British and north European summer of 1976 is the classic example.

NINE Should such a pattern of jet-stream zigzags and "blocking high" conditions recur over five or six reasonably closely spaced winters with summer sunshine insufficient to melt all the snow from each preceding winter, this may quite rapidly build snow

15

cover over the northeastern part of North America beyond the point of no return.

TEN   At the same time, "blocking highs" farther to the east may similarly build snow cover over the northern U.S.S.R.

ELEVEN   It is, of course, my duty to inform you that this is one of several models now being postulated as being the final trigger for Ice Age conditions.

TWELVE   I cannot emphasize too strongly that it is premature to draw any such dramatic conclusions from the present run of rather unusual conditions with recurrent "blocking highs."

CHAPTER 3

"It is just possible it's some kind of weapon?" asked the President of the United States. He looked out from his desk in the Oval Room of the White House, the red-white-and-blue flag with its fifty-two gold stars behind him, toward the half-circle of faces of the five men and women who made up his National Science Council and the single "guest" they had invited to meet him. The National Science Council, he thought wryly, was his own creation. It had begun as an election gimick three years ago —a political gesture to reassure intellectual America that Science would now receive the same place in the presidential pecking order as Defense. The National Science Council ranked, ostensibly at least, with the National Security Council. But scientists, it seemed, disagreed with each other even more than did the military. And a layman understood their arguments even less.

"Could this be a weapon?" he asked again. "These shots"—he tapped a pile of glossy photographs on his desk—"the ones taken by that cruise satellite—what was it, Big Bird?—well, they show it happening in an out of the way, lonely part of Siberia, just where they might try something out, I guess. And now, suddenly, it starts happening here. Twice in Alaska and now in Dakota. Have they got something going for them over there? Some way of producing freak storms, say? By golly"—it was a cautious expletive he had learned long ago from Dwight Eisenhower—"by golly, that could be tricky."

Opposite the President, Melvin Brookman, chairman of the Council, stirred uneasily. Politicians, he thought. . . they always dream in weapons. But surely this wasn't. . .

"I think not," he said decisively. "What do you say, Sto?"

The President turned his pale blue eyes to the guest who sat at the tip of the left-hand horn of the Science Council's half-circle. So this was Stovin, the wild man that some of them—privately, individually, and of course confidentially—had warned him against. Well, he wasn't a young man, which was one point in his favor. The President was becoming tired of thrusting young men who knew how to put the world right and couldn't wait to get started. He looked at Stovin again, at the thin lines of the mouth, the studied lack of expression on the face, the slight stoop to the narrow shoulders, the right index finger slowly tapping the palm of the left hand. There seemed to be a lot of tension there.

"I agree," Stovin said quietly. "It isn't a weapon."

Nine out of ten men, thought the President, would have gone on to say what, in their opinion, it *was*. But not this one. He had to be asked.

"Then what is it?" asked the President gently.

Stovin stirred, speaking almost, it seemed, unwillingly. "Did you read Melvin's 'blocking high' report, Mr. President?" He nodded toward the bulky form of the chairman of the Council, three seats away.

"I did, Dr. Stovin."

"What did you think of it?"

"I think I asked *you* the first question," said the President.

For the first time, Stovin smiled. "I asked you that, Mr. President, only because I think that the phenomenon we're talking about—the kind of thing that's just killed nineteen people in that Dakota township, Hays—is a spin-off, on a small concentrated scale, from the kind of jet stream changes that Mel Brookman is talking about. A sharp change in air pattern, a concentration of cold—

17

something we've never seen before, although Peary once reported something not unlike it from the North Pole."

"Unreliable eye-witness stuff, from an explorer, not a scientific observer," said the woman next to Stovin, dismissing it. "That's not evidence."

Surreptitiously, the President glanced down at the seating plan on the desk in front of him. This was a new one—her first meeting—Dr. Ruth Wakelin, marine biologist, CalTech. Must have been quite a looker once, with that hair and those eyes. The other three were men —Donleavy the agronomist, Chavez the botanist from Berkeley, Breitbarth—the President looked down once more at his seating plan. Yes, he was an anthropologist. Like Wakelin, first time here.

"Well, if anybody any of us loved happened to be inside one of those coffins at Hays," said the President mildly, "I guess we'd think there was evidence of something."

He turned to Stovin. "Do you think it'll happen again, Dr. Stovin?"

"I'm sure it will. But that isn't in itself important."

"It's killing people, Dr. Stovin. That's important."

Stovin shrugged. "Weather kills people every day. Drought, floods, ice, sun, cold, fog. . . they're all potential killers. We're used to them, so we take them for granted. But we're bothered about this because it's new. And I believe it's so new that it's something man has never recorded since he became man. Something that isn't in our history books. What happened at Hays— and what those photographs show happened also at Ziba—will happen again. Maybe worse."

"Worse?"

"These . . . phenomena . . . may increase in scale. They could hit a city. Suppose they hit Reykjavik . . . or Aberdeen . . . or Murmansk . . . or Seattle? There could be thousands dead. But that still wouldn't be important, Mr. President, in terms of what we're here to discuss."

"We seem to have different ideas as to what is important, Dr. Stovin."

Stovin's right index finger, the President noticed, was once more rhythmically tapping his left palm.

"What is important, Mr. President, is not what these phenomena mean in terms of local effects but what they mean ultimately. What they—to use a portentous word

—portend. And that's something which none of us here —none of us scientists, not you, or the Prime Minister of Britain, or the President of France, or the German Chancellor—is able fully yet to grasp."

"Except you, yourself, Dr. Stovin?" said the President. There was an embryonic, swiftly aborted giggle from the woman biologist. Stovin did not smile.

"I myself least of all, Mr. President. I'm a man who's pushed a door a fifth of the way open and is staring out into fog. I might be better off if I hadn't pushed the door at all. At least, I believed that, until the last few months. I thought that maybe I could live my life and die and let those who come after me deal with their own problems. Now I'm sure I can't. I'm only forty-one, Mr. President. I've got too much time left."

Melvin Brookman shifted uncomfortably in his seat. Stovin was always the same, he thought. For such a self-contained man, he generated a surprising amount of drama.

"To use your own word, Sto, this is all a shade portentous," he said. "Mr. President, I asked Dr. Stovin to join us this afternoon because he represents a point of view. It's pretty much his own point of view, though I guess he won't object if I say that parts of it, at least, he shares with other people. Parts of it"—Brookman smiled—"he shares with me."

"But I gather, Dr. Stovin," said the President, "that you do not share the view expressed by Dr. Brookman in Paragraph Twelve of his Technical Report?"

"No," said Stovin. "I do not believe that such a conclusion is premature. I believe it is overdue."

"Overdue in what sense? What exactly are you putting forward?"

Stovin was now looking at the President as though nobody else was present. "What I'm putting forward is so big that it cannot be fully comprehended," he said. "I'm putting forward things that have already happened—increased variability of weather in general, more droughts, more floods, more hot summers, more cold winters. At first, that is.

"I'm putting forward a quickening shift of climatic, agricultural, and rainfall zones toward the equator. Some of it's already with us, as you yourself, sir, know better than most . . . the southern edge of the Sahara drying out, droughts in Ethiopia, failure of the monsoon

19

in northwest India, all bringing famine to those areas. And late spring and early autumn frosts hitting crops at high altitudes, especially Canada and the Soviet Virgin Lands in Siberia, but even in Florida—of all places— and more than once in the last few years.

"I'm also putting forward extraordinary changes in the migratory patterns of birds, animals, fish. If you doubt this, Mr. President, ask your wildlife people about the caribou, the Monarch butterfly, the armadillo. And if it's more 'evidence' you're demanding, Dr. Wakelin"— he swung so sharply to the woman beside him that she flinched involuntarily—"then what about the cod? You know that cod are moving south from 'traditional' Icelandic grounds into the new British 200-mile limit. Cod are a cold-water fish, but they don't like it as cold as it is around Iceland now. Do you ever ask yourself why?"

Ruth Wakelin said nothing, and after a pause Stovin went on. "Now we have the Lithman Report."

Brookman stirred. "You may remember, Mr. President, that Lithman died last week."

"Lithman," said Stovin, "was the leading investigative climatologist in the United States. For the last fourteen years, he'd been working on a tree called the bristlecone pine in New Mexico. Bristlecones are trees that live for centuries, and you can trace known climatic fluctuations with surprising accuracy by measuring the tree rings. It's a complicated process, but it works. In many parts of the world, it's the only accurate record we have of the climatic past."

"And?" said the President.

"If you look at the pattern of the immediate past, you can often predict the immediate future," said Stovin. "Lithman's tree rings are absolutely clear. They point to the imminence of a climatic situation approximately three times more intense than that of the middle of the seventeenth century, when Londoners roasted oxen on the Thames. That period's since been called the Little Ice Age. But this one isn't going to be so little."

"And when does it begin?"

"It's begun. Look at Baffin Land. Nearly all this century, Baffin Land has had no snow in summer. Now it's permanently snow covered. The winter of 1972 was the turning point—just a few months, the merest fraction of a second on a geological time scale. But in that time, permanent snow-and-ice cover increased by 12 percent all over the northern hemisphere. And it didn't melt away the next summer."

"We've all read the Kukla-Matthews conclusions, Sto," said Brookman. "There's a lot of argument as to their validity."

"There was a lot of argument when Galileo said the earth moved around the sun," said Stovin. "But it turned out that it *did* so move."

"What exactly are the Kukla-Matthews conclusions?" asked the President mildly. "It seems I'm alone in not having read them."

"They're views put forward by two climatologists that we're on the brink of a sharp and rapid change," said Brookman. "George Kukla—he's been working at Lamont-Doherty in New York—has actually said that six more winters like 1972, spaced fairly close together, could mean a return in the northern hemisphere to the conditions of 20,000 years ago. To give you some idea of what he's talking about, Mr. President, that was a period when what is now Chicago was a mile under the ice. Farfetched, I thought when he said it. And still do."

The President poured a glass of ice water from the jug on his desk and drank slowly.

"A mile under the ice?" he said at last. "You must be joking. All I ever understood about this kind of thing was that it was a mighty slow business. Isn't it something that takes centuries?"

Stovin leaned forward and began to speak. He was speaking faster than usual, and there was a slight edge of excitement in his voice. How long had this bottled-up Englishman been in this country? thought the President. Somewhere inside him there was an American trying to get out.

"It's because I think I have an answer to that question that I've been invited here. I'm not here because I'm predicting a climatic change. There've been plenty of people doing that—Reid Bryson at Wisconsin, Stephen Schneider at Boulder, Hubert Lamb in England, Emiliani in Miami, authors like Robert Ardrey, even your own CIA."

He paused for a moment, and Breitbarth interrupted. "Ardrey? I've read his argument, if you can call it that. He's an amateur."

"Then he's a man I might understand," said the President sharply. He smiled to take the sting from his reproof. "A scientific amateur. You could say the same about most Presidents."

Stovin went on speaking as though the exchange had not taken place. "You say, Mr. President, that the process should take centuries? Well, you're in line with what a lot of climatologists have always believed. I have never believed it, but I've never been able to offer anything other than my own deductions. And then Mel" —he nodded to Brookman—"sent me those satellite photographs and the films and reports of Hays. And I suddenly saw something that no man has seen for the past 20,000 years. I saw . . . I saw"—for the first time Stovin groped for words—"I saw the outriders of the future."

Brookman shifted in his seat and the woman beside him shrugged impatiently. Stovin looked down at the single sheet of foolscap on the table in front of him and went on: "Toward the end of the last century, Mr. President, Russian scientists investigated the frozen corpse of a mammoth found near the River Berézovka in northern Siberia. The corpse was perfectly preserved—so perfectly, in fact, that the scientists ate part of its flesh. The mammoth was standing upright. In its mouth were large amounts of the vegetation it had been eating—grasses, Alpine poppies, sedge, crowsfoot. It had died approximately 40,000 years ago.

"Dozens of such mammoths have been discovered since, in similar condition and in similar circumstances. And in Pfedmost, a village in Moravia, the bones of more than 500 mammoths, lying close together, have been unearthed from a single site.

"What killed the Berezovka mammoth, Mr. President? And the others, too. What killed such enormous animals so swiftly and unexpectedly that they were still eating at the moment of death? What were the weather conditions in which at one moment poppies and crowsfoot were growing beside a Siberian stream, and the next moment the flora and fauna of that spot were frozen, undecaying, like a natural time capsule, for forty millennia? And what killed five hundred mammoths in one spot at Pfedmost?"

Stovin leaned forward, his eyes glittering. "That is why I told you earlier, Mr. President, that the deaths at Hays and in Russia were not important. I believe that what happened to those mammoths is what happened at Hays and at Ziba. We are seeing phenomena which no civi-

22

lized man has ever seen before—the catastrophic beginnings of a new Ice Age that is rushing upon us with undreamed-of speed. We don't have to wonder whether it will affect our grandchildren or even our children. We have to meet it now—within the next few years at the latest. Our civilizations have been born, have died, and have been renewed again in an interglacial dream . . . 15,000 years of warmth which have lulled us into thinking that climatic history is over, that this is the way it will always be.

"The future will not be like that. The future is ice, over a lot of the globe. The future is less food, fewer people."

Stovin paused, and the President looked across at Brookman. "How long ago did Jimmy Carter commission that third CIA report on the world food climate situation, Mel?"

"April 1978, Mr. President."

"Hm."

Donleavy looked across at the President. "Granted certain assumptions that Sto here is making, and that I myself am emphatically not prepared to make, that was a sound enough report, Mr. President. The effect on crop growth of a small drop in average temperature— say, one-degree Centigrade or one-and-three-quarters Fahrenheit—is a reduction of 27 percent. Two-and-a-half degrees Centigrade, you'd have 54 percent damage. In theory, that would be doom for about a quarter of the human race."

"That's the biological trap that Ardrey—the amateur Sto so admires—says we've all been lulled into by a fluke warm 15,000 years," said Breitbarth, smiling.

Abruptly the President stood, and the other five got awkwardly to their feet.

"Thank you, gentlemen. I'm afraid I shall soon be late for a further appointment. Mel, I'll be glad if you'll have the tapes of this meeting transcribed tonight."

The five murmured their farewells and began to file from the Oval Room when the President turned from his desk and spoke again. "Would you stay just for a moment, Mel? And you, too, Dr. Stovin."

He watched Brookman while the big man wedged himself once more into his chair. There, he thought, sits a reasonable man, a conservative man. Brookman might have made a fair politician. But he wasn't anybody's fool. He looked again at the names of the members on the list—invited by Brookman—for today's meeting. An agronomist, a marine biologist, a botanist, an anthropologist. And Stovin. A Doomsday prophet and a Doomsday team. If Brookman was completely convinced that Stovin was really a wild man, he'd never have asked that team.

"I want to thank you, Mel, for giving me the opportunity to meet Dr. Stovin. Dr. Stovin, I'm told you're a dreamer."

"Yes, Mr. President?"

"'Behold, this dreamer cometh,'" said the President, half to himself.

"Genesis, Chapter 37," said Stovin.

The President's eyebrows lifted. "You read the Bible, Dr. Stovin?"

"Sometimes."

"Do you believe in God?"

"No."

The President smiled. "Well, I do. So now we understand each other. I think . . . I think I'll be getting in contact with you soon, through Mel. Thank you for coming."

Stovin was following Brookman through the door of the Oval Room when the President asked one more question. "This scientist, Kukla, was it? Yes, Kukla. He said six more winters like 1972?"

"Yes, Mr. President."

"How many do you reckon we've had, that would qualify in his prediction?"

"Five," said Stovin.

Office of the Assistant to the President

The White House

Washington D.C.

To: Dr. William F. Stovin, University of New Mexico, Albuquerque, N.M.

I am grateful to you for your acceptance of the proposal which the President made through Dr. Brookman on the 19th: that you will spend three months in Canada and the northern United States, gathering material with which to report to the President personally on:

1. The possible significance of the so-far isolated phenomena discussed at the N.S.C. meeting on the 8th.
2. What, in your view, are the immediate climatic prospects.

You will realize, of course, that the mission and your report are essentially personal—a matter between you and the President—since a great deal of other research is currently proceeding and expanding in these particular fields.

The necessary clearances have already been arranged with the Canadian authorities. Dr. Brookman will provide you with the details of this and also of the appropriation for your mission, which will be accounted for in the general budget of the National Oceanographic and Atmospheric Administration.

I have already expressed my appreciation to Dr. Miller for releasing you temporarily from your duties at the University.

Please accept my sincerest wishes for an effective mission.

It is hardly necessary to add that the mission is strictly confidential.

CHAPTER 4

Stovin spoke abruptly, above the 160-horsepower grumble of the single engine. The little plane was turning steadily southwest, moving gradually down the ragged line of pack-ice that gleamed dully, every minute or so, through the overcast of the Gulf of Alaska no more than 3,000 feet below. Beside Stovin sat the young pilot, a map rustling on his knees, glancing down from time to time at the straight compass line he had drawn from the airfield at Anchorage along the 260 map-miles to Katmai Bay.

"How long do you reckon?"

The pilot looked down again at the map. "With this headwind, maybe two hours. But the weather's lousing up. It could be we'll have to turn back. I'll give it fifteen minutes before I make up my mind," he said.

"It'd be inconvenient to turn back at this stage," said Stovin. I've been in Alaska three weeks, he thought, and I can't afford to waste time.

"It'd sure be inconvenient to put this baby down on some place like Lake Tustumena, but that's where we'll be spending the next four days if we take chances," said the pilot dryly.

"Four days?"

"I guess that's about par for the course, for any search to locate us out here. Given fair weather for the choppers, that is."

Stovin grunted but did not reply. The little plane droned on, emerging after a few minutes from a long bank of grey cloud. Below it the sea crawled in deceptively mild-looking wrinkles—waves that from this height looked like cracked glass but which at sea level could make the Cook Inlet one of the most uncomfortable sea passages on earth. Strapped in their seats in the warmth of the plane's small cabin, they were flying over one of the bleakest, least hospitable, most dangerous regions of the globe —a mixture of ice and rock, torn tundra, and jagged coast where even the Arctic terns had to struggle to survive. Yet there was fire down there amongst the ice. Every decade or so, there were volcanoes.

Stovin looked out of the cabin's starboard window. Over to the northwest, beyond the glistening wing tip at the top of his vision and against the brighter line of the horizon, bulked a range of mountains, gunmetal grey, serrated, ominous.

The pilot saw his glance and tapped the map. "That's the Aleutian Range . . . goes way, way down the peninsula to Umnak and the Fox Islands. Mighty rough country." He turned slightly in his seat and pointed to the north. "We could turn up from Umnak and be in Russia in six hours. Just about make it on these tanks. But I guess we'd pick up a Firebar before we'd reached Provideniya."

Stovin looked at him curiously. "A Firebar?"

"Yak 28 all-weather fighter," said the pilot succinctly. "The Russians keep a clutch of them just behind that coast. They fly a mission down the Bering Strait most days, just in case anybody's figuring to come over to Uncle Sam the hard way."

He laughed again. "That's a zero-rated scenario, as

26

you might guess. But the Russians . . . they like to be sure."

"You know a lot about them?" asked Stovin.

"Just old times," said the pilot. "I flew with the Air Force awhile."

He did not elaborate, and Stovin looked at him covertly but carefully, almost for the first time since chartering the plane at Anchorage. The pilot was a youngish man, probably still under thirty. He had blue eyes and black hair, and there was a cast to his face that was unexpected, even alien. He had told Stovin that his name was Bisby, which sounded Anglo-Saxon enough. Yet, thought Stovin in surprise, he could almost be Russian. There was a flatness, a bleakness, a remote quality to his features that was neither western European nor home-grown American.

"Are we going on to Katmai?" asked Stovin.

"Guess so," said the pilot. "The cloud-base isn't too bad." He grinned, and suddenly Stovin found he liked him.

"There ain't much around here to show visitors. I guess Katmai's the best we got. But you must need to see it awful bad. It's costing you plenty." There was an interrogative lift to his voice, but now it was Stovin's turn to be silent.

After a few seconds, Bisby shrugged. "Well, if Katmai's still blowing, you'll see the glow in the sky pretty soon. About another half-hour."

Why, thought Stovin for the twentieth time, am I doing this? If there's anything new to be found about the volcano theory, it isn't going to be proved on a sightseeing tour by an academic nonspecialist in a chartered plane at 3,000 feet, but by a highly trained Air Force crew taking dust samples from a Lockheed U-2, or something like it, at 60,000 feet or more, and then having them analyzed in a computer-equipped laboratory. But I always have to be *there*, in person, he said to himself. Do I distrust other people's conclusions? Yes, I do. I've got this dream of being Renaissance man—a thinker who understands just enough about enough—enough to get a picture.

That was hard, very hard for Leonardo da Vinci, when people didn't really know very much at all. Is it still possible now, in a century when information expands at a rate far beyond the power of single human minds to comprehend? Maybe, maybe not. But one thing was sure. If Renaissance man was dead, then so—eventually—was the human race. Information was *not* knowledge. Human beings couldn't just grub away in little scientific burrows, scraping deeper, better holes. Somewhere above there was a landscape where other things happened. Somebody had to come out of the burrows, look around, and go back to tell how it really was. Somebody like Lithman. Or Stovin . . .

Well, Lithman might have been wrong about volcanoes. At least, that's what they all said. Lithman had seen volcanoes as the backcloth for climatic doom. They said he'd exaggerated the dust factor. But had he?

The trouble was that he, Stovin, was no vulcanologist. He'd only dabbled at it—typical Renaissance man. Not like Lamb in England, who'd produced the Dust Veil Index, which rated the filtering effect of all volcanoes against the dense cloud of particles that had screened the sun's rays for months after the volcanic island of Krakatoa blew itself to smithereens in 1883. According to the dust theory, the decades of high worldwide volcanic activity were the ones when temperatures fell below "normal." But *could* volcanoes spew so much dust into the air as to mask sunlight enough to trigger Ice Ages? Nine scientists out of ten laughed at the idea.

But the one thing that couldn't be denied was that the Dust Veil Index was up again. There was one hell of a lot of dust in the earth's atmosphere right now. Not surprising, with volcanoes blowing their tops in Kenya, South China, the Balkans, and Peru in the last two years. And now Mount Katmai, here in Alaska—its worst blast this century, according to records. Nobody apart from vulcanologists bothered much about Katmai, of course. What happened there didn't affect you unless you were a polar bear.

"There she is."

The pilot's voice jerked Stovin out of his thoughts. Dead ahead of the plane, beyond the blur of a single propeller, a dark cloud, with quivering pink edges, hung over the horizon. Around this center, banks of conventional cumulus rain cloud, like dirty cottonwool, bulked both above and below, so that burning Katmai blazed like a fiery eye in an ashen face. It was not an illusion that lasted. As the little plane drew closer to the volcano, the glowing heart of its central craters—there seemed to be four of them, Stovin noted—dominated the scene. A great shimmering curtain of ash towered before them, its particles

28

glowing with light from the great furnace below, so that they danced like millions of fireflies. Stovin was gazing in fascinated silence on a scene that looked like the beginning of the world, when Bisby grunted something unintelligible, grasped the wheel, and began to bank the plane sharply away.

"I don't like it," he said. "I've seen Katmai blow before, when I was a kid. But that was just a burp beside this one. I reckon we shouldn't . . . Jesus God!"

No more than three miles away, a gigantic column of fire climbed swiftly into the sky. They were flying now at about 4,500 feet, but the flame-pillar mounted far above them until its tip was lost to sight above the line of the cabin window. From its sides, smaller sprays of fire spewed out, cascading like an enormous firework down to the earth's surface, hidden in the dust cloud below.

The plane had turned so far now that Stovin was looking over his left shoulder. The column of flame and smoke and ash was now taking the form of a colossal tree—like one of the umbrella pines on the campus at Albuquerque.

"I don't like it," Bisby said again. His teeth were clenched as he peered through the window, toward clouds already lit by the red reflection of the holocaust behind them.

"There's too much damned dust—that pumice ash can be murder. And we're too close. I should have . . ."

In the same instant, the shock wave of the volcano explosion tossed the little plane like a falling leaf, twisting, spinning, up and down and sideways. Stovin was to remember afterward that he had not had time to feel frightened. Beside him Bisby's hands moved over the controls, not fighting the shock wave, not fighting the plane itself, trying to ride the air storm. At last the plane steadied, and the glow behind them began to recede. It was hard now to see the sky ahead. A greyish-white powdering of pumice ash clung to the windows. Bisby's left hand jabbed the wiper switch, the long arm of the wiper arced across the window, and in the same instant the engine stopped. The propeller turned slowly, impotent. From outside the cabin came the faint whistling of the wind.

Bisby cursed. "Ash," he said. "Pumice . . . in the intakes."

They were dropping steadily now, and through patches

in the cloud-banks, Stovin could see the long ragged rocky shoreline of Katmai Bay. There was going to be only a totally impossible choice for landing—into a jumbled detritus of rocks flung out by some long-ago eruption, or the patchy, razor-edged pack-ice just offshore. With surprising calm, he realized that he had, at the rate the plane was gliding down, no more than three minutes to live.

Bisby was altering direction. His eyes were set, staring intently through the clouded screen to a big black thunderhead cumulus below and to the right of them. The left wing tip lifted silently and the line of the horizon heaved. A moment later the wet fingers of the thunderhead closed around them. The dust on the windows changed to sludge. They were falling silently, invisibly, through a closed, blind world.

Bisby's right hand pulled the yellow lever of the starter. Somewhere deep in the engine came a deep throaty rattle. Again Bisby pumped the starter . . . and again. There was an engine cough, a stutter, and then a sustained rumble. On the gauges the oil pressure climbed to normal. The plane began to climb, up and out of the thunderhead, heading northeast toward the field at Anchorage.

Bisby looked at Stovin. "I figured I'd try a little ex-pe-ri-ment," he said, spacing the four syllables out as though saying the word for the first time.

"Where did you learn that?" Stovin tried to keep the slight quiver from his voice, but he did not entirely succeed. Bisby seemed not to notice.

"I got that from an old pilot, way back in Arizona," he said. "Fort Worth. He said you could do it with sand, if you were lucky and found a thunderhead. The cloud washes the intakes, if it gets there in time. I reckoned what goes for sand might go for pumice."

They said little after that, but the silence was unexpectedly companionable. When, an hour later, they came in low over the jumbled sprawl of Anchorage and touched down on the bleak field, Stovin held out his hand.

"Thanks," he said. "For my life. I'm glad I chose a good pilot."

Bisby laughed. "It was my life, too, sir," he said. "Not completely unselfish."

30

"I owe you a drink," said Stovin. "Tonight? I'm at the Royal Inn. West Fifth Street."

"I know it," said the pilot. "I'll be there around seven."

"Good," said Stovin. And that, he thought in surprise, is the first person, except for Diane Hilder, I've asked for a drink in the last six months.

CHAPTER 5

Bisby sat on the corner of his bed, took the tin box from his bedside drawer, and opened it. It was an old biscuit tin, tight fitting, but the lid came away easily, as though from long use. He felt inside the tin until his fingers found what he sought. It lay on his square rough palm—a narrow wedge of tiny skull, the upper jawbone with its teeth stretched in the gaping rictus of the death snarl, the lower jaw missing, the polished eye sockets gleaming dully in the light of the frilled bedside lamp.

He bent his head until the line of the dark hair on his forehead touched the skull. Then he closed his eyes and spoke in a low, harsh whisper:

"Silap-inua . . . aiyee. Sedna . . . aiyee."

Bisby remained bowed for a few moments more, smiling to himself as though half-ashamed. Absently, he stroked the skull amulet with his short blunt fingers. He sighed, replaced it in the box; and put it back in the drawer. There were four books beside the bedside lamp—Russell's *History of Western Philosophy*, Selye's *Physiology and Pathology of Exposure to Stress*, Hemingway's *Death in the Afternoon*, and the blue-and-yellow volume of the *British Admiralty Bering Sea and Strait Pilot*. He lay on his bed and read the Hemingway for three-quarters of an hour, and then got up, showered, changed into a plaid shirt and dark-blue slacks, put on his Grenfell anorak, and went out into the chill, neon-lit dark of Anchorage and around to Peggy's.

Many of the Anchorage bush pilots ate at Peggy's Airport Cafe. It was home-style cooking, and the prices were reasonable by Anchorage standards. But there was no one there tonight he wanted to talk to, so he chose a table away from the bar, ordered a sandwich and a beer, and sat thinking about the day behind him.

He was an unusual man, Stovin, the man he was meeting tonight. Didn't get excited, even when the engine cut out. Why did he want to look at Katmai? Government man, that's for sure, he thought. He'd paid for the charter with a United States Government chit—sound as the Bank of America. Why did the Government want to look at Katmai? And if they did, why didn't they fly a mission from an Air Force field? The man didn't even have a camera. It had been a near thing, though, when that engine cut. And it was my fault for taking him so near. That pumice is murder to piston engines, and I knew it; I knew it. So why did I do it? I guess it was because he was sitting there, so quiet, and I wanted to give him a fright. I gave us both one—me, maybe, more than him. Well—Bisby looked at his watch—it was time for that drink.

Sitting on the high-backed chair at the side of the hotel bar, Stovin watched Bisby come into the lobby, look around, and walk toward him. He wasn't exactly a striking-looking man, thought Stovin . . . short, almost squat, but powerfully built. He walked with a slightly rolling motion, like a seaman. But there was something about him that caught the attention, something that drew a second look. Stovin noticed a couple of girls at a table on the other side of the room giving Bisby a considering glance as he came over. And neither of them was the kind who was looking for a client. He stood and smiled as Bisby reached the bar.

"Hi."

"Hi—what'll you have?"

"Scotch, please. Ice . . . no soda. Just water."

Bisby sipped the drink critically. "That's fine Scotch, sir. Deserves good water, not soda. It's good water here."

"Really?"

Bisby nodded. "Comes all the way down from the Chugach Mountain, between us and Canada. This town taps a couple of the little lakes over to the east. Frozen a lot of the year, of course, but they've got the pipes deep under the ice. It's good water."

For a few minutes, they chatted with a casualness that was more apparent than real, each weighing the other. Yet it was a conventional-enough question by Stovin that suddenly started Bisby talking more personally.

"You lived here long?" asked Stovin.

Bisby smiled, but seemed slightly ill at ease. "I was born here, sir. At least, not here. Out on Ihovak. That's a little island, in the neck of the Bering Strait. We call it Ihovak."

"We?"

"The Ihovakmiut—the people who live on the island. The goddamn Eskimos, they . . . we . . . are called in Anchorage. They've lived there for 2,000 years."

Stovin looked at him carefully before speaking again. "You don't seem too sure whether it's 'they' or 'we.'"

Bisby's face remained expressionless, but Stovin noticed that his voice quickened slightly from its usual laconic tones, as though he were slightly excited or under some kind of pressure.

"I guess you're right, sir. That *is* something I find difficult."

Stovin smiled. "Please don't call me 'sir.' It makes me feel my age, and I don't want to be reminded of it."

Bisby was stirring the ice in his drink with the little glass bar rod that lay beside his napkin. Stovin saw in astonishment that the pilot's hand was trembling very slightly, and that he was using the rod to mask the fact.

"Don't stop now," said Stovin. "You've made me curious."

"It's nothing very remarkable," said Bisby. "I'm half Eskimo, half white American."

"You've got an American name," said Stovin. "No, I guess I don't mean that. Eskimos are American, too, I know. I mean you've got an Anglo-Saxon name."

"My father," said Bisby. "James Bisby—he was a missionary. My mother was the Eskimo half of me. She was from the Nuniungmiut, of the People themselves."

His voice quickened, changing its tone indefinably. "I mean the People with a capital P. Not . . . not a coast Eskimo. She came from Nunivak Island, about 450 miles west of here. My father married her there, in the village at Kolo. She was a Christian. He brought her with him when he moved to Ihovak."

"The People?" asked Stovin.

The tinge of bitterness in Bisby's voice deepened for a

33

moment. "That's how Eskimos think—well, thought—of themselves. There weren't many of them, even in the old days, and they're getting fewer. But we believed for 10,000 years that we were the Inuit—the whole damned human race."

"And?" said Stovin.

"We were wrong," said Bisby briefly.

Once more, that trouble with "we" and "they."

"Your parents still on the island?" he asked.

"They're dead. My mother died when I was four . . . tuberculosis. She was twenty-two. And my father was lost in the Norton Sound about seven years later, with three other Ihovakmiut, in a boat going over to Nome. Nobody knows what happened."

"I'm sorry," said Stovin, conventionally.

Bisby shrugged. "Don't be. I can hardly remember my mother, except that her name was Kikik. I just remember her as being very warm."

"And did you . . . I mean, how did you get into the Air Force? It seems . . ."

"You mean it seems mighty unlikely for an Eskimo to fly?" said Bisby. "Especially for the Air Force?" He seemed more relaxed now that he had told some of his story.

"Half an Eskimo," said Stovin, so quietly that Bisby seemed not to hear.

"I'm the one that got away, I guess," he said. "I was brought up after my father died by my uncle—my mother's brother—on Ihovak. He'd been my father's mission assistant: the three of them came from Nunivak together. His name was Oolie. After my father died, he became a boat-hunter. He meant me to be a boat-hunter, too."

"And?" Stovin prompted again.

Bisby laughed shortly. "Not *and*, Dr. Stovin. It wasn't *and*. It was *but*. But just around the time I would have started to learn boat-hunting, a friend of my father's came over from here in Anchorage. My father's father— my grandfather—was a wealthy man. He lived in California. He didn't want to see me because he didn't like my being what he called 'half Indian.' He didn't want me near him, but he wanted to do his duty. So I was sent to school in New York and then to Cornell. I lived with a foster family in Murray Hill, on Second Avenue. I've never been back to Ihovak since."

34

"And yet," said Stovin curiously, "it's not so far away from you now, is it? And you're back here in Alaska. Why exactly don't you . . ."

"I'd be ashamed," said Bisby. His hands clenched on the whiskey glass. Now why did I tell him that? he thought to himself. But Stovin said nothing and after a pause Bisby went on:

"I flunked out of Cornell—I was going to major in anthropology, but I couldn't take it. I don't like putting people into intellectual zoos. Or onto yards of film. So I went to the Air Force Academy at Colorado Springs and majored in Starfighters. It was easier. I've got good reactions."

"I know," said Stovin.

Bisby smiled easily for the first time. "You can thank my mother's side of the family for that. Her father was Katelo, and he was the best *sivooyachta* there'd ever been on Nunivak, they told me. And *his* father was Halo, and he was the best one before his son."

"What's that—*sivooyachta?*"

"The *sivooyachta* is the one who stands in the bow of the hunting boat. It's his job to spot the whale and then to strike with the spear. You need quick reactions for that."

"I'm sure," said Stovin. He hesitated for a moment and then went on. "You remember a lot of names and words and details, considering you left the island when you were still a boy."

"I learned it all by heart," said Bisby simply. Stovin waited for him to continue, but he said nothing more.

"So now you fly around Alaska," said Stovin at last. "For hire. But you don't go back to the island."

"That's right," said Bisby. "The plane's mine. I bought her with the rest of my inheritance. She's all I've got."

Except, he thought, what's in that biscuit tin, and that's no business of his. I've talked enough. He's not a difficult man to talk to. It's time to change the subject.

"And you, Dr. Stovin," he said. "You said you were going back pretty soon. Do you aim to come back and work here?"

"Maybe. But not immediately. I don't think so, anyway."

Stovin looked at Bisby and wondered. This mission was confidential; the President's aide had really laid that on the line. On the other hand, the President's aide was a politician—or, at least, a politician's man. It was a politician's instinct to keep his cards close to his chest and not to share information. But that wasn't the way he, Stovin, could play it here in Alaska. He had to talk to people who heard things, saw things, experienced things that couldn't be seen, heard, and experienced in Washington. A few days ago, he'd been up to the huge Arctic Naval Research Laboratory at Barrow, way up in the north of Alaska. There was a mass of evidence there—scores of millions of dollars worth. Sea temperatures, general circulation, insolation estimates, wind records, ice formation charts, the lot. The usual evidence, due to be fed into computers, taken out, reanalyzed, and then interpreted in twelve different ways. And not, maybe, in the vital thirteenth.

Oh, they'd make a climatic model of all the information. They wouldn't make just one; they'd probably make six. And everybody knew that climatic models, whatever impressive-sounding acronym produced them—CLIMAP, the Climate Mapping People; or GARP, the Global Atmospheric Research Project; or whoever and whatever it was—had to admit enormous margins for error. Because, he thought wearily, we only get out of a computer what we put in. We can't put in instincts, so we can't get genius out. What was it Diane—just for a moment in his mind's eye he saw that short, curling blonde hair—what was it Diane always said was the best acronym for computer-based models? GIGO, that was it, GIGO—Garbage In, Garbage Out. If the President had wanted that kind of evidence, he knew he only had to ask for it from somebody like Mel Brookman. He'd have a digest on his desk in forty-eight hours. No, that wasn't why he'd been sent to the Arctic.

"Tell me," he said to Bisby, "do you have a lot of friends up here? Eskimo friends, I mean?"

"Some," said Bisby. "I know some."

He seemed disinclined to pursue the subject, but Stovin had made up his mind. He took a small brass key from his pocket and carefully unlocked the black document case that lay on the bar beside him. He drew from it the sheaf of satellite photographs which Brookman had shown to the President.

"Have they, or you, ever seen anything like that?"

Silently, Bisby leafed through the photographs for a

full two minutes. Then he looked up at Stovin, his face expressionless. "Satellite pictures, huh?"

"Why do you say that?"

"I've seen plenty, in the Air Force. You can't mistake them; there's something about the angle. These are good, though. You wouldn't get much better from conventional reconnaissance. Siberia, I guess?" There was a faint note of interrogation in his voice.

Stovin was startled. "What makes you think it's Siberia? It looks just like any other pile of snow to me."

Bisby laughed. "You wouldn't be showing me satellite shots of Alaska, or Canada, or Norway, or Sweden. You'd have better shots at lower level. And in any case, it doesn't look like the American North."

He tapped the dark smudge of trees at the edge of one of the pictures. "See that. That's a scattering of Sitka spruce and larchpole fir, but most of it's good old birch. You don't find that combination much on this side."

"This side of what?"

"This side of the Bering Sea, Dr. Stovin."

Stovin shrugged. He felt slightly disconcerted. "Well, you're right. These shots are of Siberia."

"Whereabouts?"

"A place called Ziba, beside the Ob River. Near Igrim."

"I know it. Right on the edge of the oil field."

"You seem to know a lot about it," said Stovin.

Bisby leaned forward. "You may know something about volcanoes, sir. I don't know how much. A lot, maybe. But I'm an old Air Force flier. I know about targets. Igrim was—still is, I guess—a target. It's tucked away, warm and comfortable, Dr. Stovin, somewhere in a top-secret file at Strategic Air Command. That much I know. And as for this"—his finger drew a long swath across the glossy surface of the print—"well, I've never seen anything like it myself."

Stovin sat back and began to shuffle the prints back into their envelope.

"Pity," he said. "It was a long shot, but—well, you know—with you flying over this state a lot, I'd thought there was just a chance that you . . ."

"I've never seen anything like it *myself*," Bisby repeated steadily, "but I've spoken to those who have."

Stovin stopped putting the prints into the envelope. Bisby took the top one and drew his finger once more down its surface. "It's not possible to be certain, but if I had to bet, I'd say that . . . that feature . . . was made by a Dancer."

Stovin waited, saying nothing. Abstractedly, Bisby stirred the last scraps of the melted ice in his drink, and then went on:

"When I was about ten, I went on a trip with my father up the Inglutalik River. That's on the Seward Peninsula, well north of here. We went inland because, I think, my father had an idea of starting a mission station up in the rough country north of Umlakeet where a lot of white fur trappers were beginning to move in. He always said that wherever there were trappers there should be a mission—not for the whites, though. For the Eskimos. The idea didn't come to much, anyway, because when the trappers moved in, the Eskimos moved out.

"But there was an old Eskimo in what was left of the village. I can remember his name—Kakumi. He told stories about the Eskimo past. My father liked that kind of thing; he wrote a lot of it down, but what happened to it after he was lost I don't know. Nobody's got any of that stuff now, that's for sure. Well, my father used to tell me some of these things, and he told me how Kakumi always said that there was a piece of forest up above the Ungulik that had been visited long ago by what he called a Dancer.

"He got Kakumi to take him up there, but I was sick those two days, and I didn't go with him. He used to talk about it for weeks afterward. He said it looked like the hand of God had just rubbed along the forest, just rubbed along and left nothing behind except a big mark on the land. A mark maybe a mile long, my father said. But that wasn't how Kakumi saw it. He said it was the steps of a Dancer."

"What did he mean—a Dancer?" asked Stovin.

"Eskimos believe," said Bisby—and Stovin had a sudden, curious feeling that the pilot was studiously avoiding his gaze—"that their lives are controlled by Sedna. Sedna is the old woman who sits at the bottom of the sea. She governs the sea animals—the fish, the seal, the whale—and so she governs what the Eskimos eat. And *if* they eat. Do you follow me?"

Stovin nodded, not speaking.

"Well, in all the villages, the *shaman*, the one who

38

talks to Sedna, dances for her the harpoon dance and the other dances, to please her and make her laugh and see that the Eskimos eat. And sometimes Sedna sends her own Dancers, who come into the house when the people are gathered together, and it's dark except for the fire, and it's quiet. At least, that's what they believe."

"But surely, that wouldn't . . ."

"And every so often," continued Bisby, ignoring the interruption, "Sedna sends one of her husbands to dance, and he is bigger than a mountain and wider than a lake and deeper than a ravine. That's what Kakumi told my father."

"Why does Sedna do this?" asked Stovin. "I mean, of course, why do the Eskimos believe that Sedna does this?"

Bisby shrugged. "They say that Sedna does it when she wants to tell the Eskimos that their time has come. That is what the Dancer comes to say. I can remember my father writing it down. 'To tell the Eskimos their time has come.' "

"A sort of death warning," said Stovin reflectively. "And how long ago did this happen?"

Bisby shrugged again. "My father said that the marks on the land were so old that caribou moss had smothered the stumps of the broken trees, and there were great stones all along the glacier of the Dancer's track. And Kakumi said that his father's father had told him that *his* father's father had told him about the Dancer, and that even then the story had been old."

"How old, I wonder?"

"Well, my father said it happened not long before the year 1700, as far as he could work out. But that could only be a guess, of course."

"I see."

Stovin sat thinking for a few moments, while Bisby watched him. At last, the older man spoke again. "And that was the last Dancer the Eskimos knew?"

"No," said Bisby.

Startled, Stovin put down the document case and looked at him. "There've been others? When? Where?"

"One other," said the pilot. "At least, only one I've heard of. It was way up beside the Beaufort Sea. In the Kukpagmiut country. There's an Eskimo, a Kukpagmiut called Awliktok. I see him occasionally if I'm up around Barrow. He's got contacts right across the border. The border means 'damn all' to an Eskimo, anyway. He says there was a Dancer there, over by Mackenzie Bay. He says the Dancer took out a whole section of shore and forest, more than three-quarters of a mile long, and somewhere around 300 caribou. No Eskimos, though. Not many around this time of year, up there."

"When did this happen?"

" 'Bout a month ago."

Stovin was incredulous. "A month ago? Surely not. There's been no report, no whisper even."

"There've been plenty of Eskimos whispering, Dr. Stovin. But who in hell listens to an Eskimo's whispers? And I'll tell you one more thing—and this isn't legend. You'll be able to check it with the fisheries people. The whale are coming down early. There were six, eight maybe ten bowhead whale sighted off Barrow last week, moving south. It's early yet for bowhead to be moving south. They spend the summer in the Beaufort, feeding. Awliktok says the bowhead have lain there, on the edge of the pack-ice, and watched the Dancer. That's the way the old Eskimos talk, of course."

"Of course," said Stovin. He was thinking hard. "If I were to stay on, say, five days more, a week maybe, could you fly me over to that site? What was it, Mackenzie Bay?"

Bisby pursed his lips. "Difficult. That's Canadian territory. There's damn little chance of getting air clearance along the Beaufort, the RCAF have got a heap of Early Warning stuff back of that coastline. They won't take kindly to anybody flying over it with an itsy-bitsy airplane, taking pictures. I suppose you want to take pictures?"

Stovin nodded. "Don't worry about clearance. I can get clearance," he said.

Bisby looked at him inquisitively. "You sure about that?"

Stovin nodded again.

"Well, if you're sure, Dr. Stovin, then I guess I wouldn't mind a little trip over the Beaufort. I had an uncle used to fish the Beaufort once."

"What happened to him?"

"He drowned," said Bisby.

Extract from a letter from Dr. William Stovin to Dr. Diane Hilder, Department of Zoology, University of New Mexico, Albuquerque, N.M.

". . . it was a very unexpected coast, not much like the Norton Sound, but much more open. Bisby said there was more autumn ice than usual, but it was very broken up and there were a lot of baby bergs just offshore. The ocean is very shallow here, and quite a few caribou were running along the edge, really steaming in the sun. I guess we frightened them, because we were cruising at only about 200 feet. It seemed to me not to leave much margin for error, but Bisby's a good pilot.

"The Dancer Bisby told me about seemed to have . . . well, I don't know . . . danced? . . . happened? . . . visited? . . . just a mile or two east of Demarcation Point, which is the border with Canada, where the Mackenzie River comes in. As you'll guess, the Mackenzie water is warmer than the ocean, so it gives a largely ice-free area for about three miles out to sea. There was some snow below, but also long unexpected stretches of dying summer vegetation—much more than farther west, where the snow cover was very extensive. So when we saw the Dancer's track, it was more of a shock than I'd expected, because it had cut a swath right across a stretch of still unfrozen tundra. I was keen to land, but Bisby flew up and down a bit and then said there wasn't any remotely possible strip within twenty miles. We weren't properly equipped for walking, though it would be worth somebody who was equipped coming up and getting some samples.

"It was a really fantastic sight. Right across the shoreline, going way back, maybe half a mile into the tundra, was this enormous horizontal block of ice. There was a lot of sunshine, and it was fairly smoking with steam.

41

Some of it had melted in the last month, and I counted at least eighteen dead caribou lying around the edges. God knows, there must be many more inside—about three hundred, according to Bisby's Eskimo. And there was something that might interest you. There were a hell of a lot of wolves in the area. There must have been at least two hundred, probably more. Two large packs, maybe a hundred each, were moving together, around half a mile apart, a mile or so from the Dancer—I keep calling the thing that because I don't know what else to call it—and there were several little groups, up to half a dozen in each, lying down and quietly walking about around the Dancer itself. I guess they feed on the dead caribou which the sun melts out of the edge of the block. They seemed to be sitting around waiting, as though they knew there were a heap more caribou inside. Very intelligent anticipation.

"Diane, I'll be in Boulder next week. I have to go to Washington to talk to Brookman, and then I'm going to NCAR. *I guess you'll be back there by then—we'll have lunch. You can tell me about* canis latrans *and I'll tell you some Eskimo legends. By the way, the same rule still holds—don't talk about this. Not yet, anyway; not until I've got my appropriation through* NOOA!

"I'm going out now into downtown Barrow—eat your heart out, Manhattan!—to have a drink with Bisby. He's a good man and full of new surprises.

"See you soon, and watch that traffic on Lomax. . . ."

CHAPTER 6

Oh, Stovin, she said to herself, I miss you. Why the hell I miss you I don't know because I only get that peck on the cheek once a week. But it's been six weeks now and I miss you.

She looked down at the thick pile of typescript on the table of her little room overlooking the sun-drenched fountain and the cooler shadows of the Languages Block.

"Observations on the Hybridization of *Canis Rufus* and *Canis Latrans* in the Sangre de Cristo Mountains of New Mexico," said the neatly typed white sticker pasted to the yellow cover. "By Diane Hilder, Ph.D., University of Colorado."

Well, she thought, there it is. Eighteen months' work . . . 45, 000 words . . . 237 color slides. It won't make me a name because nobody, but nobody, is going to make a name out of investigating mating between the red wolf, of which there probably aren't more than thirty still alive in the United States, and the coyote, of which there are plenty. But it is—at least, it looks like it will be—a new species. If it can establish breeding lines as a hybrid. And if it can be protected in time from Man. So, she reflected, the old red wolf hangs on, teetering on the very edge of extinction but finally getting to pump his genes into a few receptive female coyotes. Changing but not losing. Not many animals can do that. Dogs do it, with a bit of help from us. But clever old *canis rufus* manages all by himself. Could man do it, if he had to? I wonder . . .

And now it was time to leave Albuquerque and the University of New Mexico and go back to her own campus at Boulder. She considered, only half-interested, what she might do next. There'd been a suggestion of work in Canada on seasonal migrations, but there was nothing very definite yet. In some ways, she wouldn't mind a spell back at Boulder, anyway. For a moment, her mind's eye filled with a picture of the Colorado months ahead— the chained bicycles stacked outside the red-brown buildings of the East Campus, and the college kids walking through that strangely unexpected section of downtown Boulder, past the gas stations and office blocks, beyond the geometrical bewilderment of one-way streets where you suddenly turned into an old-fashioned precinct with wide sidewalks and trees and bookshops and pastry stores. And over it all, the Flatirons bulking against the skyline with the lights of the National Center for Atmospheric Research glowing like Shangri-la, high on the mountainside in the twilight. Yes, it would be good to have another spell at Boulder. But not for too long. Nowhere, Hilder, she told herself firmly, nowhere for too long. She picked up Stovin's letter again. There were a couple of rather odd sentences. . . .

The Biology Block lay across the central campus. She walked there slowly, half luxuriating in the New Mexico sun. The late-brooded, creamy, black-barred swallow-tailed butterflies, perched on the flowering bushes along the path, stirred unwillingly as she passed. There was hardly anybody in the Block, but she went up the stairs and along the passage to the Researchers' Room and found, rather to her surprise, the man she hoped to see.

"Hi, Frank, I was looking for you."

The man at the table in the window put down his magazine—she noticed it was the British scientific journal *Nature*—and smiled. "Well, well," he said. "This was bound to happen. It's this new after-shave I've been trying. One thing I beg of you, Diane. Be gentle with me."

"Don't worry," she said laughing. "I'm not coming near you. I've got a good memory. No"—she backed away as he made an only half-playful grab—"I just want to ask you about something."

Why do I have to go through this minuet each time? she asked herself wryly. Frank Van Gelder was a heavily married man of at least forty-two, but sometimes he could be an adolescent nuisance. However, he *did* know a lot about *canis lupus*, the grey wolf, the type species, the granddaddy of them all.

"Ask away," said Van Gelder, unabashed.

"Are there many records of grey wolves actively seeking carrion—dead flesh? I mean flesh that's been dead some time."

As usual, when he was asked a serious question, Van Gelder himself became serious and intent.

"*Canis lupus* will take carrion," he said thoughtfully. "But usually only as a last resort. And then, if he can get it, it's often human carrion. You know, old graveyards. Plenty of records from Scotland and Central Europe, a few centuries ago."

In spite of herself, Diane shivered, but Van Gelder did not notice. "No," he said, "the grey wolf likes his meat fresh. When he can get it."

"So you wouldn't expect to see grey wolves—a lot of them—waiting around for carrion to appear? If there were, say, live caribou about?"

"If a grey wolf was taking carrion in those circumstances," said Van Gelder, "I guess it would be a pretty individual choice. No, I wouldn't expect to see a wolf group do that. But how do you mean, waiting for carrion to appear? You mean rubbish dumps, that kind of thing?"

"Something like that," said Diane vaguely.

"Polar bears, yes," said Van Gelder. "They raid the dumps around the Arctic bases. Somebody did a paper on that—Ingram, I think. But not wolves. Certainly not in social groups of any size."

Diane frowned. "What size, in numbers, would a grey wolf pack run to?" she asked.

Van Gelder looked at her curiously. "Not much different from any other wolf, Diane. You know as well as I do. Family groups—six, eight, ten. Maybe up to twenty when it's really cold."

"But not a hundred?"

He laughed. "Lord, no. You've been reading folklore. What kind of prey animal does it need a hundred wolves to catch and share? No point in that kind of cooperation to get three or four caribou. And nothing scatters quicker than a caribou herd."

"So it would be really startling to see a hundred wolves together?"

"Sure would. I tell you, there's no point in a hundred wolves running together. Not since the last mammoth died."

She was startled. "The last mammoth?"

"Sure," said Van Gelder. "There were only two creatures in the Pleistocene, after the last Ice Age, that could tackle the woolly mammoth. One was *canis lupus* and the other was *homo sapiens*. Wolves and men. Men invented traps and weapons; wolves developed speed and teeth. But both, both learned to cooperate within their own species. I guess you couldn't kill a mammoth by stealth, out there in the plains. So wolves did it by massed speed, weight of numbers. Big packs, a hundred or more. A couple of mammoths would go a long way toward feeding a hundred wolves. But there's been no prey animal as big as that since the mammoth disappeared. So that kind of social organization was phased out, evolutionwise. You don't need more than two or three wolves to kill a caribou or a sick moose."

"I see," said Diane thoughtfully. "Well, thanks a lot, Frank. That's about what I wanted to hear."

"It'll cost you," he said comfortably. "It'll cost you time and me money. How about dinner, next week sometime? Christine's away and I'm eating out."

"No chance," she said. "I'll be in Boulder."

"Boulder? What the hell's in Boulder?"

"My university," she said.

"You mean they've got a university now in Boulder?" said Van Gelder in mock surprise. "A real grove of academe? Why am I always the last to be told these things?"

"Very funny," she said, closing the door. All the way back to her room, past the sleepy swallowtails and the splashing fountain, she wondered about Stovin's Arctic wolves.

Dr. Melvin Brookman sat on the tall, ladderback chair outside the Oval Office and worried. In five minutes, he was going through into that Office to talk to the President of the United States. The President was well known to be a patient man. It was equally well known that he exhibited this virtue only up to a point. And it might very well be that he, Melvin Brookman, would pass that point tonight.

What am I going to say? he thought anxiously. Well, there's Stovin's report, to begin with. The President has one copy; I have the other. And what, in heaven's name, is Stovin's report? Eskimo legends, folklore, dreams. Plus some more controversial stuff about volcanoes, the sort of stuff we've all heard so often from Lithman that it's coming out of our ears. And there's that single, personal, eyewitness report of a big block of ice up on the Mackenzie estuary—not even in the United States. Observed only from the air, at that. A block of ice that could be something—well, out of the ordinary—but *could* be just a big, stranded berg. And God knows what all this is costing. Stovin seems to be renting planes like a Texas oil prospector. There's supposed to be a ten percent pruning of the scientific budget this year. Just let some anti-Administration newspaper get hold of this, and boy, oh boy, it'll be all systems go.

But, damn it, there *is* something curious going on. I feel it in my sternum, he said to himself, and my sternum's never wrong. Not the five bad winters in the last six. Nor the poor crop returns. Nor the small fails on the computerized models of sea and atmospheric temperature situations. All that has happened before. It isn't the signal for the Apocalypse, necessarily. Or even probably. In each generation there are half-a-dozen scientists to predict the End Of Civilization As We Know It—and three times as many publicists jumping on the bandwagon. But the End doesn't come—or rather, civilization

46

as we know it dies a little every year, and we just don't notice.

Nevertheless, he thought, this time there *is* something different, surely? That thing that hit Hays. That went in to the atmospheric sciences boys, and they've come up with an answer—a mathematical model. Ingenious, anyway. Correct, maybe. But why do these things happen *now?* And how about those satellite photographs? On the other hand, there hasn't been a solitary squeak out of the Russians. Not a single . . .

"Dr. Brookman, the President is ready for you now."

Only the desk lamp was lit in the Oval Office, and the Assistant to the President, having shown Brookman through the door, went over to a chair in the shadowy area on the right of the desk, under the folded flags and battle-honor streamers of the five armed services. He said nothing, but waited, listening.

"Good to see you, Mel."

"Thank you, Mr. President."

The President tapped the thin file of typescript which lay in front of him. Brookman saw that it was still marked with the red security sticker that had adorned his own copy of the Stovin Report.

"You've read this, of course." It was a statement rather than a question. Brookman nodded.

"Do you reckon he's onto something?"

"In what way, Mr. President?"

The President stared thoughtfully at Brookman. There he was again—careful, conservative, sensible, loyal, the very model of an Establishment man. Nothing wrong with being an Establishment man, of course, in spite of the sneers of folk who should know better. Establishments couldn't run without Establishment men, and the Administration was no exception. But you mustn't, you must *not* listen to them to the exclusion of all others. Just because they often said what you wanted to hear.

"I mean," he said patiently, "do you think that these . . . these Dancers have been a regular feature of Arctic life? In the past?"

"Legends of that kind sometimes have some basis in fact," Brookman found himself saying, somewhat to his own surprise.

"Because if that's so, Mel," the President went on, "then we may be starting a whole new ball game. It would mean this Arctic stuff is moving down here. Why?"

47

"Stovin thinks they're the outriders of a new Ice Age," said Brookman.

"But an Ice Age when?" asked the President.

"Stovin thinks it's already starting."

When the President spoke again, there was a faintly waspish bite to his voice. "I know what Stovin thinks, Mel. I've got it all here, in front of me. I want to know what *you* think."

Brookman rubbed his left eyebrow. It was a habit which all three of his wives had successively noticed, and deplored. It meant he was being asked a question he did not want to answer. But this was a question that couldn't be ducked any longer.

"I think," he said hesitantly, "I think . . . there may be one chance in twenty that he's right."

The President whistled. "As high as that, Mel?"

"Probably."

"The others agree with you?"

"One."

"Who?"

"Chavez."

The President opened a drawer at the side of the desk and took out a sheet of paper, running his eye down the list of names. "He's the botanist?"

"Yes, Mr. President. He's been checking on sub-Arctic plant growth. He says the pattern of the last three years bears a remarkable resemblance to fossil records from the last glacial."

"Glacial?"

"Ice Age, Mr. President."

"Hm." Abruptly, the President rose from his chair behind the desk and walked over to the ornate pier table by the window, staring for a few moments, unseeingly, at a painting of the White House that hung over it. Then he walked back, not to his desk, but to sit in one of the deep yellow armchairs by the fireplace. He smiled and nodded to Brookman to do the same. The big man sank ponderously into place.

"This thing that happened at Hays—and may have happened in Siberia—and for that matter may have happened at the Mackenzie River and for years before that . . . what is it, Mel? Stovin calls it a Dancer, but that doesn't get us very far."

Brookman leaned forward. At last there was a little positive progress to report. "I put a couple of men from

48

the Global Atmospheric team—I mean the United States component of GARP—on that, Mr. President. They came up with an answer. Seemed pretty watertight."

"Yes?"

"A couple of years ago, two Australians made a mathematical model of a tornado, which was something we knew surprisingly little about. It's been tried out pretty extensively since, and it stands up to wear and tear, as you might say. Roughly, they argued that a tornado begins as an updraught in a thunderhead cloud, which draws in air from farther out in the cloud. This air twists and spirals around the central core of the updraught, faster and faster. At the bottom end of the spiral, more air is sucked in from lower in the cloud, and gradually the tube extends earthward, like a finger. Now our boys reckon that much the same thing happened at Hays, but from a snow cloud. What we were getting, in effect, was an ice tornado. And the spiralling content of such a tornado would be unimaginably cold. It's the kind of thing, they say, that might be expected to happen in extremely cold conditions combined with a fair degree of wind—like you might get in the Arctic. I mean way up in the Arctic, around the Pole."

"And suddenly," said the President thoughtfully, "it starts happening much farther south?"

"Yes," said Brookman. "Two or three times, anyway."

"And Stovin," said the President, "believes it leads the way for a new Ice Age."

Brookman said nothing.

"How long," asked the President suddenly, "does the process take? Before the . . . the finger reaches the ground?"

"With a tornado," said Brookman, "around thirty minutes. With the Dancers, we don't have enough evidence to know. But I'd guess it to be around the same. Which may give some hope."

"Hope?"

"Well, if we could learn to identify the initial stages, Mr. President, we might be able to do something to interfere with their development."

The President shrugged. For the first time, Brookman saw, he seemed a little tired.

"Well, that might be something, Mel. At least, we'd look as though we were doing something. But we'd be dealing with the symptoms, not coming to terms with the disease. Because if these things do mean a new Ice Age, and quick, by golly, then the things themselves aren't so all-fired important. Stovin was right. They aren't important in themselves."

"No," said Brookman. He hesitated for a moment and then rose and went over to the big wall map of the world that the President had specially installed three years ago on the wall opposite the marble fireplace.

"If we assumed, Mr. President—and it's still a considerable assumption—that we *are* near a new glacial, and if we assume further that it will follow the pattern of the last glacial, 20,000 years ago, then this is what happened *then*." His finger drew a wavery line from the Pacific West Coast at Vancouver down across Montana, the Dakotas, the Great Plains, southeast through Iowa and Illinois, turning up through northern Kentucky, West Virginia, and reaching the sea near Baltimore.

"There, roughly speaking, Mr. President, was the ice frontier, 20,000 years ago."

The President rose and looked closely at the map. "Stovin said Chicago a mile under the ice," he said. "This would take in Minneapolis, Philadelphia, Pittsburgh, New York?"

Brookman nodded. "And the rest of the world"—his finger traced another line—"well, almost all of the British Isles north of a line from London to Bristol and then across Europe and European Russia. It takes in the whole of Scandinavia, the German plain, Berlin, Warsaw, Moscow, and Leningrad, of course, and east into Siberia to the Pacific."

"All would be gone?" asked the President.

"All," said Brookman.

"And how long would your . . . your hypothesis take to develop to the extent you've shown me?"

"I just don't know," said Brookman. "Stovin thinks very quickly—maybe a lot of it within a decade. He's not the only one who thinks in terms of a new glacial, of course. Nearly all the others who believe in it at all say it will be quick, too. But quick in climatic, geological terms could mean centuries. Even so, the problems of population transfer and food growing—the areas that would be affected are, as you can see, Mr. President, among the prime food-growing areas of the planet—would be gigantic. Perhaps even insuperable. The only kind of contingency plan we could make would be on

50

the basis of a world population of, at the very most, two-thirds of its present size. And using very different kinds of technology to survive."

"Are there other chief executives, in other countries, having your hypothesis put to them by their own men?" asked the President quietly.

"Very probably," said Brookman. "In fact, certainly. I know that Ledbester, in England, saw the Prime Minister last week. And there'll be others. But it'll all be under very heavy wraps. Everybody will be terrified of the kind of panic—economic, industrial, even personal—that would ensue if this got out at government level as a serious proposition."

"Nevertheless, we're going to have to talk to all the others," said the President.

"I should emphasize that what I've told you is only a hypothesis," said Brookman. "I know that's unsatisfactory, but it's all I can give you. The truth is, there's not much we know less about than we do about climate, even though we've now got weather satellites in orbit. I might be wrong. Stovin, very probably, is to some extent wrong. And the others, too. Error feeds error, any scientist will tell you. We may be wrong."

"I notice it's 'we' now, Mel," said the President dryly. "Stovin's converting you?"

"Some of the way, yes."

"And you're worried?"

"Yes."

"So am I," said the President. "By golly, so am I."

He paused for a moment, thinking. "We'll have to figure out some way of talking to the others without getting everybody hysterical," he said. "Though if we come to any kind of decision, it'll become obvious soon enough. What was it you said . . . the problems might be insuperable?"

Brookman nodded.

"I wonder," said the President. He looked, smiling, toward the ceiling. "You know, I'm not like Stovin. I've got faith in Him. He hasn't brought us this far to push us in the deep-freeze forever."

Brookman said nothing.

"You ever hear of Nathanael Greene, Mel?" asked the President.

Brookman shook his head.

"Well, I guess he's not your field," said the President.

"But old Nat's always been a hero of mine." He nodded toward the portrait of Washington over the fireplace.

"Nat Greene was Washington's lieutenant, in the early days against the British. Never won a big battle, but never lost a campaign. He used to say that 'We fight, get beat, rise and fight again.' When I was a boy, Mel, I used to think that old Nat was the kind of man I'd be happy to be. You see, the great thing that a man ought to hold close to him is that men are mighty hard creatures to put down."

He rose and held out his hand. "Thanks, Mel. I'll be in contact again, very soon. We'll have to get some of this stuff together and call some meetings. Talk, talk. There's going to be a heap of it in the next few months."

When the big man had gone, the President stood for a few moments in front of the gold-eagle sconce on the end of the marble fireplace. What was it Mel had called that thing at Hays? A finger. In spite of himself, he shivered. Unbidden, something came into his mind, and he found his lips framing long-forgotten words.

> The Moving Finger writes; and, having writ,
> Moves on: nor all your Piety nor Wit
> Shall lure it back to cancel half a line,
> Nor all your Tears wash out a Word of it.

Insuperable—that had been Brookman's word. He looked up and met Washington's eye in the portrait.

"Well, Mr. President," said the President, "we shall see."

Yevgeny Soldatov stared thoughtfully out of the window of the grey Chaika limousine taking him from central Moscow to the domestic airport at Domodedovo, twenty-five miles south of the city. The big chauffeur-driven car had picked him up at the headquarters of the Academy of Sciences, just off Leninsky Prospekt, and was now splashing in the thin autumn sleet, half snow, half rain, through Moscow's outer suburbs. Large white blocks of featureless flats reared up at intervals over the rough waste ground, already dusted with patches of the first snow. A few people, fur-hatted and thickly overcoated, walked, apparently endlessly, along the long stretches of bumpy sidewalk, or waited patiently in bus shelters for the long, mud-streaked blue buses to collect them. At last the buildings thinned out into patches of birch forest. It was Sunday afternoon, and a gang of young people—probably university volunteers, thought Soldatov sympathetically —were working in the wet, painting a concrete-and-iron bridge.

Soon the dual carriageway entered a more extensive area of forest, with the pale regiments of birch trunks standing, massed, all the way to the skyline. Soldatov's heart lifted. I'm a true Siberian, he said to himself. I have no love for Moscow. Too many people, too wrapped up in their own affairs. And the Lenin Hills are no substitute for the *taiga*.

Most Muscovites thought that to be posted to a Siberian city like Novosibirsk was the assignment they'd most like to refuse—a move to a social wasteland, the ultimate in graceless tedium. Yet he, Soldatov, had found quickly that he actually liked Novosibirsk. Oh, the city was sometimes raw, often crude. And sometimes, he remembered in amusement, it ran out of rather basic things like butter. But it had a ballet as good as the Bolshoi—well, nearly as good, anyway. And Novosibirsk, dirty old Novosibirsk and its two million people, were *going* somewhere. They stood for the future—the future unclogged by the weight of history. Best of all, in personal terms, at Novosibirsk all you had to do was to go three miles outside the city and you were in the *taiga*, the Siberian wilderness, a silvery-grey and green infinity under an ice-blue sky, where there were still elk and bear, Arctic fox and sable, and wolves—more wolves than ever this year, Kovalevsky had told him. And, for a few weeks each year, the butterflies Valentina loved so much. For a moment he saw her with his mind's eye, small and brown and determined and beautiful, and he longed to be back at once in the comfortable *dacha* at Akademgorodok, a few miles outside the city. But Novosibirsk and Akademgorodok were still 2,300 miles to the east, four hours' flight and a time zone away. It was lunchtime in Moscow, but in Akademgorodok it would be twilight.

The Chaika turned onto the muddy apron of the airport and drew up at the side doors. The airport manager came forward to greet him as the chauffeur opened the door. Making polite small talk, they went together down the small flight of steps to the private restaurant, where a single chair was drawn up at a table, and his lunch was waiting—hard-boiled eggs, red caviar, chicken in borscht, pickled cucumbers, with a glass of Tsinandali. He left the rest of the bottle. No doubt the waiter would appreciate it.

The IL-62 was full. The Novosibirsk flight was always full. The majestically proportioned blonde stewardess, with the gold Aeroflot wings pinned to the thrusting right breast of her blue uniform, had already singled him out, asking what she could bring him. But he refused the aircraft meal when it was served two hours later. It was chicken and rice, the Aeroflot mainstay, which he disliked. He was content with a glass of apple juice. I'll wait, he thought, for whatever Valentina has for me. Fresh trout, perhaps, from the Ob Sea, only half a mile from the *dacha*. He closed his eyes and slept.

There was a car at the end of the runway, and forty minutes after landing in the cold autumn night, he was home. Valentina smelled good, tasted good. And he'd guessed right. It was trout. After he had eaten, they sat companionably and talked.

"Well," she said, "did it work out? Did they listen? What did Golovine say?"

"Sat on the fence as usual," said Soldatov. "By Peter" —the expletive was peculiarly his own, arising from a childhood admiration for Peter the Great—"by Peter, it makes me wonder how the Academy functions, with men like Golovine whose one preoccupation is not to commit themselves."

She regarded him straitly. "I hope you didn't say that at the meeting, Geny. He wouldn't miss a chance like that. Nor would some of the others."

"Of course not; I'm not a fool. But they all know what I think, anyway."

"Didn't you get any backing at all?"

His face brightened a little. "Well, some. Galia, of course. I sometimes think she's got more sense than all the men put together. And I had the Siberian lobby behind me. Efrimov, Krivitsky, Mashukov . . . they all spoke up. Well"—he laughed grimly—"up to a point."

"And the others?"

"Pretty hostile. Gorshkov said he thought it was all exaggerated. He hinted I was trying to create a new little personal empire with the Investigation Unit. A lot of the others backed him, and Golvine just sat there, smiling like a Chinese image."

"But after all, you *are* Director of the Institute," Valentina said angrily. "Surely they must listen to . . ."

Soldatov laughed again, more easily this time. "There's no 'must' about it, dear. The Academy is supposed to be scientific democracy. The Siberian branch is only a component."

"But these things have been happening here, in Siberia."

"Gorshkov says they're local and temporary, and he's got a tame meteorological team to back him up. You know the sort of thing—we had a bad winter and a poor summer and we're getting freak conditions. He thinks there's absolutely no need to be seriously alarmed."

"Gorshkov's an agronomist," she said scornfully. "His *dacha* and his Zil limousine and his . . . his American hi-fi . . . by the way, did you know he'd got one? Yes, it suddenly appeared last week—all that's wrapped up in the Virgin Lands. He's not going to say 'Yes, Geny, yes, Geny, you're probably right. We'll all have to think again. Back to the planning committee.' Is he?"

"But I *am* right," said Soldatov stubbornly.

Swiftly she rose and perched on the arm of his chair, smoothing his dark hair. "Well, if you're right, my little moose—and I think you are—then it will soon be quite obvious."

"It's obvious now," he said, "if only Gorshkov had eyes to see. But it's Golvine and Gorshkov the Central Committee listens to, not me. Oh, they were polite enough. They think I'm good—the youngest Director of the Climatological Institute in Soviet history. Brilliant but *young*. Liable to get overexcited."

"Wait and see," said Valentina soothingly. He paid no attention.

"Did you know," he said, "that the Americans have had one? Colonel Koshkin showed us a satellite picture, actually at the meeting."

"What did Gorshkov say to that?"

"Said it was a blizzard, a violent blizzard. Apparently that's how their newspeople described it. Unbelievable."

"Wait and see," she said again.

"We'll wait," said Soldatov. "And one day it will be too late."

"Well, I've got a lot of questions to ask Razzle-Dazzle tomorrow," Stovin said to Diane Hilder. They sat in a polished wooden booth in the Royal Boulder Inn, looking out at the steady stream of traffic moving by in clouds of spray on the Interstate beyond the restaurant window. The waitress came to the table, her blonde pigtail swinging . . . a student, thought Diane, working her way through college. They ordered prime ribs and baked potatoes and Texas toast. Diane looked at Stovin affectionately.

"You're not exactly a computer man, are you, Stovin?" she said. "But if Razzle-Dazzle can't help you, nothing can."

"We're all computer men nowadays," he said. "Can't be anything else. Razzle-Dazzle is the best machine in the business, but it can only function with what we tell it. It's a Cray One research computer, not a genius. And we can't tell it enough. If you want accurate climatological—even meteorological—answers, you've got to feed Razzle-Dazzle everything, from zero feet up. How do we get that kind of information? There's a mountain of data at any one time . . . balloons, satellites, weather ships, climate stations, the lot. There may be ten million temperatures to be processed, but I sometimes think we'd do as well by processing the entrails of a chicken, like they did in Plato's day."

"As I said," repeated Diane, "you're not a computer man. Some people would say you're old fashioned."

Stovin did not answer but looked out through the windows of the warm room to the steady drift of thin sleety snow. It was another early snowfall—even Nature seemed to have been caught out. Between the Royal Inn and the road was the odd sight of snow dusting fully leaved trees. The sun was setting, an orange disc in a gap in the clouds which piled in purplish vapor above the Flatirons. I'm going up there tonight, he thought, and I'll ask for a cab with chains on the wheels. There are some tough gradients on the road to the Center, and I don't aim to arrive at NCAR on a stretcher. He looked again at Diane, at the narrow intelligent face framed in short, streaky blonde hair, the square shoulders, the small jutting breasts.

"I've got something to tell you about wolves, Stovin," she said. "But first let's have those Eskimo legends."

The blueberry pie had come and gone before he finished talking about Katmai and Bisby and the Dancer up by Demarcation Point, and they drank their coffee while she told him what Van Gelder had said about wolves. Stovin sat for a few moments, thinking.

"Then what explains that behavior?" he said at last. "Because I'm not mistaken, Diane. Those wolves were moving in packs of around a hundred. And there were a lot more, sitting around waiting."

"I don't know," she said slowly. "I'm damned if I know. I wish I could have seen them. But there is a possibility. It's not a factor that any zoologist likes to take too much into account because it's unquantifiable. But there's no doubt that in all animals, it's there."

"What's that?"

"Ancestral memory," she said. "It's possible that something triggered off a memory in the minds of those wolves, something buried deep in their unconscious, something that happened a long, long time ago. But it must have been a powerful trigger, and a universal one. So they began to behave like wolves did, say, 20,000 years ago. The way Van Gelder says they lived then."

"Twenty thousand years ago?"

"That's right," she said. "In the Great Ice Age."

Her cab was at the door. She stood up, patting her stomach in her usual way.

"My God, Stovin," she said. "Meals with you are death to diets. Texas toast and blueberry pie. That's playing Russian roulette with my calorie count."

"All your counts seem to be just around the right figure," he said, looking at her and smiling. He leaned forward to give her his usual peck, but abruptly she withdrew her cheek and kissed him swiftly on the mouth.

"Call me," she said. "I've always been fascinated by Russian roulette, anyhow."

He found that his heart was still thudding as the cab drew away and disappeared up the slipway to the Interstate.

Zayd ag-Akrud walked slowly over the oven-hot gravel plain toward the bull camel, which belched and wrinkled its upper lip, tearing with stained brown teeth at a lone desert thorn. Zayd was on the rim of the *reg*—a flat, dead wilderness of pebbles that stretched out for many miles to the true Sahara sand sea beyond.

The bull camel with a cow camel in milk back at the camp were all Zayd now possessed, apart from the last three goats now out at pasture with the herd. He raised his eyes to the mountains of the Ahaggar, dancing on the skyline in the afternoon heat. The sun was a shimmering white disc. A wasp, flying weakly and erratically, blundered for a moment against the blue-black Tuareg veil that masked his face against the cutting grit of the hot desert wind. He brushed it away with his hand, surprised. Apart from the bull camel and the thorn bush, the wasp was the first living thing he had seen for two hours.

Zayd was worried. He carried in his right hand the grass-plaited spring trap he must set for gazelle this evening, though he knew the chance of success was small. The long finger of stony *reg* was used by generations of gazelle on their way to evening water at the tiny pool at Zanda, ten miles away. The gazelle liked to come down on the *reg* because there they could see all around them in the level expanse, frustrating the hungry hyenas and jackals that came up from the lifeless zones of the new droughts to the south, looking for desert food. But there had been no gazelle now for several weeks. This was the sixth season in succession that the rains had failed. Without that rain the desert could not, even briefly, bloom. And without that rain, camels and goats sickened and died. Meat and milk, on which the Tuareg based their lives, died with them. The world was changing, and Zayd had decisions to make.

Carefully, pushing away the bull camel, he set the trap in the shade of the thornbush, just where a gazelle on its way to water might pause for a moment's grazing. The bull camel was lying down now. Hauling on its nose ring, while it roared angrily, he got it to its feet and began to lead it back to the camp in the flat-topped foothills of the Ahaggar. He would have ridden, but the bull camel had shown signs of weakness in the past week. Better to save its strength, because much would depend on it in the time ahead. Zayd had made up his mind.

When he entered the camp two hours later, he was weary and thirsty. A couple of lean pi-dogs scuffled in the dust around the ragged thorn fence. A score of goats, herded by two ragged children, was coming down from the sparse yellowed scrub on the slopes above the camp. Zayd straightened his back, twitched the veil more closely over his face, and stalked composedly through the dust to hobble the bull camel.

His wife Zenoba had begun the tea-making ritual as soon as one of his sons had run back from the edge of the camp to say he was coming. She boiled the battered tin kettle on the embers of her fire, outside the red goat-

skin tent. Now she made the tea in its brass pot and measured it carefully into the glass. Zayd drank. He sat on a
goatskin in the cool of the tent, spoke for a few moments to Zenoba and his young sons Hamidine and
Muhammed, patted the little boy Ibrahim on the head,
and ate a bowl of millet porridge. Then he went out. In
the middle of the little encampment of ten Tuareg families stood the tent of its chief, Moussa, its blue panels
flapping in the evening breeze. Moussa's wife Semama
scuttled away like a sand lizard as soon as Zayd entered.
He sat beside Moussa. Their slow, polite discussion—the
state of the pasturage, the progress of the drought, the
vanishing of the gazelle, the condition of the goats—continued while Semama brought coffee and then left. Zayd
looked at the older man.

"On what we spoke of a week ago, I have decided. I
leave on the day after tomorrow."

Moussa looked at him in the shadows of the tent. Outside, the sun had set. The desert wind was chill, and the
stars were diamond bright.

"And the young one, Ibrahim?"

"It is with God. He will prosper here. A lad cannot
grow without meat."

"It is true. You go to Husseyni, at Tamanrasset?"

"Yes. He is my mother's brother. He has big herds."

"It is a difficult time and a hard journey. May you
and yours be safe."

Zayd rose. "And for you, Moussa, *le-bass*. No evil."

Winter

CHAPTER 7

Irina Mikhaylovka was the first human being in Novosibirsk to hear the steps of the Dancer. The dogs in the factory down the street had already sensed it, however, and Irina was never sure afterward whether it was their howling that woke her or simply the feeling of wild unease with which she opened her eyes.

She was lying beside her husband Nikolai in the sleeping half of Apartment 131, their two-room accommodation unit on the left bank of the great Ob River. Now she struggled awake, trembling unaccountably. The familiar lights of the Birsk dredger were reflected, moving slowly, on the white plasterboard ceiling above her head, as the squat, angular vessel moved on its nightly task down the cleared ice channel. There was a sound . . . yes, a grinding and thumping, a distant roar. Abruptly, Irina climbed from the bed and crossed to the window. On the other side of the Ob, through the screen of lightly driving snow, she could see the line of the lamps along Sverdlov Street, where it joined Krasny Prospekt. She looked at her watch. Four-thirty. Another two hours yet . . . the noise was getting louder, surely?

"Nikolai," she said sharply. Her husband turned sleepily in the bed.

"Nikolai, there's something very strange. Listen. Nik . . . oh, oh."

In a crescendo of sound, the apartment block shook as though it were made of cardboard. The photograph of Nikolai's father in the uniform of the Fifth Guards Tank Army fell from the wall; the cups and plates in the wooden rack shattered where they were stacked; the window frames cracked and the double-glazed glass flew out into the Siberian night, so that freezing air, at 20 degrees below zero, rushed into Apartment 131.

Irina shrank back from the bitter blast of cold as Nikolai reached her at the gaping window.

"Look, look . . . what . . . ?"

Nikolai grasped her. "Get back, Irina."

She clung to him wordlessly but stayed beside the window. The lights of the Birsk dredger vanished. Sverdlov Street and the Krasny Prospekt were rubbed out. The long regular line of lamps on the Ob Bridge disappeared all at once, and in the same moment Nikolai and Irina saw the Dancer.

It towered above the Ob Bridge, a gigantic white column climbing into the snow-laden night sky, revolving so fast that its edges were blurred with movement. The pulsating roar of its approach continued to shake the apartment block. Through the driving snow outside their shattered window, Irina and Nikolai heard, faintly and for the last time, the dying siren of the Birsk dredger, cut off suddenly in midwail. Above it now came a new sound —the rending, splintering, thunderous rumble as the great bridge buckled under the colossal weight of the Dancer and sank, crushing and cracking the ice below, to the bed of the Ob. Stupefied, Irina and Nikolai saw that where the bridge had stood a minute before, a great wall of ice and snow now reared into the night. There was no Sverdlov Street, no Krasny Prospekt, no right bank to the river at all. In fact, there was no River Ob. Where the Novosibirsk section of the great stream had wound its ice-clogged way north toward the distant Arctic Ocean, there was now a high rampart of ice. The snow outside the window had begun to drive so thickly that through it they could only just glimpse the looming shape of the Dancer as it passed, moving diagonally across the area in which the bridge had stood, toward the main center of the city.

Irina was shaking uncontrollably, and Nikolai half dragged, half carried her back from the freezing window and into the other room of Apartment 131, where he closed the door against the onrush of the cold. Faintly from the street came a distant shouting.

"The bridge has gone," said Nikolai. "They'll be forming rescue squads. Perhaps I ought . . ." He stopped uncertainly. Irina lifted her white face toward him.

"Rescue parties?" she said, her voice cracking in a vain effort to be calm. "For what? Didn't you see what happened?"

"What?" he said stupidly.

She could control her voice no longer. "The city," she cried shrilly. "The city's gone. All gone. Everything has gone. There's nothing there, across the river. Novosibirsk has gone."

"It can't have . . ." he began, but she shook her head. "I tell you it has, Nikolai."

He seized her and shook her. "Have you gone mad, Irina? There are a million people there. They can't just go . . ."

She rocked to and fro, in paroxysms of shock.

"Novosibirsk has gone," she repeated, stuttering the words out slowly. "It is the Americans, perhaps, or the Chinese. We have been destroyed."

"Don't be such a fool," he snapped, struggling into his thick coat and pulling down the earmuffs on his fur cap. "I'm going down to the street. If the bridge has gone, they'll need some help. Now stop worrying. We're all right here, at any rate, but get that window blocked up next door. Stepan's got some plastic sheets down in the basement. Fix one across the window, or we'll damned well freeze. And let's get a bit of light . . ."

He clicked the light switch. Nothing happened. Silently Irina watched him. He shrugged.

"They'll have trouble at the power station, maybe, with a blizzard like this. The elevator probably isn't working either; I'll have to walk down. Now listen, Irina, get that window blocked. If the elevator's out, then carry the plastic upstairs. It's not heavy. But get down there quickly; we probably aren't the only ones who lost a window, and there may not be enough sheets for everybody. If Stepan's awkward, tell him I told you to do it. Have you got that?"

Dumbly she nodded. He looked at her for a moment and then, without saying more, went out of the apartment door. She sat in the little living room for a full minute before she rose and went back into the bedroom. It was now excruciatingly cold beside the window, but she clutched her dressing gown around her and gazed out at the white desert gleaming fitfully in the darkness, which stretched where she had last seen Novosibirsk.

"All gone," she whispered. "All over . . ."

"I tell you, Sto, you have no idea of the hassle there's been in and around the Council over this," said Melvin Brookman, leaning forward and speaking earnestly. "Just

65

about every climatologist in the United States wants to go to Novosibirsk. Every climatologist in the world, I guess. But the Soviets won't play. It's not just a scientific phenomenon to them, of course. Nearly 200,000 dead—it's a gigantic national tragedy. They've asked for you. You and one other. And that suits us well, in any case. Because you're the first name I put up to the President, anyway. And he agrees."

"Why me?" asked Stovin curiously. They sat in the comfortable untidy apartment that Brookman maintained in Washington, a couple of blocks from Q Street and Buffalo Bridge. Brookman had called him there that morning—just seventy-two hours after what had happened to Novosibirsk. Wryly, Stovin noticed that two of his books lay conspicuously on Brookman's desk.

"Why me, Mel?" he asked again. "Not to put too fine a point on it, we haven't always seen eye to eye in the past."

"Don't necessarily see eye to eye now, either," said Brookman dismissively. "But we've always been friends, beyond our occasional disagreements."

Stovin nodded. "That's true, but it's hardly sufficient reason to . . ."

"The President wants you," said Brookman. "You made an impression at that first meeting. Now do you want to go or not?"

Stovin laughed. "Of course I want to go. Who wouldn't? But I'm not going just as a . . . a reporter. I want to talk turkey when I'm there."

"Shouldn't be much difficulty over that," said Brookman, more cheerfully. "Apparently the Russian guy who signed the letter—Soldatov—well, he's the one who put forward your name."

"Soldatov?" said Stovin, wondering. "I know just a bit about him. He's young, if I remember right, but he's done some good work on volcanoes. . . . He's not a glaciologist, though. If he'd done any Ice Age stuff, I'd be sure to have read it."

"Well, he's the one who's got you on file," said Brookman. "Now what about the second visa? Whom do you want to go with you? I'm going to leave it as your choice."

Stovin felt a sudden, unexpected spasm of affection as he looked at the big man. Brookman's scientific world was now in process of being turned upside down, but he was already learning to come to terms with it. Brookman

66

would never be a great scientist, but his ability to respond adequately to new situations meant that he would never cease to be a useful one.

"What about you, Mel?" he said gently. "If you came along, I'd have somebody to keep me in line."

Brookman laughed. "No. That's a hell of a nice offer, Sto, but no. I'm too old and too fat and too conservative. You want a younger man—somebody who'll spark off some new ideas inside your own head. There's Fisher at Berkeley. Or I've got Bongartz at C.I.T.—he's going to be another you one day. How about him? You could do a hell of a sight worse than him."

Stovin nodded. "Yes, Bongartz would do fine. But let's take a raincheck on the second visa, just for the moment, Mel. I'll have a little think about that."

"Well, don't leave it too long. You know what the Soviets are like. They'll want those names, quick. It'll all have to go through the KGB files, that's for sure. Not that there's anything against you or Bongartz, I guess."

Stovin was thinking hard. Abruptly, he made up his mind. "There's another complication, Mel. You said they were offering two scientific visas?"

"That's correct."

"Well, I want a third. No"—he held up his hand as Brookman started to expostulate—"not a third scientific one. Just an ordinary visa. I want to take an assistant. A third man, extra to the second scientist."

"They won't stand for it," said Brookman. "Besides, Bongartz can act as your assistant."

"I don't mean another scientific assistant. I mean somebody altogether different—a man who started my mind working in all sorts of different ways a few weeks ago."

"Who?"

"Bisby. The bush pilot at Anchorage. The one who flew me up along the Beaufort Sea. You remember . . . you saw my report."

"Why in hell do you want him? Yes, I remember him. But he was Air Force. A jet pilot. They'll never allow it, over in Moscow. They'll think we're trying something on . . . some kind of intelligence trick."

"I want him, Mel, because he knows the North. Damn it, he's of the North. The man's half Eskimo. Look, I can tramp around Siberia in a warm overcoat and be told all the facts and figures, but I don't know the North. If I've got Bisby with me, I've got a whole new range of experience to filter information through. There's something about that guy. He's got a really original mind. And a gloriously untrained one."

"Well, I'll try," and Brookman dubiously. "But I don't reckon there's a chance in ten."

"No Bisby, no Stovin," said Stovin.

"You mean that?"

Stovin smiled. "Yes. You say that Moscow asked for me? Very well, there's a price. They'll understand that. The price is Bisby."

"Maybe, maybe." Brookman put his hand on Stovin's shoulder. "I thought the whole damned thing was going too well—you agreeing and all. I guess I should have known better. With you, there's always a percentage."

"With the Russians, too. You'll see. They'll huff and they'll puff, but they'll send that visa."

"I hope you're right."

Brookman unlocked a drawer in the broad leather-topped desk and drew out a stapled file. "This is your copy of what the Soviets sent us, Sto. It's a remarkable document."

"Oh?"

"Yes. It's a very, very open account to get from any agency in the Soviet Union. That's one thing I do know about," said Brookman, smiling. "I get a lot of this stuff from all over, but this is one of the frankest assessments of a domestic disaster that I've ever received. There must have been plenty of hassle in Moscow before they let Soldatov tell us all this. And they must be really, really scared . . ."

Stovin tapped the file. "Do they give any figures—temperatures, vortical speeds, anything like that?"

"Some. They had a weather monitor operating a few miles away, at that 'science city' complex they run there —Akademgorodok. It was operating just as routine, on normal parameters, and the temperature apparently just went right off the scale."

"And what was the scale?"

"They were using the Oymyakon standard. Their instrument was set to read down to 75 below, in Fahrenheit."

Stovin whistled in astonishment. "And it went off the scale—off the Oymyakon standard? Mel, that is *cold*. God knows, there's been enough in the newspapers, the last couple of days, but no hint of that."

"No, that's the really scary statistic that everybody—including you, Sto—has to keep quiet. And don't forget, that monitor burst its scale, not in the center of the damn —Dancer, whatever you call it—but out there on the fringe."

"Have they—the figures, I mean—have they been processed yet?"

"The Director at NCAR has been given them. He wants you to go to Boulder and then you'll put them through Razzle-Dazzle. The Administration is real scared of some kind of panic if folk get the idea that these things are going to start dancing all over the United States or anywhere else in the northern hemisphere. So as of now, it's just you and me and the Director who have access to those figures. And the President, of course, though I guess they won't mean much to him. We'll be able to tell him more when Razzle-Dazzle's chewed them through. Mind, I'm not sure that even Razzle-Dazzle can make much of them. As you'll see, they're a long way short of complete. Not surprising. Nobody at Akademgorodok would be remotely anticipating even a purely local temperature considerably colder, presumably, than 75 below—in October."

"No," said Stovin. He got to his feet. "Time I was going, Mel. I'm getting the evening shuttle to La Guardia."

Brookman held out his hand. "Are you flying on to Denver from New York tomorrow?"

Stovin nodded. "I've got some stuff to buy in New York. Then I was going to Boulder in any case, for . . . well, personal reasons. And, of course, I've now got a date with Razzle-Dazzle."

Brookman nodded. "No date yet for Novosibirsk naturally. The Soviets will fix that in their own good time. I'll get to you the moment I hear. And let me have the name for that second scientific visa as soon as you can. No problem if it's Bongartz. I can fix it for him to be free. And as for your guy Bisby"—his mouth puckered dubiously—"well, we'll see. . . ."

In New York next day, Stovin walked up Fifth Avenue to Brentano's where he spent ninety minutes and bought eight books. Three hours later, 42,000 feet over Illinois, he finally read the last page of Soldatov's report. He stared unseeingly from the cabin window of the United

Airlines Boeing as it cruised at 550 miles an hour high above the drifting streamers of cumulo-nimbus cloud and the grey-green misty blur far below that was the American Midwest. What do I feel now? he asked himself wryly. Justified, I suppose. Nobody will dare say anymore that what happened at Novosibirsk is some kind of aberrant climatic fluke. Not with around—he flicked back through the file and reread Soldatov's estimate with horrified fascination—not with around 180,000 dead. That was something approaching the entire population of, say, Salt Lake City.

He picked up *The New York Times* from the empty seat beside him. The story dominated the front page, with a map and an old photograph dug out of the files of Novosibirsk in better days. DEATH TOLL BELIEVED TO BE HIGH IN SOVIET ICE HORROR, said the main headline. And at the side: "Russia Declines Aid from U.N. Team." Wearily, he laid the paper back on the seat. It was the standard Soviet reaction to Soviet disasters—head back in shell, like a threatened tortoise. Show no vulnerable feature to the rest of the world. And say as little as possible. From Peking to Paris, the world's newspapers were now full of speculation supported by remarkably few facts. The very isolation of the stricken city in remote Siberia had helped the Russians to control the news flow —and prevent access by foreign journalists. The only eyewitness report was filed from Belgrade. Apparently, there'd been a small economic delegation from Yugoslavia traveling from Irkutsk to Moscow on the Trans-Siberian Express, and the train had to stop near Novosibirsk after the bridge went. But it was a pretty confused report even so, because the Yugoslavs hadn't arrived until about four hours after the Dancer, and they hadn't seen much. Just a few hundred bodies laid out in the snow beside the track. All that the Russians had admitted on the Tass agency was "a tragedy" with "many dead." No figures, no assessment; above all, no prediction. Only Soldatov seemed able to get the facts out of Russia—facts that were, according to Mel Brookman, to be treated, even here, as strictly under wraps.

"Ladies and gentlemen, good afternoon." It was the captain's voice. "Over on the left of the aircraft now, you can pick out the line of the Mississippi River. And that white patch in the distance, way out beyond . . . that's Springfield, the State capital. We're crossing into Missouri now. The weather at Denver is cool, around 55 degrees Fahrenheit, and there's a little rain. We expect to land on time. . . ."

There it was, Ol' Man River, the Mississippi itself. Stovin had seen it on this flight a hundred times. It had always been there, strong, ineradicable, a permanent wrinkle on the face of America, as familiar as a line on your mother's face. Thirteen thousand miles from Minnesota to the Gulf of Mexico, watering a chain of cities —St. Paul, Dubuque, Hannibal, St. Louis, Memphis, Vicksburg, New Orleans. And now what? What, he wondered suddenly, had been the geography of the Mississippi—the detailed geography—20,000 years ago? Ruefully, he confessed to himself that he didn't know. But the next generation might be due to find out. Would some future airline captain, flying some future jetliner over the snows of Illinois, point out a different line for the Mississippi? The thought staggered the imagination in terms of what that could mean for human life in North America. A remark of Robert Ardrey's came back to haunt him, as it sometimes had in the past three years, ". . . the defect is in our imagination, not natures . . ."

There was a local cab strike at Stapleton Airport, just outside Denver, but several cabdrivers were tacitly ignoring picket lines by using their own cars to pick up passengers, and Stovin found no difficulty in getting a car to Boulder. The University had kept a room for him, and as soon as he checked in, he phoned Diane. The ringing tone pealed, again and again, but there was no answer. More upset than he liked to admit to himself, he lay on the narrow bed in the little university guest room and tried to doze. But images kept flicking through his mind, jerking him back from the edge of sleep . . . the corpses those Yugoslavs had glimpsed beside the Trans-Siberian Railway, Brookman's worried face as he handed over the Soldatov file, Bisby telling him about the bowhead whales, and last of all, the faint silver line of the Mississippi eight miles below his aircraft seat. At six he showered, went into the cafeteria, ate alone, took a Mogadon tablet and went back to his room to sleep. This time sleep came, heavy and stifling but sure, and when he woke next morning he felt better. He looked at his watch. It was eight o'clock. On an impulse, he reached for the bedside phone and rang Diane again. With pleasure, he heard her voice.

"Hi, Stovin. What's this, an alarm call?"

"No, I phoned you last night, but you weren't there."

"I was out trying to get a job."

"Yes?"

"The Bureau of Animal Breeding and Genetics," she said in explanation. "They want a wolf-lady—wolf-person, I suppose I should say."

His heart sank a little. "Did you get it?"

"Don't know. The Director was in Cheyenne for a meeting, and he asked me up to see him. He said he's got a couple more to see first, but it sounded good. I think I may have it."

"Where would you be based?"

"London, England, for the first six months," she said laughing. "After that, anywhere, I guess."

"Oh."

There was an awkward little pause.

"You don't sound too bright, Stovin."

"No," he said, a little desperately. "I mean, yes. I have to go up to NCAR this morning; I'm going to have some stuff processed. I'm lunching with the Director, but how about dinner tonight?"

"All right, Stovin. But no more blueberry pie. No more Texas toast."

"It'll be the smallest calorie count east of the Flatirons," he promised.

When he took a cab out to NCAR an hour later, the temperature had dropped and a thin sleety snow was falling. A steady stream of cars splashed by on US 36, and a patchy sun climbed painfully into the sky, looming as a white-gold disc through the purplish background of massed cloud over the Flatirons.

"Real early for snow," said the driver. He was an old man in a red-checked anorak and a battered blue uniform cap. "Looks like it's goin' to be last year all over again. Hope not."

"It was bad last year," Stovin agreed.

"We got it early," said the old man, "and it just kept a-comin' and a-comin'."

The complex of angular brown buildings that made up the National Center for Atmospheric Research jutted up from a little plateau beneath the Flatirons. Stovin hurried in out of the gusting snow, up the wide steps, past the geometric designs of modern art on the staircase walls, past the big color prints of ice crystals along the

72

corridor. The Director greeted him briefly, and they walked down to the computer room together. The Director was carrying his own copy of the Soldatov file.

"You read this, Sto?"

"Yes."

"Doesn't look good, does it? Of course, there's just the chance they're isolated phenomena. But I guess you don't think so?"

"No."

"Nor do I. Mind you, even as isolated phenomena they wouldn't be classed as reassuring, exactly. Except for the aftereffects, what hit that city had rather more effect than a Hiroshima-style atomic bomb. Well, let's see what Razzle-Dazzle utters. Sto, I've had to ask one of the scientific assistants to be in on this, because he's going to have to operate the machine. He's a good boy; he won't talk. I've really laid that on the line to him. His name's Harmon. Dave Harmon."

The computer room lay at the base of the NCAR complex, in an underground chamber buried beneath the mesa below the Flatirons. Four feet of earth covered it as an insulator; inside its silent halls the temperature was kept rigidly constant at 68 degrees Fahrenheit. Stovin and the Director walked together across the red-paneled floor. Each panel, Stovin knew, was individually balanced; each was individually removable; and each gave access to some piece of vital equipment. In the center sat Razzle-Dazzle, the great Cray One research computer, looking like a large fluted barrel painted in brown-and-orange stripes. Grouped around it were the twelve slave computers that fed it. This was the giant processing brain of GARP, the Global Atmospheric Research Project, set to handle up to eighty million instructions a second.

As Stovin and the Director reached the computer area, Harmon came forward. He was a fresh-faced, burly young man who looked as though he might be more at home feeding passes to a quarterback than feeding statistics into Razzle-Dazzle.

"Now we've got this to ourselves, Dave, haven't we?" said the Director. It was half a statement, half a question.

"We have," said Harmon. "All other users have been called off. We've got direct access on the central teletype —no waiting, no time sharing."

"Good," said the Director. "You've got the tapes?"

Harmon nodded toward a plastic table on which sat

the five cans of magnetic tapes sent from Moscow—flat, circular steel-blue containers that held all that instruments could measure about what had happened to the big city of Novosibirsk on the River Ob in central Siberia a week ago. Harmon picked up the cans, checked the numbers, and placed them one by one onto the mounting spindle of one of the peripheral computers—an oblong white box about ten feet by eight, against the near wall. There was a faint hissing as the tapes revolved successively in their inner vacuum. Three minutes later, the tapes were read. The sustained hiss from the tape drive ceased. All the information sent from Novosibirsk was now stored in the magnetic memory of the central computer. Stovin walked over to where Harmon stood beside Razzle-Dazzle. The young man watched him curiously.

"Here's the tape for my programme," said Stovin. Again Harmon opened a compartment on the central machine, installed the tape, and pressed the operating button. Steadily, as the questions on Stovin's tape were processed inside the computer, the line printer poured out the answers on its long cream-colored strip of paper, like a giant supermarket bill. Stovin and the Director carried it over to the end of the room, where a table and chairs waited for them. For several minutes, they read steadily, each of them making a series of notes on a pad in front of him. At last, Stovin looked up.

"Well, as far as it goes, it seems clear. To the north and the east of Novosibirsk, temperatures started to fall dramatically about two-and-a-half hours after midnight. That sucked in the air and started the vortex . . . it was a real-life demonstration, you might say, of that Australian tornado model."

The Director nodded. "Still begs the main question, though, doesn't it, Sto?"

"You mean exactly how the temperatures dropped? Well, that happened outside the area covered by the Akademgorodok weather monitor—way, way outside. So there's nothing Razzle-Dazzle can tell us about that."

"No," said the Director. "But you saw the other very curious thing?"

Stovin rose suddenly and walked over to a chart of the stratosphere which hung along one wall. At last he swung back. The Director watched him without speaking.

"If Razzle-Dazzle's getting the right information," said Stovin, "we're into a whole new situation. Because it looks . . . it looks as though the jet stream took a dip. Now we know, of course, that the jet stream does become unstable when the planet enters a cooling period, that the atmospheric winds swing north and south and cause unexpected climatic changes. But nobody's ever thought of a jet-stream aberration *downward*. Have they?"

"No," said the Director. "It took Razzle-Dazzle to do that. Trouble is, we know so damn little about the atmosphere. Are we suddenly getting a downward drift of the jet stream? My God, if we are, it can bring unimaginable cold locally, and very low temperatures over wider surrounding areas. Exactly what happened to that poor city."

"Because," said Stovin, "that was a cold that was not of this earth. Literally not of this earth. What's the temperature twelve miles up—even above the Equator? Somewhere around 112 Fahrenheit below, if I remember the textbooks?"

The Director nodded without speaking.

"Well, it's all beginning to figure," said Stovin. "The jet stream certainly zigzags a hell of a lot more than twelve miles laterally, and when that happens it sets off the depressions that track west to east around the world. And if we're now getting *vertical* swings in the jet, we're tapping the deep freeze of outer space. If that's so, we know *what* a Dancer is, but we still don't know *why* it is. Is this what always happens in an Ice Age? Or is this special, something Nature's reserved just for us?"

"Maybe you'll find out more over there in Novosibirsk," said the Director. His voice seemed tired.

"Maybe," said Stovin. "There are one or two procedures we can try that they may not be familiar with. The ice itself, for instance. There must be plenty of air bubbles from that Dancer still trapped inside it. We could try analyzing it to see if it contains any isotopes characteristic of very high altitudes. It would at least confirm the *how*, though still not the *why*."

"Well, that's ingenious, Sto, and worth trying. But I don't reckon the *how* is going to concern us in the immediate future. Nor even the *why*. All that everybody's going to ask us for the next few months is the *when*. And that's going to be very hard to answer. . . ."

Harmon walked over to them, carrying five lengths of lineprinter strips that he had now mounted on black cards.

"Here are Razzle-Dazzle's maps and diagrams, sir," he said to the Director. "I can have them photocopied and give Dr. Stovin a set."

"No," said the Director. He put out his hand and took the cards from Harmon. "I'll copy them myself, in my office. Sto, have you got those printouts?"

"Yes," said Stovin. "I'll take the tape cans back too."

Together they walked up the carpeted steps to ground level. The Director came out to the main doors, where Stovin's car was waiting. "Don't worry about Dave," he said. "He knows how to keep his mouth shut."

"Do you think he got much of it?"

"Enough," said the Director. "He's no fool and he's a quick printout reader. He'll have got enough."

"In that case," said Stovin grimly, "I hope he can sleep tonight."

The Director laughed shortly. "It's you and me need the sleeping pills, Sto. Harmon's young. The young are resilient."

Stovin got into his cab. There was still a dusting of snow in the north wind, and the sky was like a sheet of white metal. The Director shivered. Stovin wound down the window and looked at him.

"You remember a few minutes ago," he said, "I asked if these things are what always happens when an Ice Age begins?" The other man nodded.

"Well," said Stovin, "there's something that keeps coming back into my mind, ever since I saw that Dancer up by Demarcation Point. I'd always thought there was no record of these things, but . . ."

"Yes?" said the Director.

"It was an account by Sebastian Munster, the geographer—something he saw in the Rhone Valley, in the Alps, in 1546. There's a copy of Munster in the library —part of the Schuster bequest, I think. Take a look at it. It's instructive. Page 330, or thereabouts."

With a scrunch of chained tires on the snowy gravel, the car drew away. The Director walked inside the Center, and into the library. He asked one of the girls for a copy of Munster. With a look of surprise, she took a key from the desk and opened a locked cabinet behind her, carrying the book over to the desk where the Director was now sitting. It was a large leather-bound volume, its title page headed, in archaic curling script: *Cosmographiae*

76

Universalis lib. VI, published in Basel in 1552. With a sinking heart, the Director turned to page 332, riffling through the yellowed sheets adorned with wood engravings of monks' heads and thumbnail landscapes. Here it was:

> *Anno Christi 1546, quarta Augusti, quando trajeci cum equo Furcam montem, veniam ad immensem molen glaciei cujus densitas, quantum conjicere potui, fui duum aut trium phalangarum militarum; latitudo vero continebat jactum fortis arcus . . . Dissilierat portio una et altera a corpore totius molis magnitudine domus, quod horrorem magis augebat . . .*

Wryly, the Director smiled. Munster, of course, had written in Latin, the *lingua franca* of civilized scholarly intercourse in the sixteenth century. It would be Stovin's view that you couldn't be truly scientifically literate even now unless you had a working knowledge of Latin. But he, the Director, didn't. And he doubted if anybody else in NCAR did, either. He carried the big volume back to the assistant.

"Could you get somebody to copy this passage for me?" he asked, smiling. "I'll take it down and get somebody at the University to give me a translation."

She looked at the passage. "Oh, Dr. Stovin was looking at it the other day," she said. "I think there's a translation in Ladurie. He mentioned it."

She took from a shelf behind her the claret-colored volume of Ladurie's *Times of Feast, Times of Famine,* a history of climate over the past thousand years. The Director flicked through the index. There it was, Chapter Four.

"On August 4, 1546, as I was riding toward Furka, I came to an immense mass of ice. As far as I could judge, it was about two or three pike-lengths thick, and as wide as the range of a strong bow. It's length stretched indefinitely upward, so that you could not see its end. To anyone looking at it, it was a terrifying spectacle, its horror enhanced by one or two blocks the size of a house which had detached itself from the main mass . . ."

Ladurie had translated the measurements into modern terms. Forty to fifty feet high, 600 feet wide. The Director sat looking at the book and suddenly spoke aloud. The girl at the library desk looked up startled, unsure whether he was speaking to her or not. The Director looked at her as though continuing a conversation.

"I guess," he said, "that could have been a Dancer, all right. Just one Dancer. It signalled a Little Ice Age that froze central Europe for a century and a half. And we've had four Dancers already. What are they telling us?"

CHAPTER 8

Hundreds of animals and many people attacked as packs proliferate

BIG BAD WOLF RETURNS TO MENACE RUSSIANS

From Michael Binyon,
Moscow, March 20.

Once again the cry "wolf" is echoing through Soviet forests and villages. The peasants' traditional enemy is back in force, attacking sheep, dogs, and even people in alarming numbers. . . .

Last winter wolves killed thirty dogs in the Kirov region, northeast of Moscow, and countless huskies were attacked. Wolves even ventured into the city, and a few miles from Kirov a large pack was discovered.

All over the country, it seems, the wolf population has been increasing. In the Russian Federation there were an estimated 2,500 wolves in 1960; now there are about 12,000. The same is true of Byelorussia, the Ukraine, and the Baltic republics.

Wolves are particularly numerous in the steppes. In Kazakhstan, central Asia, there are an estimated 30,000, and they have recently reappeared on the outskirts of Moscow . . . Attacks on people have increased.

Extract from a report in the
London Times, March 21, 1978.

"Well, what's this about wolves, Stovin?" asked Diane, scuffing her thick walking shoes through the mess of leaves, covered with part snow, part slush, beside the winding road that led up to NCAR from the road outside Boulder. The snow-sleet showers of earlier in the day had stopped while they were eating an hour before. It was cold, very cold. Diane, thought Stovin, was the only woman he knew who would have accepted his invitation to walk.

"Just that there was an interesting piece of that Soviet report, that they'd come into the city—well, what's left of the city, I imagine—in big numbers," he said. "Plenty of food for them, I suppose."

Diane shivered, but Stovin did not appear to notice.

"The thing that puzzled me," he went on, "was that they were close enough in sufficient numbers to take advantage of the situation."

She shrugged the shoulders of her white duffel coat. They'd left the car half a mile behind them and were walking together toward the western afterglow of the autumn evening above the Flatirons. Long streaks of pink and gold ribanded the horizon, the slablike mountains rearing through the gilded light like puffs of dark smoke.

"There's said to have been a big explosion in the Siberian wolf population in the last few years," she said. "The Russians don't really give progressive details, just an occasional global figure. There've been some newspaper stories, but not many facts. And not many of our people are able to get more than a brief visit over there. But, yes, I'd guess there just could be enough wolves around Novosibirsk to cause trouble. On the whole, though, they usually keep clear of human beings. Especially if the humans are armed . . . and I imagine they will be around Novosibirsk now? I mean, the Soviet army will be there, stopping looting, and so on?"

"There's something about that in the report," he said. "They give a figure for wolves shot in the last week. Something around 300."

She whistled. Above the Flatirons, the gold streamers were now sinking into inky gloom, and the first drift of stars shone in the evening sky.

"Three hundred? That's more than I would have thought—a lot more. Can I see the report?"

"You're not supposed to, but you can."

Abruptly she stopped, and turned to face him, half laughing, half serious. "You make your own rules, don't you, Stovin?"

"Only some of them," he said. She thought that his voice had a surprisingly flat, bitter tinge. She slipped her arm through his.

"I wouldn't be out here walking with you if you didn't," she said.

It was dark now, and they walked back across the short tufty grass to where Diane had left her little car. When they were once more sitting inside it, she felt for the switch, but his hand reached out and checked hers. In the faint light from the windscreen, his face was intent.

"I want you to see what the report says about wolves because it may . . . concern . . . you."

"How?"

"You know I'm going out there?"

"I guessed."

"I can take two others. I'm taking Bisby—he's the pilot who flew me over the Beaufort Sea."

"I remember," she said. Her heart, she realized, had begun to beat very fast.

"And I can take another scientist. Mel Brookman wants me to take Bongartz."

"Bongartz . . . didn't he do a lot of work on the Dust Veil? I remember seeing something about it in one of the journals. Not my field, though, as you know."

"Exactly," he said. "Not your field. Any more than *canis lupus* is Bongartz's. I don't want Bongartz. I know he's good, but I don't want him. When I was up in Alaska, I talked a lot to Bisby. It taught me one thing— something I'd always known, I suppose, but it needed Bisby to get it straight in my mind. We aren't going to understand what's happening by looking at climate alone. We've got to think bigger than that. We've got to understand what's happening *because* of what's happening. Do you see what I mean?"

She nodded in the darkness.

"It'll be a waste to take Bongartz. We don't need two climatologists to report to the President. So I'm going to take somebody else. You, Diane, if you want to come. No"—he raised his hand—"don't say anything for a minute. Listen . . . I need a zoologist, and a zoologist who understands what I'm talking about."

80

He sounded urgent, almost desperate.

"All right, all right," she said mildly. "You don't have to twist my arm. If I'm doubtful about coming, it's because of something else."

"What?"

"Look, Stovin, am I good enough? This is a pretty important trip. I doubt if anybody in Washington, let alone Moscow, has ever heard of me. Are they really going to let you take a zoologist who's not an international name? When there's a man like Van Gelder in New Mexico who'd jump at the chance. Your own university, too."

"Van Gelder would drive me raving crazy in forty-eight hours," said Stovin irritably. "And in any case, Van Gelder himself said you were the best of the generation coming up. He's often said so."

"Van Gelder said that?"

"He did."

"Well, well. I always thought it was my blue eyes he fancied."

"I have to call Brookman tonight," said Stovin.

"He'll blow his top," she said. She found her voice sounded slightly unsteady. For the first time, Stovin himself chuckled.

"Not him. He's sweating too hard trying to get a visa for Bisby. He'll find an accredited zoologist a lot easier. But . . . you're coming?"

"You know I'm coming."

"Well, that's that, then. Let's get back to Boulder. I have to get to a phone. To start off, I have to call Bisby."

"What's he like—Bisby?"

"Oh," he said vaguely, "Bisby's a good guy. A guy you can talk to. You'll like him . . . you wait and see."

"Good," she said. She leaned across and kissed him lightly on the cheek. He could smell the sweet scent of her hair. He turned and kissed her on the mouth. She did not draw back, but she made no more than a token response. He felt slightly disconcerted.

"It could be complicated," he said gruffly. "I don't think . . . that your academic abilities are the only reason I want you to come."

She pressed the starter and the busy little Volkswagen engine spluttered into life.

"Don't worry about that," she said. "They aren't the only reason I'm coming."

81

Bisby drove slowly south out of Anchorage, listening to the chains on the car wheels cutting into the hard-packed snow. The road wound along beside the lumpy ice of the Ninilchik River, through a little slum of campers and abandoned car lots, where the rusting ends of forgotten vehicles stuck out of the white mantling of the snow. After two or three miles he reached the house he sought. House, he thought, was an overly dignified word to describe it. It consisted of two campers, axle deep in the frozen ground where they had settled in the mud of last summer, joined by a little linking tunnel of dirty fiberglass. Beyond the site was the river and a straggling stand of stunted alder trees. It was already twilight.

The flaking door of the bigger camper was closed. He did not knock, but turned the knob and entered. For a moment he stood, until his eyes were accustomed to the light. A television set, the sound turned down, flickered some faraway ballgame in the corner; a single lamp, frayed flex trailing, was switched on above the shelving at the side. He went over to the other side of the camper, near the little cubicle that housed the cooking stove, and sat down.

The interior of the camper was warm, redolent of the body odor of the eight Eskimos who crowded in a silent circle, waiting. Once or twice the doorknob turned and another figure stole in, briefly outlined, until the door closed, against the ghostly glimmer of the snow outside. Soon the little cabin was so crowded that there was room for no more. The Eskimo beside Bisby, a young fat man, breathed heavily, snuffling and clearing his throat. There was a sound of movement in the other section of the camper, and the young Eskimo abruptly reached across and switched off the television set. The lamp went off with it, and the camper was now almost dark, reflecting only the twilight glow of its small window and the occasional lights of a truck howling by on the highway outside. Opposite Bisby sat a middle-aged woman in a stout plaid anorak, talking in a low voice to the girl next to her. The remainder of the people in the camper were no more than dark hulks in the shadows . . . an occasional clearing of a throat, a muffled giggle, and once, three times repeated, a shrill whisper—*até,até,até.*

Bisby was not sure at what moment the squat figure of the shaman Julius Ohoto entered the room. The wind was getting up outside, and the whole camper creaked as the

82

gusts buffeted it, so that the sound of any arrival was deadened. One moment, it seemed, the center circle was empty. The next he was there. Any *katkalik*, of course, was said to have the power of seeing in the dark—what was it his father had told him? "The *katkalik*, they believe, has an inner fire, by which he lights the path of his soul." They believe . . . that's how his father had put it. What would his father think of him now? In any case, this Julius Ohoto didn't trust to inner fire. In the shadows beside his seat, Bisby saw the big rubber-covered torch that Ohoto used. Nevertheless, as though from long habit, the pilot's fingers went up to his chest and under his anorak, and he grasped the smooth bone of the little skull amulet. He looked at the shaman. Ohoto was a middle-aged man; he worked, Bisby suddenly remembered, as a clerk in an Anchorage real-estate office. He wore heavy executive-type spectacles which, on his flat face, made him look slightly absurd, and he had a gold filling in one of his front teeth. Bisby could see how it glinted when the shaman moved his head. Ohoto was holding a bottle of beer which he suddenly raised to his mouth, drinking heavily. He made no move to offer anything to anyone else present but picked up a long wooden wand that lay beside him and tapped it on the bottle. The young fat Eskimo beside Bisby began to sing. It was a song about the caribou, an old song that Bisby had heard as a child on Ihovak, a high strange piping lilt to which all in the room listened silently, remaining quiet after its last incongruous echoes died away. The shaman Ohoto sat as though waiting. At last he held out his hand, stretching out in the darkness to the other side of the room, away from Bisby. One by one, the Eskimos reached out their hands—the men the right hand, the women the left—and briefly clasped his fingers. A baby in the corner cried briefly; its mother hushed it but pushed its tiny fist against Ohoto's palm. Then it was Bisby's turn. The shaman's fingers felt rough and cold, like a fish's skin. When Bisby took his hand away, he grasped his amulet again.

Ohoto squatted in the center circle and took from his belt a leather glove. He placed it beside him, stood, and touched it with the point of his wooden wand—again and again and again. Each time he touched it, it seemed harder to raise the point of the wand. At last, the shaman struggled with the wand as though its point were buried deep in the earth. As he flung back his head in the darkness, Bisby felt a drop of Ohoto's sweat fall onto his own hand. A few moments later, the shaman had reached the last stage of his spell. He could no longer lift the wand at all. He spoke harshly, gasping.

"My *tornaq* is with us."

A shuddering sigh ran through the Eskimos. Bisby felt the hairs on the back of his own neck prickle and rise. With each Eskimo in turn, Ohoto now held a muttered conversation. For each Eskimo, Ohoto asked the *tornaq* a single question: Should I buy this boat, this car? Will this woman help me? Will my debtor repay? Each time he pulled at the wand. If it rose swiftly, easily, when a question was asked, the Eskimo who had asked scrambled, gratified, from the house. Sometimes the wand was immovable. The woman in the plaid anorak asked her question, "Will my son recover?" As though bolted to the earth, the wand remained down. Sobbing, she crawled from the circle.

As Ohoto reached him, Bisby realized that he was the last in the room, and that he and the shaman were now alone. He sensed that he was being watched by the shaman in the darkness. The shaman picked up the beer bottle, drank heavily, and pitched it, clattering, to the far end of the camper. Then he began to chant, so quickly that the words seemed to run together into one. It was an Ihovakmiut chant; there was an occasional word in the mounting gabble that Bisby recognized. His head was spinning. Dully he wondered how Ohoto knew that he was from Ihovak Island.

At last the torrent of words ceased. The shaman grasped the wand, "Put your question," he said.

"I have been invited to go on a far journey," said Bisby. "Will it profit me to go?"

There was no movement from the wand. It remained point down, but Ohoto did not struggle with it as he had for previous questioners.

"What is the answer?" asked Bisby at last.

"There is no answer," said Ohoto. "I just can't hold the wand. See . . ."

He took his hand away. The wand stayed point down, as though sprouting from the floor. "You must ask another question."

Bisby moistened his lips. "Is it my destiny to go?"

The wand soared upward, as though floating on air.

"It is your destiny," said Ohoto.

Bisby began to rise, but the shaman raised his free hand.

"You have another question," he said. "Ask the *tornaq.*"

Bisby's hand was damp on his amulet.

"Shall I return?"

Suddenly, there was a breath of icy air, and a clattering, rushing sound, as though the room were full of beating wings. Startled Bisby raised his head, and missed what happened to the wand. When he looked back at the shaman, the wand was no longer there.

"What . . . ?" he began to say, but Ohoto shook his head and placed a finger on his lips.

"My *tornaq* has answered," he said. "He is gone."

The gravelly ledge where the wolf lay was more than a hundred feet above the jumbled pack-ice of the lake. Thirty thousand years ago, before the ice came and the lake shrank into its frozen bed, the ledge had been a beach. The shells of ancient sea creatures still littered it, and around the wolf were also scattered the evidence of an earlier occupation by other hunters of the Siberian tundra—long, pointed quartz flakes, as sharp as on the prehistoric day they had been chipped into arrowheads. Unblinkingly, the wolf stared over the bare, bleak land. The landscape was treeless; the last tiny flowers of the Arctic summer had long gone; in the lee of the boulders at the lakeside, the last, sheltered remnants of the multi-colored summer lichen clung dead and discolored in the crevices. It was a landscape that at first sight appeared to be devoid of life, but the wolf knew better. Beside the lake lay a caribou skull; from across the water came the short, scratchy wick-wick birdcall of a late-migrating phalarope. The wolf's attention, however, was concentrated on the ragged line of distant dots that was winding over the snowcrest three-quarters of a mile away. He raised his head and wrinkled his nose, sniffing, as the dots came nearer, moving at a steady three miles an hour, their lean rangy shapes became instantly identifiable, though the wolf had long known what they were. He rose abruptly on the ledge, bracing the four padded toes of each foot against the looseness of the shale, digging in the fifth toe, the dewclaw, to hold himself firm. He flicked his long darting tongue over his narrow muzzle, threw back his head and howled. At once the leader of the wolves in the line, now less than half a mile away, howled also.

The wolf on the ledge turned and made his way down to the lake, swinging north when he reached it, loping steadily away up a long glacier-carved corry of smashed rocks. At the end a jumble of granite slabs formed a little natural amphitheater, and here the fourteen other wolves of the pack lay waiting. First he greeted his mate, with a rough nuzzling and pawing. For the rest of their lives, they were the mated pair of this pack, and he was the leader. He was in his prime. No wolf of his pack would yet challenge him; every decision that affected the life of the pack would be taken by him alone.

When he finished with his mate, it was time for the other wolves to welcome him. There was a flourishing of tails, a placing of paws upon neck, an excited yipping, a series of mock advances and retreats. These formalities over, the big wolf, tail up, trotted back down the corry. The other wolves followed him, in hunting-pack formation single file, well spaced. The pack he had seen from the ledge—it numbered a dozen—was already beside the lake when they arrived, and for a few moments an age-old ritual took over. In each group of wolves the ears went back, hackles stood up, bodies were stretched to make the maximum bulk, and a low threatening growling began. The leader of the other pack, an old animal with a badly torn muzzle, urinated sharply beside a rock, and the first wolf leader sniffed at it consideringly. For a moment the two bounded away, making half-serious feints at each other, until suddenly the older animal lay in a position of submission, crouching low against the snow, his tail firmly between his legs. The other leader sniffed him and turned away. At once, though with a little snarling and pushing, the two packs merged. They were one pack now—one pack of twenty-seven wolves. They trotted in single file up the corry, led by the first wolf leader, his tail high. He did not stop in the little amphitheater where his own pack had spent the last two days. The short day was merging into an early twilight, and the cutting wind was flecked with snow. As surely as if he held a compass, the wolf leader loped on. He had the dark-red disc of the sun humped on the horizon behind his right shoulder as he led the pack south.

CHAPTER 9

Stovin abandoned his attempt to sleep, opened his eyes, pulled at the tab of the window blind, and looked through the small square porthole into the blackness of the night. For a few minutes he had thought that the deep rushing roar of the Boeing's engines would be soporific, but questions kept forming in his mind, and sleep would not come. There were a few stars sprinkled in the night sky, almost eclipsed by the pulsing red-orange glow of the port wing light. He looked at his watch. They were an hour and a quarter out from London Heathrow. Three more hours to Moscow . . . Beside him Diane sat with her eyes closed. It was impossible to tell if she was asleep or not. Beyond her was Bisby, quietly reading. Stovin screwed up his eyes to read the title at the top of the open page. Faintly surprised, he noticed that it was Thor Heyerdahl's *Early Man and the Ocean*. Typical Bisby, he thought. Never does what you expect. He looked again through the porthole. A cluster of lights was coming up under the port wing—Denmark, perhaps? I don't know, he thought to himself. Just one more thing I don't know.

Why had the Russians refused to grant visas to other scientists? Ledbester had been angry, really angry. The big British scientist—physically he wasn't unlike Mel Brookman—had been shaking with rage. "We're in this damned situation up to our eyeballs," he'd told Stovin. "If there's trouble coming at the pace you think—and, Stovin, I'm beginning to agree with you—then we're going to be worse hit than any other major industrial nation. We could have a very, very difficult time practically anywhere north of the Thames. If there's knowledge to be gained at Novosibirsk, there's knowledge to be shared. . . ."

Well, you could see Ledbester's point. And the President had made it very clear to the British Prime Minister that Britain would get a copy of whatever report Stovin

87

made—if, he thought desperately, Stovin found anything. By God, I have to. Ledbester was right, of course. Britain would take a beating; anything that could lessen or even explain that beating would be vital to the British. Why do I call them the British? I'm one of them myself. No, I'm not. I'm American. I chose to be American. I'm glad to be American. But . . . there is that trace of fellow feeling for those cold, damp, shabby, stuffy, civilized little islands. I never knew my father, he thought. He died before I was three years old. My mother always said he was British of the British. She told me that often enough, sitting in that little apartment in Santa Monica, remembering. "I didn't dream," she used to say, "that I'd ever long for rain. But I do. Our sort of rain, anyway." He'd never properly understood what she was talking about, of course. But he'd—well, it wasn't a word he often used—he'd loved her. And now she was gone, too. All that was left of their bit of Britain was pumping around in his veins. He wouldn't be himself, William Stovin, without it. Nevertheless, he thought, closing his eyes and suddenly beginning to doze, I'm an American. Now and forever.

He woke to an indefinable sensation in the aircraft seat beneath him. He looked at his watch and knew what it was. They must now be within a hundred miles of Moscow, and the Boeing was beginning its letdown. There was a bustle in the cabin a few minutes later as the seat belt sign came on. Diane stirred and woke, talking for a few moments to Bisby. Stovin could not hear what they said, though he noticed somewhat to his own surprise, that he wanted to. As the jetliner came down into the lower air, it began to descend through swirling snow, and when it came in on its final approach half an hour later, the chains of blue runway lights were half obscured by the gusting white flurries. It was not an easy landing. The Boeing's captain came in once, wheels down, aborted in the last few seconds, and climbed away to circle once more over the dark sprawl of the city before making a second, successful approach through the grey-white murk. Bisby had laid down his book and was listening thoughtfully to the changing note of the engines. He looked across at Stovin and grinned, nodding toward the flight deck forward of their seats.

"It's a poor night for flying. I'm glad I'm not in that chair."

It was snowing hard as the Boeing taxied up to the

circular canopy of Sheremetyevo's central complex. Curiously, Stovin took his first sight of the Soviet Union. A few muffled figures stood outside the complex in the hard white-yellow lights. Beyond them were parked two big jets—an Alitalia Boeing and a big high-winged Aeroflot aircraft which Stovin did not recognize.

"Antonov," said Bisby briefly when Stovin asked him. "They have a bomber version, as well."

There were banks of hard-packed snow beyond the runways. Two yellow airport buses came out, and the temperature in the aircraft cabin dropped sharply as the doors were opened. Stovin and the other two began to move out with the shuffling line of passengers, but a stewardess came up smiling.

"Please sit down," she said. "We're told there are special arrangements for you."

Awkwardly, they wedged themselves back into their seats. Outside, a large and angular machine moved steadily up and down, breathing hot air onto the freezing ground. It was followed by another machine mopping up the melted ice and, a few moments later, by a black limousine, sidelights glowing. Bisby leaned across, watching curiously.

"Here comes the Zil," he said. "I guess somebody out there's got his orders."

The stewardess beckoned, and they went down the center gangway and out of the aircraft. Although Stovin was already muffled in his short thick duffel coat, the cold as he stood at the top of the aircraft steps made him gasp. Beside the door of the Zil, drawn up at the foot of the steps, a fur-hatted guard stepped smartly forward and opened the door, ushering them into the broad back seat. A youngish man with glasses sat beside the uniformed chauffeur. He turned to greet them as they settled into the car, speaking in grammatically perfect English but with a heavy guttural accent.

"My name is Grigori Volkov," he said, smiling. "From the Ministry of Foreign Affairs. I am at your service while you are in Moscow—though I regret that you will not be in Moscow very long."

The Zil began to pull away, moving out along a wide road toward the airport gates.

"Don't we go through immigration?" asked Diane in surprise.

"Not necessary," said Volkov flatly. "You are our

89

honored guests. If you will simply pass me your passports and visas . . ."

He opened a black plastic briefcase, took out a rubber stamp, and franked their visas, carefully noting down the numbers and details in a notebook, and even copying in details of other visas from Stovin's passport. He saw Stovin's look of astonishment and laughed uneasily as he passed the passport back. "We are a document-conscious country," he said, apologetically.

The car plowed on along the broad highway to Moscow. Stovin looked at his watch. It was nearly midnight, but even so the lack of traffic seemed remarkable. They passed a snowplow, toiling in the opposite carriageway.

"A bad night to be out," he said to Volkov.

The Russian shrugged. "This road was closed for two hours earlier today, before we could clear it. The snow is bad now, but it was much worse at midday. People do not come out in this weather."

"I imagine you're used to it?"

"In January, yes. But this is early. This is a cold land, Dr. Stovin, as you know, but it is very early to get this weather. We are now at the beginning of our winter, but I have known midwinters that were less cold."

Dimly, through the driving flakes, a gaunt skeletal construction loomed up on the right-hand, near side of the road—a projection of girderlike forms, like a giant tank trap.

"Our weather did one thing for us," said Volkov. "It helped us stop the Germans in 1941."

He nodded toward the monument. "That marks the nearest point they reached to Moscow. Some of them believed they could see the towers of the Kremlin from there."

"Do many Germans come to Moscow now?" asked Diane.

"Of course," said Volkov. "Germany is democratic now." He smiled in the darkness of the front seat, and they caught the flash of a gold-filled tooth. "Some of it, at any rate," he added.

"You say," said Stovin interrogatively, "that we won't be long in Moscow?"

"Just tonight," said Volkov. "You are booked on the morning flight to Novosibirsk tomorrow. It's not a long flight—about four hours."

"Who will meet us there?"

Volkov shrugged again. "I do not yet know the names. Probably somebody from the Siberian Academy of Sciences."

He looked at Stovin, his expression indefinable. "The situation in Novosibirsk is unpredictable . . . irregular, you understand?"

Stovin nodded.

"But be assured," said Volkov. "You will be met."

The car had now reached central Moscow and was turning down a wide, shop-lined boulevard.

Volkov jerked his thumb at the deserted highway. "Gorky Street," he said. "Your hotel is at the end, near Red Square."

The hotel was big, impersonal, international. They were on the 17th floor, and Stovin looked out briefly through the smeared double-glazing before getting into the narrow bed. The lights of Moscow—nothing like those of New York, he thought—showed at intervals through the drifting snowflakes. On some building nearby, a great red star glowed into the night. He climbed into bed and opened one of the books he had brought from New York. It contained Herman Flohn's *Background of a Geophysical Model of the Initiation of the Next Glaciation*, an examination of the triggering of past ice ages, written in 1974. He took out the page marker and began to read.

"In view of the rapidity of development, the initial stages must have lasted less than a century, only a few decades. What kind of atmosphere/ocean circulation anomalies are able to produce such catastrophic events? Any answer to this question can only be more or less speculative . . ."

Wearily, too tired to go on, he closed the book.

"You can say that again," he thought, as he started to settle into sleep.

"By God, that's an ice blink," said the second officer of the British coastal survey ship *Orca*, laying his binoculars down on the polished ledge in front of him staring out from the enclosed bridge. Far to the north, along the horizon where the grey sea met the grey sky, a white streak of light rippled for a second or two, then died, then rippled again.

"Nonsense, it can't be," said the first officer brusquely. "Not in these waters. We're 200 miles south of the maximum limit of drift ice." He raised his own binoculars and looked at the horizon for several seconds. At last he turned to the other man.

"Something distinctly odd, I agree. Anything on radar yet?"

"It's a long way away yet, whatever it is," said the second officer. "Still, there might be something . . . I'll see what's on the set."

He disappeared down the companionway, leaving the first officer with his binoculars once more at his eyes. The first officer was acutely aware that he had less experience in Arctic and sub-Arctic waters than his junior, and he did not wish to look a fool. The *Orca* was heaving her 1000-odd tons over the 600-fathom depths of the Iceland-Faroe Rise, far to the northwest of the Shetland Isles and the Faroes themselves. You wouldn't expect to find that kind of sea ice here, he told himself firmly, and certainly not on the scale that produced the visual phenomenon, caused by the distant reflection of the ice-pack on low clouds, which seamen called "a blink." The second officer was back beside him now, his face so noncommittal that the other man knew he was triumphant.

"Well?" he said.

"There's a lot of sea-and-rain clutter, but there *is* something on the screen," said the second officer. "It's vague but it goes right across the screen. Much too far away yet to be sure what it is. But I've seen the same thing before—once with a heavy snowstorm, over the East Jan Mayen Ridge."

The first officer looked out at a glassy sea and then up at a sky where a watery sun was trying to put in an intermittent appearance.

"The Jan Mayen Ridge," he said, trying to keep the incredulity out of his voice. "But that's far north of here. And there's no sign of snow."

"And the only other time I've seen it like that on the radar and from the bridge," said the second officer carefully, "well . . . it was an ice blink."

It was two hours before the men on the bridge of the *Orca* sighted the first ice. It dotted the sea in small grey hummocks, like the glistening backs of whales. The *Orca* lowered a net and hauled some on board. The two officers went down to the foredeck and looked at the catch.

"Well, I'll be damned," said the second officer slowly. He reached a gloved hand into the crevice in the block of ice and pulled out two small dead fish. "I saw that once before, but a lot nearer the Pole than this. . . ."

"What do you mean?" said the other curiously.

The second officer straightened up, still holding the fish. He jabbed the ice block with his foot.

"I mean that's old ice, what we call rotten ice," he said brusquely. "That ice has been around for years, so long it's got algae living in it, and fish living off the algae. It's not newly formed. It's off some really big berg. Something very, very big."

"So?"

"So where's that berg?" said the second officer. "It must be a hell of a long way south of where it should be, to be breaking up like this. Look at that lot . . ." He pointed out to where the ice hummocks dotted the sea. "And there's one thing for sure," he went on. "Wherever that berg is, there'll be others. Bergs are like whales. They rarely travel alone. By God, I'll tell you one place I'm thankful not to be."

"Where's that?"

"On some bloody oil rig, out in the Forties Field or wherever."

"You're right," said the first officer. "Pass me a signal pad."

"There's one thing you can't do on an oil rig," said the second officer. "You can't run in front of the weather. Or anything else, for that matter. . . ."

Extract from memorandum, Chairman, National Science Council, to the Assistant to the President

". . . so that the information in the attached presentation might briefly be summarized for appropriate nonscientific Government agencies as follows (Note: Most if not all of this information is, of course, available to foreign governments as a consequence of standard international cooperation on these matters, and also of their own scientific monitoring of climatic phenomena.)"

1. *Variations in Sea Surface Temperatures are now very marked: a fall of 1.7 degrees being recorded in October, for instance, off the coast of northwest Spain, and a further fall of 1.9 degrees off the coast of*

Peru. This last fall confirms a trend that has been evident in SST *records since 1970 (see Dept. of Agriculture Report* PCTC/A/31075: Failure of Peruvian Anchovy Fisheries).*

2. *The* SST *variations are additional evidence of what has now become a basic shift in weather pattern. With the equipment currently at our disposal, the effects of changed* SST *on the jet stream are not fully quantifiable but are nevertheless striking. Certain conclusions can readily be drawn:*

    a. *The polar air mass is no longer receding to the north in spring and early summer.*

    b. *The temperate air masses that normally follow it are thus held back.*

    c. *The result is a southward shift in climatic bands, i.e., the weather currently regarded as "normal" in Alaska may be expected to become characteristic of the northern United States and southern Canada. As a consequence, the present temperate zone of the United States—the corn belt— will be infiltrated by colder weather, while itself pushing down into what are at present the subtropical regions of Florida, California, and New Mexico.*

    d. *This southward shift, paradoxically, has already been evidenced in Africa by the catastrophic droughts of the past few years in the Sahel regions south of the Sahara, comprising southern Algeria, Mauretania, Mali, Niger, Upper Volta, Ethiopia, and southern Sudan. These have followed the steady movement south of the Sahara Desert—an advance of several miles a year—in response to changes in the jet stream and the subsequent shift of the climatic band. The repeated failure of the monsoon rains of the Indian subcontinent must be ascribed to the same cause.*

    e. *In terms of the next 200 years, this change must now be considered to be permanent. There is no evidence that the Sahel region will again, within foreseeable historical parameters, be suitable for anything more than the minimal human nomadic population which it barely sustained until the so-called agricultural revolution in the region two decades ago.*

94

f. In the case of the Indian subcontinent, the evidence is less clear, owing to the unpredictable character of jet-stream changes over the Himalayas. Nevertheless, monsoon failure and consequent famine, rising from the level of disaster to that of catastrophe, may confidently be expected in the next twenty-four months.

3. The effect of a southward climatic band shift on the northern United States, Canada, Siberia, Britain, and northern Europe may also be expected to be dramatic, though the time scale is less certain. Evidence on this is inconclusive. An extreme position, postulating very rapid change, is taken by Dr. Stovin, partly on the evidence of the highly unusual climatic phenomena which he is at present investigating at Novosibirsk in western Siberia. A computer model, produced at Connecticut Institute of Technology, gives a longer time scale of approximately 125 years before a full glaciation is established, though this would be characterized by "spurts" of unquantifiable intensity while world climate is moving in that direction.

4. In any event, the effect on world population and food and energy production will clearly be very considerable within measurable time to come, and on this I attach a report from Dr. Conor Donleavy, the agronomist seconded to the National Science Council. . . .

CHAPTER 10

Seated in the Special Reception Area of the airport at Novosibirsk, Yevgeny Soldatov dozed uneasily, his head sunk on his chest. Sounds at the door disturbed him, and he struggled awake, half rising to his feet. But it was only one of the airport security officers holding a muttered and—from where Soldatov sat—inaudible conversation with the young woman behind the desk. Soldatov sat back wearily. He had barely slept for forty-eight hours, and he hadn't seen Valentina for four days. And now, though in the circumstances not surprisingly, the Moscow plane was late—nearly an hour late. He could, of course, have left the actual process of meeting the Stovin party to somebody else. He could have met them tomorrow, after all of them had grabbed a few hours' sleep. But, for some reason he did not himself entirely understand, he wanted to meet Stovin personally. At intervals over the past few days, he had reminded himself that Stovin was coming. It had begun as a comfort to him; it was now, he knew wryly, more of an article of faith. He smiled grimly. Oh, what a row there'd been when the Ministry in Moscow had told him they were withdrawing the offer to Stovin because Stovin wanted the extra visa. It wasn't often that even an Academician could trounce a Ministry man, but this was one of the times. What had happened at Novosibirsk changed everything. Oh, they hadn't grasped it yet in Moscow—not fully. He looked down at the plastic folders he had been asked to hand to the Stovin party. One each . . . neat little paperback books of the kind available, free, to foreign visitors at many Soviet airports, Vasily Orlov's *Foundation of the Party,* Alexander Guber's *How Heavy Industry Was Built,* Karpenko's *Mechanism of Planning.* What did they think these things —he pushed them away from him contemptuously—what effect did they really think these things would have on a man like Stovin? Make him join the Party? Sometimes, he thought, the people in Moscow seemed to live in a dream world. But he, Soldatov, was living now in a new world, a world which this American was one of the few qualified to understand. A new stir came at the door, and beyond the fur-hatted officials, Soldatov glimpsed the angular features and slightly stooped frame he recognized from photographs. They were here. He got quickly to his feet and went forward. Suddenly, unexpectedly, in spite of his fatigue he felt slightly shy. He held out his hand.

"Dr. Stovin? It is a great pleasure to meet you. My name is Yevgeny Soldatov. Please come with me. You must all"—he smiled quickly at the girl and Bisby—"be tired."

At least, he thought with satisfaction, they were all wearing sound winter clothing—fur-lined leather coats, and what seemed to be fur-lined boots. Expensive American clothing. But it was just as well because there wasn't any to spare in Novosibirsk. Not now.

"I'm just glad to be here," said Stovin. Soldatov looked at him more closely. He was slightly younger, slightly less grey, than Soldatov had imagined him to be. There was about him, thought the Siberian, an unmistakable feeling of authority, but it was intellectual and not political or executive authority. Stovin seemed a man confident, perhaps even arrogantly confident, in the power of his own mind. Soldatov jerked himself back to actualities. Stovin was introducing the others.

"Diane Hilder," he was saying. "From the University of Colorado."

Soldatov sketched the tiniest of bows. So this was the woman. He'd been told—better not to speculate about how the information had been obtained—that Stovin was interested in her, and that was why she'd been given the second scientific visa. Maybe. At all events, she looked intelligent enough. And attractive, with that streaky fair hair and that wide mouth. A zoologist, they said. She'd worked on wolves. He thought of what he'd seen that very morning, and his mouth twisted.

"And this is Paul Bisby," said Stovin. "My assistant . . ."

Now here was an unexpected face. There were faces like this further east, around Irkutsk and the Baikal Sea, not so far from the Mongolian border. And up around the Lena River. That was it, of course. This was a Lena face—a Yakut face. At least, he thought as he gripped Bisby's proffered hand, it was a Yakut face some of the time. As soon as Bisby spoke in the normal American tones, his face slipped back, in some way, into nondescript Anglo-Saxon.

"I have a car downstairs," Soldatov said. "I think it will be best if we go now to Akademgorodok where we have your accommodation. I'm afraid you will not be all together. Novosibirsk is quite impossible, of course, because neither of the hotels now exist. But we were left relatively unharmed at Akademgorodok. Our little town is full, as you can imagine . . ."

The lights in the room flickered briefly and went out, plunging them into black darkness through which Soldatov's voice, in its grammatically perfect but slightly stilted formal English, continued as though nothing had happened.

". . . and so I hope very much that you will be as comfortable as we can make you."

The lights came back on, and he led them to the door and down the steps, past the fur-hatted security men outside on the steel-railed landing, and past the Red Army sentry who stood, Kalashnikov assault rifle cradled across his chest, at the swing doors leading out to the airport apron. There was a steady pulsating of small engines around them as they moved outside, and Soldatov sensed Bisby's curiosity.

"Generators," he said to the young American. "You know . . . you know roughly what happened here?"

Bisby nodded.

"Virtually every power line into the city, above and below ground, was destroyed," said Soldatov. "Naturally, they're now under repair, but it isn't easy. Tomorrow you will see. So we're using army generators for the moment—eighty of them, to be exact. They've been flown in from the north. We have bases not so very . . . you were in the Air Force, I think?"

"Yes," said Bisby.

"Then, of course," said Soldatov cheerfully, "you will know already that we have bases not so far away."

Five minutes later the three Americans were wedged in the back of Soldatov's chauffeur-driven Chaika, with Soldatov himself in the pulldown bucket seat opposite them. The car drove swiftly along a swept road that was already dusted with fresh snow. There was relatively little traffic, though once they passed a small convoy of three big trucks, headed by a tracked army vehicle, heading in the opposite direction, toward the airport. All at once, however, the situation changed. Ahead of the car, the long bare horizon began to glow with light. Groups of people loomed up in the headlights, furred, muffled, walking along the road. A minute or two later they passed the grey-white angular shapes of the first tents. Some were dark and apparently untenanted; some were lit by the inner glow of oil lamps; and outside some, dark figures moved around open fires flaring into the Siberian night.

Stovin leaned forward. "Tents?" he said questioningly. "They must be damned cold. What's the temperature outside?"

Soldatov shrugged. "Not really cold yet, I'm glad to say. Not Siberian cold. I haven't seen tonight's temperature figures, but it's about the same as last night. And that was around 20 degrees below freezing, Fahrenheit."

"Oh, God," said Diane.

"We've got around half a million homeless people here, and about 100,000 of them are either very young or very old or very ill," said Soldatov quietly. "We're around 1,400 miles from Moscow, and even Omsk is nearly 400 miles away. There's absolutely no way we can evacuate people on that scale; there's nowhere to evacuate them to. The ones with tents are the lucky ones. But we're working on what we've got. Would you like to stop for a moment and see?"

The Chaika slowed and turned off the road onto a broad track marked by spaced-out oil lamps. In front of the car now was a bank of floodlights, so powerful after the darkness of the road that Soldatov and the three Americans shielded their eyes as they climbed from the car. The dry biting cold cut into them at once, but what was happening in front of them was so arresting that each of the Americans virtually ignored the temperature. The noise was deafening. At least forty power saws were working within a few hundred yards, progressively felling a long tongue of birch forest, comprising tens of thousands of trees, which reached down almost to the road. Tractors were hauling the felled logs to a clearing where hundreds of men and women swinging hand axes under the glaring lights, were trimming them into smooth poles. Beyond the trimming site, log huts were beginning to go up. There was a steady hammering, sawing, clattering from the site. More than a thousand people were toiling there with desperate, almost frantic urgency. A medical tent with a big red cross painted on its canvas stood at the side. Even as they watched, a middle-aged man helping to carry a felled birch log to the trimming site relaxed his hold and slipped, kneeling, to the ground. He held his chest. A woman in a green uniform came out from the tent and knelt beside him. No one spoke to, or even looked at, the three Americans where they stood, watching, with Soldatov beside them.

"Two things we're not short of," said Soldatov. "Wood —there's not much except silver birches for the next 700 miles east—and we have people . . . labor. Log huts are better than tents."

They looked on in silence for a few moments more before Soldatov led the way back to the car. The cold had really begun to bite now, and they settled gratefully into the warm, stuffy interior. The Chaika pushed on for a mile or so, horn constantly blaring, against what had now become a steady stream of construction traffic—much of it people on foot carrying spades and lamps and axes—moving in the opposite direction. When these groups of men and vehicles finally thinned out, the car entered a broad, dark plain, with snow piled at the sides of the road. Beyond the road they could sense, rather than actually see, the serried ranks of the birch trees which stretched like a sea to the horizon.

Soldatov twisted in his seat and looked over the driver's shoulder. "We haven't far to go," he said. "Here is the Ob River."

The night was clear and the black water, streaked with grey ice, gleamed in the starlight. There was a very faint prickle of lights on both river banks but nothing that would indicate the presence of a large city. A thumping, drumming sound came from underneath the Chaika. They were crossing, slowly, a long pontoon.

"We are about eight miles north of the old Ob Bridge," said Soldatov. "You knew that the bridge was gone?"

"Yes," said Stovin. "Was this as near as you could get?"

"I'm afraid so. The problem—well, you will see it tomorrow—wasn't just that the bridge had gone. We might have done something about that, something temporary but effective. No, Dr. Stovin, you will see that the Ob River has also gone—at least in the sense that it used to flow through the city. The whole course has changed, about four miles down from here. We have had to blast a new channel, or we would have had floods even as high upriver as this by now. Luckily, at this time of year the ice is thick and the Ob moves slowly, underneath. It gave us an extra forty-eight hours. But even now, this bridge is twice as long as the old Ob Bridge, though the river here used to be a little narrower than it was at Novosibirsk."

The drumming ceased, and the Chaika moved slowly down a road where there were once more groups of people. The big car stopped at a barrier flanked by a small wooden hut outside of which stood three or four soldiers with lamps. An NCO came up and looked inquisitively through the driver's window. There was a quick exchange in Russian, and the driver passed some papers through. The NCO looked through them carefully. Soldatov sat quietly, saying nothing. At last the NCO stood back, said something curtly to the driver, and waved the Chaika through. A couple of men warming themselves at

100

a glowing brazier looked up. The car was almost past the brazier when there came the unmistakable tearing crack of a rifle, and the driver stopped abruptly. One of the men at the brazier shouted something into the darkness and turned back to the car, laughing and pointing. About twenty yards away, two soldiers came into the circle of light, dragging a black body behind them.

"What's that?" asked Bisby incredulously. "A looter?"

Soldatov laughed shortly. "You could call it that," he said. He turned quickly to Diane Hilder. "It's your field, I think," he said, smiling. "It's a wolf."

"Can I see it?" asked Diane swiftly.

"Of course."

Soldatov spoke quietly to the driver and then got out and opened the door. Followed by the other two Americans, Diane walked with Soldatov over to where the corpse of the wolf lay in the circle of reddish light around the brazier. The two soldiers beside it drew away when Soldatov spoke to them but watched her curiously. She knelt beside the wolf.

It had been a good shot. The bullet had severed the wolf's spine in the nape of the neck, and there was only a small, saucer-sized area of matted blood, already congealing with cold, to show where it had entered. One yellow eye was opened, staring upward toward her; the other was closed. The long red tongue lolled, stiffening rapidly in the frost, from the fleshy lips. She put out her hand and gently opened the mouth. At a word from Soldatov one of the soldiers came forward to help her, drawing a rubber-sheathed torch from his belt. His strong blunt hands held the wolf's jaws apart while she peered inside with the torch. The saberlike upper corner incisors, long and yellow and slightly curved, were unlocked in the moment of death from the similarly sized canines of the lower jaw, or she knew there would have been no chance of opening the jaw so easily. Farther back were the massive carnassial teeth, capable of crushing the bones of a horse or a bison. They projected smooth and strong in the cooling saliva of the mouth. At last she drew back and nodded to the soldier above her. He released his hold on the jaws, which remained open as she walked back to the car with the others.

"Well?" said Stovin as they settled back into the warmth of the seats.

"That was interesting," she said, though she spoke to

Soldatov rather than to Stovin. "A young male, about 120 pounds, I'd guess. And no more than two years old—there was hardly any wear on the carnassials. I thought he might be an old wolf, to come scavenging around this site. But he's in—at least, he *was* in—the prime of life. Not an animal I'd have expected to see looking for . . ." She hesitated.

"Bodies," said Soldatov flatly.

She nodded. At the back of her mind stirred the memory of the conversation she'd had with Van Gelder that hot afternoon in Albuquerque . . . in another time, another world, it seemed now. What was it he'd said? *"Canis lupus* will take carrion, but he likes human carrion. You know . . . graveyards." She jerked her mind back to the present.

Soldatov was speaking. "It is interesting that you use that word 'scavenging,'" he said. "I used the same word to Valentina, but she said that I shouldn't prejudge the question."

"Valentina?" said Diane.

Soldatov smiled. "Of course . . . I'm sorry. Valentina is my wife. You, Miss Hilder, will be meeting her tonight because you are staying with us in the *dacha* at Akademgorodok."

He turned in the darkness of the car to where Bisby and Stovin sat side by side. "I'm afraid that since we have only two bedrooms in the *dacha,* you will be accommodated separately. It's a school—School No.2, where I myself attended, not long ago. But you won't be too uncomfortable. And there'll be others in the same position; School No.2 has, I think, around forty scientists sleeping in its classrooms tonight."

"International scientists?" asked Stovin.

"Soviet scientists," said Soldatov.

There was an awkward little pause, broken by Diane Hilder. "And Mme. Soldatov . . . she knows about wolves?"

"She knows more about butterflies," said Soldatov. He seemed glad to change the subject. "She's a lepidopterist. But here in Siberia, a zoologist is bound to find interests in other fields. As you will, too, Miss Hilder."

"What did she mean, 'prejudge the question'?"

Soldatov looked out of the misted car window into the darkness. "We are almost in Akademgorodok. You will be able to ask her yourself."

102

For the three weary Americans, the next half-hour was a blur. The Chaika stopped outside a large concrete building. The snow was coming down again, fast out of a black sky, and the cold bit at Bisby and Stovin as they hurried past a stand of ornamental birch trees into the entrance hall of School No.2. It was, Stovin noted tiredly, a school like any other school, giving off the strange, indefinable atmosphere compounded of floor polish, paper, canteen meals, and sweat that marked every school on both sides of the Atlantic. Quickly Soldatov showed them to their quarters: a classroom with old-fashioned desks pushed to one side, and four Red Army iron-and-canvas beds in a row against the far wall. Above the beds hung a double row of framed portraits: Byron, Hemingway, Mark Twain, Dickens, George Bernard Shaw, Shelley amongst them. Two large bright pressure lamps stood at each end of the room, and on two of the beds sprawled two Russians, reading. They stood as Stovin and Bisby came in, and Soldatov introduced them formally.

"Sannikov, catalyst chemist. Skripyzyn, agronomist for this *oblast*."

The two Russians nodded and shook hands politely, but seemed disinclined to talk, returning almost immediately to their books. Stovin pushed his suitcase against his bed and looked up for a moment at Hemingway's bearded face above his head. He turned and saw that Soldatov was watching him.

"This is the classroom for advanced English," said the Russian. "Here the students speak only English, read only English and American books, think only English and American. I was taught in this classroom myself."

"*Think* only English and American?" said Stovin, regretting the ironic words as soon as they were out of his mouth. Soldatov did not seem, however, to find them a challenge.

"*Think?*" he said. "Well, that is why we have School No.2, is it not? To teach students to think the right way . . . for themselves."

Diane was dozing in the warm depths of the car when Soldatov rejoined her. The Chaika moved off through the snow, nosing its way forward into an opaque maelstrom that flung back its headlight beams as solidly as a white wall. A few minutes later the car stopped, its chained wheels sliding, then gripping, in the snow. Soldatov scrambled out, holding the car door open with difficulty against

103

the gusting blizzard, so that Diane could follow him. Beyond him, in the grey-white gloom, a yellow rectangle of light suddenly swelled. It was the doorway of the *dacha*. Grasping her arm, Soldatov hurried her inside, leaving the fur-clad and muffled chauffeur to get the bags out of the Chaika's trunk. A small, brown-haired woman came forward into the momentary confusion of the *dacha*'s little entrance hall where Soldatov and Diane were stamping the snow from their shoes. They followed her into a long, low-ceilinged room with a blazing log fire at one end and hot-water radiator pipes at the other. It was lit by three large pressure lamps. There were paintings and drawings along one wall, and a multidrawered cabinet, with books and papers piled on top of it, stood against the wall opposite. Bright woollen rugs covered the polished pine floor. Valentina Soldatova held out both hands.

"Welcome to our house," she said. "I am relieved that you are here. The weather is so bad that I thought you might have to spend the night at the airport—or even that your flight might be diverted to Omsk. It happens sometimes."

"The snow wasn't too bad at the airport," said Soldatov. "It got much worse after we passed the tent camp. They'll have had to stop work there by now."

His face puckered momentarily with worry, but then he turned to the two women. "First, though, I must introduce you. Valentina, this is Dr. Hilder. Dr. Hilder . . . my wife, Valentina. She also"—he smiled broadly and proudly—"is 'doctor.' "

"I think I would much prefer to be Valentina," said the Russian girl. "And perhaps you . . . your name is Diane? May I call you Diane?"

"Please," said Diane. She looked more closely, for the first time, at the other woman. Valentina Soldatova was slightly built, pretty, no more than twenty-eight years old —a little younger, perhaps, than Soldatov himself. Her face was warm with intelligence.

"You must be tired," said Diane, "of being told what good English you speak."

"You are kind," said Valentina. "But you will find this is not unusual in Akademgorodok. Many of us here were taught at School No.2—where your two friends are sleeping tonight."

She turned to her husband. "Who is with them in their classroom?"

"Sannikov and Skripyzyn," said Soldatov.

"Skripyzyn?" said Valentina, wrinkling her nose, laughing.

"What's wrong with Skripyzyn?" asked Diane, smiling. "I didn't get out of the car, so I didn't see him myself."

"He stayed here, at the *dacha,* once. The hotel was full. He snores. He makes a noise like an icebreaker. Your friends will find it hard to sleep."

"Not tonight, they won't," said Diane. Now that the first formalities were over, she was beginning to feel very tired.

Valentina rose swiftly from her chair. "Of course. You will be quite exhausted. Come with me. But first . . . a little milk with brandy in it. You will sleep like a true Siberian. Geny"—she nodded toward Soldatov—"says that Siberians don't sleep, they hibernate."

Soldatov walked with the two women to the door of the long living room. He was standing in the full glare of one of the pressure lamps, and for the first time, Diane realized how grey, pinched, even haunted was his face. He held out his hand, and slightly surprised by the sudden gesture, she took it. He put his other hand over hers so that her palm was enclosed between his two.

"Sleep now," he said. "Tomorrow . . . there is much to do."

"Bismillah ar rahman ar adhim," prayed Zayd ag-Akrud from his swollen throat, his head touching the coarse Sahara sand. "In the name of God, the Compassionate, the Merciful . . ." He remained bowed for a few moments more, and then twitched the blue-black veil back across his face, reaching up his left hand to his neck and fingering the red leather wallet, containing a single verse from the Koran, which hung there. He stared into the eastern darkness, trying to make up his mind. Behind him, the last dying blue of the desert sky was darkening rapidly into the shadows that would briefly precede the blackness of night. Twenty yards away, beside the deep hole of the well, squatted his wife Zenoba, her face a mask of misery. Zayd's sons Hamidine and Muhammed lay beside her on the cooling sand. The third son, little Ibrahim, had his head in her lap but was ominously quiet.

Painfully, Zayd got to his feet and walked back across to the well, staring into its shadows as though he could will back the water it had once contained. The well was no

105

more than a hole in the sand, perhaps six feet wide, fifteen feet deep. Zayd had known of it since he was a child of five, riding with his father to the camel markets fifty miles to the south. He had never known it to be dry before. The harder-packed area of sand leading to its edge was cracked and veined with tracks, strewn with the small hard balls of camel dung, which showed where other travellers had rested. Beyond it was a more chilling sight, a dead camel. The sun had already reduced its skin to a brittle leather, and a desert rodent, probably a fox, had torn open the stomach. Nothing remotely eatable was left. Zayd looked at his own animals.

His three goats remained and two riding camels, one in milk. The bull camel was sick, down on its haunches in the shadows beyond the well. Five minutes ago, Zenoba had pulled at the teats of its companion but had got little more than a cupful. No milk camel, Zayd knew, could be expected to give milk without food. And neither camel had eaten for many days. The goats were in slightly better shape, because Zenoba had brought a little thorn hay with her. Three goats . . . but his mind was made up. Hamidine and Muhammed were twelve years old and thirteen years old, respectively, almost men. They might last yet for days. But Ibrahim was seven. If the bull camel died tomorrow, the child would have to walk. And Zenoba? For a moment her name flicked across his mind, but he dismissed it impatiently. Zenoba would walk as long as he told her to. Zayd drew his knife and walked over to the oldest of the remaining goats, grasping it by the mane of rough hair at the back of its neck and slashing open its throat in one swift stroke. It shrieked once, gurgling and bubbling in its own blood as it died, and Zenoba came quickly over to where he stood over its body. She caught the spurting blood in a bowl and, in a fever of anxiety to eat, began to drag the goat back across to the well. But Zayd swore at her angrily: "This is the evening meal. I am not a jackal. Do what you have to do."

Submissively, Zenoba crossed to the bull camel and pulled from its back three or four of the dried thorn branches which hung from the pannier. She piled them together, poured a little of the remaining water from a goatskin *guerbo* container into the old tin kettle, struck a match, and waited while the water boiled. From her neck she drew the small bag that contained the tea, measured it into the brass teapot, and waited till it boiled.

106

She began to pour the mixture from one brass bowl into another, and then back again, in the time honored fashion, but Zayd could no longer bear to watch her. He held out his hand and she gave him the bowl, watching him as he sipped its scalding contents. He allowed two or three mouthfuls to trickle down his parched throat and then nodded. She poured more tea into the bowl and took it across to the two older boys. They, too, drank, while she sat once more with Ibrahim's head in her lap. She tried to give him some of the cup of milk she had squeezed from the camel, but he turned his head away apathetically. Patiently, she dipped the end of her scarf into the bowl, soaking it in the camel milk. Then she wiped it across Ibrahim's mouth, so that his lips opened, and some milk trickled in. As the taste of it stimulated him, he took the bowl in his hands and began to sip at it more determinedly. Satisfied, she made a little more tea and, for the first time, drank herself.

The two boys, bickering dispiritedly, raised the square wooden frames of the little tent draping it with the black-and-blue cloth from the second pannier of the bull camel. Zenoba cut a haunch from the dead goat and butchered the rest into smaller pieces, wrapping each in dark cloth tied with leather cords. The cooking haunch she placed in the embers of the fire. There was not enough heat to do the job properly, and she could afford no more thorn sticks. The haunch was no more than a quarter cooked, in places still raw and bleeding, when she drew it out. Zayd ate first, followed by the two older boys, their faces tense with hunger, the fat trickling down their chins as their teeth tore at the meat. Zenoba chewed a little of the meat herself before taking it out of her mouth to give to Ibrahim. The boy ate little. Tomorrow would be difficult.

"Sleep," Zayd said to Zenoba. "Until the moon is high. Then we ride again."

She began to speak, surprised, but he waved his hand at her impatiently, and she drew back into the shadows of the little tent, taking Ibrahim with her. This would be the first time they had travelled at night, but Zayd knew that another day under the high Sahara sun might be Ibrahim's last. Eighty miles to the east lay Tamanrasset. At Tamanrasset there would be the Algerian government medical mission, water, tourists even. At Tamanrasset, Ibrahim would not die. But Tamanrasset was many days away. He picked up the *guerbo* and drank a little water, shivering. The desert wind was cold now, and he longed for the warmth of the other bodies in the tent. But there was just the chance that some small desert animal—a gazelle, perhaps—might, like him, make the mistake of believing that there would be water where there had always been water before. If the world had changed, then that was the will of God. But under God, a man—better than a man, a Tuareg—must do what he could. He went out beyond the empty water hole and squatted down in the darkness, his rifle—a forty-year-old 7.02mm Mauser that had once belonged to one of Rommel's infantrymen —across his knees. It would cost him an hour's sleep, but it was worth the chance.

An hour later, he returned to the tent. Nothing, not as much as a sand scorpion had stirred near the water hole. He lifted the edge of the tent covering and looked down in the starlight at Zenoba's face. Her black hair was parted in the middle, and one of its tightly twisted braids lay across her mouth. For a moment Zayd's loins stirred briefly with desire, but he put the thought out of his mind. Tomorrow they would be riding into a world where nothing was certain. There was a second water hole at Lissa. Would there be water there? How long would the bull camel last? Zenoba would need all the rest she could get. Because if the bull camel died, she would have to walk, and she was not a man, with a man's strength. With no Zenoba, there would be no Ibrahim. The moon would be up in another three hours. Until then, they would all sleep.

CHAPTER 11

Stovin leaned against the blizzard as a man might lean against a wall, but then gathered his strength and jogged forward after the blurred forms of Bisby and Soldatov just ahead of him. The snow, driving down so thickly that it was impossible to see more than a few yards in the twilight gloom of the Siberian early afternoon, tossed around him in a shrieking, piercing fury of cold. Its particles, whipped from the frozen ground by the storm, bit and stung through the furs that muffled his face. Sometimes, unbelievably, they seemed to penetrate to his body itself. Even under the thick layers of padded clothing that Soldatov had provided, he felt an extraordinary impression of vulnerable nakedness. Occasionally a dark form passed them, moving the other way, also at a run. This lumbering trot, Soldatov had warned them, was the only safe way to move at a temperature of 40 degrees below. "Slow down," he had said, "and your blood could freeze in your veins . . ."

Stovin was finding that it needed tremendous mental effort to put aside his physical misery so that he could pay some sort of reasoned attention to his surroundings. They were moving now across what had once been the approaches to Novosibirsk's big railway station, one of the principal stops on the Trans-Siberian line from Moscow to the Pacific. There was nothing to indicate now that any major installation had ever stood there, and the approaches were no more than a hummocky desert of ice, obliterated by the passing of the Dancer a fortnight ago. Through the twilight snowstorm, thought Stovin, it seemed as lonely and as untenanted as the Pole itself. Ahead of him, Bisby and Soldatov were slowing down. All three began to pant heavily as they climbed a ridge of ice from which the blizzard tore ice fragments and powdered snow in an unceasing bombardment. They moved forward slowly against the blast, like men wading through glue, but once over the crest, they dropped out of the wind.

For the first time, Stovin saw that the lee of the ice ridge was peopled by a crowd of dark figures, perhaps 200 of them. From the other side of the ridge, the distant shriek of the wind could still be heard, but it was dominated now by a new sound—the rattle and roar of dozens of compressor drills held by small teams of men boring into the ice. Above this crescendo of sound, Soldatov was shouting, his exhaled breath crackling from his mouth in a cloud of tiny crystals. He pointed across a pile of metal rods and jumbled engineering equipment in front of him.

"You see," he yelled, "the first of our two main problems here. This railway is vital. We must . . . ah!"

He stopped speaking as an officer in a high-collared

greatcoat stepped swiftly across to them, sliding and slithering on the slope, and holding up his hand. Around them, the noise of the drills died away. The site workers —some of them women, Stovin noticed—were silent, staring fixedly across the frozen ground into the grey-white blur of the twilight and the falling snow. And then, a few hundred yards away in the gloom, a violet flash streaked upward from the ground, and the ice plateau erupted in a column of pinkish-red flame and grey-white debris, falling raggedly back to earth, near enough to spatter them with fragments of ice. The rumbling roar of the blast was so loud that Stovin whipped his gloved hands to his muffled ears. The officer relaxed, nodded to Soldatov, and waved them forward. Soldatov led them forward until they stood at the side of a small prefabricated hut guarded by a single soldier, his Kalashnikov assault rifle cradled across his chest. The side of the hut cut off some of the renewed noise of the drilling, and Soldatov spoke again in more normal tones:

"Well, there you see it. We must clear this line. Here we're four days from Moscow and two from Irkutsk. And beyond Irkutsk is Trans-Baikalia with about a third of all the oil in the Soviet Union. And, in the short term, we need food. We still have a big surviving population here, and we depend on the railway."

A big twin-rotor Army helicopter clattered overhead, navigation lights winking red, descending somewhere in the murk ahead of them.

"Yes, there is air supply, of course. It's better than nothing. But it's not enough for three-quarters of a million people. And we aren't the only ones in trouble. There aren't enough . . ."

"How do you mean," said Stovin, "you aren't the only ones in trouble?"

"This weather," said Soldatov, "is . . . just one moment." He looked at Bisby and Stovin. Ahead of the hut, the noise of the power drills had again died sway, and three or four men were hacking carefully with handpicks around a dark object in the snow.

Soldatov glanced at Stovin's muffled face and said again, "Perhaps it would be better not to . . ."

Bisby spoke before Stovin could say anything. "It's all right," he said steadily. "We may as well get used to it."

As one of the men moved aside, Stovin saw again the unmistakable shape around which they were working. It

110

was a small overcoated arm, with a woollen mitten still on the hand, projecting from the ice. Carefully, almost tenderly, the picks scraped deeper and deeper. Stovin would have liked to have wrenched his eyes from the sight, but some indefinable impulse now kept him watching. One of the diggers dropped his pickaxe, drew a sheath knife from his belt, and probed into the ice, scraping at the surface. Through its milky screen there now appeared a human face, a small pinched face, eyes closed, short fair hair frozen into an absurd fringe. It was that of a boy about ten years old.

"I think, perhaps, that his parents or older brother or sister will be somewhere here near him," said Soldatov quietly. "This was the site of the main waiting room; they will have been waiting for the Rossiya, the Trans-Siberian express. We find them all the time; he's just one of scores of thousands in the city. But, for the diggers, it's never easy . . ."

"No," said Stovin. An unaccustomed feeling was stealing over him. Mentally, he examined it and found to his surprise that it was shame. The theories of climatic change that he had argued were one thing. That small dead face was another. He knew now, bitterly, that in the past few weeks he had even felt a grim satisfaction that at last he, the controversial Stovin, was being proved right; that eminent contemporaries who had doubted him must now listen attentively to all he had to say. But there was more to being a man than pride in the power of a mind. And yet . . . it was going to take minds, good minds, a lot of good minds, to attempt to deal with what had happened here. What might—what *would*— happen elsewhere.

"You said there were two main problems. What was the other?" he asked evenly. Bisby looked at him swiftly, almost incredulously, but he had schooled his face to show no emotion. Soldatov turned from the dead child, who was now being lifted from the ice, and walked around the side of the hut to the door. Beyond it, Stovin now saw for the first time, was a compound, about a hundred yards square, marked only by rough trestle fences. Here, from under snow-smothered tarpaulins, lay other bodies, hundreds upon hundreds of them.

"They were dug out of the workers' flats, just off Sverdlova Street," said Soldatov. "About 4,000 people lived there. I'm told that not one survived.".

111

A couple of Russian officers came out of the hut as they entered it, and the sentry slapped his gloved hand on his rifle butt in salute. The hut itself was empty, warm, almost stuffy, with a charcoal brazier glowing at one end. There was a long trestle table strewn with plans and drawings, and a dogeared map of Siberia was pinned along the wall opposite the window. It was so wonderful to be out of the cold that Stovin almost missed what Soldatov was now saying.

". . . so our second problem is there." He jabbed his finger toward the snow-smeared window. "This is not the snow we are used to. Oh, of course, of course, we Siberians are no strangers to snow. But I have never seen snow like this—falling almost without cease. It is making it virtually impossible to work outside for many hours of the day."

"What are conditions like elsewhere?" asked Stovin.

Soldatov shrugged. "The area is so enormous, of course, that conditions differ sharply."

He pointed to the map. "Can you read the Russian alphabet, Dr. Stovin?"

Stovin shook his head.

"Ah, then I'll explain." He passed his hand over the whole area of the map. "More than nine million square miles. But divided, as you see, roughly into two by the latitude 50 degrees north. That is the wind divide. To the west of it, west of the Ob River, we have something like the weather of northwest Europe. More extreme, perhaps, but something like. North of it, we get colder weather. And northeast, coldest of all. Every few miles northeast brings a drop in temperature, until we reach Verkyoyansk and Oymyakon in the Yakut Republic, about 200 miles south of the coast of the Laptev Sea. Those are the coldest places in the northern hemisphere."

"How cold?" asked Stovin.

"Minus 90 degrees Fahrenheit," said Soldatov. "And all over the Yakut area, temperatures of around minus 70 degrees are to be expected. Almost all Siberia has a January average of below zero. And the summers are short but warm; we've had up to 100 degrees Fahrenheit in Yakutsk itself, in July. It's near enough to the sea. The Arctic Ocean warms it. But not, apparently, any more."

"No?" said Stovin. "I don't remember any Sea Surface Temperature figures for the Laptev Sea in the material that came to Washington."

"When we get back to the *dacha,* I will show you the figures," promised Soldatov. "There is a drop. You will see. And the summer in Yakut was short, three-four weeks, not the usual eight. We normally get a sharp drop in temperature there between October-November. This year, between September-October. The Yakut weather is coming south. South and west. And then, of course, this . . . this thing . . . that hit us a fortnight ago. We think . . . changes in the jet stream."

"I think so too," said Stovin. Soldatov looked at him for a moment without replying. Bisby saw how ravaged, even haunted, was the Russian's face.

He spoke again, "The temperature when this happened at Novosibirsk. You saw that, of course?"

Stovin nodded.

"We have a basic standard here for weather stations," said Soldatov to Bisby. "We have machines capable of monitoring down to the extreme Oymyakon standard—the Yakut temperatures. Ninety degrees below. At Novosibirsk, we went right off the Oymyakon standard. The temperature was unimaginable. There is no precise measurement, because we did not have a machine capable of measuring it on the spot. But I think it may have been colder than any temperature ever recorded, anywhere in the world."

"I agree," said Stovin. Soldatov said nothing but sighed.

"About twenty years ago, your Vostok station on the other side of the world, in the Antarctic, recorded minus 126 degrees, didn't it?" Stovin went on. "But I think you're right. I think Novosibirsk, that night, was colder than that. When we get back, you show me those figures and I'll tell you why I think so."

"Yes, yes," said Soldatov. Suddenly he seemed to be barely interested in the conversation. A Red Army engineer-lieutenant came in through the door of the hut in a flurry of snow and a piercing blast of cold. Soldatov spoke to him briefly and then turned back to the others.

"They will send an army vehicle to take us back to the *dacha,*" he said. "It will have tracks. The weather is getting much worse. We cannot go on using the car."

Ten minutes later, the door opened once more, and the greatcoated officer, outlined against the driving snow, beckoned urgently. Soldatov rose to his feet and put his hand on Stovin's shoulder. He jerked his thumb toward the door.

113

"I very much fear it is a new world out there," he said. "I am glad you are with me."

"Who was assigned to be with him?" asked the Chairman of the State Security Commission. He stood with his back to Grigori Volkov, looking out of the high Kremlin window toward the long yellow wall of the Arsenal and the snow-encrusted tops of the larch trees in the Alexander Gardens beyond. Volkov shifted his feet uncomfortably before replying, and the movement did not escape the Chairman. He swung around from the window and looked directly at the young Foreign Ministry official, waiting.

"It was Katkov, Comrade Chairman. From the office at Tomsk. He was the nearest suitable officer."

"And?"

Volkov hesitated. "I gather it's very difficult at Novosibirsk, Comrade Chairman. I am told that Katkov's helicopter had to turn back. The weather was too bad. Otherwise he would have been there today. Now it may be tomorrow, or even longer."

"I see."

"I could use someone from Novosibirsk itself. Gunchenko is available."

The Chairman shook his head, frowning. He turned back to the window. Volkov sat waiting, looking at a big oil painting of Gorky Street on the opposite wall. A nicely composed picture, he thought irrelevantly. It looked like a Pimenov. Surely it couldn't be? There weren't any Pimenovs in private hands outside of Leonid Brezhnev's *dacha* in Zhukovka One. No, it must be a reproduction. But he'd never seen it on sale.

Without speaking, the Chairman opened a drawer in his big green-topped desk and drew out a bright blue file. To Volkov, on the other side of the desk, it was upside down, but he knew what it was without straining to read the typed label in reverse. It was Yevgeny Soldatov's special *pervy otdel*—an amplified version of the lifetime file kept on every Soviet citizen, showing his work, party affiliations, academic status, and political history. The Chairman leafed through until he found what he wanted, tapping the page with his forefinger.

"I see that Katkov has worked with Academician Soldatov before," he said.

"Yes," said Volkov. "They know each other."

114

"In that case, I think Katov is not the ideal choice," said the Chairman. "Better to have someone whom Soldatov does not know well, and who does not know him well."

"But . . . Soldatov . . . ?" said Volkov, betraying his surprise.

The Chairman waved a hand. "Don't misunderstand me, please. There is nothing, nothing whatever, against Soldatov. His record proves that he is a loyal servant of the State, though"—he smiled—"perhaps a scientifically unconventional one. Perhaps that is just as well. I know nothing of these things, but some of those who do tell me that Academician Soldatov is right. We shall see. But this is a new situation, Comrade Volkov, . . . these Americans, this man Stovin. Even for Soldatov, it is a new situation. I want someone there with a fresh mind, not Katkov. And certainly not some bumpkin from Novosibirsk."

"No," said Volkov and waited. But the Chairman seemed to have dropped the subject quite suddenly.

"I drove in by the Yaroslavsky Station this morning," he said. "It was snowing so hard I didn't think we'd make it. But the station . . . it was a fantastic sight. Have you seen it?"

Volkov shook his head.

"There must have been twenty thousand people there . . . the Army have put up tents all around the Leningradskaya. Just temporary accommodation, of course, until they can be properly housed. Though that's not going to be easy."

Volkov nodded. "They're coming in on the Trans-Siberian from Kargat, Comrade Chairman. That's the nearest working portion of the line to Novosibirsk. They're being taken there by helicopter and lorry, and then put on the train. Some are being dropped off at Omsk and Sverdlovsk but most are sent on to Moscow. They're the lucky ones. I wouldn't fancy being in Novosibirsk tonight, myself."

The Chairman sighed. Sometimes, thought Volkov, he looked quite an old man.

"It's going to be a hard winter, Volkov. Let's hope that Soldatov and this American can come up with some answers. Of course, you met them when they arrived, didn't you?"

"I did."

"What did you think?"

115

Volkov thought for a few moments before replying. "I didn't see them for long, Comrade Chairman. But I formed a few impressions. Stovin, the scientist . . . formidable, withdrawn, a little austere. Highly intelligent, of course—and probably not just in his own field. The woman . . . attractive, thoughtful, vulnerable to the right man. Perhaps a little sexually immature. A rather narrow intelligence, I should say. And I had just a slight feeling . . ." He hesitated.

"Yes?" said the Chairman.

"That there was something . . . some sexual interaction . . . between her and Stovin. Difficult to be sure."

"Interesting. And the other, the pilot . . . Bisby?"

"A nobody. Of no importance. Why he's here is hard to guess. I'm told that Stovin is a deliberately eccentric man who likes to demonstrate it. It might explain the presence of Bisby."

"Hm."

The Chairman rose. The interview was over.

"Let me know as soon as you get to Novosibirsk. There'll be an Army plane at Domodedovo at six o'clock. Decide for yourself, depending on the weather. You may be able to fly right in, or land on the way and go on by road."

Volkov stuttered in surprise. "I . . . I . . . Comrade Chairman? To Novosibirsk?"

"I think you are the best man."

Volkov swallowed. "Thank you, but . . . tomorrow I have a delegation from Finland. It has been arranged for weeks. I have done all the preparatory work. There is no one else who . . ."

"True, you are an official of the Foreign Ministry," said the Chairman patiently. "You are also an officer of the KGB. You know which takes priority. I want an independent mind assessing what goes on between the American Stovin and our own Soldatov. You are the best man. Make your arrangements. I will clear your departure with the Minister."

"Thank you, Comrade Chairman."

When Volkov had left the room, the Chairman put Soldatov's special *pervy otdel* back into the drawer and locked it. Then he opened another drawer and took out a similar file. It was Volkov's own *pervy otdel*. The Chairman leafed through it until he came to the page he wanted. He knew what was written there already, but he was a man who had a superstitious habit of reassuring himself.

"*Political attitude,*" he read once more. "*Completely reliable.*"

He nodded, smiled to himself, and put the file back in its drawer.

"What I want from Stovin," said the President moodily, "is a prediction. A scenario for the next couple of years." He laughed shortly. "Couple of months, maybe."

The Director of the Central Intelligence Agency stirred uneasily. He reached out and absently shuffled through the sheaf of satellite photographs on the Oval Office desk. "These should help give us that, Mr. President," he said. "They show all that weather coming in right across Siberia, over the Arctic Ocean and the Barents Sea. Look at this one . . . see, they've even got trouble at Murmansk. And all their oil stuff around Igrim and up around the mouth of the Ob—that's all having a rough time. They'll be really worried about that."

"There's not much satisfaction there," said the President, "if we get the same thing in Alaska. And we will, won't we, Mel? Our oil situation's going to get even worse."

Melvin Brookman stirred his bulky form at the other end of the desk.

"Looks that way, Mr. President," he said. "And soon. I've got a computer model, based on the latest Sea Surface Temperatures and atmospheric data, which gives some idea. And if it's right, the affected area will certainly take in Prudhoe Bay in the north, and maybe south down the Alaska coast to Valdez."

"And that might interdict the Alaska pipeline for an indeterminate time to come," said the President.

Brookman nodded. The Director of the CIA spoke again. "We've been talking to the British, Mr. President. They're pretty worried about their own North Sea oil. They've got nearly all their eggs in one basket, of course, up in the Shetlands."

"It looks like a poor time to buy an automobile, gentlemen," said the President. "And there's not been time yet to hear anything from Stovin."

It was put like a statement but Brookman knew it was a question.

"Not yet. Of course, it won't be the same from Russia

117

as from, say, Britain or West Germany. The Soviets haven't asked him out there to help us, but to help *them*. And if they think he's liable to learn too much about any crucial difficulties—the kind the director here has just described—well, they might put up the shutters."

"What would that mean?"

Brookman did not reply but looked at the CIA man. The Director leaned forward. "Dr. Brookman and I were discussing this just before we came into the Office, Mr. President," he said. "It seems to me that Dr. Stovin might have . . . well, a little difficulty . . . in reporting promptly. It's not just oil that's being affected, though the implications of that are serious enough. There are more obvious defense factors involved up there—ports, air bases, missile silos. I mean, let's be frank, if it were the other way around, and this Soldatov was being shown up and down the Alaska coast . . . well, I might put one or two perfectly natural-seeming obstacles in the way of his getting all that stuff back to Russia as fast as maybe he'd like. And that's something they can do a lot easier than we can. If Soldatov were over here, he'd have half the United States press corps following him around. But I'll bet there isn't as much as one junior legman from *Pravda* following Stovin—unless that legman happens also to be a colonel in the KGB."

The President nodded but made no comment. Instead he turned to Brookman and said, "A computer model?"

"Yes," said Brookman. "We ran it up at C.I.T. There'll be scores of similar ones being made all over the world now, of course. The trouble is that mapping the atmosphere involves an amount of computation that even advanced computers—like the Cray model that the boys at NCAR call Razzle-Dazzle—can't handle. We need multiple correlated observation from around 100,000 points in the atmosphere to get even a very rough idea of global weather. And then it only gives us the 'how.' Not the 'why.' "

"And the average head of state will be lucky if he grasps a fifth of it," said the President dryly. "I'll be glad to see Stovin again. I'd rather talk to a man than a model."

He rose and the others got to their feet. "I'm sorry, gentlemen, that's all the time I have. I have to see a deputation from the central African republics—the Sahel countries. A question of stepping up food supplies. More

118

dollars. It's going to be mighty hard to explain to the American public that extra snow in Alaska means drought and starvation south of the Sahara."

"Well, it's simple enough," said Brookman. "If you think of the world in terms of climatic bands . . ."

"Most of us don't, Mel," said the President gently, but he smiled to take any sting out of the words. "That's why I like talking to Stovin."

He walked with them to the door of the Oval Room, noticing again how the Director of the CIA took pains to step around the gold American eagle crest that was woven into the blue carpet, while Brookman merely lumbered straight across it. The Director turned and gave him a half wave, half salute as he disappeared into the hallway. The President shivered suddenly. I feel cold, he thought —maybe I'm getting old. What's wrong with me, anyway? The Director is a patriot. The CIA sees opportunities in all this—opportunities for America. No doubt in Moscow there are people who think in exactly the same way. Everybody imagines there are political solutions to everything nowadays, that governments can wave magic wands. The free world—whatever that is—will succeed. Or socialism—whatever that is—will triumph over crisis. I don't see it that way, he thought. Not any longer. I think it's too late for solutions. All we can hope for now is sensible reactions to the inevitable. Maybe, like Noah, we're going to have to go in two by two. But how long have we got? And what will it be like in the Ark?

Diane Hilder experienced a moment of sick disgust before, with an effort that was almost physical, she forced herself to return to an attitude of clinical detachment. The young Russian laboratory assistant had less self-control, however. He retched for a moment behind his green theater mask and rushed from the table where the dead wolf lay stretched. Diane took the forceps from the tray and, using the blunt side of the scalpel in her other hand as a lever, once more gently raised the flap of the long incision she had made in the wolf's shaven, pear-shaped stomach. The strong rank scent of the dead animal's gastric juices penetrated even the antiseptic screen of her own surgical mask. Yes, there it was . . . and there was no doubt at all about *what* it was. The left hand and lower wrist of a human being. Partly digested, the skin had wrinkled, and all color was gone from it. The bones

119

and nails were crushed. Not surprising, of course—given the power of a wolf's carnassial teeth. This was—she forced herself to look at it more closely—yes, the hand of a woman. Or could it be a boy's? It was slim and hairless. But no, it was a woman's. There was the proof. Carefully, using the forceps, she picked from the splintered sliver of bone a small wristwatch. A lady's watch, rolled gold, on a thin metal strap. Cheap, not even an automatic, she thought absurdly. It was a prominent winding spindle. And grotesquely, it was still ticking. The sickness came over her again. I really can't go on with this any more, she said to herself, but she explored the stomach cavity more thoroughly. No, there was nothing else there. That had been the wolf's share. Just the hand and the wrist.

The laboratory boy was back beside her now. He had taken off his mask and looked slightly ashamed. She walked away from the table, and he helped her to take off the gloves and theater gown. It was an oddly companionable moment: He spoke no English and she no Russian, but the shared horror of the hand had drawn them together. He showed her to the waiting room and then left her, pantomiming that he was needed elsewhere. The room was empty, and there were ten minutes to wait before the car was due back for her. She sat thinking.

In a way, it had been a bonus, that wolf. She'd asked Soldatov to save it for her before she went to bed last night, and he'd rung the army post and arranged for it to be taken to the half-deserted Biological Institute so that she could do a post-mortem. Otherwise it would have been skinned by now, he said. Well, Stovin had said he wanted a zoologist with him, and no zoologist worth her salt would pass up a prime specimen of *canis lupus*, the type species itself. Especially one from the Soviet Union. She'd never seen a Siberian specimen before. One hundred and twenty-eight pounds, it had weighed, which was ten pounds over what the textbooks gave as the maximum for a male adult in this region. And in any case, the behavior of these wolves was atypical. Wolves didn't come into areas like that tent site last night, full of the noise and bustle of human beings, especially not if they were feeding off bodies, as that one obviously had been. Presumably there weren't any bodies around the campsite itself. They'd have been cleared away days before. Very curious . . .

120

Although the Biological Institute of Akademgorodok was no more than three-quarters of a mile from the Soldatov *dacha*, the driving snow she had glimpsed from its barred window as she worked on the wolf had made her doubt if the car would be able to get through to bring her back. But she saw now through the tall glass double doors of the waiting room that the blizzard had quietened for the moment to what was no more than a brisk snowfall. The car came on time, and they moved off along a wide avenue on which two snow-sweeping vehicles were already working, clearing a two-lane strip and piling the moved snow in towering banks on each side of the road. It was noticeable, she thought, that here in Akademgorodok there seemed to be no shortage of machinery and effort to keep life working as smoothly as possible. It would have been difficult for anyone who did not know to have grasped that a few kilometers away, a modern city had been crushed and torn and was in desperate need of help. Akademgorodok was crowded, certainly, but that was all. There were muffled, fur-clad men and women plodding on foot along the road where the car was making its painful, low-geared way. She would have been willing to bet that each was a scientist, a technician, a laboratory or institute worker—perhaps brought in from some scientific establishment distant from this region. But there were no refugees from Novosibirsk, in spite of the science town's proximity and suitability to receive them. There were no tents, no military patrols. Life went on here, she imagined, much the same as before the Dancer came. A little speeded up, perhaps, a little more urgent, but basically little different. In Soviet Russia, Akademgorodok had a role, and nothing, nothing at all, was going to be allowed to interfere with it.

They were almost at the *dacha* now. The road passed beside the shore of the great reservoir, the artificial Ob Sea. Through the snow-flecked car window, between gaps in the snow banks, she glimpsed from time to time the dark expanse of the Ob ice.

It had changed. Now it was sprinkled with hundreds of tiny points of light, some of them moving, some apparently motionless. Before she could lean forward to ask the driver what they were, the car turned away from the frozen water and entered the birch woods of Akademgorodok. The big department store on the corner by the scientists' restaurant was still lighted and open as they went by. A long queue of furred and overcoated figures stretched into the restaurant. A minute or so later, the car was stopping in front of the door of Soldatov's *dacha*, and Valentina was fussing over her, exclaiming and tut-tutting at the paleness of her face. Valentina brought her some coffee. Stovin wasn't back yet, and she wished desperately that he was. In Colorado, it had seemed to her that this trip together might do something for each of them—act as a catalyst in their relationship. It hadn't. Stovin was too intellectually excited by what he imagined lay before him to have room for sexual emotion at the moment. She knew that, and in a way it made her love him more. She did love him. She knew that. And she could have sworn that there'd been at least a flicker in his eye from time to time when he looked at her. Had he really brought her all the way out here because he thought she was the ideal zoologist? I'll have to tell him about that wolf, she thought. In a way I want to tell him. But not yet. Perhaps it's as well he isn't here right now. I don't want to think about it again just yet. . . .

CHAPTER 12

"Now this butterfly," said Valentina Soldatova, picking it up in a pair of silver tweezers so that its set, spread wings stirred faintly in the warm air of the *dacha*'s central heating, "is quite remarkable."

Sitting beside her at the long trestle table, piled high with Valentina's boxes of butterflies and Soldatov's working papers which occupied one wall of the *dacha*'s single living room, Bisby leaned forward. Valentina's face was alert with interest, and she was wearing a pair of spectacles that tipped forward on her nose in what Bisby knew was an absurdly attractive way. In fact, he reflected, she was a very attractive woman. But she did nothing for him. Nothing at all. Mind you, he thought wryly, the women who do nothing at all for you, Bisby, are becoming a very large club. There hadn't been one in the last five years.

"What's its name?" he asked.

"How do you mean?"

"Has it got a name, in Russian? Do you see it often?"

She laughed. "How must I say its name in American? 'Wizard,' I think. 'Arctic Wizard.' But in science, of course, in Latin—*oeneis jutta.*"

"Of course," he said, and grinned.

She made a contrite face. "I am sorry, Paul . . . I may call you Paul?"

He nodded.

"I am forgetting, Paul, that you are not a scientist. You must find it difficult sometimes? When you are talking to Dr. Stovin?"

"Sometimes," he said vaguely. He looked across the room to where Soldatov, Diane, and Stovin were deep in conversation around the central stove that supplemented the central heating. Soldatov sat with a large map spread across his knees, tapping it vigorously from time to time as he spoke. Bisby turned back to Valentina. At least she was trying to keep him interested.

"Why is it remarkable?" he asked, looking at the butterfly more closely. It was a dark, smoky brown, about two inches across, with a pattern of black eye spots and yellow borders down the edge of each wing.

"The Wizard has learned," she said simply. "It lives in the north of both continents, west in Alaska, east in Siberia, and in Greenland, too. When there is sun, it sits on the rocks, and you cannot distinguish it from the lichens around it. And when the cold wind blows—and sometimes it blows in summer, too—then the Wizard falls to one side, so that the wind sweeps over it, and its body stays warm. I know no other butterfly that does this. That is why I like the Wizard best of all. I have been in the North in deep water up by the River Lena, when it was so cold that our breath became star whispers, and I have looked across a wilderness of snow and ice and I have thought, Under there are still the butterflies, sleeping. Or what will one day become the butterflies, of course. And next summer they will fly again."

"Very remarkable," said Bisby, smiling at her. "And what are star whispers?"

Valentina chuckled. "When it is very cold and you breathe out, you will see a cloud of—how do you say? —ice crystals coming from your mouth, because your breath is freezing as soon as it leaves the warmth of your lungs. This is what in Siberia we call star whispers."

"I saw them this morning from my own mouth," said Diane Hilder. Bisby looked up quickly. She had joined them unnoticed, leaving the two men still deep in discussion over the map. "Oh, I see, you're showing your favorite butterfly."

"As I told you this morning," said Valentina, "I like to see any animal adapt."

"Even wolves?" asked Bisby. Valentina stopped smiling, looking a little anxiously at Diane Hilder. The American girl's face had paled slightly, and her mouth was set. Oh, God, thought Diane, why does he have to bring that up again? I know, I know I ought to be looking at it purely scientifically, but I can't. And he knows it, and it gives him some sort of kick to remind me. Maybe he *wants* me to be a really lousy zoologist. But he's shrewd, that one. And he was the only one to spot, straightaway, the significance of that watch. "It was still ticking?" he'd said. "Then it's likely the wearer was alive immediately before the hand was eaten. An automatic watch might have gone on working inside the wolf, but a cheap winding watch would run down quite quickly. It's a pity you didn't bring it back to get it examined. Then we could have calculated when it was last wound. . . ." She shuddered. He was right, of course. That wolf hadn't been scavenging, pulling to pieces a dead body, frozen since the Dancer hit Novosibirsk more than a week ago. No, he and the rest of the pack—the ones that had presumably shared the rest of the body— must have cut out that poor woman from the mass of refugees around that tent site, maybe only an hour or so before we got there ourselves. According to Soldatov, people were reported missing every day—not surprisingly, in this weather and in these circumstances. But how many were being picked off by wolves, then? It was simply unheard of for wolves to tackle a mass of human beings in this way—more like Red Riding Hood than serious zoology. Nevertheless, if, for the sake of argument, it could be assumed that . . .

"Even wolves?" asked Bisby again. Diane shrugged. She had recovered her composure.

"It's a new situation for wolves, too," she said. "You can never entirely predict how an animal will react to a new ecological situation. The only thing you can be sure of is that it won't—in fact, it can't—behave out of character. It can only do what's already in it to do. We shall have to learn exactly what that is."

"Of course," said Valentina. She was anxious to change the subject, and she saw with relief that Yevgeny and Stovin were joining them. Bisby looked at Stovin, an indefinable expression on his face. Stovin did not appear to notice.

Soldatov twitched aside the curtain at the long triple-glazed window. "The snow is back," he said moodily. They peered out into an opaque, swirling whiteness. In the warmth of the *dacha,* they could hear only a faint moan from the wind, but it was clear that the blizzard was blowing in powerful, snow-laden gusts. Every so often, the white curtain would part for a moment, so that they could see the dark, empty expanse of the Ob Sea ice.

"No lights there now," said Diane.

Soldatov laughed shortly. "No chance of that. Those lights were people, fishing. They will have had to stop when the snow began again. Nobody would stand a chance out on the Ob ice in this weather. In normal times, people come out here for sport. Sometimes by night, but usually by day. They wear warm furs, bring a bottle of brandy, perhaps even a book, bore a hole in the ice, and fish with a hand line for hours. It's a hobby, not an economic activity."

"Do they catch much?" asked Diane curiously.

Soldatov shrugged. "A few lake perch, perhaps, if they're lucky. But not the big fish. The big fish go deep in winter."

"Then why are they fishing now . . . and so many of them?" said Diane.

"For food," said Soldatov. "They're short of food over there in Novosibirsk. The troops are bringing in what they can, but there are still hundreds of thousands of people there. Even a few lake perch are better than nothing. The troops have been told to allow a certain number of men through—men with families."

Diane was surprised. "Through? Through what?"

"Of course," said Soldatov, "you will not have seen. There are military checkpoints on the road outside Akademgorodok. It is not possible at the moment, to come into the town without a permit. These men are simply being given a permit to fish."

"But why can't the others come in?"

Soldatov did not duck the question. "If we are to make a contribution toward meeting the problems ahead, we must think and work without distraction. It is more important for the people out there that we do this than that we open our science town to a few hundred of them and allow our work to be disturbed."

It was, Stovin thought wryly, exactly what he had been thinking beside the mass graveyard of Novosibirsk's station that morning. Bisby, however, was more challenging.

"Although they're dying, those few hundred? And starving, too, you say? You aren't short of food here are you? You gave us"—he turned to Valentina—"a good meal tonight."

"That was moose, from the deep freeze," she said. "It has been in the freezer for six months. But no, we shall not starve. There is not a great variety of food in Akademgorodok, and already we are working a rationing system, but we shall not go hungry. Even though there are more than three hundred extra scientists here. There is special treatment for Akademgorodok. Always. This is where our institutes do their work. It's where our science is based."

"I see," said Bisby. He seemed disposed, thought Stovin with a twinge of disquiet, to start arguing the point, but at that moment the telephone bell gave a single long peal. Soldatov crossed to the desk at the other side of the room and picked up the handset. Then he took a pencil from his pocket and began to scribble down a series of numbers on a writing pad. After a couple of minutes, he spoke a few words in Russian into the telephone and replaced the receiver. He turned to Stovin.

"That was the Permafrost Institute, at Yakutsk," he said. "Apparently the Army has now restored the telephone link, through its own temporary exchange. The Institute is handling climate data for the moment since we're having difficulty at Novosibirsk. I have a colleague up there—Galia Kalmykova, my deputy. She has sent me"—he tapped the writing pad—"some of the figures that are available. They are quite astonishing."

The two men bent over them, and Diane and Bisby, drawn together for the moment by mutual incomprehension of what was going on, watched silently. The murmured conversation went on for five minutes . . . "very sharply increased reflected surface albedo, of course, after the heavier precipitation of the last two winters . . ." and Stovin nodding and working out some calculation on an empty page of his diary, and then Soldatov again . . . "given a surface albedo of 55 percent plus this terrestrial radiation, we could expect the feedback to be quite extraordinary . . ." and then, once more, Stovin ". . . it's been staring us in the face for long enough, but we've just put on snowglasses and refused to look . . ."

At last Stovin glanced over to where Bisby and Diane sat together and got to his feet abruptly. The one thing he didn't want, he reminded himself, was for Bisby to feel left out of what was being discussed. And Diane? Well, Diane was, at any rate, a scientist if not a climatologist. She knew how conclusions were arrived at even if she didn't understand these particular arguments. She could take care of herself. But he owed Bisby an explanation.

"Well, it's coming, Paul, and coming fast," he said.

"Oh?"

"Those figures Geny was just showing me—they're radiation and albedo figures for the snow cover up on the north coast, at the edge of the Arctic Ocean. They aren't good. They aren't reassuring at all."

Bisby stirred impatiently. There was an expression on his face, thought the watching Soldatov, that was close to anger.

"Sto, I don't know what albedo is, never mind the rest."

Stovin paused, trying to put it into words. "Albedo is the amount of reflectivity from the surface of the earth. The sun shines on the earth, and some of its sunlight is absorbed into the earth, warming it. But some sunlight, of course, is reflected off the earth's surface back into space. Snow-and-ice cover have the effect of increasing the reflectivity—the albedo. That throws a greater proportion of sunlight back, so the surface temperature drops. Now if other factors—say sunspots, or volcanic dust, or man-made interference, or a combination of all three—interfere with sunlight at the same time as snow-and-ice cover are giving off more albedo, then the snow-and-ice cover begins to increase across a cooling surface. It's an inevitable feedback mechanism. More snow and ice, more albedo, less sunlight absorbed, then more snow and ice, and so on. There's nothing startlingly new in this; it began more than ten years ago, in Baffin Land."

"Then why's there been all the argument?"

"For a lot of us," said Stovin patiently, "the argument hasn't been over whether the earth was cooling. We thought we knew that. But even those who realized what was happening clung to the belief that climatic change has always been thought to be a slow, slow business. The pessimists thought there might be a semiglacial—a Little Ice Age—in about 500 years' time. The optimists thought 10,000 years was nearer the mark. But there's a man in England who said fifty years would see us into the start of Ice Age, at least—and I've always thought it could be a lot sooner even than that. So did Geny here, apparently. And we were right."

Bisby was looking at Stovin intently, eyes narrowed. The older man looked back at him curiously, doubt stirring in his mind. If the thought hadn't been incongruous he would have sworn that Bisby was . . . well, almost triumphant.

"How do you know?" asked Bisby.

"We're getting snow blitz here in Siberia," said Stovin. "And it's marching south. For all I know we're getting it in Alaska and northern Canada as well, and maybe the northern United States. I haven't been in touch with Boulder today, but I'll call them tomorrow."

"Snow blitz?" said Diane.

"That's when you get snow falling, freezing, not melting at all as it does under normal climatic conditions and then being added to by more and more snow. When that happens, you can practically see it roll across the map. Up to now, snow blitz has been no more than a mathematical hypothesis—something we were sure could happen, given a certain combination of circumstances. I'll give you an example. Herman Flohn—he's a German meteorologist who works at Bonn—estimated a year or two ago that given a comparatively modest rise in surface albedo, a forest fifty feet high would be completely covered by snow and ice in a matter of about twenty-two years. The kind of figures that Geny was just given from the Permafrost Institute would give a time scale divided by ten. Two years, perhaps much less."

"Two years, and the snow-and-ice cover will be fifty feet high," said Diane incredulously. "But how far south?"

Soldatov had been watching the conversation between

the Americans inquisitively, with Valentina standing silent beside him.

"How far? Ah, that is the—how do you say in America —the sixty-five dollar question."

"Sixty-four," said Bisby, grinning for the first time.

"Sixty-four? I see. Paul . . . Diane . . . look here." He spread the map he had been using earlier.

"Already there is great trouble up on the north coast, the White Sea, the Kara Sea, the island of Novya Zemlya. This has happened, literally, in the past four days. Fortunately there is not much population up there, though there are oil installations, important ones. People are having to be evacuated."

"What's happening in America?" asked Diane.

Soldatov shrugged. "I have no information. I will check tomorrow. But I would imagine that there will be difficulties in Alaska. And our television news said tonight there had been an unparalleled snowfall in New York, which, of course, is much farther south than the Siberian coast."

"It gets damn awful winters all the same," said Bisby thoughtfully. He tapped the map, tracing a line from the inverted crescent of the island of Novya Zemlya onto the mainland and down to the town of Vorkuta. "This is part of the area that's in trouble?"

Soldatov nodded. "Yes. They had a . . . what you have called, I think, a Dancer at Vorkuta. Quite near a tributary of the Ob, not far from the mouth," he said, turning to Stovin. "Curious how these things seem to respond to the presence of water, isn't it?"

Stovin put a hand to his chin. "Now that's something I hadn't . . ."

Bisby was speaking, still staring at the map. "But all that area, that's . . . are you sure you're able to tell us all this?"

"Of course, of course," said Soldatov in surprise. "What do you mean?"

"Well, that's kind of a sensitive area," said Bisby slowly. "Don't you have any security wraps on that?"

Soldatov laughed, and patted him on the shoulder. "Oh, my dear Paul, this is more important than such security," he said. "It won't be the armies, or the navies, or the air forces, even"—he smiled at the young American—"who will have to work out the answers to this. It will be scientists, like Sto here, and me, and Valentina and Diane. Each in our fields. We cannot work unless we know, each of us, everything we need to know. So don't worry about . . ."

"What's that?" said Valentina.

Even through the sound-muffling, triple-glazed windows, a steady pulsating hum began to make itself heard. The *dacha* shook very, very slightly, so that a little snow plumped down from its steep roof. Soldatov pulled aside the window curtain. The snow still poured down, but the noise was getting louder now, and as they looked up into the blizzard, they caught, every so often, the winking red navigation lights of successive aircraft coming in to land. They watched for several minutes.

"But there are scores and scores of planes," said Soldatov. "Who would order flights on a night like this? There will be crashes."

"It's what I thought," said Bisby. "Up there, where you were showing us on the map, that's the air defense belt for incoming hostiles over the Pole. I reckon you're having to evacuate those bases right now. The airfield here's still working, and it's a fair way south, in spite of the Dancer. So they're putting one of those Arctic groups in here for the moment—maybe a couple of groups, even. They must be in real trouble up there, or they'd never risk flying in this. They're sure to have lost some aircraft. That's why I asked you about security. We wouldn't want you to get into trouble, Geny."

It was the first time he had called Soldatov by his first name, and the Russian felt irrationally pleased.

"Oh, there's no question of . . ."

"There's a vehicle outside, I think," said Valentina. "It looks like an army snow track." Alone of the five, she had wrenched her eyes from the sky. A loud knock came at the side of the *dacha*, and she hurried to the double doors, opening the outer one. A furred, overcoated figure stood there, stamping the snow from ankle-high boots. Two soldiers, having each deposited a suitcase, were trotting back through the freezing storm to the waiting shape, just discernible through the snow gusts, of a small tracked carrier. With a slight feeling of shock, Stovin recognized the man in the doorway.

The newcomer quickly shut the door and took off his fur hat, brushing a fringe of snow from his face, which was already becoming red and damp with condensation in the warmth of the *dacha*.

130

"Comrade Soldatov?" he said, looking toward the Russian.

"Of course."

The newcomer nodded briskly. "Grigori Volkov, Foreign Ministry," he said. "From Moscow. Dr. Soldatov, it is a pleasure to meet you and your wife. I have heard much about you."

He turned to the Americans. "We have met already, of course. I hope you have not been uncomfortable. We don't usually give our guests such a cold welcome, even in Siberia. What a night!"

"Have you been billeted here by the Council?" asked Valentina, coming forward to lead him into the living room. "We have not much space since Dr. Hilder is here, too, but we would be happy to help."

"For a few days," said Volkov. He did not seem inclined to elaborate.

"I imagine you're here on Foreign Ministry business?" said Soldatov. He sounded, thought Stovin, suddenly a little uncertain.

"In a way," said Volkov. He turned to Stovin.

"I am here," he said, "to see that you get everything you need."

"How many more men to go, Wally?" asked the engineer-in-charge, watching the big orange Sikorsky S-61 helicopter lift off from the dirty yellow circle on the uppermost of Geranium One's three decks.

"Ten, plus you and me," said the crew boss tersely. "Listen, I'm going down to B Deck to get my boots. A hundred and twenty dollars they cost me, in Houston last year, and I'm not leaving 'em on this lump of oversized Meccano. One more load'll do it. I spoke to Cruden Bay five minutes ago. The last chopper's on its way out now. Left about an hour ago."

"None too bloody soon, either," said the engineer-in-charge. "I definitely don't like the look of that thing."

He picked up his binoculars again and peered through the salt-encrusted window of the derrick control office, midway up the soaring grey struts of the oil production platform. Doing a quick sum in his head, he worked out the likely arrival time of the helicopter. Geranium One was one of four giant oil production platforms that reared three hundred feet out of the North Sea, northeast of Aberdeen. They were, he reflected nearly 200 miles from

Cruden Bay on the Scottish mainland, from where the Sikorsky had lifted off. Assuming it was flying at its normal 120 knots, it should be here in, yes . . . fifty minutes more. Allowing for this head wind. He stepped out of the door of the derrick office for a moment, and instantly the familiar creaking and groaning of the 35,000-ton structure assailed his ears. Far below, the steel-grey sea, scudded with misty white foam, blurred into the long ripples of what at sea level would be considerable waves. The wind —half snow, half sleet—whipped over the wet and slippery deck, howling through the struts that thrust upward into the murk above him. It wasn't, however, the storm that worried him.

He focused his glasses again and looked over to the North. There it was, a line of white on the horizon, rather like a distant cliff line, but where no cliff could be. It glimmered faintly in the fitful afternoon light. Hell, it couldn't be more than nine, ten miles away. He went quickly down the iron staircase, past the living quarters on B Deck, and down to the control room on the bottom deck. There he picked up the radio-telephone.

"Geranium One to Cruden Bay, do you read me?"

"I read you," crackled the laconic reply from the Scottish coast.

"Frank, what's the latest on that iceberg? It looks to be coming down on us pretty fast."

"Well, it's still bang in line with you, so it's just as well we're flying you all off. The RAF people have plotted the course and speed. They say it's doing a bit more than two knots."

"Listen, Frank, that gives us not much more than three hours, by my reckoning. I hope to Christ that chopper doesn't get engine trouble, or something. That berg's going to be knocking on our door very soon. I've never seen anything like it. It looks as big as the Isle of Wight."

There was a short laugh from Cruden Bay. "So they tell me. But you don't need to get excited. The chopper's well on its way—they gave us a fix ten minutes ago. The other three platforms are evacuated now, aren't they?"

"Yes."

"Then not to worry, old lad. You leave Head Office to do the worrying. And Lloyds. It's going to cost one of them around £100 million."

"I suppose so. Are we covered against bergs?"

Another laugh. "I wouldn't know—I have enough trou-

132

ble with my car insurance, thanks. Listen, I'll buy you a large Scotch tonight; I'm off duty at six. I'll meet you at the Royal—about eight, say?"

"If I can make it. God knows how much paperwork all this is going to mean. They might want some of it straight-away."

"Tell 'em you're suffering from stress," said the voice from the mainland.

"I bloody well am," said the engineer-in-charge. He replaced the receiver and went back up the iron staircase to B Deck. Better tell the lads the chopper's nearly here, he thought. They'll be getting edgy.

Three hours later, the last twelve men from Production Platform Geranium One, which until forty-eight hours ago had been delivering 130,000 barrels of oil a day into the mainland storage tanks, were back at Cruden Bay, clambering stiffly from the Sikorsky's narrow seats. Only a circling RAF photo-reconnaissance Nimrod, cameras working busily, recorded the moments when the thousand million tons of ice in the half-mile-long berg, moving through the heaving sea at the pace of a walking man, drew near to the skeletal structure of the production platform. Beside the Nimrod's captain sat a marine glaciologist sent by the Air Ministry as a special observer. He watched in fascinated concentration, shaking his head. He turned to the captain.

"That thing simply shouldn't be there," he said quietly. "Not at this time of year, anyway. We were really surprised when we got the first report three days ago. Spring is the iceberg season, not winter. And even allowing for the fact that it's here, it isn't the kind that *should* be here. It ought to be a glacier berg, like the ones that start somewhere off the Greenland coast. But look at this one. It's a tabular berg . . . look, the damned thing's like a moving island. It's the kind you get when a whole ice shelf breaks away from a coastline. You get them in the Antarctic, but not here. That kind of berg's got no business here."

"Somebody should have explained that to the iceberg," said the pilot dryly. "My God . . . just look at that."

Below them the great iceberg struck the rig. Geranium One's great steel legs, each anchored by forty 50-ton piles, were plucked from the seabed like straws. The empty decks canted, then tilted more steeply, and in grotesque cartwheels the giant derrick, the outbuildings, and the winches poured from the rig, slithering and crashing their way down the blue-green sides of the berg, which towered above them. For a moment the derrick, caught on an ice ledge, teetered like a balancing arm, and then slid beneath the waves. Four-hundred-and-fifty feet beneath the surface superstructure of Geranium One, the thirty-two-inch pipe that had linked the platform to Cruden Bay was torn effortlessly from the sand of the seabed, its broken end spouting the residue of hundreds of tons of oil which had remained in it after the supply valves had been closed on the previous day. The whole structure was going now, literally overwhelmed by the enormous mass of the berg. Two minutes later, the outer edge of the iceberg caught the neighboring tower of Geranium Four, rubbing it from the sea's surface like a boot crushing a matchbox. The crew of the Nimrod, 2,000 feet above, watched in awed silence.

The captain turned to the Air Ministry man. "Well, that's something I'll never forget," he said. "I hope those cameras did their job. Come on, let's go home."

The glaciologist put a hand to his head, speaking as though to himself.

"It needs colossal changes in Arctic coastline stress and pressure to produce an iceberg like that. And a whole changed pattern of Arctic ocean currents. What the hell is going on?"

"Evacuate Anchorage?" said the Secretary of the Interior. "But that's 50,000 people. Never!"

"Mr. Secretary," said the Governor of Alaska tiredly, "I have to deal in realities, not in slogans. It's a whole new situation up there now."

He passed his hand across his forehead. God damn it, he thought, I just must get some sleep soon. Across the desk in the office high in the Interior Department Building the Secretary looked at him with sudden concern. He pressed a button on the desk console, and a young, grey-flannelled aide came in from the outer office.

"The Governor and I will take some coffee," said the Secretary. He gave the other man a little time to compose himself, looking abstractedly out of the window toward the snow-dusted tulip magnolias in the park gardens of Rawlins Square.

"When did you get in from Juneau?" he said at last.

"I landed about an hour ago," said the Governor. "But not from Juneau. I came straight in from Point Hope—

I guess we were just about the last plane out. You know we've had to quit the Oceanographic Institute?"

"Yes," said the Secretary. "For the moment."

"Jim," said the Governor earnestly. "I wish I could get it through to you people down here. It's not for the moment. It's for good—well, as far ahead as we can see, anyway. And the oil people—they're going to have to get out of Barrow."

He leaned forward, speaking rapidly. "It's not snow like we used to know, even in Alaska. And it's nothing at all like that"—he waved a hand contemptuously toward Rawlins Square. "It's snowing like there's no tomorrow— and for all I know, Jim, there *is* no tomorrow. It's been coming in all day, all night, all week, all month. Living up there, I guess we thought we knew all about winter— you know, it could be tough, but we could handle it. Not this time, Jim. You could put every bulldozer and snow- plow in the United States in a ring around Anchorage, and you wouldn't make a dent in what's happening up there. To start with, there's nowhere to put the damned snow. The snowbanks at the side of the highways are forty feet high now—and we're getting houses over- whelmed every day. There are folk sleeping in every restaurant room and hotel corridor in town. Yesterday we had to clear every automobile out of a multistory park and use it for accommodation. And God knows what's happening to the Eskimos in those campers parked along the Ninilchik River; the State road patrol cleared a piece of the highway south of the town three days ago, and I had an engineer drive along it. He said you wouldn't even have known there'd been campers or huts there. Just a damned great piece of snow and river ice. And no Eski- mos standing around, asking for help. Of course, a hell of a lot of them are back in the city now, probably bedded down in that car park. It's hard to keep track of Eskimos even in normal times."

"Hm," said the Secretary. "Assuming it does become necessary to evacuate 50,000 people . . ."

"It does, and it has," said the Governor tersely.

". . . assuming it does," said the Secretary, "what con- tingency plans do you have?"

"We can take some, say, 10,000 in Juneau, but no more," said the Governor. "Yes, yes, I know Juneau's the State capital, but I know and you know it's only a small town. And we could probably get a few more thousand into places like Fairbanks, because at the moment they're better off there than places on the coast. But we'll need certain conditions. And a hell of a lot of Federal help."

"What conditions?" asked the Secretary.

"Conditions that neither you nor I can do anything about, Jim. The weather's got to slacken off a bit, or we're going to be in trouble even down as far as Juneau. The Canadians—you know about the Canadians?"

"I had a report this morning," began the Secretary, but the other man interrupted.

"They're flying rescue missions—full-scale Air Force rescue missions—all over the Yukon Territory, bringing folk out. It looks like we're going to have to do the same."

"And we'll be flying them back next spring," said the Secretary.

The other man sighed. "Jim, if I were you I'd get this morning's briefing from your Department scientists. There isn't going to be any relief in the spring—not the way you mean. My information, and it comes right from the Institute—what *was* the Institute—at Point Hope, is that even if we started to get spring temperatures tomorrow and then a normal summer, there's no way this mass of snow and ice could be even half melted before next winter. And even a normal snowfall next winter will just pile it on. We're going to have to redraw the maps, Jim."

"Maybe, maybe," said the Secretary soothingly. "But I can't help feeling that by next winter we'll have come up with something that'll help deal with all this . . ."

Jim's talking like a damned fool, said the Governor to himself, sitting back in the car taking him to his hotel in Georgetown half an hour later. No, maybe he's not . . . I'm not being fair. He's like most of the rest of the people here; they read reports, estimates, calculations. In a way they understand it, but they don't really believe it. It's natural enough, he thought wearily. If you haven't seen it, you can't believe it. But once you *have* seen it . . . well, that's something else again.

"What I want," said the British Prime Minister, looking up at the portrait of Sir Robert Peel above the Downing Street fireplace, "is a firm forecast of when Sullum Voe will be fully operational again, Christopher. Heaven knows what all this will do to the balance of payments. I want to go to the House and say next May, or June, or even July for that matter. But I want a date—something that will steady the market. We can't hedge our bets any more where North Sea oil is concerned."

"I can't give you a date, Prime Minister," said the chief government scientist, Sir Christopher Ledbester. "There's nobody in the world could give you a date. But I'll give you an opinion. Sullum Voe won't be open for oil landings on any considerable scale next May, June, or July. And probably not open next year at all. And the Shetlands won't be fit for human habitation, apart from research teams, over the same period. We've got to start thinking again, in terms of a new technology for getting out oil in Arctic conditions. It won't be a quick business. And Sullum Voe and the Shetlands may not be part of it. We're lucky, in a way. We've got the fields that are being developed over on the other side, in the Western Approaches. We could land that oil near Bristol. Should have more chance there. But on the east coast—well, I wouldn't recommend an oil terminal anywhere north of Harwich."

"As bad as that?"

"Not yet, of course, Prime Minister," said the scientist. "But it's coming. The question is: how soon? I must say, I'd like to hear something from Siberia. The best climatologist in the world is out there, and he hasn't said a word yet, either to Washington or to us. Assuming, of course, that Washington is keeping to the American end of the deal and letting us have everything he sends."

"Oh, they'll do that, Christopher, even if it's only to keep the French off their backs. The whole of Europe's getting pretty worked up, and there've been some wild scenarios from the Economic Commission. All sorts of Doomsday stuff."

"The trouble with Doomsday," said Ledbester heavily —at Cambridge he had been known as "Leadjester" because of the ponderous weight of his wit—"is that we may not recognize the Doom when we're shown it or know the Day when it finally arrives."

CHAPTER 13

Bisby was happy. He was sitting at the end of the wooden infantry bench which stretched down the center of the armored personnel carrier. Immediately in front of him, the Red Army lieutenant in command stood in his own small compartment, alternately swaying and bracing himself in response to the carrier's movements as it lurched on its wide tracks through the snowy forest thirty miles north of Novosibirsk. To the front of the lieutenant himself, but below him in the sloping front of the carrier, sat the driver. Bisby could just see his head, in its close-fitting helmet, moving and bobbing in the tiny driving hatch. Above both of them projected the short barrel of the 75mm gun, though no gunner sat in the cramped turret. This wasn't, Bisby reflected, an operational patrol. In fact, it was hard to say what exactly it was . . . Not that it mattered. Because it was good, good, to be away, even for a few hours, from the scientific claustrophobia of Akademgorodok.

He took a look at the carrier's other occupants. Fur-hatted and muffled against the icy wind that blew over the carrier's steep but open sides, Soldatov and Stovin sat beside him, neither of them speaking very much. Farther up the bench, Diane and Valentina Soldatov were talking to each other, though it was impossible to hear what they were saying above the sustained roar of the engine. Occasionally Diane laughed while the Russian girl leaned forward, expressing herself earnestly with vigorous movements of her hands. Bisby watched her covertly. Diane looked altogether different when she laughed. Her slightly arrogant expression vanished, and she seemed more vulnerable, more open. Open to what? Open to Stovin, I guess, he thought. I reckon he'd just have to crook his finger, and she'd be all his. He glanced across at the older man. Stovin's face was set, unsmiling. Now there was a man who wasn't one little bit happy right now. And that wasn't surprising. Suddenly all the flow of scientific and technical information—in fact, of any information at all about the outside world or even what was happening in Russia—seemed to have dried up. "When am I going to see those isotopes, Geny?" Bisby had heard Stovin ask Soldatov that morning. "I'm not supposed to be here just as a tourist, surely?" Soldatov had been embarrased, awkwardly saying something about delays and promising to try to speed things up. Ten minutes later, he'd been in earnest conversation with Volkov. But he'd got nothing out of that stone face. Bisby looked along to the far end of the bench. There was Volkov, still writing busily on a white pad clipped to a board, indifferent to the lurching of the carrier. What was it he'd said when they arrived in Moscow? "This is a document-conscious country." Now he was proving it. And, of course, Stovin knew, everybody knew the reason why the information Stovin needed was no longer available. Volkov was the reason. Nothing you could really put your finger on, of course. His techinque was simple. Stovin would ask for something, and Volkov would say, "But of course . . . immediately." And then, somehow, it wasn't immediate. Things seemed to crop up. There would be delays. The delays would, of course, be dealt with "immediately." But meanwhile, he, Volkov, would have to ask Stovin, with regret, to be patient. Like this morning. Stovin had wanted to go to one of the institutes in Akademgorodok with Soldatov to get access to a computer. It turned out that the computer was suddenly under repair. "All right," Stovin had said, "Geny and I will go back to the *dacha* and work some of it out in our heads." "Of course, of course," Volkov said. And then, "But perhaps it would be better if we went out today to look at the site where the 'extraordinary phenomenon' that hit Novisibirsk originated—out in the forest." Even Soldatov had protested warmly that their time would be much better spent in Akademgorodok itself, but Volkov had insisted. They would have to go today, he said, because this was the only day the Army could supply two vehicles for the trip. Why would they need two vehicles? Volkov had raised an admonitory finger, "One vehicle may break down, have difficulty, strip off one of its tracks. It is an Army rule: Vehicles never travel alone in the *taiga*." Actually, thought Bisby, that was the first thing Volkov had said that made good practical common sense. Two vehicles were *better* than one. The Siberian winter day was short, and he wouldn't much care for a night in a frozen carrier in these conditions, even though it had almost stopped snowing for the moment.

He looked out to the right of their own carrier to where the second vehicle plowed along on their flank, leaving a long hanging wake of driven snow behind it. Its eight Russian infantrymen sat in the rear, the muzzles of their automatic rifles dancing in a jagged pattern above the carrier's dirty white camouflage. They'll be wedged pretty tight in that carrier, thought Bisby. We've got more space in this one.

In front of him, the lieutenant began to speak into his throat microphone, and the carrier veered left, moving over the lumpy ice hummocks toward what Bisby knew to be the line of the River Ob, which was marked by occasional sparse stands of stunted spruce and larch. The area down to the broad frozen stream was open, though about half a mile beyond it rose the great tree wall of the *taiga*—hundreds of thousands of tall silver birches, stretching in close-packed regiments to the horizon. The carrier was slowing now, almost stopping. It began to slue and slide on its track as it picked its way across broken ground. Then it halted, with the other carrier a little farther away, about a hundred-and-fifty yards from the rim of a circular, snow-covered depression on the forward slope leading down to the River Ob. Stiffly, they all scrambled out of the vehicle. The soldiers, Bisby noted, adopted instant defensive positions, lumbering outward across the craterlike depression until they had established a hundred yards in diameter. It seemed to be a tactical drill learned by a long practice.

Nothing else in the desolate landscape moved, save overhead where a single eagle swung effortlessly, quartering the long ice-jumbled banks of the Ob for the tiniest movement that meant food. Beyond the black wall of birch and spruce to the west, and low in the darkening Arctic sky, hung the deep-orange disc of the sun, only just above the horizon. To the east the sky had assumed the blue-gray cotton-wool appearance that heralded more snow, and already there were streaks and large flakes in Bisby's face as he turned it upward to watch the eagle.

Volkov, Stovin, and Soldatov walked together up the

steep, snowy slope that led to the high rim of the natural bowl in which they stood. Valentina, a small pair of binoculars at her eyes, was concentrated on the eagle. Diane stood beside Bisby, thrusting the toe of her boot into the snow in front of her. She turned to him, surprise in her voice.

"Look, Paul, that's all pretty new snow. And loose. Look . . ." She bent down and thrust her gloved hand into it up to the wrist, scooping it out in a flurry of white crystals. Bisby, too, bent down and did the same. When he brought up his glove, a little moist sphagnum moss, greyish-yellow, clung to the fingertips. He stared at it in astonishment, turning to Diane.

"But look at this . . . this moss should be way down in the permafrost. And the snow above it should be packed hard until next summer."

She nodded, looking around her in wonder. "It's not a natural hollow at all, this," she said. "It seems that way at first because it's snowed since it was made, and that disguises what's happened. But if you look at it closely, it's far too round and regular for something that's been here for a long time. It's more like an impact crater."

"It's a crater, all right, but it's not an impact crater, exactly. We might start a whole new jargon and call it an extract crater," said Stovin. Unnoticed, he and Soldatov had joined them, leaving Volkov in earnest conversation with the young lieutenant.

Soldatov looked up at the darkening sky. "You mean . . . the jet stream, of course?"

Stovin nodded. "It reached down like . . . well, like a finger. God knows how deep it drove into this river bank, because the snow that's fallen since has masked it. But when it came it bored into the earth like God's pneumatic drill. All this rim on which we stand now is spoil—earth spoil—from that drill. Frozen hard again now, of course, and covered with snow. But that's why there's sphagnum moss from twelve–fifteen feet down in the permafrost so near the surface now. It's part of that earth spoil."

"We need special machines to drill into the permafrost," said Soldatov. "It is very, very difficult. But not, it seems, for a Dancer."

"And then, once it had established itself here," said Stovin reflectively, "it presumably stabilized itself much nearer to the surface and began to move. Toward Novosibirsk. And at that point it was travelling more or less on the surface, because otherwise we wouldn't have a twenty-foot-deep crater, but a twenty-foot-deep channel, all the way to the city."

He turned to Soldatov. "You remember what you said to me the other day—that it was curious how these things seemed to be associated with the presence of water? I'm sure that's significant . . . but there's something else."

"What?" asked Bisby. He shivered for a moment under his thick parka, looking out over the rim into the thickening twilight that, beside the edge of the forest, was already almost darkness. There had been something . . . or had there? The faintest flicker of movement against the towering stand of the birches, perhaps. He strained his eyes, only half hearing Stovin's reply.

"The Dancer seeks warmth," said Stovin. "Not necessarily warmth in human terms, but something that's warmer than the rest of the landscape where it operates. Water—beside a coast or a river. A town like Hays. A city like Novosibirsk. And even, perhaps 20,000 years ago, the Berezovka mammoths. A mammoth herd must have given off warmth. So a Dancer touched them. And forty centuries later, men could eat their flesh."

There was a shout from one of the soldiers on the opposite edge of the rim, about eighty yards away. He was pointing over toward the forest. The Soviet lieutenant scrambled up beside him and then walked back to Volkov, smiling and offering his binoculars. Bisby joined them, straining his eyes into the deepening gloom. There it was again, that movement.

At his side, Volkov gave a pleased exclamation and courteously passed him the binoculars. "Something not many visitors see, Mr. Bisby," he said. "You are lucky."

Bisby focused the glasses, and the source of that barely glimpsed movement suddenly filled the lens. It was an Arctic wolf, a male, almost totally white with a thick, deep ruff around its face. It stood on a slight rocky eminence just forward of the tree line, tail down, one foot raised in what seemed almost a self-conscious sculptural pose. It was looking toward them, but even as he watched, it turned its great head to the side and gazed over to where the black shape of the farther personnel carrier bulked large on the slope.

"I guess that carrier puzzles him," said Bisby to Diane,

142

who had borrowed Valentina's binoculars and was standing beside him. "Look, he's put his tail up."

The wolf was now trotting slowly, parallel with the river bank, out on their flank. Behind him in the trees there was another flicker of movement, and Diane grasped Bisby's arm. He remembered later that it was the first physical contact he had ever had with her, and that even in that dank twilight, absorbed by what was happening out on the snow, he had felt an unmistakable, rising sexual clamor inside himself.

"See?" she was saying. "There are more of them. One . . . three . . . four."

The five wolves, with the original male in the lead, were moving steadily, unhurriedly, but purposefully along the line of the river. They betrayed no curiosity, as far as could be seen, about the two personnel carriers or about the party of human beings grouped in the crater. Suddenly, in a long rippling movement, they seemed to vanish altogether.

"They're lying down," said Diane. Her voice sounded slightly edgy.

"When they do that, they merge with the snow," Bisby said admiringly. "But what the hell are they playing at?"

Diane was still watching the five wolves intently. Volkov had retrieved his binoculars and was standing beside her. "What do you imagine they are doing, Miss Hilder?" he said. "You are, after all, the expert."

She turned to them both, her face troubled and puzzled in the fur fringe of her parka hood. "I can tell you one thing," she said. "Those are hunting tactics. Those wolves are maneuvering for prey."

"But what is the prey?" said Volkov. "We have been here for half an hour now, and we shall have frightened off any other animals that might have been nearby. I would imagine that there won't be an elk within two miles."

His voice—just like Diane's, Bisby realized—sounded slightly strained.

"I agree," said Diane. "There are no elk. So they're hunting us."

Bisby laughed. "Then they've got a rush of blood to the head," he said. "Delusions of grandeur. Five wolves, even if they're kamikaze crazy, aren't going to do much damage to a couple of armored vehicles and ten armed soldiers."

"You're right," said Diane. She sounded more relaxed now. "They'd never attack so many of us, even if there were more of them. Most unwolflike behavior. Though, of course, they don't know that we're armed."

"Then perhaps we should show them," said Volkov briskly. He shouted to the lieutenant, who waved back and called an order up to one of the infantrymen crouched at the crater's rim. Three seconds later came the tearing crack of a rifle shot. Later, Bisby was absolutely sure that he had in the same instant heard the dull *thwack* of the 7.62mm bullet striking the nearest wolf. However, the sound—if indeed he had heard it—was at once obliterated by the dreadful screaming of the wolf. The great animal rose as though catapulted into the air fully six feet from the ground, turned over, and lay on its back, kicking in a flurry of reddening snow. After a second or so, the doglike screams subsided into low whimpering. There came the tearing crack of a second shot, and the whimpering ceased.

Diane swung around to where Volkov stood beside her. "I don't think that was a very good . . ."

He interrupted before she could finish. "We must teach them a lesson," he said. "They mustn't think they can play games with human beings."

For one brief second, her mind's eye flicked back to the moment on the dissecting table when she had opened the wolf's stomach and found the hand. But the conservationist training of years of study and research immediately took over, and she spoke savagely to the Russian, "There was no need for that. They have as much right here as we have. That was a form of murder, and I don't want . . ."

"Jesus God!" said Bisby. He was pointing toward the dark bulk of the forest tree line. What at first appeared to be a ragged, broken white wave was rushing down upon them. It was fully three seconds before Diane realized that the wave was composed of wolves—dozens, scores, perhaps a hundred of them. With low, excited hunting calls, they swept down toward the more distant of the two armored carriers, where only the driver and the radio operator still sat in their seats. The wave of wolves seemed to flow along the ground with astonishing speed in the Siberian twilight. The lieutenant ran to the rim of the crater, and two of the infantrymen beside him

144

opened a methodical fire, sending two, three . . . five . . . seven shots into the advancing mass of animals.

Bisby seized Diane's arm. He was pointing back to where the four remaining wolves of the original five, on the other side of the crater, had been lying. All four had now risen and were facing the crater. The leader was standing slightly forward of them, in the posture they had first seen him, one paw raised. He threw back his head, and the thin sound of his howl sounded above the shouts of the soldiers and the baying of the pack. The noise around the crater was so loud now that it was impossible for Diane to hear what Bisby was saying, but he jabbed his finger desperately to where the wolf leader stood, and she grasped what he meant. She pulled at Volkov's shoulder. The Russian had been standing transfixed. He turned to her, his face a mask of bewilderment. She pointed back to the leader of the pack.

"Shoot that one," she cried. "Quickly—that's the one who's organizing it."

Volkov looked at her for a few seconds as though not comprehending but then lumbered forward to where the lieutenant, with the Soldatovs and Stovin at his side, stood at the crater's rim. He, too, pointed back toward the leader. But it was too late. The big wolf and his companions had vanished, their simple tactic of engaging the party's attention completed. In any case, what was happening around the farthest carrier was beyond anything that any of them, even Diane, could have imagined. The first wolves had reached the carrier. Two large animals were slipping and sliding on the sloping steel front. Even as they watched, one of them managed to seize the driver by the head. From the turret above came a long burst of machine-gun fire, directed into the middle of the milling mob of wolves. There were yelps and cries. One or two animals went down, and a large wolf, half white, half grey, crawled from the melee around the vehicle and lay in the snow. A moment later the dense mass of wolves was all over the vehicle, covering it in a snapping, snarling flood. Valentina turned her head aside and put her hand over her eyes. From the edge of the crater came the sharp cracks of intermittent rifle fire, but the infantrymen up there were seriously inhibited from firing into the wolves on the carrier itself because of the danger of hitting the two men aboard it. The lieutenant gave a hoarse cry, seized a rifle from the nearest soldier, and ran forward over the rim of the crater, slipping and sliding toward the wolf pack around the carrier. As he ran, he fired from the hip. A wolf dropped; another screamed. And then, from somewhere behind him, came the four white forms of the pack leader and his companions. They struck him almost together in a snarling worrying mass. He was no more than thirty yards from his own infantrymen, but it was impossible for any of them to get an aimed shot without risking hitting him.

Within a further minute or so, it was all over. It was now so dark that the group of human beings huddled in the crater could discern only faintly what was happening as the wolves withdrew into the forest. Four or five of them, snapping and snarling, dragged the body of the radio operator with them. Of the driver's body there was no sign. Presumably, cramped in the narrow driving compartment, it had been too wedged for the wolves to pull it clear. Not all of it had been so protected however. One wolf, trotting into the forest, dropped something from its mouth for a moment, pushed it with its muzzle to turn it over, and then fixed its teeth in the object to get a better grip. Sick with horror, the onlookers saw that the wolf was carrying the driver's head.

"What are we going to do about that poor fellow?" It was Stovin's voice, unnaturally calm. He pointed to where the lieutenant lay dead in the snow. Beside him, his arm around Valentina's shoulders, Soldatov stared at the black forest, saying nothing. Her head was buried in the thick stuff of his parka, and her body heaved with convulsive sobbing. Bisby, Stovin noticed, was also looking out to where the wolf pack had disappeared. His face was strange, almost avid. From the forest came the sound of tearing snarls.

"Hear that?" said Bisby. "The bastards are still there."

"They're eating," said Diane dully.

"Eating? There must be a hundred wolves there— maybe more. And they've got only one body to eat."

"The leader will be eating, and perhaps the wolves that dragged back the body," said Diane. "The others will wait."

"For us, you mean?"

"I think so."

Stovin looked out again to the forest. Volkov had scrambled across the crater to talk to the Soviet sergeant who the lieutenant's death had left in command of the little patrol. Covered by the remaining riflemen, two soldiers had gone out thirty yards in the darkness and were bringing back the officer's body. Volkov pointed to the second carrier, about 200 yards away, but the sergeant shook his head. Volkov shrugged and rejoined the Americans.

"I think we would be better to get into the carrier and get clear of here," he said, "but the sergeant thinks we shall be too exposed as we cross the open ground to reach it, if the wolves come again."

"He's right," said Diane. She found, rather to her own astonishment, that her brain was functioning clearly, and that her own fears were under control. "They'll certainly attack if we try to get to the carrier. I think in some way it was the carriers that triggered the whole thing off; I simply don't understand it. Why didn't they come straight to the crater? There was more . . . food . . . here, and it was easier to get at."

"Maybe they didn't come to the crater because they're frightened of it," said Stovin. "Is that possible?" He huddled deeper into his parka as an icy little wind stirred the ruffled snow.

She looked at him for a moment without speaking.

"Yes," she said at last. "You remember—I was talking a while ago about ancestral memory. This could be part of the same behavior syndrome. A Dancer came down here. The wolves either saw it or, deep in their subconscious, 'remember' it. And either way they respect it: they're in awe of it. So while we stay in the crater, we're all right. Try to cross to the carrier, and we'll be in trouble."

"But the radio's in the carrier," said Bisby. "And that's the only way we can tell Novosibirsk how we're placed."

Volkov spoke sharply to the sergeant and then turned to them, smiling.

"That is no problem," he said. "It seems there is a routine procedure for a forest patrol. As soon as we are forty-five minutes overdue, they will send out a search helicopter from Novosibirsk. They know exactly where we are supposed to be, so it should not take long. Until then, we will wait . . ."

"And until then, we will be very, very cold," said Bisby shivering. For the next hour, they stood and squatted close together for warmth. Luckily, although it snowed a little, the fall was light. Once, when two soldiers climbed over the rim of the crater in an attempt to reach the carrier, the swift, ghostly shapes of several wolves brushed through the snow ahead of them, so that the men turned and ran, gasping, back to safety. A little to one side of the waiting party, the body of the lieutenant, lying on its stomach, was guarded by a single infantryman. Death from wolves, thought Bisby, was neither clean nor neat. He had glimpsed the ragged mess that had been the lieutenant's face when they brought the body in. It was noteworthy, in strictly clinical terms, that even the thick Soviet winter uniform, which he would have wagered was impenetrable by the teeth of even the most savage carnivore, had been torn to shreds by the fangs of these superbly adapted animal killing machines. The lieutenant's left arm was gone, but the leader and his three companions had abandoned the body before having time for more dismemberment.

At last, with a glow from its searchlight, above the dark bulk of the forest, the helicopter came. For a moment it dazzled them, sweeping the spotlight to and fro until it picked out the silent shapes of the two carriers. Then, navigation and landing lights winking, it racketed down to a level stretch of snow about fifteen yards from the crater. An officer jumped down, and Volkov went forward to meet hm. A few seconds later he came back.

"This machine holds eight," he shouted above the noise of the rotors. "We will go back now. They will send out another for the soldiers."

Silently, they stumbled over to the helicopter, and a fur-hatted soldier helped Valentina Soldatova, her face ashen in the hard white lights from the cabin, up inside. Diane and Soldatov got in beside her and the others followed, so stiff with cold that they moved with difficulty. With a roaring, whirring clatter, the big machine lifted off, sending a thick blizzard of driven snow over the shadowy forms of the infantrymen left below. The forest lurched beneath them. Stovin rubbed the misted panel window and looked down, but there was only blackness. Somewhere below were the wolves, still waiting. But that's over, he thought, a reaction of utter weariness sweeping over him as the helicopter roared toward Novosibirsk. In relief, he said it aloud. "Well, that's over."

Beside him Bisby stirred, rubbing his cold hands.

"I've never figured you for an optimist before, Sto," he said. "It's not over. It's barely begun."

148

The Chairman of the Council of Ministers sat in his Moscow office and picked up the red telephone on his desk.

"Andrei?"

"Yes, Comrade Chairman?"

"I have read your report, based on what Volkov sent from Novosibirsk. The report is clear enough, but the implications are hard to understand."

"I agree."

There was a pause. At the other end of the line, the Chief of the State Security Commission waited, wondering, until at last the Chairman spoke again.

"We must know more. From now on, the American party should be given everything they need."

"Everything?"

"All that our own scientists receive. The Americans will be no use to us if they are kept in the dark. . . ."

Extract from a letter from Dr. Diane Hilder to Dr. Francis Van Gelder, Director of the Hahn Institute of Comparative Zoology, University of New Mexico, Albuquerque, N.M.

". . . and third, but by no means least important, it appeared to be completely aberrant behavior, totally untypical of everything we have understood—or thought we understood, Frank—about canis lupus.

"The size of the pack—at least four times as big as anything we've ever imagined to be a working social unit; the deliberate singling out of human beings as prey; the simple but effective tactics, almost like a long-learned battle drill.

"What struck me most, after I managed to come to terms with the sheer horror of what had happened, was

that this behavior was the kind of thing we've always scoffed at in myth and legend, where the wolf is a ravening enemy of man, whether it's the one that fancied Red Riding Hood (not a story I'll ever read comfortably to any child of mine) or the Fenriswolf of the Norse demonology, descended from a spirit of evil.

"We know that wolves and men were the two creatures that hunted most successfully over the tundra of past ice ages. We've always assumed that man soon gained the upper hand; that the wolf turned into what was relatively a blind alley, in terms of evolution, and that it was man who profited from the challenge of the ice age to become what he now is. But, I'm beginning to wonder, how easily did man win this competition? Was it a much closer-fought contest than we've imagined? And even at the back of my mind, I'm half-ashamed to say, I have a prickly feeling that maybe it isn't quite over yet.

"The other thing that occurred to me, that you might like to have a good look at, was what triggered off the attack on those two vehicles. Was it some kind of echo from the remote past? Did they, in some spasm of ancestral memory, relate those two bulky objects on the snow to some buried memory of mammoths? Because those were mammoth-hunting tactics, and that pack was the kind of size which you yourself told me—remember that afternoon in Albuquerque—would combine to attack and cut out one or two very large animals.

"And yet even that doesn't really make sense. Because there are no mammoths. So why would a pack form to hunt them? The pack was already in existence when it saw the two vehicles; it was a mammoth-hunting pack in a country where there hasn't been a mammoth for several thousand years, and probably very few surviving beyond the last Ice Age. The only solution that occurred to me was that some more general factor changed their behavior—temperature, perhaps, or atmospheric pressure. In other words, that they were experiencing once more the conditions that operated when there were mammoths, in the last ice age. And so they went out looking for mammoths and found . . . well, we know what they found.

"Maybe wolves are now better equipped than men, in some respects at least, to appreciate that things are changing. . . ."

150

CHAPTER 14

The renewed onset, in late December, of the blizzards in the northern hemisphere seemed for the first few hours to watching meteorologists to be no more than an extreme example of the kind of freak conditions they had been monitoring for some years, notably in the "bad" winters of 1976 and 1978. "The worst storm of the century," said the newspapers and news broadcasts in fifteen languages on the fourth day, and waited for the thaw. By the standards of earlier years, climate monitoring, following the Global Weather Experiment of 1979, was exceptionally good: Ships, aircraft, satellites from the United States, Soviet Russia, France and Japan, balloons, ocean buoys, all provided a mass of information, methodically processed by computers, giving detailed pictures from points dotted all over the earth, probing deep into the oceans and more than twenty miles above the planet. And yet . . . it was five days before scientists realized that what was happening was on a new, cosmic scale that first masked, then overwhelmed all available means of scientific information. By that time, the extent of the catastrophe was evident to less-tutored eyes, though there were puzzling features. The drought in the Sahel countries south of the Sahara intensified; set along the desert's northern border, rain was falling for the first time in living memory, and a Libyan dictator claimed that Allah loved him. In the Antarctic, more remarkably, the temperature at McMurdo Base reached 51 degrees Fahrenheit, the highest ever recorded, and the South Pole itself basked in the relative warmth of 9 degrees.

The northern hemisphere itself was too deep in crisis to pay attention to these anomalies. The snow came sweeping in over the North Pole, across Arctic Canada and down into the wheat lands, over Greenland, Scandinavia, over the Barents Sea, across northern Germany, the Baltic, Denmark, Poland, northern Russia and Siberia. It rolled south across temperate Britain and steadily down into the northern United States. The great northern cities froze to a standstill: Pack-ice, formed with astonishing rapidity, clogged northern ports in both continents. The remarkable thing about the weather was that it rolled over such a broad band of the hemisphere virtually simultaneously, and that it continued without respite for more than two weeks. It snowed and froze, snowed and froze. A puzzled French climatologist at the Government weather station high in the Massif Central turned to a colleague and said, "It is like a successful military offensive—wherever there is a weak spot, the enemy pours in." At Bergamo, in the Italian Dolomites, the Italian duty meteorologist, more dramatic but also more perceptive, said sadly on the telephone from his already isolated station: *"E finito il nostro mondo"*—our world is over.

The speed with which disaster attained overwhelming proportions bewildered even the scientific pessimists who had preached Doomsday warnings for the past three decades. Suddenly the delicate apparatus that supplied and sustained modern technological civilization was seen to be inadequate to deal with a situation in which snow simply fell for two . . . five . . . ten . . . fourteen days, without cease. Whole landscapes changed. Familiar landmarks sometimes vanished. The entire technological resources of civilized nations were now devoted to frantic attempts to keep open a limited number of roads and a smaller number of ports and airfields, so that populations numbered in tens of millions should not go desperately cold and hungry. The world was changing. From now on, it seemed, nothing could be taken for granted.

Pyotr Bilibin came from a hamlet in eastern Siberia, on the banks of Lake Baikal, the inland sea which froze so hard in the winter that the great lorries could rumble across its solid expanse until late into the spring, their routes marked by tree branches thrust into the ice. But he knew he had never seen anything like this. He sat in the open driving hatch of his tank and peered through the white wall of driving snow toward the red taillights of the tank in front of him. Bilibin's tank was, in fact, the hundredth in a long line of 210 tanks gradually picking their way due north across East Germany in the worst blizzard Bilibin had ever seen. The entire mechanized division—tanks, armored carriers, countless lorries and 11,000 men—was on the move over the seventy-three miles between last night's halting point at Pritzwalk and their destination of Rostock on the Baltic coast, where they were due to embark for the Soviet Union. Occasionally the almost unnaturally calm voice of Bilibin's tank commander, huddled papooselike in the turret above him, came over the intercom, but Bilibin knew the tank commander would be able to see no more than he could. They had been travelling now for about two hours, and they had so far come five miles. They had just gone through the village of Falkenhagen, driving in what seemed to be a tunnel of ice, since the snow cleared by the earlier tanks lay in the banks thirty feet high beside the road. The only way, indeed, that Bilibin knew that it was Falkenhagen they had passed through was that he had driven unknowingly over its road sign, which had flopped momentarily across the front of his tank so that he had glimpsed it for a revealing second. From the tank, no house, no lighted lamp, no tree could be seen. Simply the white tunnel ahead and the red taillights.

When the taillights abruptly vanished a quarter of an hour later, he hoped for a moment that they had simply been masked by a momentary drift of snow. But they did not reappear. A few seconds later, the noise from the drumming tracks changed in character. Suddenly all was snow. They were driving, helplessly disoriented, through the snowbank on the right-hand side of the road. For a moment or two, they moved through a wall of snow and ice, and then they burst through and the drumming of the tracks changed in character. They had now left the metalled road and were grinding slowly over what seemed to be a frozen field. The snow here was already twelve or more feet deep, and for Bilibin it was like driving continuously into a soft wall. Nothing could be seen on either side, and there was no sign now of any vehicle ahead. Behind him, obediently following his own taillight, the remaining tanks of the division were coming disastrously on. There was a muffled curse over the intercom from the turret above him, and his tank commander ordered Bilibin to halt. A moment later, carrying a large electric torch, the commander scrambled down the sloping sides of the tank and disappeared into the swirling snow, moving back toward the rest of the column. Keeping his engine at no more than a throaty

153

murmur, Bilibin sat and waited. He glanced proudly at his new German watch. Nine o'clock. Cold and cramped, he tried to doze. Above him the wireless operator, cut off completely from the divisional network by the blanketing interference of the blizzard, leaned his head wearily against his set and closed his eyes. An hour later, with the snow high above his closed-down turret, Bilibin stirred, held his cold wrist up to the small light in the roof of the driving compartment. It was half-past ten, and the tank commander had not yet returned . . . .

In the division's rear headquarters in the schoolhouse at Pritzwalk, the senior staff captain spoke to a lieutenant. "Have they gone through Meyenburg yet?"

"Not as far as I can make out. There's absolutely no radio communication and no chance at all of getting a motorcycle dispatch rider down that column. Who'd move a mechanized division on a night like this?"

"Army headquarters would," said the staff captain brusquely.

"But why?"

"That's not your business, Savinkov. Or mine, either. We do what we're told. Though I should have thought it was obvious why we're being moved back to Russia."

"Yes?"

"We're going back," said the captain patiently, "because we're a mechanized division. We have a couple of hundred tanks and a lot of heavy-duty stuff like artillery tractors and armored recovery vehicles. You know what the situation's like here; can't you imagine what it's like at home? We're not going back because we're soldiers, but because we can organize and maintain and drive supertractors—tanks. In Russia, we're urgently short of tractive power—the kind of vehicle that can haul loads through snow and pull other vehicles out of snow. Every country in Europe will be short of tractive power. So we've got a new role. And there's a new strategic balance. Not guns. Tractors."

He laughed grimly and patted the lieutenant on the shoulder. "At last we've all found a use for the tanks. You didn't think when you joined the Army that you'd be running a tractor fleet, did you? But I'd give a week's leave for a radio report from the division."

It was four hours before the captain, white-faced, finally reported by telephone to army headquarters that the tanks were lost.

"Lost?" said the general's angry voice. "What do you mean?"

"We don't know where they are, sir. Eighteen tanks passed through Meyenburg and they're safe—halted in the forest about three miles north. The others—we simply don't know."

"Helicopters, then. At dawn. I'll take a ride in one myself. We'll soon see where they are."

Below the whirring rotors of the general's helicopter, nine hours later, stretched a white desert. The blizzard itself had died away for the moment. The landscape above which the helicopter moved, its black shadow racing ahead in the pale sunlight on the snow, rolled like an undulating sea to the horizon. No road was visible, though the tops of the houses of Falkenhagen thrust through the white mantle. On their roof, a few people waved desperately as the helicopter clattered above them. Only a mile farther on came the first evidence of the division. A ragged line of slim metal rods sprouted from the snow, like weird surrealist plants in a Dali painting. The general peered below as the pilot tapped his shoulder.

"Radio aerials, sir," the pilot was shouting above the roar of the engine. "Twenty . . . thirty. There's a lot of tanks underneath that lot. And there'll be more farther on."

The general slumped in his seat.

"That's my division?" he said at last. And again, hopelessly, "That's my division?"

A strange cold wind blew the dust into stinging little vortexes of grit along the long straight road of Janpath in Delhi. The wind was dry but icy. The ragged men who could always be seen playing complicated chesslike games in the pavement dust had abandoned them two days ago and were huddled in doorways around the collonnades of Connaught Square, looking at the sky and talking. The sellers of nails and metal tools on the pavement of Chandni Chowk had packed up and vanished. A few tricycle rickshaws braved the cold. Here and there a legless beggar pushed himself through the swirling dust on his wheeled tray, holding out a hand to occasional Europeans hurrying back from brief shopping expeditions to the warmth of the Imperial Hotel.

"I thought this was supposed to be the best time of the year here," said an English lady to the tall Indian

155

with whom she was drinking tea in a window seat in the hotel's shadowy lounge. The Indian worked for the National Agricultural Office. He had spent the morning in anxious discussion with his immediate superior.

"Normally, of course, yes," he said. "Warm and pleasant by day, if cool at night. But we are having a difficult time lately. I have never known it so cold by day in December, and I am told there is very heavy snow in Kashmir, far below the usual snow line. And all along the southern slope of the Himalayas. Perhaps"—he smiled politely—"we Indians should pay more attention to winter sports."

"It is *really* cold," said the lady severely. "I might as well be in Manchester."

I wish she were, thought the Indian. But she had to be entertained. She was the wife of the United Nations official who was at this moment discussing with his immediate superior exactly how to alleviate the famine that would hit them in the summer and autumn if the monsoon failed like last year's; in fact, he reminded himself, the new climatological bureau at Simla said it would be *worse* than last year. It was almost inconceivable as a possibility, but would there be a monsoon at all this year? Without that summer rain, nothing would grow. He thought again of what he had found in the archives of the City Library; a photocopy had gone to his superior. An Englishman had kept a Delhi diary, nearly 200 years ago. He had described just such a wind, just such December cold. And that year, there had been no monsoon. And there had been appalling famine, at a time when the population was smaller and less city oriented than now. He shivered. Overhead six or seven kites, black wings spread, buffeted their way over the hotel gardens. There wasn't another bird to be seen—not one of the mynah birds, green parakeets, or small iridescent finches that normally flashed through the trees. The kites would be hungry. But, he wondered suddenly, for how long?

The bull camel went down again, slipping and sliding in the soft Sahara sand on the crest of the long ridge. Zenoba, walking beside it, was in time to clutch the small form of Ibrahim as he tumbled from its arched back. Zayd ag-Akrud turned back from the top of the sun-scorched slope, calling to Hamidine and Muhammed as they pulled up on the second camel. Cursing and shouting, the man

156

and the two boys hauled on the rope that passed through the bull camel's nose ring, while Zenoba, with Ibrahim beside her, watched dumbly from the side of the ridge. The bull camel roared and bellowed, pawed and thrashed with its feet, but stayed on its side. At last, gasping in the heat, Zayd stopped pulling. He went over to where the other camel stood patiently, ignoring the struggle taking place about its companion only a few yards away. From the blanket pack on its flank, he took a handful of Zenoba's thorn sticks, thrust them under the camel, and struck a match. Rolling its eyes, the camel bellowed desperately, the smell of its scorched hair and flesh stinging their nostrils. Convulsively, it scrambled to its knees, and with a shout of triumph, Zayd hauled on the rope. A moment later it was once more on its feet. Zayd took from the blanket pack a palmful of the grease from the dead goat of two nights ago—grease that Zenoba had kept carefully in the old tin box which she carried always with her. He smeared it on the blistering patch on the camel's side, looking meanwhile at the load the animal had to carry. This was a young camel, barely twenty years old, and it would now be entering its time of full maturity. A load of 600 pounds or more should be easy for it, and it was carrying much less. Ibrahim and Zenoba between them weighed less than 200 pounds, and the two packs on its flanks no more than another 150. It was obviously sick, but he could not lighten the load unless Zenoba walked for more of each day. She would have to walk. It would slow them—there would now be at least six more days to Tamanrasset, and three even to Lissa. He spoke quietly to Zenoba, and she mixed a little of the congealed blood from the dead goat, carried in a covered bowl, with some of the last of the water in the big leather bottle. They sat for half an hour on the hard side of the dune where the sand was packed into concretelike masses by the steady pressure of centuries of prevailing desert winds. The bull camel must be given a little time to recover from its treatment. And Ibrahim was fretful. They drank a cupful each of the blood and water, and briefly Zayd prayed, facing east. They then moved on toward Lissa and Tamanrasset, using the hard sides of the ridges, where possible, and the shade of the steeper ones wherever they could find it. The bull camel slipped and staggered occasionally, but it followed Zenoba obediently enough where she walked holding its head rope, steadily east.

The Director of the National Center for Atmospheric Research sat in his cold administration office above Boulder and waited for the two hours of central heating due to begin in ten minutes' time. He crossed to the white-flecked window and looked out, shivering in his overcoat, through a confusion of whirling snow. It was not possible to see more than about twenty yards, but he knew he was looking down toward the open area of vehicle bays behind the administration building. Nothing could now be seen of these bays or the vehicles they contained; the snow had obliterated them days ago, rising high above their tops and then freezing into solid blocks which every few hours would vanish beneath new falls of snow. And somewhere down there below was the little town of Boulder. The mountain road between the town and the Center had been completely impassable for many days. Already they were short of fuel, short of food.

I'm sitting here, he thought, in a place that is virtually a temple dedicated to global weather research, and I don't really know what's happening. Already there were people dead in Boulder—at least forty, according to the strictly rationed, sparse radio broadcasts which the power shortage allowed. It seemed absurd, even indecent that . . . oh, God, not more? The door opened and an anoraked assistant, carrying a tray of pins, came in. She crossed to the great wall maps of the countries of the world on the wall opposite his desk and began to push in a series of orange-covered pins. The Director crossed to her side and watched. Each, he knew, marked a snow-crisis area—a place where local weather conditions were, at least temporarily, out of control. One by one, they joined a broad swath of similar pins sweeping in a broad belt across Canada and the northern United States: around Edmonton in Alberta and Regina in Saskatchewan, around Butte in Montana, Anoka outside Minneapolis-St. Paul, and at somewhere called—he peered more closely—Faribault, south of the same city. It was a pattern with which the Director had become familiar over the past few days. But as the girl drove in her last orange pins, he gave a little gasp of surprise. One went in at Solomon, west of Abilene in Kansas; the other, unbelievably, at Kingfisher, only a little north of Oklahoma City.

"So far south?" he said. "Already?"

She nodded. "That's eighty-six up to six A.M. today," she said, "in the United States and Canada. And a lot more from Britain and Europe; the information from there is very full. Virtually nothing, though, from the Soviet Union."

She began fixing blue-tipped pins into the large-scale map of Britain: Sumburgh in the Shetland Islands, Elrick outside Aberdeen, Inverurie to the north. There was already a patch of pins, the Director noted absently, along the southern side of Scotland's Moray Firth . . . Elgin, Banff, Nairn, Lossiemouth, Cullen. But here came new ones—he whistled silently to himself—down the long stretch of the North Sea coast deep into England, stretching out toward embattled Newcastle. He peered at the pins as she pushed them in. Blyth in Northumberland, Whitley Bay near the mouth of the Tyne. The Director, as a young man, had once done a year's exchange at Newcastle University and had spent his free weekends exploring the long stretches of silver sand and the small ports and ruined castles that marched north across the border into Scotland. He crossed to his desk and looked again at last night's GARP report. It was unbelievable; at least, he reminded himself, it would have been unbelievable three weeks or even a fortnight ago. But there it was, checked, double-checked, clearly typed in front of him. England's great city of Newcastle upon Tyne, throbbing with enterprise, technological know-how, and industry, had been cut off from contact with the rest of the country for five days. Literally cut off. It had been snowing there for more than two weeks—not just snowing, in fact, but blizzarding. No road into the city was now open; apparently the best available, the one coming in from the south through Durham, was still under more than thirty feet of snow, and about half the British Army was toiling there to cut a way through. The airport had been buried for days, and no port within thirty miles was operational. Helicopters had been able to get into the city until—he flicked through the report—the day before yesterday. Now, unable to risk landing in the deepening, drifting snow, they were reduced to winching up urgent medical cases and then dropping food. The estimates of casualties varied, even in Newcastle itself. The British Prime Minister had told the President that there were at least 2,000 dead in the city and its suburbs, and possibly nearly as many again in the Northumbrian countryside. In Scotland, perhaps a thousand. The countryside estimates were the hardest to arrive at accurately; there was some evidence that isolated communities were simply going into a state of siege, cut off from all contact, and waiting for a slackening in the snow-blitz. Nevertheless, people died in their cars, in their un-heated, fuelless homes, in the snow canyons of the city streets while looking for food. Discipline, apparently, was surprisingly good, and there was said to have been little or no food looting in the first two weeks. That would be changing now, of course. Hunger, the Director reminded himself, drives men to greater excess even than sex. What had happened at Newcastle was one of the greatest natu-ral catastrophes of the century, killing more than twice as many people as had died in the San Francisco earth-quake of 1906. If only, thought the Director, we could think of it in those terms—simply as a disaster—how comforting that would be. But it wasn't a disaster. It was a change . . . a gigantic, irreversible change, a change of unbelievable, deadly speed. And not, of course, simply in Britain, the Soviet Union, and the United States. Look at northern France and the north German plain. Yet, of course, he reminded himself, there had been something worse than Newcastle. There had been Novosibirsk. Funny how we don't really count it when it happens to Russians, he thought, ashamed. And where were Stovin and his party? They might even be dead in whatever was happening in Siberia.

Nothing, nothing was coming out of Russia. The early satellite photographs had shown disaster areas around Archangel, but now the snow itself and the total occlusion of the low, snow-bearing cloud covers masked all pictures. All that was certain was that in the northern Soviet Union, they were having a very, very hard time. Moscow Radio referred guardedly to "considerable difficulties" which were "under control." In Moscow itself, it was harder to hide the facts. There was already food rationing more stringent than that of the war, and power was switched to private homes for no more than two hours a day. And that in a temperature of 40 below . . .

The red flasher of his desk telephone began to glow. It was the call the Director had been waiting for, and he picked up the handset.

"Dr. Brookman for you, sir," said the voice of the girl at the Center switchboard.

"Mel?"

"That's me," said Brookman's voice. Astonishingly,

thought the Director, Brookman sounded more cheerful, less harassed, than at any time in the past few weeks.

"Where are you, Mel?"

"Connecticut—at C.I.T. I ought to be in Washington, but it's not too easy to get there at the moment. I've been using the train in from Westport, but it's getting very unpredictable, and in any case La Guardia's closed again today, so there'll be no shuttle."

"Can't you fix an Air Force plane?"

"I guess I could try, but it seems to me I might as well be here. We've got a lot of facilities, Director, even though we don't have Razzle-Dazzle. How is Razzle-Dazzle, by the way?"

"We're using him on rationed fuel," said the Director. "It means we've had to get together a jury rig to seal off the heating to keep the computer room at constant temperature, and that means we have to ration ourselves to two hours' heating by day and four by night. It's pretty damned cold."

"How long have you got?" asked Brookman, soberly.

"For Razzle-Dazzle, you mean? Well, I think we can keep the computer room at constant temperature for maybe another three weeks, though it could mean a shade less heating for the rest of us."

"How many of you are still there?"

"Thirty-eight, counting me. That's a full scientific monitoring staff and a skeleton staff of all the ancillaries."

"Any trouble persuading people to stay?"

The Director laughed. "The trouble was making some of them leave while we could still get helicopters in. Everybody wanted to be in on the Robinson Crusoe act."

Brookman sighed. "Well, when we put the Center way up there in Colorado, we weren't anticipating anything quite like this. I guess there's no chance of getting more fuel?"

"Not unless this snow lets up for a couple of days. If it does, we might be able to clear a landing pad for helicopters. But, Mel, even that won't be easy. One of our scientific assistants, young fellow called Selden, got about fifteen yards out through the main doors yesterday—literally cut his way through, in a private tunnel. He measured the depth. The snow outside was around fifty-two feet deep as of noon yesterday. And it hasn't stopped snowing since."

"Hm. Well, Director, I've one piece of news for you.

Good news. We've had Stovin's first report. A Russian brought it in yesterday evening, special flight to Kennedy. Thank God the airport was open. Ehrlich went from there to get it—he said the Russian couldn't have been more cooperative. Suddenly that was the word. Cooperation. After weeks of stalling."

"That's something, at any rate," said the Director, "because as you know, all the indications are that this weather —in fact, we can't even call it weather—this latest shift in climate started up in northern Siberia. Perhaps I should qualify that. I should say that the *evidence,* the first *evidence* of what we're experiencing now came from there."

"I've had a first look at what Stovin says, and a copy has gone to the White House," said Brookman. "He reckons he's confirmed his jet-stream theory, and that he's on the way to deciding just why the stream is becoming subject to these extraordinary vertical aberrations. There's a lot more stuff, too, and some of it is typical Stovin. It's always damned hard to fault Sto on climatology, but you know what he's like—he doesn't think climatology tells the whole story."

"What sort of stuff?" asked the Director cautiously.

"Oh, you know Sto," said the other again. "He believes in the indivisibility of knowledge. He seems more interested at the moment in what that girl, Hilder, tells him than in exactly *why* the climate's changed."

"It's not the indivisibility of knowledge that worries me," said the Director. "It's the impossibility of assimilating more than a hundredth of what's available. You talk to a biologist or a zoologist or a botanist, and suddenly you're in a different world. And you're no more than a child in that world. Just as they are in yours."

"That's why the President trusts Stovin," said Brookman. "The White House sees science as a lot of pressure groups—all talking a language, a series of different languages, that the President or any other layman can't understand. They all demand money, facilities, support, and the President doesn't know whether they're right or wrong. But Stovin . . . well, Stovin tells him. Stovin makes a point of studying other disciplines. He picks people's brains. Churchill did the same thing, you know. He had a pet scientist called Lindemann—used to keep him in touch with all sorts of things . . ."

"I wouldn't exactly call Stovin a pet," said the Director. "And he's the best climatologist I know."

"Incidentally," said the other, "some of the jet-stream conclusions you'll be reading—well, they're being backed up to a great extent by the data from the University of East Anglia, in England. They're deep, deep in trouble in that area, as you know better than most of us, but they're like you. They're holding on well at the new university weather station, and the British have actually moved a cabinet minister and all his staff in with them. A sort of battle headquarters."

"A cabinet minister, as well as everything else?" said the Director. "Please, please don't let anybody here think of that. When do I get Stovin?"

"On the private telex, starting in about ten minutes. But we can do better than that. We can bring you to Stovin himself. He's coming out from the Soviet Union, tomorrow or the day after. The Russians want to take part in a really big northern hemisphere conference, and I guess they'll fall over backward to be as helpful as possible. He's bringing a whole party with him—Soldatov and the pilot, Bisby, and young Dr. Hilder, and some other woman. I think somebody said it was Mrs. Soldatov, but I'm not sure. Anyway, you'll see them all at the meeting. I'll let you know as soon as it's fixed."

"How am I going to get there? Nobody's going to land a chopper here unless the weather changes."

Brookman laughed again. "Hope you've got a head for heights, Director. I spoke to General Weightman at the emergency base, Truscott Field, this morning. He said they could get a helicopter over and winch you up. Then from Truscott they'll fly you to wherever the conference is. Santa Fe, I heard suggested. It can hardly be snowing there yet."

"I see," said the Director. "My God, Mel, I'm getting too old to be Superman. But I'll be glad to talk to Stovin. Razzle-Dazzle's great for providing scenarios, but he's short on inspiration. What we're beginning to need now is an inspired guess."

"And you think Stovin can provide some of that?"

"He's a good guesser," said the Director. "He has an excellent track record."

"A good guesser? Not much of a compliment to a scientist."

"Mel," said the Director soberly, "it's the greatest compliment that can be paid. You know that and I know that . . ."

There was a pause before the Director spoke again. "You know about the information I've had logged on my map?"

"I guess you mean the trouble in Kansas?" said Brookman. "Yes, I do. It doesn't look like being exactly a good year for wheat, does it?"

"There's absolutely no way," said the Director, "unless we have a long summer—and. the chances of that are now zero—that the corn belt is going to produce anything like its normal output. And maybe no output at all. We're going to have to rethink the whole food-growing policy for the world, and a lot of people are going to die while we're doing it."

"There are cold-weather strains of wheat, of course," said Brookman.

"How many acres are planted? Mel we're talking about next year's loaves, next year's cattle food. We're going to have to empty the strategic stockpiles, and then what? I watch those damned pins spreading over my map and I'm frightened. Look at what happened to Alaska. Is there anybody in Anchorage now?"

"There's some sort of Eskimo community up there— about a couple of thousand Eskimos and a few whites still living around the city. I spoke to a pilot who'd been up there a week ago. It's still snowing, of course, and there's not much of Anchorage to be seen now. A modern city . . . vanished. He says you would never have known it was there. And a month ago, it was taking tourist bookings."

"Well, full marks to the Governor," said the Director. "He was the one who persuaded the Administration to get them all out in time. Luckily Alaska isn't exactly overpopulated at the best of times. But I look at my map and I think of other places . . . Illinois . . . Chicago. It's not something that's good to think about before turning out the bedside lamp."

"No," said Brookman. "Well, I'll see you in Santa Fe or wherever. It's going to be a pretty high-flying conference—the President will be there."

"How's he taking all this?" asked the Director.

"He gave me a message for you," Brookman said. "He thought it might help. Genesis, 8:22. Just that . . ."

A minute or so later, the Director pressed the desk

buzzer for his assistant. "Jennifer," he said, "have we a Bible in the house? I suppose not. . . ."

"Of course we've a Bible," she said indignantly. "I've got one in my desk."

She brought it to him, and he turned to Genesis, 8:22, reading the lines carefully and then saying the verse aloud to her:

"While the earth remaineth, seedtime and harvest, and cold and heat, and summer and winter, and day and night shall not cease."

He looked up at her and spoke in a neutral voice. "He's a good man, the President, isn't he?"

She was a plain woman, but her smile illuminated her face. "Yes," she said. "He's certainly that."

CHAPTER 15

Annex One to the Report by Dr. William F. Stovin, Visiting Professor (Climatology), University of New Mexico, and Dr. Y. M. Soldatov, Academy of Sciences, USSR: Initiation and Predicted Short-term Development of the Present Glaciation

Subject: Interpretative Summary for Heads of Government

ONE   *The most surprising and, initially, the most difficult factor with which we have to deal in the present glaciation is the totally unexpected speed with which it has attained considerable and (for the forseeable future) irreversible proportions. Each of the authors of the attached report has in the past estimated to various scientific and governmental agencies that such a climatic development was overdue and could be expected to make swift progress. These* views have been supported by a growing number of climatologists in several countries. None of us, however, thought that irreversible changes could take place in a matter of weeks: the more "pessimistic" estimates (i.e., those by the present authors) postulated two-to-three years as a conceivable time scenario.

TWO We consider, with the benefit of hindsight, that the evidence of the possibility of dramatically rapid change has, in fact, always been available, though it has been masked by the compartmenting of scientific research into strictly defined areas such as zoology, botany, geology, meteorology, and so on. For example, we believe that evidence from zoology and paleozoology has been insufficiently correlated with that of more conventional climatology: i.e., the remarkable mass deaths of mammoths along the northern Siberian coast 40,000 years ago; and changes in the present behavior syndromes of animals such as wolves (see the Hilder Report in Annex Four), caribou, armadillos, certain species of migratory butterflies and birds, and in the movements of cold-water fish like cod and herring, and marine mammals like the white-and-blue whale.

THREE Since it is of surpassing importance that the extent and time span of the new glaciation be accurately monitored, we recommend that new international research projects should be established at once in relevant areas of the world; and that the other mammals, reptiles, fishes and insects of the planet should be studied urgently to determine their own response to the new situation and the extent to which they receive instinctive warning of further climatic change.

FOUR The abilities of men at the edge of climatic areas in which community survival is practicable will also obviously come under sharp scrutiny; it will be important that all such communities contain research scientists and that the education of children should be undertaken with this in mind.

FIVE *The full extent of the present glaciation has not yet been reached; it is our conclusion that the present winter and the next will establish the basis of a very rapid return to an approximation of the Wurm (or Wisconsin) period, which began about 80,000 years ago and ended about 12,000 years ago. During this period, the ice sheet covered virtually all of Canada, extended deep into the northern United States, and stretched across northern and central Britain, much of northern Europe, and the northern and central Soviet Union.*

SIX *The accompanying changes caused by the southward shift of climatic bands (i.e., southern France can be expected quite rapidly to develop a climate approximating to that of recent years in northern Britain and parts of Scandinavia) will cause considerable changes in the rain-growth-food patterns of other parts of the planet. The Sahel droughts, for instance, will be balanced—this has already become evident —by new rainy seasons in the north. It is possible that, after a painful period of adjustment, the continent of Africa will be able to retain its ecological and population balance.*

SEVEN *This will not be true of North America, northern Europe, and the northern USSR, nor of India, Pakistan, and a considerable proportion of Southeast Asia. The enormous unknown factor of the People's Republic of China, containing about a quarter of the world's human individuals, is never far from the authors' minds. Unfortunately, for obvious political reasons, neither the USSR nor the United States is able to put together any coherent picture of the impact of climatic change in this huge area. Recent relaxations of attitude have not so far extended to giving full information about what is regarded as a national disaster. Satellite observation by the Soviet Union (photograph series C/102/4/5/ 6/7, Annex Eight) reveals, however, that northern China is experiencing comparably rigorous conditions, and that the phenomena now known as Dancers have occurred near*

167

Palikun in Sinkiang and also much farther east at Wuchuan in Inner Mongolia.

EIGHT

It is clearly not the province of the authors of this report to attempt to quantify the extent of human organizational (and thus political) change that will be necessary to deal with the new climatic situation. But they would emphasize that although "panic" solutions will inevitably be offered (i.e., the nuclear destruction of the North Polar icecap has already been suggested in certain quarters both in the United States and the USSR), these would be certain to be disastrous. It is possible that mankind will be able to respond to this situation, with the help of food-producing sciences, without widespread human anarchy and within the developing framework of existing systems of government. What will be necessary is international cooperation of an unprecedented kind.

NINE

The question will be asked: Since the New Ice Age came quickly, might it not go equally speedily? The answer, in the authors' view, is No. The immediate result of a glaciation is an increase in surface albedo (reflectivity), so that even quite strong sunlight fails to warm the new glacial areas of the Earth. The most optimistic forecast that could be made is that this new glaciation may begin to change to an interglacial epoch within, perhaps, 3,000 years. However, when the progress of past glaciations is examined, such a conclusion must be regarded as very optimistic. There are sound climatic reasons for believing the Earth is now a glacial planet. Many Polar areas of it, in fact, have never left the conditions of the last glacial, which ended elsewhere (as noted above) around 12,000 years ago, enabling the spread and development of human civilization. And even throughout this warmer period, of course, great inhabited areas of the planet have . . returned each winter to Ice-Age conditions. We do not yet understand the underlying factors, possibly of planetary alignment or solar

radiation or volcanic activity—or a combination
of these—which occasionally interrupt the
"normal" glacial condition of the Earth to bring
the warmer interglacials. But there is at present
no reason to believe that this new glacial will
not follow the pattern of previous glacials. On
this basis, it can be expected to last
approximately 40,000 years. . . .

"It is an extraordinary document to be given official sanction without suitable censorship," said the Chief of the State Security Commission. "It refers even to changes in the political structure. I can see our dilemma, of course. No doubt some of the rules must be broken. But even so . . . I admit to doubts, Comráde Chairman."

The Chairman of the Council of Ministers leaned back in his padded chair. How many back aches, he thought. It's my damned kidneys again. Please, please, not another operation. He looked out of the window to the snow drifting steadily across the walls of the old Moscow fortress.

"I know, Andrei, I know," he said at last. "But the situation demands it. I have this northern hemisphere conference in America next week. How can I go there if we have not given full information? Indeed, how can I if Soldatov and Stovin are there, and I can be shown not to have done so? We can at least reap considerable propaganda value from the fact that young Soldatov has played a great part in this Report, though I imagine that propaganda will count for little at the talks."

"If it is finally necessary, Stovin and Soldatov could be . . . well, delayed," said the security chief.

The other shook his head. "No, Andrei. I have decided, and the Council is in agreement, to publish the entire report to the Soviet people, in *Pravda,* to coincide with the conference. It will mean a special issue, and it will be hard to distribute it in present conditions, I'm told. But it will be done."

"All the report?" asked the security man quietly.

"All of it. We have evolved a political system, Andrei, not perhaps a perfect system"—the other gaped in momentary astonishment—"but one that should be well suited to deal with this situation. Of all nations, we are worst hit. Either our system works, or it doesn't. Now we must find out."

"It has not always worked before," said the security man carefully, "on the basis of full disclosure of every problem to every person in the Soviet Union."

"Except, perhaps, during the Great Patriotic War," said the Chairman. "Then we all knew. I was still a child, but I knew."

He shuffled dismissively in his chair. "Thank you for coming, Andrei," he said. "And for your advice and concern."

The security man rose. "I will make personally the arrangements for the Stovin-Soldatov party to leave," he said. "There is only one proviso I would like you to accept. I think it better not to bring them out through Moscow. The city is full of troops; as you know, we have brought back more than half of those committed to the Warsaw Pact because we need the labor. So I will have them flown out by the Pacific down to Los Angeles. I see no reason to give the CIA an intelligence present from somebody like the man Bisby, who will certainly be keeping his eyes open."

The Chairman waved a hand. "As you wish, Andrei. The details I leave to you. . . ."

"Well, what did you think of it?" asked Stovin, looking up from his chair in the Soldatov *dacha* as Bisby closed the blue covers on the last page of the photocopy of the Stovin Report.

"To be honest, Sto, the only bits I could get close to understanding were the ones you put in the Annex for heads of Government. It was very interesting, especially sections Three and Four. I think you got Section Four wrong."

"Oh?" Stovin said sharply.

"The other stuff," said Bisby, "all the stuff about the why and the wherefore—well, I don't understand it, and I'll lay that not many people who'll read it will, either. And it doesn't matter, anyway."

"No?" said Stovin. He tried to keep any note of irony out of his voice, but he did not altogether succeed because Bisby looked at him sharply.

"All that matters now," he said, "is that it *has* happened, not *why* it happened. What was it you were talking about in Section Four?"—he flipped through the pages—"Yes, '. . . the abilities of men at the edge of climatic areas in which community survival is practicable.' There've been people in those areas for thousands of years, Sto."

Stovin stared at him. "You mean Eskimos, of course."

Bisby laughed bitterly. "Yes, Eskimos. My people. Poor damned stupid Eskimos. Have you ever heard how a Kallunaat—that's a white, to you—talks about Eskimos? 'They're nice people,' he'll tell you. 'But feckless, childlike, can't cope with the modern world. Probably don't feel pain like we do. They need looking after, need to try to learn our ways. But you'll never make much out of an Eskimo. He's just a guy who's in the way of the oil drill, or the road, or the logging camp, or whatever. And he's just going to have to move over, isn't he? Because that's the way of the world. Survival of the fittest. And we whites, we Kallunaat, are the fittest, aren't we? No, you'll never make much of an Eskimo. He's got no conception of law, like we have. He's strictly Stone Age.' That's how a white talks about an Eskimo."

"They made a jet pilot out of you," said Stovin mildly.

Bisby was standing at the window, looking out at the surging ridges of snow which stretched down to the frozen Ob Sea. He turned fiercely to face Stovin.

"But I'm not an Eskimo, am I? I wish to God I was. I'm half Nuniungmiut, half Kallunaat. So I don't count. Oh, at school in New York and at Cornell, it was kind of an advantage to be half Eskimo. A bit of a freak—the sort of racial freak all the progressives could get warm and cozy about. And it made the girls look at you. You know, what's it like below zero? All the jokes. Not that any of them would actually have *married* a real Eskimo. It was hard enough for my father. When he married my mother, do you know that there were only about twenty white people in the whole area? And that half of them never spoke to him again. The other half . . . well, some shook their heads sadly. And others sniggered. It was as well for me I left when I did. But I didn't want to be a jet pilot. I'd rather have been *sivooyachta*, standing with a spear in the bow of an Eskimo father's boat."

"I wonder," said Stovin. And then, "You blame your father?"

Bisby shook his head. For a second there flashed into his mind the old tin box under his bed and the worn book with its stained red covers.

171

"No," he said. "I wish he had been like my mother, of the People. But he knew things which few other men knew. He knew that everything must change. That is what he taught me. I have been waiting ever since."

"Why?"

"I have been told to wait," said Bisby. His voice suddenly sounded vague, far away.

"Who told you?"

Bisby looked at him for a few seconds, but did not answer the question, instead asking one of his own. "Why did you bring me out here, Sto? It can't have been easy."

Stovin hesitated. "I don't really know. I had a feeling about you; in a way, what you've been telling me reinforces it. That you knew the North, were a child of the North. I'm ashamed to say I haven't given it much thought since."

He pointed to the long trestle table crowded with papers and computer printouts with which he and Soldatov had worked over the past two weeks. "We've been busy. But I should have . . ."

Bisby interrupted him. He seemed scarcely to have heard the last few words Stovin said. "A feeling? You had a feeling?"

"Yes."

Bisby dug his hands into his pockets and turned back to the window. Suddenly he sounded awkward, slightly embarrassed. "You remember Anchorage . . . that road going out past the campers along the Ninilchik River? We went along there once, on the way to the airfield."

"Yes."

"There was a man who lived there, a man called Julius . . ."

Outside in the *dacha*'s little entrance hall, there was a sudden commotion. A second later the door opened and Diane and Valentina came in, followed by the smiling Soldatov and, after a moment or two by the tall form of Volkov. The Foreign Ministry man, thought Stovin, looked like a cat full of cream.

"All is arranged," said Volkov. "We fly to America tomorrow."

"All of us," said Valentina. Her eyes were shining and she laughed excitedly. That's why Volkov looks so pleased with himself, thought Stovin. He's coming, too. Nevertheless, Stovin was glad. The Foreign Ministry man had suddenly become extraordinarily useful. Somewhere in the Soviet hierarchy—and it must have been high up—there had been a change of heart. Perhaps it was the imminence of the hemisphere conference. But it had everything. The information made available to him and Soldatov, with Volkov smoothing the way was of a kind which no Western scientist had ever had available to him before. All had been provided: sea surface temperatures from the Kara Sea, the Laptev Sea, the East Siberian Sea, the Okhotsk Sea; the volcanic output of the smoking, glowing cones of the Kamchatka Peninsula—"the Land of Fire," as the Russians called it; the albedo of land surfaces, taken at regular intervals all along the north Siberian coast, taking into account both vegetation and snow cover; the height and spread of ice sheets and pack ice over the past ten years. Some of this information had been acquired by routine monitoring set up long ago. But the rest of it, Stovin knew came from desperately urgent scientific surveying conducted in the past three months. The size of the scientific effort was staggering, and the amount of money spent, he reflected, must have been astronomical. Whatever he or Soldatov had demanded, they had received. Volkov had seen to that. And every computer in Akademgorodok had been at their disposal. The only other country in the world where such an effort could have been made in so short a time, Stovin knew, was his own—the United States.

"I have never been to the United States," said Valentina. "I have never been outside the Soviet Union, except once to Prague. I cannot believe"—she looked covertly at Volkov—"even now that I am going. And perhaps I shall see New York."

"It is normal for the wife of a man like Dr. Soldatov to accompany him," Volkov said dismissively. "But I am afraid I must disappoint you. You are not going to New York. Ah"—as her face crumpled—"do not misunderstand me. You are going to America. But we are flying the Pacific route to Los Angeles. Not New York."

"Why is that?" asked Bisby.

"We have been luckier here in Novosibirsk, in the past few days, than the people of Moscow," said Volkov. "They have had very bad weather indeed, whereas here the snow has slackened a little."

"Only a temporary respite, I am afraid," said Soldatov.

"Nevertheless," said Volkov, "the airport here is better than at Sheremetyevo, outside Moscow. There they have

173

two runways closed, and last week the airport was closed for two days completely. And in any case, the air traffic there is very heavy, much heavier than usual. We are moving a good deal of snow-clearing equipment."

"I see," said Bisby. "But I didn't know there was any service from here to the Pacific coast—the American Pacific coast, I mean."

"Of no importance," said Volkov, grinning slyly. "Aeroflot has put a jetliner at our service. It is here already; it came in from Alma Ata today."

Bisby was grinning too. It was curious, thought the watching Stovin, that Bisby and Volkov, although engaged in a perpetual thrust-and-parry conversational fencing match, seemed to understand each other and get on very well together.

"Nice," said Bisby. "Nice to have a tame State airline."

"Indeed," said Volkov. "Perhaps, in America, you should try it?"

They ate their supper together, and afterward Stovin and Soldatov settled down at the big trestle table. They were working on a new annex to the report, trying to establish the effect of climatic change on the Caucasus and the oil regions of Iran. Bisby and Volkov played chess, though the American knew he was not in the Russian's class. Valentina and Diane were packing, and after the third chess game was over and Volkov had, as always, explained exactly where Bisby went wrong, the Russian got to his feet.

"Please," he said to Stovin, "you stay here tonight. I will go back to School No.2 with Mr. Bisby. You and Dr. Soldatov still have work to do. It will give you an extra hour or so . . ."

New gusts of wind were shaking the little house, and the snow had started again. Stovin made only perfunctory protests when the army carrier came a few minutes later. After Soldatov had seen Volkov to the door, he rejoined Stovin at the table, and they worked on for another hour before the American yawned.

"We have a long day tomorrow," said Soldatov. "Perhaps we should finish now. We can take some of this material with us to Santa Fe. There will be computers close by, at the University in Albuquerque?"

"Of course," said Stovin. I could stand to see that campus, he thought. I didn't appreciate the sunshine enough last time. In a sudden almost shy gesture of friendship, Soldatov patted his arm.

"Goodnight," he said.

On the priority telephone in School No.2, it took Volkov twenty minutes to get through to the code number of the Chairman of the State Security Commission in Moscow. Volkov had expected a subordinate and could not hide his surprise when the Chairman answered.

"I am sleeping in my office," said the Security Chief. "Many of us in Moscow do that now. Traveling in and out is too difficult at the moment. Now . . . is your journey arranged?"

"Yes," said Volkov. "An Aeroflot Antonov—they argued about it in Alma Ata, of course, but they backed down in the end."

"Yes," said the Chairman. "And Valentina Soldatova —you have told her?"

"She's delighted," said Volkov.

"I never knew a woman who wasn't delighted to go to America," said the Chairman dryly.

"I was a little surprised," said Volkov. His voice was cautious, the Chairman noted with amusement.

"I know," Volkov went on, "that it is not unusual, in normal circumstances, for the wife to accompany the man. It is a reasonable privilege. But these, after all, are not normal circumstances."

"Just so," said the Chairman. "And you gave me the answer yourself, in your own report. You described Soldatov as an exceptionally happily married man."

"Yes," said Volkov. "But . . ."

"A man devoted to his wife will worry if he has to leave her behind in Novosibirsk in what, as you say, are not normal circumstances. If Dr. Soldatov worries, he will not do good work. It is important, for everyone's sake, that he does do good work. So Valentina Soldatova accompanies him."

"I see," said Volkov.

"You should be glad, Colonel Volkov, that she is going. It has given you a chance of some sunshine."

"Oh?"

"If Valentina Soldatova were not going," said the Chairman, "then you yourself would not be going. I trust you to keep an eye on her. On them both. Goodnight."

175

~~Diane Hilder lay~~ reading in the narrow bed in her little
room at the *dacha,* listening to the low moan of the snow
wind across the ice of the Ob Sea, and was glad she was
going home. None of them talked any more about what
had happened out in the forest, when the wolves had
killed the soldiers, but it still haunted them. Though she
had found to her surprise that horrible though it was, it
had not matched in horror her earlier experience of finding that unknown hand in the wolf's stomach. The work
she had done on wolves out here had been valuable and
important, aided by the material supplied by the Zoologi-
cal Institute. Stovin had said it had been a vital annex to
the report—"possibly, in the long run, it's the most important part of the report," he had said. That was typical
Stovin. He was a man who loved paradox. But she would
never, after this, be able to work on wolves again. She'd
find something else, back in the United States. But not
wolves . . . So she wasn't tough enough to be a really
good scientist, it seemed. Not like Stovin. Nothing seemed
to touch him through the barrier of that intellect. Certainly I don't touch him, either, physically or metaphori-
cally, she thought. I imagined when he asked me to come
here . . . well, what did I imagine? That, maybe . . . God,
I'm lonely, I'd like Stovin here with me right now—here
beside me. She smiled suddenly. Here on top of me, I
suppose.

On a sudden impulse, she slipped from the bed and carried the pressure lamp, which was all that was available
now when the power was rationed after nine P.M.,
over to the little table with the looking-glass above it
which served as her dressing table. She picked up a brush
and vigorously attacked her short shining hair until it
gleamed gold in the hard white light. Then, experimentally, she put a little of the duty-free scent she'd bought on
the Pan Am plane, during the flight to Moscow, behind
her ears. Not bad, she said, looking at herself critically.
Distinctly sexy. If I were a man I think I'd fancy you.
Hilder. She pushed her hair away from her face. Yes, it
looked better like that.

There was a creak at the end of the stairs. Stovin coming
up to sleep . . . of course, he was in Volkov's room. She sat
there, irresolute, thinking that tomorrow they were going
back . . . they'd never be together in exactly this way
again. She pushed at her hair once more. Her whole body
seemed to be trembling. Abruptly she got up from the

dressing table and opened the door. The room occupied by the Soldatovs, at the end of the passage, was dark, but there was a line of light beneath Stovin's doorway, next to hers. Gently, she opened the door.

He was sitting up in bed, a book propped against the blankets. He looked up, startled, as she came into the room, carefully closing the door behind her. She found it strangely difficult to speak.

"What are you reading?" she asked, absurdly.

"Herman Flohn," he said. His face was in the shadow cast by his pressure light, and it was impossible to see his eyes.

"Are you . . ." he began, but she put a finger to her lips, pantomiming the need for silence. He went on looking at her, saying nothing.

"I'm awfully cold," she said.

He put the book down and stretched out his hand. "Let me see . . . yes, you are."

He looked up at her where she stood above him. She could see a small pulse beating at the end of his left eyebrow.

"My, you smell good," he said.

"Do I?"

"Sit here . . . that's better."

He put up his hand and gently stroked her hair. Then he kissed her, so easily that it was hard to believe it was only the second time he had ever kissed her lips. She found herself half responding, half drawing away. He sounded strangely breathless, pulling back the blanket.

"If you're cold," he said, "you'd better get in."

She lay against him so that their bodies touched down their whole lengths—toe, knee, stomach, lips. He passed his hands searchingly over her body. She put her own hands behind his neck, grasping the thick grey hair behind his head and kissing him fiercely.

"Do you feel warmer now?" he said, when he'd got his breath. "Are you glad you got in my bed?"

"Stovin," she said, "I thought you'd never ask."

It was the kind of lovemaking she had hoped for, a sort of sexual comradeship she hadn't found before. She was not, she knew, a woman of much sexual experience. There had been only two previous occasions—within a few months of each other, and with two different men, more than two years ago. They'd been no more than experimental . . . exciting, in a way. But they hadn't made her feel particularly happy afterward. Stovin was better . . . much, much better. Tender and considerate, but strong and unexpectedly dominating. She lay beside him, more contented than she had been for as long as she could remember.

"What took you so long?" she said, absently stroking his bare shoulder.

"What do you mean . . . long? I thought it didn't go on long enough."

She raised herself on her elbow and looked down at him. His face was still damp with effort and activity.

"I don't mean that, and you know it. I mean . . . why didn't you try me before?"

He shifted, a little uncomfortably. "I'm sort of a private person, Diane. I never understand people. I'm better with ideas. I think I just didn't want to get involved."

"Do you feel involved now, Stovin? I think I'm involved."

He looked at her intently, his hand on her body. "I'm older than you are, Diane. I'm going to be quite an old man before you're even middle-aged. There'll be problems. And in any case, the way things are in the world, there's no way of even guessing what the future holds."

She laughed at him. "I'm not exactly a chicken myself, Stovin. I'm nearly thirty."

"My, my," he said, grinning suddenly. "I don't know how you bear the burden of the years."

He was above her again, and momentarily she gasped as she was pressed back into the bed. "It looks like it's not the only burden I'm going to bear," she said, her mouth muffled against his shoulder. "You realize this bed creaks, Stovin?"

"No problem," he said. "So does the Soldatovs' bed. It was going great guns not so long ago. They're a steady married couple—they'll be happily asleep by now."

"Is that what happens to steady married couples?" she asked, linking her hands behind his back.

"If they're lucky," said Stovin.

Half a mile away, in the shadowed corner of the classroom in School No.2, Bisby leaned beneath his bunk-bed and drew out the tin biscuit box. Carefully he sorted through its contents—the shining white skull amulet, a book with stained brown covers, an old photograph of a man standing beside a wooden house. He placed them in

178

order on the wooden chair beside the bed. There were other things, too—a flaked flint scraper of the sort found in the Stone-Age rooms of museums, a handful of nails, and incongruously, a red switch marked in white letters, "EJECT." At last he found what he sought, at the bottom of the box. Tenderly he drew it out. It was the skin of a young fish eagle, its black-white-grey feathers slightly ruffled, shining in the light of his torch. He put his hand upon it and spoke aloud, five or six words said so quickly that no listener would have been able to separate them. He remained staring into the darkened classroom for a full minute, and then slowly replaced the things in the box.

"I am flying tomorrow," he said. "Is there a sign?"

He waited for five minutes before he undressed and climbed into bed. On the opposite bunk, the sleeping Volkov stirred and flung out an arm. There is no sign, thought Bisby. Why is there never a sign?

CHAPTER 16

Regional Headquarters: State Security Service of the USSR Chukchi Autonomous Region (Province of Magadan); Anadyr Area Weekly Intelligence Summary

There have been disturbing developments in the past five days:

ONE   *Considerable illegal movement of population has been taking place in the northeastern sector of the Autonomous Region. This movement has largely involved people of the Chukchi ethnic group, but has also included appreciable numbers of Evenk, Yakut, and Eskimo family groups. Total numbers involved so far are in excess of 3,000 individuals.*

TWO   *The illegal movement, which has consisted of about 200 vehicles, as well as reindeer and dog*

179

sleds, has been in a northeasterly direction.
This is puzzling since, though climatic
conditions here are unusually severe even for
this time of year, the ground conditions into
which the illegal movement is extending are
appreciably worse.

THREE   The city of Anadyr is now being partly
evacuated, without permission from the
Administration of the Autonomous Region, or
even from the District Soviet.

FOUR   The illegal movement appears to be
spontaneous and without recognizable
leadership.

FIVE   Attempts by Army units stationed at the
Ugoinaya Early Warning Station (two infantry
companies consisting largely of Chukchi
nationals) to interfere with the illegal
movement of population have been
unsuccessful. A temporary barrier and
check-point north of Anadyr was bypassed. No
shots were fired. A number of soldiers of
Chukchi ethnic origin, including an officer,
appear themselves to have joined the eastward
movement.

SIX   In present climatic conditions, attempts to
reinforce this area with troops from other ethnic
groups would not be possible. The airport west
of the city has been closed for three days, and
even helicopter landings are at present
impracticable. Troops could be brought from
Khabarovsk to Magadan on the K-Highway
and held in Magadan until the weather situation
improves.

SEVEN   Again owing to weather conditions, monitoring
of the illegal movement in its early stages by air
has proved very difficult. The three Army
helicopters stationed at Anadyr flew nine
missions during the first two days; one
helicopter and crew were lost. Air photographs
taken at that time show that the illegal
population movement straggled over
approximately fifty miles, still heading
northeast. Some casualties appear to have been
suffered, almost certainly from extreme climatic
conditions. Seventeen bodies were counted on

180

the coast road near Geikal, fifty miles northeast
of Anadyr.

EIGHT *Further photographic missions cannot at present*
be undertaken. It is important to retain the
two remaining helicopters for the movement
or evacuation of key personnel.

Volkov sat in the cold temporary office made available
for him at the headquarters of the District Soviet in
Anadyr, and worried. Through the glass doors he could
see the remnants of the staff standing and talking. Occasionally a telephone would ring. Sometimes it would
be answered, sometimes not. There was an air of general
confusion; outside in the passages, men and women milled
about, all talking loudly, protesting, cajoling. Virtually
no organizational effort was being made, he told himself
fiercely. It was more like a town awaiting occupation by
enemy troops than the capital of an Autonomous Region
—though it was an Autonomous Region with a population of only 80,000 over its whole vast peninsula, the
very tip of northeast Siberia, opposite Alaska. He picked
up his own telephone once more, trying Moscow, Magadan, and Khabarovsk, in that order. He could get no
ringing tone through the automatic exchange. He glanced
at the number written on the pad in front of him and
again tried the airfield outside the town. This time he
got a ringing tone and—after three minutes—a reply.
It was a rough, unprofessional voice, not one of the regular operators, he realized.

"Yes?"

"This is Colonel Volkov . . . State Security . . . in
Anadyr." He would never normally have said such a
thing on the telephone even though, no doubt, his position in the KGB was a matter of common conjecture. But
something had to be done to move these people off their
buttons.

"Yes?" said the voice.

"Is there any runway open yet?"

A laugh. "What do you mean . . . any runway? There's
only one runway here. And it isn't open."

"When, then?"

There was a deep breath from the other end of the
line. "There are just about six people on this airfield now.

181

The runway's under eight feet of snow after last night. It would take all the troops in Khabarovsk a week to clear it for one hour. And it's still snowing."

"Is my aircraft there?"

"What aircraft was that?"

I must be patient, thought Volkov. I must not lose my temper. "An Aeroflot Antonov," he said steadily. "We came in about eighteen hours ago, in the blizzard. It was an emergency, and we needed fuel."

"It's been an emergency here for the last ten days," said the voice morosely. "Yes, there is an Antonov on the parking bay opposite. We don't usually get many like that in here, so it's probably yours. I'll tell you now . . . it might as well be in Khabarovsk for all the good it is to you. It'll be iced up like a frozen reindeer, and in any case there's no runway. And the radar tower's finished."

"Why?"

"Cables have gone—no way to get at them now. And no operators, as of this morning."

"Why?"

"Chief radar officer was a man called Kotegrine. He was a Chukchi—practically everybody is in this hole. He packed up and went yesterday, and the others went with him."

"Where?" said Volkov. He felt dazed. If only he could talk to Moscow . . .

"Oh, you know," said the other vaguely. "East . . ."

"You're not Chukchi?"

Another laugh. "Me? No. I'm from Leningrad. I'll wager they've got it bad back there now. But I wish to hell I was there myself."

"Are you staying on?"

"Yes, I'll stay on for today, anyway. I'm damned if I know why."

"Just look at them," said Diane. "I've never seen anything like it. Where on earth are they all going?"

In the reddish twilight of the midwinter noon, past the snow-mantled front of the District Publishing House, opposite the hotel windows, streamed a steady exodus of human beings. Some were in vehicles, headlights blazing in the murk—cars, trucks, lorries, and an occasional small tracked vehicle like a miniature snowmobile. Many were on foot, and there were also scores of dog and deer teams pulling sledges loaded high with boxes, tarpaulins, children. Inside the hotel itself, the lobby was crammed with people shouting, talking, gesticulating. Every so often families would meet there, embrace, and go out to join the exodus. There was now no food available in the hotel. An hour ago, Soldatov and Valentina had gone down to the empty kitchens and found a loaf of bread and an overlooked tin of Bulgarian plum jam. With this, seated in the empty lounge, they had made a meal while they waited for Volkov.

"They're nearly all Chukchi," said Bisby. "A few Eskimo amongst them."

Diane looked out at a group of men near them—sturdy, well-made men wearing thick anoraks and fur caps, or sometimes bare headed, their bluish-black hair cut short and combed down in short fringes over their brows. Two women stood beside them. One turned her face toward the hotel for a moment. Her broad flat face bore a thin tracery of black lines on the brow, nose, and chin. Bisby, watching Diane, saw her surprise.

"Tattooing," he said. "They still do it, some of them. Some Eskimos do the same thing. Different patterns, though."

"Is that how you tell they're Chukchi, not Eskimo?" she asked. "They all look so alike."

"Oh, it takes one to know one," he said. "And in any case"—grinning—"I'm a failed anthropologist. So I know a bit about the Chukchi. They're a mixture—maybe part Mongol, part Indian. But they aren't Eskimo—at least, they aren't modern Eskimo. They and the Eskimo probably came from the same stock a long, long time ago. There are resemblances . . . hunting techniques, even language. For instance, the Chukchi have a word *aliuit*. It means 'islander'—very like the Eskimo word for the same thing. Probably gave its name to the Aleutian Islands. They *do* look alike. But if you're an Eskimo, you know the difference."

"Surely they don't still hunt in the old ways?" she said, changing the subject.

"Some do," he said. "There's a lot of seal and walrus up here, around the Bering Strait, and down the Koryak coast, and all the way down the other side. And whale, a lot of whale."

"We have shore collectives for that," said Soldatov,

183

joining the conversation. "And, of course, for reindeer herding."

Bisby laughed, openly derisive. "You show me a Chukchi or an Eskimo who says he believes in politically based shore collectives, and I'll show you a liar," he said. "Eskimos and Chukchi had their own collectives ten thousand years before Lenin."

"Things have changed," said Soldatov. "The Chukchi are part of the USSR. They have entered the modern world, perhaps better than your own Eskimos in the United States. We have Chukchi doctors, Chukchi teachers. A Chukchi has been head of the Institute for Non-Ferrous Metals in Magadan. There's a Chukchi in the Academy of Sciences; he's a linguistics researcher, a fine man. They've left the Stone Age. They're part of our society."

Bisby swung around and pointed at the window.

"Then where are they going?" he said. Soldatov looked at him, saying nothing.

"We're a long, long way from Moscow here," said Bisby. "Nearly as far as you get in the Soviet Union. We're only about 400 miles from Alaska and the United States. I wouldn't count on any feeling of Chukchi solidarity with the rest of you. You made this an autonomous region, and they seem to have taken you literally. They're leaving. Autonomously."

"Then they're leaving in order to die," said Soldatov. For the first time he sounded angry.

"That's as may be," said Bisby. "A lot of these people know more about this particular kind of world than the rest of us, including me. We'll see what happens. And where they're going."

"What's more to the point is where *we* are going," said Stovin. He had watched Valentina's discomfort as her husband, usually so mild mannered, clashed with Bisby, and he thought it time to intervene. Now he looked up. Volkov looked harassed but determined.

"I am sorry to have kept you waiting so long," he said. "But I have been making arrangements. We are going to move."

"You mean they've got that runway open?" asked Bisby in genuine surprise. "I should have thought there was about as much chance of lifting an Antonov off as of jumping from here to Seattle. I'll tell you now—I didn't think all that much of our chances when we came in yesterday. Whoever was flying it must have been able to see mighty little, and the radar wasn't too good on the approach."

"How do you know that?" said Volkov sharply.

"I was sitting right forward, and the flight deck door kept coming open. There wasn't much air-ground conversation going on, and so I reckon he was coming in on the seat of his pants. Not much incoming or outgoing traffic here, of course, but he did a fine job."

"Yes, we were lucky," said Volkov after a pause. "We were lucky there was an airport at Anadyr and that we didn't have to go on to Anchorage—we had flight clearance to there. But the airport there, it seems, is finally closed."

"So what now?" asked Bisby.

Volkov shrugged. "We have difficulties here. I will be frank—I do not know what is going on. These people . . . they can behave unpredictably."

Bisby grinned, but Volkov ignored him.

"And so," the Russian went on, "the problem remains. We must get to Seattle—from there it will be easy to get to Los Angeles. The airport here is not operating for the next few days—for the foreseeable future, in fact. There are difficulties of communication with Moscow by the ordinary telephone network because of the weather conditions. It should be easier from a military post; they will have radio communication on their own networks. And so we will go to Uelen. It's northeast of Egvenikot, there is a small air force weather survey station there. They will fly us back to Khabarovsk, and from there we will fly to Seattle. All the flight clearances can be arranged at Khabarovsk. It is the best thing to do."

"How far is this place . . .?" asked Stovin.

"Uelen? By road, more than 300 miles."

Bisby whistled.

"Do not fear," Volkov said, smiling. "I have a vehicle. It is not comfortable, but it works. And I have an escort. See . . ."

He pointed out of the window to where a Soviet soldier stood beside a grey Tatra truck, its bright sidelights glowing through the gloom.

"A truck, in this weather, for a distance like that, with what looks like the California gold rush on the roads all around it?" said Bisby.

185

"It is the best that can be done. We cannot stay here. In two days' time, I think this town will be empty, except for a few miners coming in from the outside. Frankly, we must move while we can."

"The snow has stopped—for the moment, at any rate," said Stovin. "What are the road conditions like?"

"It will be slow, because . . . well, you need only a look from this window. But they have snowplows ahead, I am told. Almost everything that will move is on the road."

Valentina was holding her husband's arm. He spoke to her soothingly, but behind his spectacles his eyes were alert, worried.

He spoke directly to Volkov. "What is happening out there? Where are they going?"

"I do not know," said Volkov. "I am wondering if they know themselves, Dr. Soldatov. With such people, one cannot ever be certain. I saw some of them outside as they came in. They had a raven in a cage. There was a man beside it, beating a drum. A sealskin drum. Unbelievable, in the twentieth century."

Bisby looked up sharply. His voice had an edge to it, Stovin noticed, watching.

"They had a raven and a drum, did they? I wonder how many of those there are, amongst all those people." He pointed out of the window, where the post-noon twilight was already gathering. His voice was abstracted, almost remote.

"You don't understand, Volkov. Nor any of you—how could you? The raven is important to Chukchi and to Eskimos. You see, it was Raven who guided them long ago. He was a human with a raven's bill. He sought a land where the People could live; it's because of him that humans can live in the world. He guided them."

Suddenly his voice was shy, embarrassed. "At least, that's what the Chukchi and the Eskimos think . . . thought, I mean. Though I suppose some of them still believe it—these things die hard."

There was a pause, and then Stovin spoke. "Yes," he said, "I see. And the drum?"

Bisby had recovered his composure. "Oh, we all follow a drummer," he said easily. "Even you, Sto. But some men hear a different drummer, and they march to a different tune."

No one spoke for a moment or two, and then Volkov looked at his watch. "It is too late now. We will leave

186

as soon as we can get a little light. We need to get used to the road. Meanwhile, I will try to find the air crew who brought us in yesterday. It would be better to have them with us, I think; we may need a crew later, and it may prove hard to find one. They were in the hotel last night, but they are no longer in their rooms. Perhaps they are sleeping nearer the airfield."

"Perhaps," said Bisby. "But I don't think you'll find them."

"We're on a knife-edge in the north, Mr. President," said Brookman. Across the long table with its dull green cloth, white sets of note pads and blotting paper, and carafes of water, the lantern-jawed Secretary of the Interior, an industrialist from Illinois, nodded emphatically. He sat next to the President. Around them, on the newly formed National Emergency Committee, sat some of the key figures in the crisis: the Secretaries for Defense, Agriculture, and the Treasury; the general commanding the Army Communications Center at Fort Huachua in Arizona; Brookman himself; and the official in charge of the Office of Civil and Defense Mobilization. They had never met together as a group before this morning. On the other side of the President sat a man whom they had never seen—nor ever dreamed might be present at a meeting concerning the domestic security of the United States. He was a small, bright-eyed French Canadian, fresh in two hours ago from Ottawa. Officially designated Minister to the President.

"A knife-edge," said Brookman again, and the President looked at him for a moment without replying. Instead, he turned to the Canadian.

"You, too, of course?" he said.

"It is very bad," said the Canadian. His voice had a very faint but unmistakable French accent. "The Northwest Territories, the Yukon . . . well, of course, they were evacuated at the same time you cleared Anchorage and northern Alaska. It was difficult, but not so very bad—a matter of about 65,000 people in all. We're using British Columbia as a reception area, you know, Mr. President."

The President nodded.

"The weather is bad there," said the Canadian. "Much rain, some snow. But nothing like as bad as farther north.

"The weather is coming steadily from the north and

the west, right down across Alberta and Saskatchewan. Now that's not an unusual pattern, but nevertheless, there is something wrong. Something different. We don't have any sign of a *chinook*. I imagine, Mr. President . . . gentlemen . . . that only Dr. Brookman and the Secretary here"—he nodded toward the Secretary of Agriculture —"will have much idea what a *chinook* is. Well, gentlemen, it's what makes wheat growing possible in Alberta and Saskatchewan and right down into the United States."

"We're having the same problem," said the Secretary, so quietly that the Canadian did not hear him.

"The *chinook*," said the Canadian Minister, "is a winter-spring wind. It normally blows down the side of any east-moving depression, like we're getting a series of right now. It's a very useful wind, relatively warm and dry, and it can raise atmospheric temperature by as much as 30 degrees in a quarter of an hour. It makes pasture and grain growing possible right down the spine of this continent, down from our Mackenzie River into your Colorado."

"And?" said the President.

"It does not blow any more," said the Canadian. "Some of the temperatures we are getting in Saskatchewan are unbelieveably low—and there's nothing to alleviate them. We came to a decision in Ottawa yesterday that will be announced tomorrow. We're going to have to evacuate Winnipeg, Mr. President. Three-quarters of a million people. But we've had nearly 600 deaths in the city in the last week—mostly folk whose heating has failed, or who're old and ill. But the Prime Minister has been told the situation will get steadily worse. So we're moving out of Winnipeg. God help us and them."

"I've got news for you, Minister," said the Secretary of Defense briskly. "You talk about Winnipeg. I'm talking about Chicago. We're going to . . ."

The President held up his hand, and the Secretary of Defense subsided.

"How are you doing along that stretch of the Canadian-United States frontier, south of Winnipeg?"

The Canadian pursed his lips. "I'm afraid a lot of people are coming across, Mr. President. It's a human instinct, I guess, to head south, even though they're heading into what are probably much the same conditions. People are seeing their homes, their towns, steadily overwhelmed. They won't worry about any frontier."

188

"Nevertheless, we can't cope with tens of thousands of Canadian refugees," said the Secretary of Defense. "We have very much the same problem ourselves in the north. We're pulling virtually every old person, woman and child out of Fargo, in North Dakota, for instance. And now there's Chicago . . ."

"Yes?" said the Canadian. Suddenly he sounded tired, defeated.

"We're going to evacuate Chicago, suburb by suburb. That's around three million people, Minister. Our second biggest city. It's going to need a lot of discipline, and it's going to need every available kind of transport from helicopters to farm carts. Above all, it's going to need clear roads. There's only a limited number of roads, even now, that we can keep clear. We can't take in Canadians on the scale that seemed to be developing."

He turned to the President. "I've moved additional National Guard units up around that section of the border, Mr. President. As of this morning. They have orders to turn back those who are not United States nationals."

"But what if . . ." said the Canadian. He saw the President's face and stopped in time. The President's voice was so mild that Brookman, who now knew him better than any of the others, looked up sharply and felt a prickle of fear down his spine.

"What did you say you had done, Henry?"

"Given orders to turn them back," said the Secretary.

"That frontier hasn't needed soldiers for a very long time," said the President. "It doesn't need them now. Get them out of there, Henry. At least, keep them there —but to help, not to hinder. You do that."

"But surely," said the Secretary desperately, "we can't be sentimental. These are our own people who're being put at risk if the roads get any more jammed than they are."

"We *can* be sentimental," said the President. "Because if we aren't, by golly, we may as well be ants or wolves or rats. So you change those orders, Henry."

"I'll do it as soon as the meeting's over," said the Secretary.

"Do it now," said the President gently. The Secretary looked at him for two long seconds, and then rose to his feet and left the room.

"Thank you, Mr. President," said the Canadian.

The President laughed shortly. "Don't thank me, Jean-Pierre—I may call you Jean-Pierre?"

"Please . . . of course."

"You may be able to help us, as well as we can help you. We're in all sorts of trouble in Washington state, and northern Oregon. Could be we'll ask you to let some people move into British Columbia. You say that area's clear?"

"It's much better than the areas to the east," said the Canadian. "There are parts that have even had heavy rain but no snow. As to what you suggest, I shall, of course, inform the Prime Minister immediately. I feel sure, however . . . well, we are one continent, are we not?"

"That's how I see it," said the President. "We, too, have snow-free areas, even in parts where you wouldn't imagine that could be so—there's a big stretch of South Dakota, isn't there, Mel?"

Brookman leaned forward. "That's so, Mr. President. Of course, nobody could guarantee how long such areas will be clear, or if they'll still be clear next winter. But in the short term, in the next two–three months, they could save a lot of lives. You see, after all, we have no real idea of what it was like in the last glaciation. Climatologists tend to be seduced by their own maps—maps that show the whole of the north of the continent under the ice. It may not have been quite like that. For years, maybe centuries . . . there may have been . . . pockets."

The President turned to the man from the Office of Mobilization. "The movement of people into these areas, on some sort of progressive short-term time scale . . . is that going to be practicable?"

The mobilization expert rubbed his hands. He seemed almost to be enjoying the situation.

"I don't know, Mr. President. That's the only answer I can give. But we're going to try. I guess it just may be done."

"Good," said the President. "Mel, how about food?"

"Well, there won't be nearly enough food, in the way we've been used to consuming it, Mr. President. The Secretary over there"—he nodded across the table—"has given me three models of crop yield forecasts, based on different computer information and prediction. I would recommend taking the worst of these forecasts. The yields will be down dramatically, not only here but in every major grain-producing country.

"On the other hand, there *are* the strategic food stock-piles here and in Europe, and I guess they've got a lot salted away in the Soviet Union. So, for maybe a year, there'll be almost enough."

"Almost?" said the President.

"There are going to be some deaths, sir. A lot of deaths. There's always been starvation in the Third World, of course, though we've made at least some effort to help. Well, now we're going to find it difficult to help at all. So their starvation will intensify. You can multiply past Third World starvation by ten, and you'll still be under-estimating it. Nevertheless, the hope for the world lies here, in the United States—and in Britain, Europe, the Soviet Union. Because if we're going to crack this thing, that's where it will be done. Not in the Third World. If we go under, they go under anyway."

The President raised his eyebrows. This was a new Brookman. A Brookman who could bite.

"You really think there's anything we can do, in the long term, to crack it?" he asked.

"Well, there are possibilities," said Brookman cautiously. "You read Annex Nine to the Stovin-Soldatov Report, sir?"

"Yes."

"It sounds fanciful, but it might turn out to be a practical possibility. Animals migrate, to and fro, from winter to summer and back, so that they can feed and breed in the best conditions. Now Stovin's idea, as you know, was that we could, relatively quickly, organize our societies so that at least while the next few winters were affecting us, before the new glaciation hardened, so to speak, we could move people from, say, Iowa down to Florida and New Mexico and Texas, and back north during what will be a much shorter summer than we've grown accustomed to. The Europeans could do the same to the Mediterranean or even to North Africa, and the Russians to the Caucasus. It would certainly be a gigantic project, but it would buy us a little time to look around."

"We're good at gigantic projects," the President said.

"Yes," said Brookman. "But we're going to have to change some of the other things we're good at. We've always been good eaters of certain kinds of food. Did you know, Mr. President, that an average man in an advanced country needs nearly a ton of grain a year to keep him going? He takes it in grain for bread, and for cattle food so that he can eat meat. Even in Africa, a man takes around 400 pounds. Well we're going to have to come down to an African level, and they'll be going lower still. They'll be lucky to get 200, though if they can eventually develop some of their potential arable land, they will gradually increase that figure."

"That's in the longer term," said the President. "What of the short term?"

Brookman leaned forward earnestly. "Our hope is chemistry. It's possible to produce chemical, microbiological rations that will keep a man going over a period of time, at any rate. We've done it with astronauts, as you know. I had a transatlantic call yesterday from Ledbester in England—he's their government scientific adviser— does the same sort of thing I do here. He says their Imperial Chemical Industries have had a few people working on chemical food packages for a couple of years. They've got some good ideas and some good formulas. Our own people have gotten hold of something pretty good, too. The problem isn't going to be the formula. It's going to be mass production. The scale of mass production that would give all of us, say, seven supplementary meals a week in a chemical pack. It will be a staggering target. And some of the areas where the factories are situated—Pennsylvania, say, or northern France, or Hamburg, or Manchester—they'll be under the snow before they produce an ounce."

He paused, shuffling a sheaf of typescript on the white blotter in front of him.

"Nevertheless, Mr. President, we're starting. I've got the vice-presidents of our four biggest combines coming to see me tomorrow, and Ledbester and a couple of their people are flying over to join us. Plus a German from Dusseldorf. We've got a lot of lost time to make up. Of course, the results of a prolonged diet of chemical food— even of a considerable proportion of chemical food on the human body, digestion, elimination, blood count, growth of the fetus in the womb . . . well, there's no way we can do more than guess. We may have some surprises."

"Nevertheless, it's something we could send out to the Third World, as well as to our own people," said the President thoughtfully. "It wouldn't be impossibly bulky."

"No," said Brookman. "But we shall need an awful lot, just for ourselves."

"Mel," said the President, "we're going to have to share. Because if we don't share, we're going to have to fight. And we can't afford to do that. People who're starving have nothing to lose. If we don't give, they'll try to take. So we're going to have to share. Talking of which, in strictly domestic terms, how far have we got with the rationing project?"

"The ration cards are printed, Mr. President," said the Secretary of the Interior. "The press have got hold of it, of course—no way of keeping a project that size under wraps. But people are pretty well prepared for something of the kind, anyway. And all those in the north will welcome it. For the rest . . . well, they won't find it comfortable. But every television screen every night shows what's happening in the north. They know it has to be done."

"None of us is going to be comfortable for a long time to come," said Brookman. He, too, sounded tired. He's . . . what, sixty? thought the President. A little older than I am. And I guess he's colder then I am most of the time. It's time I stopped treating him like some kind of answering machine. A few minutes later, the President closed the meeting. As its members filed out, he stretched out a hand and drew Brookman back into the room.

"Pretty chilly up there in Connecticut, Mel? You going back soon?"

"Tomorrow night," said Brookman. "But I'll be in Santa Fe next week. Yes, it's pretty cold in Connecticut. I wear my overcoat in my office."

"Hm. Mel . . ."

"Yes, Mr. President?"

"I thought when I picked you as Chairman of the National Science Council I'd got the right man. Now I know that to be so."

Brookman sounded surprisingly embarrassed. "That's kind of you, Mr. President. That's very kind."

CHAPTER 17

A column of trucks and automobiles wound steadily away from the front of the great building, picking a way out along a cleared boulevard, following a route marked by police cars, red lights flashing. Although it was not yet midday, the snow piled two stories high on either side cut down the daylight to such an extent that the line of traffic moved in a sort of twilight. The cars were packed with families, and every so often one of them might be seen to contain a smuggled dog or cat. It was strictly against the new emergency regulations to take pets from the city, but that particular regulation, though it was made to conserve badly needed food, was one which many people would ignore.

This was the third day of the evacuation of Chicago. Now it was the turn of the inhabitants of Marina City, the sixty-storied twin towers that rose high above the Chicago River, housing thousands of families. Marina City had been built in 1964, two cylindrical, balconied towers thrusting into the blue sky of Illinois, a confident architectural monument to the needs and the technological power of urban America. Today, although it throbbed with the steady passage of those leaving (forever, although they did not then know this), it was cold and dark. Except for the emergency generators installed purely temporarily by the United States Army to power, for this day only, the machinery in the lower floors where the cars vital to the evacuation were parked in their accustomed bays, Marina City had been without light or heat for a week. And it was also rapidly running short of food.

Nevertheless, it was still better off than many other parts of Chicago. The evacuation of America's second biggest city was a gamble—a gamble that had been undertaken only because the scale of death in some areas had become disastrously high. In icy, unheated apartments, families literally froze to death, and the very young and

194

old suffered from growing hunger. The supermarkets held food, but the difficulty of getting to them often outweighed the advantage. Men would go out from apartment blocks in gangs of twenty or more to burrow through the snow wall to a store they knew to be no more than a block away. Men died in these foraging parties; occasionally an entire party would fail to return. It proved appallingly easy to become disoriented. In the suffocating white wilderness, landmarks printed on people's minds since childhood had vanished forever.

Very early in the crisis, the police established permanent small garrisons in every major supermarket—normally three or four officers rotating duty around the clock so that they could give out carefully rationed canned food to those who came. Even against these guards, food raids were attempted, though the difficulty of getting away through the snow proved to be a better deterrent than the police themselves. In the dubious areas down on South Side and Division Street, however, the crime situation was particularly critical, and forty-two food raiders were shot by police during that last week.

Only one course seemed open to officials toiling to deal with the catastrophe of Chicago: to get people out in every vehicle that could be driven, while fuel could still be pumped with Army assistance from frozen but disinterred gas stations. The very nature of Chicago's situation had made it peculiarly vulnerable to a snow disaster. The winds pushing a virtually continuous blizzard across Lake Michigan had no buffer to divert them from the tall streets. First they had piled snow over the vast complex of industry, steel mills, and refineries along the lakefront to the south, where frozen-in freighters simply disappeared beneath mountains of snow. Then the snow had taken over the city itself, piling sixty . . . eighty feet high along Jackson Boulevard, obliterating the great grain exchange, covering State and Madison, collapsing the elevated tramway of the El in many places. Chicago had known bad winters before—many of them. This was altogether different. This was an urban apocalypse.

And so the evacuation began, suburb by stricken suburb, day by day . . . Evanston, Highwood with its Italian-Americans, Wilmette, Winnetka. And now, Marina City —close to the center of town. The people of Marina City were being taken to the Quad Cities of Moline, East Moline, Davenport and Rock Island, which lay nearly

200 miles west. The snow there had been light so far, by comparison with the blizzards that had destroyed Chicago.

In the Quad Cities, temporary reception areas were being constructed with frantic haste to hold hundreds of thousands of people until even more urgent efforts could be made to ship them south. The scale of the dislocation of human lives was terrifying. No operation as enormous as the evacuation of Chicago had ever been seriously considered in the United States, even as a contingency plan in the event of nuclear war. And now it was an operation conducted in impossible climatic conditions.

The escape road to the Quad Cities, now being held open by thousands of toiling soldiers, was State 173, running west for more than eighty miles to Rockford, where the solidly frozen Rock River offered a broader, more easily swept surface down to Moline. But State 173 was becoming a graveyard. Police and soldiers marshalled the traffic along its narrow, cleared snow channel, bulldozing stranded vehicles into the icy mountains stacked at the roadsides. And every so often, the winding column, following its own chain of red taillights in the snow twilight, passed broken-down vehicles, beside which stood desperately waving people, begging for lifts from anything that passed. Yet everything that passed was full, crammed with as many people as it was possible to hold.

Medical teams, in cleared spaces in the snow, fought to save those who were lucky enough to reach them or be brought to them. But there could not be enough medical teams for a road packed with hundreds of thousands of refugees heading west in a blizzard. Things were going wrong. By the second day, many of the groups of people beside the road were no longer waving. They were indistinguishable heaps in the snow, already dead. The column moved on past them, full of hoping, praying human beings. Yet it did not simply contain men, women, children. Chicago had been a very, very rich city . . .

Waiting in the big olive-drab truck outside the towers of Marina City, the United States Army Captain was well aware of the hell of State 173. He had driven along it two days ago, on the first day of the evacuation, and had returned under orders in one of the few State police cars moving east. He had picked up his load, followed the flashing lights of an escorting police car through a temporarily cleared intersection at Jackson and Wells, and was now waiting, parked, below the twin towers. All he expected was to be slotted into a place in the line crawling out through the suburbs and west.

His truck was a big one, capable of holding up to twenty people. At this moment, it held six: himself and the soldier-driver in front, and three carbine-armed soldiers behind. The fourth man in the rear was a civilian —a tall, grey-haired man from the Art Institute of Chicago. Around him lay what occupied the rest of the space in the truck: stack upon stack of wrapped, framed paintings. The captain, squinting through the windshield as he waited for the signal to move, cared nothing for art. But his commanding officer had told him this was one of the greatest collections of Impressionist paintings in the world. And his orders were to get the paintings to Rock City, where they could be picked up by a helicopter which had tried—and failed—to land beside the Institute itself. What was in the back of the Army truck, guarded by the armed soldiers and watched over lovingly by the Institute man, was valued, very conservatively, at seventy million dollars. And, in terms of art, it was totally irreplaceable.

There was a sudden new confusion amongst the vehicles crawling away from Marina City. A big long-distance bus, full of people, was being towed by an Army tractor to one side. It wasn't the first that had broken down, thought the Captain grimly, and it wouldn't be the last. Better here than out on State 173. Or was it? Nobody who had to go back into that icy building would last long— a day maybe, or even two. Look at them getting out of that bus—there must be at least seventy. And quite a lot were kids. A policeman he hadn't seen before came out from behind the bus and floundered over to the truck. The Captain wound down the window, letting in a blast of icy air.

"You waiting to go out on State 173, Captain?"

"Yes."

"O.K. You can help us some. We've got a problem here. There's around eighty people in that bus who aren't goin' to make it unless they crowd in somewhere else. I reckon you've got"—the policeman looked carefully at the truck—"well, you could probably take at least twenty-five. All the kids, anyhow, and some of the women. We'll help you unload all this." He jerked a thumb at the stacked paintings.

The Army man shook his head. "Can't do that, I'm afraid."

The policeman looked at him, his upturned face dusted by snowflakes. "I guess you didn't hear me, Captain. There's twenty-five women and kids out there that you can get in this truck."

The Captain shook his head again. "Can't do it. I've got orders to deliver this load, and deliver this load is what I'm going to do."

There was a tapping at the window between the rear of the cab and the loading space of the truck. He turned in his seat and pulled back the sliding panel of glass. It was the man from the Institute of Art. "What's the delay, Captain?"

Before he could answer, the policeman cut in. "I'll tell you what the delay is. I want him to unload this goddamn truck so he can take some kids out to Rock City, and he won't do it. That's the delay."

"What children . . . where?"

The policeman pointed to the people huddled beside the stranded bus. "Those kids there."

The Institute of Art man looked at his paintings, wet his lips, and spoke to the Captain.

"It's all right, Captain. Unload the paintings. I authorize you to do that."

"No," said the Captain. "You can't authorize me, sir. The only person who can change my orders is the Colonel, and he's not here. That load stays where it is until Rock City."

"But I tell you . . . I authorize you."

The Captain ignored him. He spoke to the policeman. "Now, do you see me into that column, or do we just tag on in our own way? Because I'm moving out."

The policeman stared at him silently and then stepped back. The big truck moved forward, past the group of people beside the bus, and followed a big Chevrolet limousine out onto the boulevard. In the back of the truck, the civilian stared desperately at the three soldiers.

"But . . . I told him . . . he could have . . . I was prepared to . . ."

The wrapping of stout cloth around the painting nearest to him fell away for a moment. Mechanically, he moved forward to push it back into place. He looked down. It was Georges Seurat's *"Un dimanche d' été"*—a painting of a Sunday afternoon beside the water, warm bright sunlight, ladies with parasols, moustachioed men lying on the grass. He stared at it, almost with horror, and then turned abruptly away. That was a lost world.

Tamanrasset was a ghost town. Walking beside the bull camel—God be thanked, the beast seemed to have recovered its strength in the past three days—Zayd ag-Akrud stared about him in bewilderment. Dust and Sahara sand and dry thorn branches blew along the broad main street, clattering the loose shutters of the empty cafés where the rich European and American tourists and their shameless women had sat, watching the tall Tuareg pace to the mosque for an hour of evening prayer. The bank where Zayd's uncle had kept, against the advice of the family, some of the money he had earned with the goats . . . the bank was closed. Where, then, was his uncle? He looked back at where Zenoba and Ibrahim perched on the second camel. The boy, too, seemed a little stronger, though still weak. He needed medicine.

A couple of scabby pi-dogs scuffled through the dust; a very old woman, seated in a doorway chewing a pomegranate skin, watched them pass. There was a little flurry of activity on the far side of the main square, where the empty tourist hotel's smashed windows gaped to the sky. A small queue of very old people had formed, pressing eagerly forward to the back of a green truck painted with white letters: United Nations Famine Relief. In the back of the truck, dipping her ladle into a bucket of white grain porridge, a French girl wearing torn jeans was serving out food to those who held out their bowls. Zayd had eaten nothing since God had put the desert hare into the sights of his rifle the day before yesterday, deeming it better that Zenoba and the boys should take all its meat. But no Tuareg could take help from a woman. Nevertheless, they were hungry . . . He turned and called sharply to Zenoba. She slid from the camel, helping Ibrahim down.

"I will see to the boy," he said. "Take two bowls and get food."

She went over and stood in the queue. The girl began to argue when she held up two bowls, but Zenoba turned and pointed to where he stood with Ibrahim and Hamidine and Muhammed beside him. Comprehending, the girl nodded and smiled. Zayd turned his face away. It was shame to eat from such a source, but it was not such bad shame that death was preferable. Then a man, previously unseen, climbed down from the driving seat of the truck and walked over to them. He spoke in a mixture of very bad Tuareg and slow, careful French.

"You go north?"

"Why north? I have come to Tamanrasset."

The other laughed. "There is nothing here, not now. It's all different now. It is better in the north. They are having rain. That is where people are going. You should go north."

Zayd shrugged, though he was thinking hard. "If God wills."

The driver looked sharply at the small form of Ibrahim. "He looks hot; he has a fever?"

"He is sick," said Zayd.

The other went back to the truck and returned a few moments later with a small bottle of white tablets. "This is all we have," he said. "They are aspirin. You know what aspirin are?"

Zayd said nothing.

"They are . . . well, they will be some use, anyway," said the driver. "Give him one every three hours, for a day and a half. As you go north. You can get water for your camels behind the hotel. There is still a little."

"How far is north?" said Zayd.

The driver shrugged. "Three hundred miles, perhaps more," he said. My God, I'm talking to a dead man, he thought. They haven't got a chance of making it, not him, or the girl, or the children. But the driver had seen more than three hundred people die, around Tamanrasset, in the past weeks. Five more were just five more.

"Keep going," he said. "And good luck."

"As God wills," said Zayd.

CHAPTER 18

"It's like the edge of the world," said Stovin. Beside him, wedged in the warm cab of the Tatra truck, Volkov grunted, refolding the small road map he had taken from the side pocket of the truck. He seemed uneasy, a little lost.

"It *is* the edge of the world . . . of our Soviet world, at any rate," he said. "But we're getting nearer to Uelen. We've come a long way since Egvekinot."

Stovin nodded. Egvekinot, nearly 200 miles northeast of Anadyr, was where they had spent the night, in an empty village school, sleeping with their blankets made up on the bare wooden floor. And they had been alone there. Although the school had offered shelter, the Chukchi exodus—somewhat thinned out now from the numbers they had seen back in Anadyr—had streamed purposefully past it without stopping, travelling steadily on into the snowy night. Volkov had got their little party moving again as soon as possible in the morning, though the road north from Egvekinot—unmarked on any map Stovin had seen—was surprisingly good. There had been a couple of snowplows in the Chukchi exodus, which had helped a great deal. Nevertheless, the Tatra had many times passed ditched vehicles, some with fur-swathed figures standing beside them. For the most part, the roadsides were piled high with snow cleared by the plows, giving the eerie effect of driving down a long twilit tunnel. It was not totally dark because, although the low red sun had long ago slid below the horizon, the snow had stopped and the moon was up. The snow beside the road was banked too high for them to be able to see the moon itself. But the moonlight, filtering into the snow tunnel and reflecting on the piled whiteness, gave a ghostly light to which Stovin's eyes had quickly become accustomed. At least, thought Stovin, if the truck skidded off the road and they had to dismount, they were well equipped. Volkov had used the remnants of his authority at the maintenance store beside Anadyr airfield to get them Siberian gear—fur-lined and hooded parkas, and lined boots—of the type worn by airfield maintenance workers. He had contemptuously dismissed their American equipment. "The cold you will experience here," he said, "is nothing like a winter's day in New York. Those . . . garments . . . are useless." Stovin snuggled deeper into his parka. It itched a little at the neck, but it was comfortable.

Beside Volkov, the soldier—a stocky Chukchi with the usual black fringe of hair beneath his ear-flapped Army cap—sat at the wheel. He drove competently but said little. Bisby, before they started, had tried him with some words of St. Lawrence Island Eskimo, and he had

201

seemed to have at least a slight understanding. But Volkov had been uneasy and had asked Bisby to stop.

"I do not like your speaking to a Soviet soldier in a language I cannot understand," he said. "It is unsettling for him. He is a Chukchi and our escort. This is not a time to unsettle him."

Then he had spoken sharply to the Chukchi in Russian, and the soldier had replied, stumbling, in the same language. Although Bisby, when Volkov's back was turned, had tried him again in Eskimo, he had kept his broad face impassive and had turned quickly away as though not understanding. Not hard to see why Volkov was worried, decided Stovin. This was an unexpectedly excellent road—a military road. Only a real emergency had allowed Americans to see it.

Stovin peered through the misted windshield. Ahead of them was a reindeer sled containing a man and two women, and piled high with bundles. At the rear swung a lighted lantern—presumably acting as a rear light to warn traffic coming up behind. The two reindeer were harnessed as a pair, side by side, a strap around each neck and a leather thong passing under their bodies and tied to a bow-shaped piece of metal on the front of the sled. The sled was spanking along at about eight miles an hour, and it was several seconds before the big Tatra drew clear. Its occupants looked searchingly at the truck in the moonlight, and Stovin could see their broad faces, fringed by the fur of their hoods, quite clearly in the moonlight. They did not smile or wave.

Abruptly, as the Tatra pounded on, the snowbanks on either side of the road fell away, and they moved out onto the ridge of a broad escarpment. On each side in the light of the moon stretched a vast barren tundra. The chained tires drummed briefly on a wooden bridge. They were crossing a frozen river—not wholly frozen yet, for jagged leads of black water gleamed here and there amongst the snow-covered ice. Above them, dark freezing vapor swirled in blackish clouds. Volkov took the map from the car pocket again and studied it carefully, saying once more, "We are getting closer."

The landscape was now so infinitely desolate that it had acquired a strange lunar beauty, and Stovin hoped that Diane and Bisby and the Soldatovs, surrounded in the back of the Tatra with all the blankets and covers and fur-lined coats they had taken from the store cupboards

202

of the Anadyr Hotel, were awake and could see it. Below stretched the gleaming tussocky plain, broken at first, near the river, by countless channel ways, frozen hard. As they left the area of the Kamchalan, these features became fewer and finally petered out. All that broke the white wilderness ahead now was an occasional greyish-black line meandering through the snow, each marking one of many streams. The exodus from Anadyr, so thick and swollen when they left the little town, had now thinned out to no more than an occasional vehicle. They were now the only vehicle moving; the other three or four they passed were drawn up at the side of the white ridge, with tarpaulins or what seemed to be deerskins stretched beside them and fur-coated or anoraked figures moving dimly in the light of fires. Ahead, as they left the last of these, loomed a cone-shaped mountain—perhaps, Stovin estimated, 3,000 feet high, though it was hard to be sure in this light and in these conditions.

Volkov looked at his watch. "We are making good progress," he said. "We have no more than fifty miles to go. We shall have supper at Uelen; the Air Force will feed us."

In almost the same instant, it began to snow again. The moon vanished as though switched off, hidden by racing clouds of snow. The storm blew up astonishingly quickly and with ferocious intensity, scudding the snow from the road in long horizontal streaks, peppering the windshield like tracer bullets. Even above the roar of the engine, they could hear the hiss and the howl of the wind. The windscreen wipers were fighting a losing battle with the snow.

Beside Volkov, the Chukchi soldier took his hand from the wheel for a moment and jabbed it toward the swirling whiteness outside. His eyes rolled. *"Poorga,"* he said.

"What's that?" asked Stovin.

Volkov was peering anxiously through the windshield. *"Poorga* is a Siberian wind, I think. I have heard of it; it can blow for hours. But I do not know, Dr. Stovin. The Soviet Union is a big country; we have many time zones within our frontiers. I have never been in this tip of Siberia. I know no more of it than you. I would not have undertaken this journey if I had not known that the new road would take us all the way to Uelen. Even now, I am not sure I acted correctly. I may be rebuked by my superiors. But we could not remain where we were, in those

203

circumstances. And it is of the greatest importance that you and Dr. Soldatov arrive on time in Santa Fe."

"Yes," said Stovin. "That's important."

For a moment the Tatra's engine missed a beat . . . two . . . three . . . but picked up again just as the big truck began to falter to a halt. The Chukchi took a hand from the wheel again and made a despairing gesture, saying something inaudible above the hiss of the storm to Volkov.

"What is it?" said Stovin. He found that he had to shout.

"It's too cold," Volkov shouted back. "It's too cold for the engine. I see now why the others, the others on the road, had stopped. They knew."

The truck labored on, but already its chained wheels slid and slued on the road as the snow packed, froze, packed, and froze ahead of them. Stovin began to worry about Diane and the others, but it would have been madness to stop to see how they were managing. He shuffled around in his seat and peered through the plastic window in the rear of the cab. But it was misted on the other, inaccessible side, and he could make out no more than a blur of heavily wrapped forms, partly sitting, partly lying amongst a mass of blankets. He tapped on the plastic several times, but there was no answer.

Volkov gripped his arm, pointing through the blur of the windshield. "There is something . . . something. There. Do you see it?"

Stovin remembered later, ironically, that if ever there was a moment in his life that he could be said to have believed in the power or prayer, this was it. Unbelievably, hard beside the road, a light gleamed . . . and behind it the dark bulk loomed of some single-story structure. It was hard to distinguish its outlines in the driving snow, but it looked like a house. With a surprised grunt, the Chukchi wrenched the wheel. For a moment, the truck slid over the snow, sideways, as though it were flying. There was a splintering crash on the off side, and Stovin saw a length of snow-covered fencing, with a post hanging from its end, rear into the air. Canted to one side, the Tatra came to a halt. Obeying a long-learned drill, the soldier seized his automatic rifle from the clip beside the door and jumped down from the truck, while Volkov and Stovin scrambled out of the other side. The roar and hiss of the blizzard were like the sound of water pouring into a furnace.

"Quick," Stovin bellowed above the din. "The others . . ."

Bisby and Soldatov, unrecognizable in their bulky fur-lined coats, were already at the tailboard of the truck, and the two women jumped one by one. Valentina pitched forward as she fell, but she put out her gloved hands and vanished, up to her neck, in a bank of snow. Soldatov turned with a cry that sounded thin and lost above the noise of the storm and pulled her out. The soldier had already reached the hut. For a moment the door opened, and a flood of lamplight shone out into the scudding snow. One by one, gasping, they tumbled through the door, landing in a heap inside. The Chukchi pulled in Volkov, who was the last to get through the doorway, and together they put their shoulders against the door and forced it closed against the power of the wind. Three simple wooden batten bolts secured it. Magically, the howling of the *poorga* stopped, although its muted, suppressed roar still sounded through the wooden walls, and its strength occasionally shook the structure of the hut itself. His breath rasping in his throat and his chest heaving, Stovin looked about him. It was a totally unexpected sight.

He was standing in a fair-sized, square room with three doors at the farther end. The room was lighted by three powerful oil lamps and heated by a large iron stove at its center. A few skins, mostly, as far as he could see, of white Arctic hare and an occasional fox, were pinned around the walls. Near the stove was a round wooden table with a wooden chair drawn up on each side. The table was set for a meal: knife, fork, spoon beside each of two plates. The plates bore a meal, still steaming. Bisby was already standing beside one of them. Stovin watched as he put down a finger and touched a strip of meat.

"Still hot," he said. "Looks like moose—elk, they call it here. And turnips."

One by one, Volkov opened the doors at the end of the room. One led into a small cell-like pantry in which hung the skinned bodies, still apparently fresh, of two hares. A large joint of dark-colored meat was spitted on a hook on the opposite wall. One or two cans and jars stood on the shelves. The other door led into a slightly larger kitchen, with a china sink and a large pitcher of water standing beside it. A rush mat was on the floor, and a row of knives and kitchen implements hung on a rack above the sink. There was no sign that anybody other than they themselves was in the hut. Volkov opened the last door, gave a sharp exclamation, and quickly shut it behind him. After a second or two, the door reopened and he appeared in the doorway, beckoning to Bisby and Stovin. They walked across the room toward him, but when Valentina followed, Volkov held up his hand.

"Please wait," he said, "it is better . . ."

He turned and pointed, so that his back blocked the doorway to the Russian girl but allowed the two men to see. They peered past him. The room was a bedroom, with a large old-fashioned double bed in the center and a small table with a photograph and a telephone at its side. Half on the bed, but with its head and shoulders drooping down to the cheap red carpet on the bedroom floor, sprawled the body of a man. His head, lolling, looked up at them from this grotesque upside-down position. His hair, black and greasy, lay lank into a pool of blood.

Only Bisby moved. He knelt beside the body and gently dipped a forefinger into the blood. "His throat's been cut," he said, "and not very long ago, maybe only three or four minutes ago. His blood's still quite warm."

Suddenly, the Chukchi soldier was standing beside Bisby, looking down at the dead man, his face expressionless. After a few moments he, too, knelt down and drew back the blood-stained sleeve of the man's arm. A cheap-looking wristwatch gleamed on the dead wrist. Carefully, the Chukchi unfastened it and put it into his uniform pocket. Volkov watched him, silent. No one said anything. There was a gasp from the door where Valentina and Diane had pushed in to see what had happened. Volkov turned, waited until all, including the soldier, had left the bedroom and then came out himself, closing the door behind him.

"But who killed him?" said Valentina, half weeping.

"We cannot know," said Volkov heavily. "This is a strange land, a strange people. You have seen. And strange things are happening. We cannot know."

"But . . . you mean, they're fighting amongst themselves now?" said Diane. "Killing each other?"

"Not each other," said Bisby swiftly. "Killing, yes. But not each other."

He turned to Stovin. "You saw that man's face, Sto.

That wasn't a Chukchi face, or even an Eskimo, or a Yakut. That was a Russian face. I'll lay that guy wasn't born very far from Moscow. And he had a telephone. Not many Chukchi with a telephone."

Stovin pointed to the far wall, where a large-scale map was pinned between two hare skins.

"He had a map, too."

Volkov walked over and looked at it. When he turned back to them, some of the puzzlement had gone from his face.

"Of course," he said. "This is a road overseer's hut. We keep them, on new highways, every hundred miles or so. It will have been his duty to look after the new road. So he might well be, as you say, Russian. It is mostly Russians who can be relied on for such duties."

"Then why . . ." whispered Valentina.

Bisby gave a short, grunting laugh. "Not hard to see why," he said. "The Chukchi are on the move. I guess Russians with telephones—any kind of Russian, for that matter—aren't exactly popular. Whoever did it . . . well, it must have been happening almost as we got here. And whoever killed him saw the truck stop, and then our soldier friend here"—he pointed to the Chukchi who was watching them impassively—"got out with a rifle. So *they* got out, quickly. Didn't wait to find out whether it was friend or foe."

"Got out?" said Volkov unbelievingly. "In that storm?"

"The people who killed him," said Bisby, "were very probably Chukchi. They'd have something outside, a sled maybe. A Chukchi can move in a storm where a Russian would die. But there's something else strange about this whole setup."

Diane, feeling weak and sick, had sat down on one of the wooden chairs beside the table. Bisby walked over and pointed at the plate and knife and fork beside her.

"Haven't you noticed?" he said. "The table's set for two."

Volkov looked at him for a moment and then walked determinedly back into the death room. After a second of hesitation, Stovin followed him. The Russian was down on his knees beside the body, lifting the heavy, old-fashioned bed coverlet which stretched almost to the rush matting on the floor.

"It seemed to me," said the Russian, over his shoulder,

"that there just might be someone . . . but no, there is nothing."

He got to his feet again beside the body. "I think it better to leave him here. The authorities may wish to see him exactly as he is."

Bisby's voice came from the doorway. "What authorities, Volkov? There are no authorities."

Volkov frowned. "Of course there are authorities. They must be told."

"Try the telephone," said Bisby. He seems almost to be enjoying the situation, thought Stovin, surprised. Volkov picked it up, listened experimentally, then placed it back on its rest.

"Dead," he said. "The lines . . . probably blown down in this storm."

"Or cut," said Bisby.

With a conscious effort, Stovin had turned back the coverlet beside the body. He pointed now to what lay there, neatly folded: a man's thick flannel nightgown and a slightly thinner one with pink rose embroidery at its neck.

"So the second person—the missing one—is a woman," said Volkov. He went across to the little table and opened a drawer. A few printed papers fell out, among them two fairly old photographs. One showed an old couple, probably man and wife. The other was clearly of the man on the bed. Beside him stood a youngish woman, smiling into the sun, her dark hair braided above her head.

"His wife, I guess," said Bisby, looking over Volkov's shoulder. "And she wasn't a Chukchi. That's a European face."

"Then," said Volkov, "where . . ."

For the first time, there was the faintest hint of concern in Bisby's voice. "I think it's all over for her, Grigori," he said. The Russian looked up sharply, obviously surprised by the use of his given name.

"Either," said Bisby, "she ran out into the storm when . . . whoever it was came and killed her husband. Or, more likely, they took her with them. Either way, her chances are pretty small."

The Chukchi pushed past Bisby in the doorway and came back into the room. This time he ignored the body but went carefully through the oddments of clothing in the table drawer, taking out some socks and stuffing them into his tunic pocket. The nightgowns on the bed caught his eye, and he picked them up. The man's he threw contemptuously into a corner, but he turned the woman's over and over, fingering it interestedly. At last he folded it and pushed it into his open tunic. Then, without speaking, he went back into the main room where Diane and the Soldatovs were waiting. Volkov, who had watched him silently, carefully, then beckoned to the two Americans. They followed him out and he shut the bedroom door, this time sliding its single wooden batten into place. The Chukchi—Diane, staring at him uneasily, thought he was beginning to look less and less like the smart Soviet soldier who had guarded their truck, it seemed an age ago in Anadyr—was seated at the table, busy devouring both the meals from the plates. Grease from the moose meat ran down his chin, and he grunted a little as he ate. His automatic rifle, within easy reach of his right hand, leaned against the tabletop.

It was, unexpectedly, Valentina Soldatova who broke the silence. "We, too, must eat," she said. "There is food there." She walked over to the little pantry and took out the large joint of cold dark cooked meat from the spit. In the cupboard below were two long loaves of coarse grainy bread with bags of flour. Valentina pinched the bread experimentally.

"This is new," she said. "Whoever she was—is, perhaps—she baked her own."

"What did you think she'd do, out here?" asked Bisby. "She can't trot around to the nearest shop."

In the same instant, he swung around and, with deceptive casualness, stretched out his hand toward the rifle as though he were going to move it so that he could sit down in the other chair. The Chukchi's right hand moved so swiftly that it seemed to the watching Stovin as though it had been on the rifle from the beginning. The muzzle came up, pointing at Bisby's stomach. The Chukchi said something, fast, guttural. Bisby listened carefully and replied with a couple of equally unintelligible words. Slowly the Chukchi lowered the muzzle and then cradled the rifle in his lap.

"What did he say?" asked Soldatov. His face was pale. Bisby shrugged. "Chukchi talk isn't Eskimo talk, not by a long way, though some of it's very similar. I think he told me to be careful. I told him I was his friend."

"And are you?" said Stovin. It seemed a strange question.

"He can't make me out," said Bisby. "I think that's

209

what bugs him. Trouble is, from his point of view I don't look like anything he's ever seen before. I look a bit Eskimo. At least, he thinks he knows. And that may be a useful mistake from our point of view."

"Why?" asked Diane.

Bisby seemed suddenly to tire of the subject and began to pile plates on the table, ready for food.

"Well, Chukchis don't much like Europeans, as you can see. But they hate Eskimos. They hate them most of all. At least, they always did . . . Maybe that'll change. But I doubt it."

A reaction, compounded of physical weariness and mental bewilderment and exhaustion, was now beginning to set in for all of them. The Chukchi, clutching his rifle, now sprawled on a reindeer skin rug beside the stove. The others sat or stood at the table, eating bread and the cold meat sliced up by Valentina with the butcher's knife from the kitchen. Afterward as unobtrusively as possible, the three men looked around the cabin for the hunting rifle which Volkov thought the dead man would be sure to have possessed—"both recreation and income in this wilderness," he said. But there was no sign of it. Whoever had killed the man next door had presumably taken it away.

The cabin was warm. There was a pile of cut wood beside the stove. Stovin picked up a log and looked at it critically. Small gleaming particles were embedded in its silvery bark. He moistened a finger and rubbed it on the wood and then touched his lips. Salt . . . this was driftwood. Plenty on this coast, no doubt, and the sea wasn't far away. The Ob and the Yenisei and even the Canadian Mackenzie fed enormous quantities of continental forests into the Polar seas. This wood might have travelled a couple of thousand miles, down from the East Siberian Sea or the Beaufort Sea, through some crosscurrent in the Bering Straits in the summer, into the Bering Sea, and finally into the great Bay of Anadyr.

There were blankets in the truck, but the storm was raging with undiminished intensity outside, shaking the wooden structure of the cabin, while an occasional cross gust blew wood smoke back down its narrow chimney pipe and back into the room. It would have been too dangerous to attempt to go even twenty yards to the Tatra in such conditions. By tacit consent, too, they ignored the fact that next door the bed was piled with coverings.

They arranged themselves on the floor, the Soldatovs using the deerskin mat as a covering, and Stovin and Diane the rough red blanket which had served the previous owners as a tablecloth.

Diane pushed herself up against his body, so that the softness of her fair hair felt agreeable against his cheek. He looked across the room and saw Valentina Soldatova watching them, smiling, for the first time that night. She said something quietly to Soldatov, who raised his head above the deerskin and looked at them. A broad smile spread over his face, and he took his hand from under the skin, making the thumbs-up sign. Slightly embarrassed, Stovin smiled back. Volkov, who had spread his fur anorak beside Bisby's near the stove, walked over to where they lay and stood above them. Covertly he nodded toward the Chukchi, who was sitting on the other side of the stove, leaning against the table, apparently three-quarters asleep.

"I think," said Volkov, "that we should leave the lamps burning. And that one of us four men should remain awake. If it suits you, I will take the first watch. I will wake you, Dr. Stovin, after two hours, and after two more hours you can wake Dr. Soldatov. And then he can wake Paul Bisby. I think this may be safer."

"I agree," said Stovin. "That suits . . ."

At that moment, the Chukchi struggled to his feet. Without a word, he went over to the bedroom, lifted the wooden batten, and went inside, staggering out a few seconds later with the dead man across his shoulders. He nodded fiercely toward the outer door. Bisby, watching him closely, saw that he had kept his rifle slung at his right shoulder so that he could instantly have dropped the dead man and covered them from the hip. Slowly Bisby walked over to the outer door, lifted the three wooden bolt battens, and opened it. A howling maelstrom of snow and icy air swept for a moment into the room. The Chukchi moved to the door and, with a grunting cry, pitched the body outside. Bisby helped him once more to close and bolt the door. The Chukchi nodded toward the bedroom as though asking a question. Bisby shook his head. The Chukchi shrugged contemptuously and went into the bedroom, taking the rifle with him and closing the door. Almost immediately, they heard the bed creak, and within a few seconds a steady, rhythmic snoring began. Like a ghost, Volkov glided across the floor and secured the outer batten.

"I think perhaps, we can all sleep. It would be impossible to get out of there quietly. Goodnight."

For Diane, her cheek warm against Stovin's woollen sweater, it was a strange, disturbed night. Stovin himself slept fairly easily. His left hand moved to her face as he slept and tangled with her hair. For more than an hour she lay awake, listening as the fury of the storm made the wooden building creak with its pressure. Occasionally too, there seemed to be other, new sounds—a banging and thumping at the far wall and, once, a deep muffled bellowing. Was it the wind? For a moment she thought of waking Stovin, but he was sleeping well, and it seemed foolish.

Better sleep while they could. It was a whole new world outside with everything up for grabs. Including maybe me, she thought. She had seen the Chukchi look at her covertly once yesterday. Again she shivered. What's happening to us all, she thought, drifting slowly into something approximating sleep.

"Have you seen this garbage?" said Richie McPhee, standing on the verandah. He passed a can of cold beer to the tall, grey-haired man who sat beside him on a wicker chair, and tapped a blue-covered document. The house seemed slowly to be cooking on its wooden stilts in the fierce heat of the January sun, burning down from the baked azure of the western Australian summer sky.

"You mean the Perth Warning?" said the other slowly. "Yes. I've seen it."

"I reckon it's about overdue for some of the weary Willies in Perth to get off their arses and come and find out what cattle farming's all about," said McPhee. "Do you think they've even heard about Camballin? That we've moved the bloody Fitzroy River and watered 8,000 bloody acres? We aren't going to get the Kimberley cattle wiped out, not while the Fitzroy's still there."

He picked up the blue-covered document and read aloud, sarcastically:

"Listen to this garbage, Denis: 'The decline in rainfall across Australia could in general be 50 percent, with pockets of wetter conditions. In western Australia, conditions at present marginally suitable for sheep and cattle

212

farming will dry out to become totally unsuitable, at least for present breeds. The most optimistic forecast that can be made is that annual precipitation will certainly be at least 30 percent less than today. This change is likely to take place within a five-year time span.' Why the hell do they talk about 'precipitation,' Denis? What's wrong with calling it rain?"

"That's how they talk," said the other briefly. "I dunno, Richie . . . they could be right. We've had damn-all rain this year—worst I can remember. We lost some head, on the south edge of the Kimberley. We turned in around a thousand head—hell of a lot of 'em cleanskins, wild, unbranded, off the station. That's not a high total for 1,400 square miles. And they were around 500 pounds and didn't fatten up to more than 900 in the feedlot. Not much in that. It's been a damn-awful year, and it won't be better next."

"Aaah, it's always the worst year ever in the Kimberley," said McPhee. He picked up the empty beer can and hurled it at a green-crested pigeon that was foraging in the dust around the stilts.

"Look at that damn bird," he said. "You'd think it was a household pet."

"It's thirsty," said the other.

"Then it should fly down to the Fitzroy," said McPhee. "Lovely country down there now, cattle or pigeons. Ever since we moved the river. Who'd ever have thought we'd raise cattle along the Great Sandy, eh? There'll always be water down there, Denis."

"You see they're forecasting snow in the southeast, a real freeze-up?" said the other. "Seems they're havin' to pull out of all the Antarctic bases. A real Ice Age, they say."

McPhee laughed. "The character who wrote this garbage ought to come down here to Olive Station and see what an Ice Age's like," he said.

"Seems that's what it *is* like," said Denis. "Cold for some, drier for others. Too bloody dry."

"There'll always be water on Olive," said McPhee. "As long as we've got the Fitzroy River. And what's goin' to stop the Fitzroy? Tell me that, Denis."

The other tapped the blue-backed report.

"Maybe some Willie in Perth just has, Richie," he said.

The great Indian rhinoceros thrust his prehistoric, armor plated head out of the almost impenetrable wall of twenty-foot-high *saccharum* grass. His little nearsighted eyes rested incuriously on the sandy stretch of river flats ahead of him. He was almost the last of his line: no more than 900 of his species still dwelt in the whole vast Indian subcontinent, and none elsewhere. But now he had no potential enemy except man, and he had learned that even man, though sometimes an irritation with his elephants and his cameras, was no longer a danger in the Chitawan reserve.

The rhinoceros was uncomfortable. In these January days in Nepal, he liked to find the deep muddy water-holes where he could wallow in the Chitawan streams, filled by rains that always averaged nearly 100 inches a year. Hole after hole, he had found, was dry. Emerging finally from the grass jungle, he trotted down to the river-bank, followed by two cow rhinos and a small calf. The river was an inadequate trickle. He lifted his great horned head once more and grunted in anger. Then he crossed the line of the river and followed by the other three, lumbered slowly down the smooth yellowish sward in front of him. In the little grass-roofed hut at the end of the Chitawan airstrip, the man who blew the horn to scare off the grazing buffalo, when the plane from Katmandu came in to land, watched in awe-struck astonishment. The four rhino had long disappeared down the valley when the Chitawan Land Rover arrived in a flurry of dust, ready to meet the plane.

"I have not seen such a thing before," said the man with the horn to the ex-Gurkha soldier who drove the Land Rover. "I have never seen them go down the valley. They will soon be in the village. The rhino will be killed."

The Gurkha had soldiered the world from Aldershot to Adelaide, and he had little time for peasants, even the sophisticated kind who worked on airstrips.

"That is strictly forbidden," he said coldly.

"But this has never happened before," said the peasant.

CHAPTER 19

Stovin woke first, struggling in those early moments to re-member where he was, and then flooded by a feeling of wild unease. Something seemed to be missing, and for a few seconds he lay still, wondering what it was. Then he realized. The hut no longer creaked and groaned. The storm was gone. Gently he moved Diane's head from his stiff shoulder. She moved convulsively, murmuring some-thing in her sleep. He lowered her head onto a fold of her rolled anorak and got clumsily to his feet. He felt constrained, uncomfortable, and old. In the far bedroom, the Chukchi could be heard, breathing loudly and grunt-ing in his sleep. Volkov lay face downward by the stove. Beside him sat Bisby, whose eyes were now open. He smiled slowly at Stovin but said nothing. The Soldatovs, lying in each other's arms, were still asleep. The room was cool. He crossed to the stove, turned up the draught inlet, and dropped in two more logs. Then he crossed to the door, lifted the wooden bolts, and pushed it open, staring out into a wilderness of white as the piercingly cold air rushed in. Luckily the door had been on the wind-ward side of the hut, so that the force of the *poorga* had piled comparatively little snow in front of it. It was still as dark as night outside. He looked at his wristwatch and found that it was nearly eight o'clock in the morning. The dead man beside the door was no more than a huddle of snow. A white bulk against the line of the road, still faintly visible, lay the big Tatra truck, slued half on its side. It was buried in snow, and in any case, its engine would now be frozen solid. There would be no way out in the Tatra. The fence through which they had crashed reared grotesquely into the air, mantled in snow and pointing like white fingers toward the sky. The unbroken part of this fence surrounded the hut in a rough rectangle. Beside the house was another, cruder wooden building, roofed but with no chimney pipe above it. Below that

215

was a small cell-like structure, not much bigger than an old-fashioned sentry box. The lavatory, I imagine, he thought. An outside lavatory, in this weather.

It was so cold outside that every breath he took seemed to burn his lungs until, after a minute or two, his body temperature began to adjust. When he had finished in the sentry box, he came out to find Bisby waiting outside. The young American frowned at him, watching him zip up his trousers.

"Never do that, Sto. Never take a chance like that in this weather. Only expose yourself where you've got some kind of shelter, even if you have to make it yourself. Just one last touch of that *poorga* across this corral, and you'll be missing something you value. So you watch it."

"What did you say . . . . corral?"

"Yes," said Bisby. "Wait till I've finished. I'll show you."

When Bisby came out, they walked over to the second structure adjoining the house. Bisby pulled open one of the stout wooden shutters, and they peered in. There was a clumping and snorting and a rank gamy smell. The shed, for it was little more, seemed to contain animals, though in the darkness it was difficult to see what they were.

"See those lovelies," said Bisby. "Best thing I've seen for a long time."

He saw Stovin's uncomprehending face, and laughed. "Reindeer, Sto. Four of them. We should have guessed. I thought I heard them thumping about, next to the outer wall, last night. And I guess they're harness reindeer, too. If they were meat reindeer, they'd be out in the country, taking their chance. But these'll be smaller, trained. They'll have dried moss in there. You'd never get a meat reindeer to eat that."

Together they went back into the main cabin where the others were now stirring.

"You mean, *we* could eat them?" said Stovin slowly. He realized the stupidity of the question as soon as it was out of his mouth.

"Eat them hell," said Bisby. "Sto, they're transport. There'll be sledges in there or somewhere around the building. Bound to be. I reckon they're a lot more reliable than automobile transport up here, and there's a lot more moss for fuel than there are gas stations. That dead man out there, he used them. That's how he got around his piece of the road."

"But can we use them? We don't know anything about reindeer."

"I do," said Bisby promptly. "Mind, it's been a long time. But the United States Government brought them in to St. Lawrence Island twenty years ago, after they tried to stop the Eskimo taking a fair share of the whales."

He laughed bitterly. "Government wanted to try them for meat, as a substitute for the whales, you see. Big herd, 8,000 head, maybe more. They didn't take too well. Funny creatures, reindeer. They'll eat only one moss, and it seems like it has to be their home moss. But my father . . . well, he was keen to try them for the sleds, instead of dogs. He bought some and tried them out on Ihovak for years, before . . . well, he taught me and some of my cousins. I know a bit about reindeer."

Volkov came over to them, rubbing his eyes, and Stovin went across to where Diane was now sitting where she had slept.

"My God, Sto, I could do with a bath," she said, tousling her hair. "Are there any . . . you know, facilities?"

He jerked his finger out of the door. "Out there," he said.

"You're joking?"

"No, that's where you have to go. And Diane . . . be careful. It's really, really cold, like you've never known before. Put everything on before you go out."

She hesitated. "That man . . . is he still . . . ? What a damned fool I am. Obviously he is."

"Yes," said Stovin. "He's still there. But he's covered in snow. You can't see him."

One by one, Diane and the Soldatovs went outside. Volkov, who had already been, called a conference as soon as they got back, while Valentina cut up more bread and meat. She had found some tea in a cupboard, and a pot was boiling on the stove.

"I think," said Volkov, "that there is only one thing to do. My friend here"—he nodded toward Bisby—"says there are reindeer in the shed. There will certainly be sledges there, in that case. We must use them to get to Uelen. Paul"—it was the first time he had used Bisby's first name—"believes that he can handle one sled. But there are five of us, and we shall need two."

"Six of us, if you count the soldier," said Soldatov quietly.

"We can't count the Chukchi," said Bisby. His voice was brusque. "He won't be staying with us. He'll be away to join the other Chukchi first chance he gets. And that's one reason we should move as soon as possible, taking all four reindeer and two sleds. It will be dangerous to stay."

"Why?" said Soldatov. "If we stay, there is certain to be transport up this road within a day or two. We have a little food. We can hold out."

Volkov began to speak, but Bisby interrupted him. "The Chukchi won't stay," he said again. "He'll be off, the moment he's out of that door."

He nodded toward the bedroom. "And he'll bring back his friends. There are things . . . people . . . here that they might want. I'm not trying to be scary, but I'm looking at you, Diane, and you, Valentina."

Valentina grasped her husband's arm. Soldatov spoke angrily. "What do you mean? He is a Soviet soldier."

"Geny," said Bisby. "He's not a Soviet soldier any more. He's a reindeer Chukchi—one of the fiercest, cruellest fighters in the Arctic. It took you Russians a hundred years to hold down the Chukchi—you didn't manage to do it until forty years ago. And this particular reindeer Chukchi is in possession of an automatic rifle, which is more than most of them have, thank God. But he'll be back with his friends today, tomorrow at the latest. That's why we've got to get out now. We'll have one further advantage with the reindeer and the sleds."

"What's that?" asked Stovin. He felt bewildered but Volkov was nodding slowly as though knowing in advance what Bisby would say.

"With the reindeer, and all muffled up, we shall look like Chukchi. They won't think we're Eskimos because nearly all Eskimos use dogs. And that's good because I reckon they'll be hunting Eskimos. The question now is, Who can handle the second sled?"

He looked around the group thoughtfully. Volkov spoke first. "I will try," he said, smiling. "A Foreign Ministry man can do anything."

Bisby shook his head. "I think not, Grigori. It needs sensitive hands—I think one of the women. You, Valentina. You understand animals."

"Why not me?" said Diane. "I understand animals, too." She felt vaguely annoyed at being passed over, although she did not relish the thought of driving reindeer.

"No," said Bisby again. "Valentina understands animals right here." He patted his stomach. "But you . . . with you, Diane, it's mostly in the head."

He turned to Volkov. "How far do you reckon to this place—Uelen?"

"About forty-five miles."

"Good. Now listen. A reindeer pair with a sled behind can make about six or seven miles an hour on a fair surface, maybe a bit more where it's really smooth, like a road. But they have to stop, much more often than horses. Every two hours, say. They need rest and they need moss. If they can find any. That snow may be too deep."

There was a sound of movement from the bedroom and a deep belch from the Chukchi. They heard him get to his feet and push at the door. He called out to them, sharply thumping on the wood.

"We could leave him there," whispered Diane. "The door's bolted."

Bisby shook his head. "Not a chance. He's got that rifle in there. First thing he'd do would be to start banging away to try to blow the bolt off. And it wouldn't be good to be in here while he was doing it. No, he'd better come out where we can see him."

He crossed to the door and lifted the wooden batten. The Chukchi shambled out, looking at them suspiciously. The transformation in him was increasingly disturbing. Two days ago, even the previous morning, he had been a smart Soviet infantryman in clean uniform, shaved and washed. Today he had a day's growth of beard. His tunic was stained with grease from his supper. He looked unkempt, wild. He crossed to the table, tore a piece of meat from the elk joint, and crammed it into his mouth. There was a thump as one of the reindeer next door backed momentarily against the dividing wall, but the Chukchi, eating greedily, seemed not to have heard it. After he had finished, he looked at them all, loweringly, and went to the door, his rifle slung over his left arm. He pushed it open and stood in the entrance, giving a strange guttural cry. From somewhere out beyond the road, a smiliar cry sounded, thin, reedy, but no more than a quarter of a mile away. The Chukchi kicked idly at the body of the dead man where it lay mantled in snow. The others watched him, silent, fascinated. There was a flurry of snow up on the road. When it cleared, they saw that a sled drawn by two reindeer stood there. Three Chukchi, dressed in heavy furs, climbed down and came over to where the Chukchi soldier stood. They talked quickly in heavy guttural tones for a few moments, and one of them laughed loudly and clapped him on the shoulder. Grinning, he turned back into the house where the Americans and Russians were waiting. He looked at them impassively as though making a choice. Finally he jerked his thumb at Valentina, loosening the rifle on his shoulder. He said a single guttural word to her and again jerked his thumb at the door. She shrank back beside a white-faced Soldatov. With an impatient grunt, the Chukchi moved his rifle, one-handed, into a competent covering arc, reached out, and grabbed her by the hair. She screamed. The Chukchi half laughed, half snarled, and began to pull her to the door, holding the rifle pointing outward toward the others, waist high. Hopelessly, Soldatov began to move forward. But Bisby was quicker. Diane, watching in chilled horror as Valentina was dragged to the door, remembered later that no one had even seen Bisby move. Somehow, suddenly he was at the soldier's side. The point of the razor-sharp meat knife, with which Valentina had carved the elk joint, was pressed to the Chukchi's throat so firmly that a little blood from the broken skin began to trickle down his neck onto his tunic collar. The Chukchi's eyes rolled. Bisby pressed the point in a little more, and the Chukchi released his hold on Valentina's hair. She stumbled back into the room.

Bisby was now standing with his body hard against the Chukchi, almost as though they were dancing. His knife remained pressed against the Chukchi's throat. Although the Chukchi still held the rifle behind Bisby's back, there was no way he could slide his hand down to the trigger without Bisby's knowing.

Bisby spoke, "Take it, Sto. And when I step back, give it straight to me."

Stovin pulled the rifle from the Chukchi's hand. In the same instant, Bisby gave the soldier a violent push and took the rifle from Stovin. He stood back, the muzzle pointed at the Chukchi's stomach. The three Chukchi in the morning darkness outside the door watched silently, making no move. Bisby pointed up to the reindeer sled and said a single word. Slowly, looking back from time to time, the four Chukchi floundered through the snow toward it. Halfway there they began a violent discussion, and the soldier and one of the others turned back toward the house. Instantly there was a tearing crack from the rifle and snow spurted up at the soldier's feet. All four turned and half ran, half scrambled back to the sled, moving off a few seconds later in a hanging trail of driven snow. Bisby smiled and patted the rifle affectionately.

"Useful, this," he said. "I was hoping he'd get a rush of blood to the head."

Volkov stretched out a hand. "I think perhaps I . . . well, that is Soviet equipment."

Bisby looked at him. His voice was expressionless. "No, Grigori. I got it, so I'll keep it. For the moment."

Valentina, palefaced and tearstained, put a hand on his shoulder, reached up, and kissed his cheek. He was smiling now, and the tension relaxed.

"I'll do it again if you go on like that," he said. "Any time . . ."

They all laughed shakily, including Volkov. But Stovin noticed that Bisby kept a firm hand on the rifle. And that Volkov was watching him.

CHAPTER 20

Volkov watched the preparations for departure with a mounting sense of unreality. He had been able to suppress his doubts and fears, both from the others and himself, as long as he remained in charge of the group. But that situation had now changed. In effect, the leadership had suddenly passed to Bisby because it was apparent to all of them that only Bisby had any grasp of the nature of the world into which they were now moving. Not one of the others understood Bisby. And now he, Volkov, found that he felt isolated, alone, among Americans. True, he reminded himself, the Soldatovs were also Soviet citizens. But Soldatov, though undoubtedly of high intelligence in his field, seemed in other respects to be naive. And Valentina Soldatova was . . . well, his wife. For the first time in his life, Volkov was out of contact with superior authority. He knew that whatever he did would be likely to be blamed. Nevertheless, his task remained. He had to get the Stovin party to the United States, and he must do so without risking their lives any more than was absolutely necessary. This extraordinary Chukchi revolt, which certainly should not be witnessed by Americans, had not been—*could* not have been—envisaged by his superiors in Moscow, any more than the emergency that had forced him and his party to land at Anadyr. I have to act within the possibilities open to me, he thought. My job is to get them there somehow.

Bisby was checking the sleds. He had found three, propped against the walls of the reindeer shed. They were almost identical, but he chose the two that seemed in the best condition. Each sled was about fourteen feet long and a little more than three feet wide. The floor of the sled was raised on a wooden framework linking its steel runners, roughly a foot above the snow. The whole structure was surrounded by a rail a few inches high with, in front of it, a stout wooden bow to which the harness was attached. Carefully, methodically, Bisby was checking the runners for cracks or distortion. Satisfied, he went back into the main cabin. There Valentina, wrinkling her nose, had boiled a big iron saucepan full of the hard-frozen mud from a pile in the reindeer shed. Grinning at her distaste, he took it out to the sleds and began to smear it, wrapping his hands in cloths so that they should never touch the bare cold metal on the runners. He looked up and met her eye as she watched him curiously.

"This'll make it a lot easier for us to drive," he said. "Steel isn't the best stuff for runners—whalebone or white birchwood are better—but steel wears harder. Trouble is, it collects snow, and the snow gets frozen." He finished smearing the mud, and she brought him what he asked for—a thick cloth soaked in hot water. Quickly he ran it up and down the runners. The water froze onto the already frozen mud almost as soon as it touched, leaving a surface of smooth ice. Bisby pulled out one sled onto a level stretch of packed snow and gave it a light tap with the palm of his gloved hand. It glided away effortlessly, almost as though it were flying. He nodded, satisfied, and began to repeat the process with the second sled.

"Where did you learn that?" asked Stovin.

Bisby's voice was vague, slightly remote, as it always seemed to be when he was asked about his Eskimo days. "Oh, Ihovak, in the old time," he said. "You can't rely on steel runners when it's really cold. But I guess that poor guy was no Eskimo. He trusted in steel."

When he went to the shed to lead out the reindeer,

Bisby looked at them critically. Two were youngish beasts —one, especially, being half sullen, half refractory, kicking up its heels when harnessed with the sealskin strap, which passed around its neck and between its legs, before being secured to the wooden bow at the front of the sled. The other two were older and more docile—a better pair for Valentina. He harnessed them carefully to the smaller sled, double-checking the lashings at their shoulders. Then he called Valentina over and began to explain.

"Let them go at their own pace unless they slow down too much. They look as though they're pretty used to harness, and they'll know what they can do. The real important thing is to stop as often as possible, because they're animals that have to eat. But I'll be leading, in the first sled, so I'll do the timing. We'll take all the dried moss with us; it's probably enough. The snow out there" —he pointed out into the undulating white wilderness beyond the immediate ridge of the road—"looks pretty deep to me. So they may not be able to get their mouths down to the moss on the rocks if it's frozen too hard."

He looked at the sky, and shrugged. "What's more, it looks like more snow. That'll make it hard to travel, but it may at least keep the Chukchi off our backs. We'd better move as soon as we're packed up."

The packing and loading of the sleds took nearly an hour. It was done by Bisby and the women. Stovin, determined to play his part, had led the other two men to the ridge of the road where, spaced out, they could watch for Chukchi. It was intensely cold, and each of them was wrapped so comprehensively that barely their eyes, with the lashes already uncomfortably frost fringed, showed in their head coverings. Crouched on the rim of the road and looking out across the grey-white featureless snowplain bounded on each side by a low but bulky mountain range—the ridge of the Chukotskiy Kherbet to the north and the line of hills of the Chukotskiy Peninsula to the south, according to Soldatov—Stovin peered through the star whispers of his exhaled breath. Nothing moved in that empty landscape. Behind him the line of the road, now deep in snow and unswept for vehicles, wound down into a shallow valley. It was distinguishable only because the new snow on it lay whiter than the same snow on the land on each side. Wherever the four Chukchi had moved earlier that day, they'd gone now. Almost in the same instant, he saw a black speck far in the distance. The uniform, washed-out grey-white of the landscape made it impossible to judge range, but he estimated as best he could that the black speck was about three-quarters of a mile away, to the east. The daylight—if you could call it that in January only a hundred miles south of the Arctic Circle, he thought—was now at its low maximum for the day—a sort of super twilight, like the glimmering menace of a sky that in Europe or America might precede a storm. He watched carefully for a moment, and then called to Volkov who was stationed about 200 yards to his left. The Russian scrambled up beside him a minute or so later, puffing a little with the effort so that he was surrounded by a cloud of tiny snow crystals. His voice was muffled—"Talk down into your furs," Bisby had warned them, "and don't pull back those hoods unless you want to lose a lip, or your nose. You can get a frozen face in a couple of minutes if the wind's right, but it takes a hell of a time longer to unfreeze it, and bits of it may come off when you do."

Putting his head close to Volkov's furs, Stovin raised his voice and pointed. "Over there . . . just about two o'clock of that hummocky ridge. Can you see it? . . . there's something . . ."

Volkov screwed up his eyes. It took him a few seconds to pick up the black mark on the snow, and then he nodded vigorously. A few moments later he began to pick his way down the slope, back toward Bisby. Stovin stayed where he was. Ostensibly, he was watching, but a tiny, half-ignored voice inside him told him that he stayed because he could no longer be troubled to move. Out on his right, Soldatov also seemed to have spotted the distant speck and was sliding and lumbering back toward the hut. He seemed to be moving in a strange zigzag, thought Stovin. He found that he felt no curiosity about it. His brain seemed to be shrinking where he squatted, becoming like a small frozen stone in the center of his skull. Coldness pervaded him, as though he had never previously in his life been warm. He could think of nothing else. Uncomprehending, he registered with this new dulled mind that the speck had moved, though only infinitesimally, in the white expanse. Suddenly Bisby was beside him, squinting out through his furs to the hummocky ridge, three-quarters of a mile—or was it more or less? —away. What was it Bisby was saying?

"Reindeer," said Bisby. "Only one, I think. There'll be

Chukchi near it somewhere. Probably the ones who came for the soldier this morning."

Somehow Stovin forced himself to make an effort at rational thought. He seemed to be standing outside himself, listening to his own voice.

"Can't see Chukchi," he mumbled like a child. "Only one deer. Could be a wild one."

Bisby shook his head, glancing at him with sudden, sharp attention. "That's no caribou," he said. "You'd never get a loner like that. It would either be dead or with the herd. That's a sled reindeer. Sto, you don't look good. Can you move?"

With difficulty, Stovin nodded. He found, absurdly, that he was protesting as Bisby pulled him to his feet. The younger man half bent, half crouched in front of him.

"Put your weight on me," he said. "All of it." His voice was commanding, almost hectoring. Stovin looked at him dully, but made no move. Bisby drew back his gloved hand and punched him hard on the shoulder. The force of the blow made Stovin stagger, though he felt no bruising impact beneath his layers of clothing. The momentary movement, however, seemed to jerk him away again, and he partly stepped, partly flopped forward until he was sprawled across Bisby's back. Panting in a cloud of snow crystals, Bisby floundered down the slope toward the hut. Diane saw them coming and ran forward, falling on her face in the snow. As she scrambled to her feet, Bisby reached her. A moment later Valentina hurried over from her sled.

"Get him inside," said Bisby. "And not too near that damned stove. Take a look at his hands. And you, Valentina, make some tea. Geny, go back to the road and watch for Chukchi."

They pulled Stovin into the hut, and Diane, her face tight with anxiety, began to pull off his thick boots.

"Leave them," said Bisby. She looked up at him, not understanding.

"But his feet . . . he can hardly stand. They must be frozen. Surely we must . . ."

"Leave them," said Bisby again. "Leave them until I can look at them. They won't be too bad yet, and they won't get any worse in here. I'm going back to look at that Chukchi reindeer."

Diane brought the hot tea and forced Stovin to drink.

Volkov, watching with concern, joined Valentina at his side and began to massage Stovin's hand. The hand which Valentina held had already started to look waxy toward the fingertips, and the Russian shook his head.

"You were lucky," he said. "Another quarter of an hour, and you might have lost the upper joints of all four fingers. Do you know what the temperature is outside?"

Stovin shook his head. He was already beginning to feel better, and his hands burned painfully. There was also some sensation of returning sensitivity in his feet. Volkov took from his pocket a small cheap thermometer.

"The roadkeeper kept this in the reindeer shed," he said. "When I looked at it this morning it was 38 degrees below zero. And that was in the shed, Dr. Stovin. It was probably at least 4 degrees colder outside. I have seen frostbite before. It is very unpleasant. You must be very careful. Try to keep moving your fingers, inside your gloves, when you are out. And do not rest your hands, even in gloves, in one place for more than a few seconds. Especially not on snow, or ice, or metal."

Remembering how he had positioned his gloved hands on the ground beside him, to steady himself while he squatted, Stovin gave a wry grin. His faintness had passed, and, although his feet hurt, he felt much stronger. When Bisby came back a few minutes later, Diane asked if she could unlace Stovin's boots. Bisby nodded. She got the boots off with difficulty, and Stovin could not repress a cry of pain. His feet were red in parts, waxen in others, and here and there there were small raw patches where the skin had been pulled away by the removal of the frozen socks. Diane began to massage the feet, almost weeping, but Bisby seemed unconcerned. He went into the little pantry and came back with a tobacco tin wedged with dirty grey, fishy-smelling grease and a bottle of oil.

"Seal fat," he said. "I guess the roadman traded it, somewhere down the coast, with Eskimos. Eskimos use it all the time, all kinds of things. Rub a bit of oil and fat into his feet. They aren't too bad—he won't lose any toes. But just for two minutes, not even a second more. Otherwise, his feet'll start swelling, and he won't be able to get those boots on again. And that'll be real trouble."

The two women got Stovin's boots back on after a struggle. His feet were now acutely painful, which Bisby said was a good sign.

"Why me?" said Stovin. "Why didn't Volkov and Geny get frostbitten? We were all there together, doing pretty much the same thing."

Bisby laughed. "You're . . . well, a little older than we are, Sto. If you were a seal Eskimo, or even a reindeer Chukchi, you'd be pretty much at the end of your useful life. Your blood circulation . . . it isn't as good as ours. The cold will hit you harder. What was it outside, Grigori?"

"Forty below," said the Russian.

"There you are, then," said Bisby. "You'll have to watch it, Sto."

He turned to the others. "That Chukchi reindeer's foraging around for food, I think," he said. "The Chukchi will be bedded down beside it, which means they aim to travel tonight, probably. I'd say they don't know we have reindeer—that soldier didn't look too bright. So we'd best get moving."

"Bedded down?" said Diane. She sounded incredulous. "In this?"

"They're reindeer Chukchi," said Bisby patiently. "They're nomads. They hunt, live, move, and raise kids, travelling around this stretch of country. They'll have made a snow bivouac this morning and eaten something —bit of dried reindeer, maybe—and now they'll be asleep. They intend to come and get us tonight. They think we'll still be here, and they think we'll find it harder to use this baby when it's even darker than it is now." He patted the automatic rifle, which hung from his shoulder.

The sleds were packed tight with virtually everything portable—the iron cooking pot, a small Primus stove, the food, all the blankets except the bloodstained ones, the knives, even the skins from the walls. They had nothing else, apart from the hand baggage they had brought from the plane—it seemed centuries ago now—in Anadyr. The rest, presumably, was still at the airport or already looted. Yet Volkov had frowned at the wholesale commandeering of the contents of the hut. Bisby brushed his objections aside.

"The poor guy out there doesn't need this any more," he said. "Nor does his wife, wherever she is, and whether she's dead or alive. But we might. We don't know what we're going into out there, or how long it'll

227

take. Nothing's certain, Grigori. We don't know where we're going."

"We're going to the air station at Uelen," said Volkov. "And then we'll be back where these things"—he waved a hand at the packed sleds—"will be the subject of an inquiry. We must be careful."

"First of all," said Bisby, "we're careful with our lives. And what we don't take, the Chukchi will. There's nothing on those sleds that we might not need, except . . ." He hesitated, looking at Stovin.

"Except what?" said Stovin.

"Except your books," said Bisby, and went out to the sleds. Diane was silent, beginning to feel a slow anger. But Valentina reached out her hand and touched Stovin's sore fingers.

"He's young," she said. "When you are young, you are insensitive. But we have a saying in Siberia—in our part of Siberia, of course, not in this . . . this snow desert. 'Forty years is not yet a woman, and forty below is not yet a frost.' Forty years is not yet a man, either, my dear. One day, he will discover it. . . ."

It was almost like flying, thought Diane. Unbelievably warm and comfortable. Settled deep into her blankets and furs, with Stovin dozing and muffled beside her, she reclined in the back of the sled. In front of her, swaying against the deep dark blue of the late noon sky already sprinkled with countless thousands of stars, was the hunched form of Bisby, occasionally uttering a strange hoarse cry as he pushed the side of his long pointed stick into the flank of the more mutinous of the two reindeer, or hauled back to slow down and let Valentina's pair, following in their tracks, keep up. She twisted around and gazed through the tiny spy hole Bisby had left in the packed goods behind her head. About a hundred yards back, the other sled came steadily on, plumes of whitish vapor from the reindeer muzzles streaming above the harnessed pair. Valentina was doing well—much better, Diane acknowledged mentally, than she herself would have done. Bisby had been right. Twice now they had stopped to allow the reindeer to eat, but they were still making good time over level snow. Eight miles to every hour, Bisby said. She looked at her watch. In that case, they'd now come nearly forty miles. More than halfway there. She looked out at the surrounding wilderness. For mile after mile, it had been a pale grey monotone, unrelieved by any other color, nor even by any appreciable lightening or deepening of its own characteristic hue. There was nothing to which to anchor the eye, no way of judging distance, no lines of horizon to mark where the frozen land met the freezing sky. How Bisby knew where he was headed was beyond her understanding. She had seen him, each time they stopped, looking attentively at the stars. So at least they were going in approximately the right direction.

Quite suddenly, the twilight of midday had deepened into the darkness of afternoon. All that could be seen now through the tiny spy hole behind Diane's head was the whitish flurry of the other sled and an occasional plume of reindeer vapor masking, for a moment, the bright stars. Bisby was looking around him. Beside the road—if this *was* the road—a long low ridge stretched into the darkness. Bisby reined back on the deer and slowly the sled came to a halt. A few moments later, Valentina's sled stopped, rather more clumsily, a few yards away. The reindeer stamped, snorting in clouds of crystals, on the hard pack of the snow. Bisby raised his head and sniffed at the night. A slight but perceptible wind was blowing from them toward the road, strengthened occasionally by more powerful gusts. He nodded to himself as though confirming some theory, and prodded the reindeer into motion again, turning the sled, followed by Valentina, away from their previous direction of travel and up over the ridge. He did not stop until they were halfway down its slightly steeper, windward side. Then he climbed down and walked over to where the Soldatovs and Volkov waited with the other sled. The reindeer stood with stoic patience, occasionally thrusting their heads down into the snow of the ridge in a vain effort to find rocks and lichen.

"There's another storm coming up," said Bisby. "What the whalers call a williwaw along this coast. We could be covered in a few minutes. We'd best get our heads down for the night. This ridge will be good protection; it might have been made for us."

Stiffly, Stovin and Diane, followed by the Soldatovs and Volkov, got down from the sleds. After the warmth of the sled coverings, the outside air was piercingly cold, stinging the face like showers of hot metal. Stovin's feet hurt badly, although Diane had bandaged the worst of the torn patches with pieces of an old nightshirt from the cabin. The wind was growing stronger, whipping the snow from the top of the ridge in little scuds of flying icy particles. Bisby picked up the long, metal-tipped stick he used on the reindeer and pushed it experimentally into the snow along the length of the ridge, coming back a few moments later, apparently satisfied. He took from his pack the big whalebone knife they had brought from the cabin, and spoke to the three men.

"I'm going to cut some blocks—enough to make a shelter," he said. "You come with me and carry them back to where we're standing. Don't pile them on top of each other, or they'll freeze together. I'll come back and fix them when I've cut enough."

He turned to Diane and Valentina. "Take the blankets and the tarpaulin out of the sleds," he said. "They're packed so you don't have to disturb anything else."

A moment later he was walking away up the ridge. Stovin and the Russians stumbled in his wake. Even in the physical misery that was now oppressing him, Stovin felt a surge of unexpected admiration for the way Bisby cut the blocks. Swiftly the sharp knife carved at the frozen snow, separating it into rectangular slabs, each no larger than a man could cradle across his chest. One by one, they staggered back with the cut snow. Stovin felt his heart pounding. As he passed Soldatov on his way up the ridge, he saw that the Russian, too, was moving with difficulty. Only Volkov seemed relatively unaffected by the rigors of the night. The wind was growing stronger every minute. Stovin found to his intense discomfort that he was sweating inside his parka, the sweat freezing and encasing him in a light layer of ice.

When Bisby was satisfied that they had enough blocks, he began to build. Again, he seemed extraordinarily swift in his actions, shaving and tamping each block at a slightly different angle from its predecessor so that they fitted into a rapidly growing, small triangular wall, its base resting on the side of the ridge, with a narrow opening at the tip. By now Stovin was beyond any kind of admiration for this technique, or even of wonder at what was happening. His whole being was concentrated on his desire to get out of the cutting wind that was freezing all of his body. He longed for the ice wall to rise enough for him to cower behind it. Bisby worked on, never slackening, never seeming to hurry. When the wall was a little more than three feet high, he stopped. All the men, working together, raised one of the sleds across it so that it acted as a roof for about half the space. When they went back for the second sled, Soldatov slipped, holding his chest. Valentina hurried over to him, and Diane at once took his place in lifting the second sled into position. Bisby packed snow around the area where the sled runners were propped against the ridge. At last he was satisfied. The storm was gusting fiercely, blowing clouds of frozen snow above their heads, some of it raining down upon them in stinging showers. Gasping and breathing heavily, they dragged the tarpaulin, the blankets, and the food and Primus stove into the bivouac. One by one, they wedged themselves inside. It was just large enough for the six of them to lie together, their furred bodies in close contact, and just high enough for them to sit. Incredibly, it seemed warm. The wind, in occasional maverick downward gusts from the top of the ridge, plucked at its walls, but inside all was still. They lay there, panting, while Valentina pulled back the hood from Soldatov's face and looked at him. It was difficult to see his features in the ghostly glimmer of the bivouac's interior, but he smiled shakily at her and his breathing was easier.

Bisby's voice came again. It was sharp. "We can't lie here like this. You'll get cold again. Get the Primus going. I'll make a lamp."

He took from his blanket roll a small tin bowl Stovin remembered seeing in the cabin and poured in some of the seal oil from the bottle. Then he placed into it a wedge of flannel from the old torn nightshirt, struck a match, and lit it. It smoked for a minute or two and then burned with a steady, pulsing flame. Gradually its warmth seemed to seep into the bivouac. They sat and drank the tea which Diane had brewed, and gnawed a piece of the moose meat from the cabin. Suddenly they found that the tension of the past hours had evaporated and they they were talking again. All his life afterward, Stovin remembered the warmth and comfort of the north Siberian bivouac, the gentle splutter and fishy smell of the seal-oil lamp, the shadowed face of Diane beside him. It seemed to him that nowhere else in the world had he ever been so at ease. He could not bear the thought that tomorrow this tranquillity must end.

"You learned all this on Ihovak, I guess," he said to Bisby.

"Yes, my uncles taught me, a long time ago. When you learn young, you don't forget. Mind, they wouldn't have thought much of this, even as a bivouac. And if you were making an igloo—a winter house—well, I'm not nearly good enough to make that. You can live in the cold much like you live in the sun, though. All you have to do is to learn."

Bisby leaned over toward Soldatov, his body pressing for the moment against Diane's, so that even in his thick furs he felt again that momentary unexpected, unwanted stir of desire.

"How do you feel, Geny? You didn't look too good."

Soldatov shook his head. "I'm better now. I was like Sto back at the cabin—I got cold."

"You're out of condition," said Bisby, but his voice was gentle enough to take the edge from the words. "Not surprising, the life you lead—led, I suppose. You'll all have to learn to try not to hurry unless you have to—and then to be very quick, real quick. Did you sweat?"

"I did," said Stovin and the two women, almost together.

"Then you have to get your clothes off, right now. Turn the Primus up high. You must dry them out, quick as you can, or they'll freeze on you again tomorrow, and you'll have mighty sore bodies."

It was curious, thought Stovin afterward, how little embarrassment or even shyness anyone displayed in the bivouac. Within a minute or two they were out of their damp, cold underclothes and wrapped once more in blankets, while Bisby placed the clothes, linings inward, around the stove. For several seconds both Valentina and Diane were naked from the waist up, but none of the men seemed even to notice the fact. And when the time for their bodily needs arrived, they crawled singly into the recess which Bisby had burrowed in the corner beyond the lamp, and crouched in the darkness.

When all was over, Bisby poured more oil into the lamp, and they lay back. Stovin was on his side, with Diane hard against him, face to face. She slept easily, almost at once, but he lay awake, listening to her steady breathing and that of the Soldatovs beyond. Volkov and Bisby talked a little in low voices, but he could not hear what they were saying. Gradually their voices trailed off. Volkov belched once, heavily. Stovin watched the yellow, smoke-edged reflection of the seal-oil lamp on the snow ceiling, and slowly drifted into sleep. It was a sleep disturbed by strange dreams, and he was still half dreaming when Bisby, crouched above him, shook him awake.

"Get yourself dressed and get your boots on," he hissed. "And start packing up: wake the others. I'm going outside again. There's a light over the ridge, not three hundred yards away. A bivouac, I guess, like this. It'll be Chuckchi—probably those four. I was wrong about them. They must have followed us the whole day until the storm came."

It was perilously near the hour of prayer when Zayd saw the sand gazelles. There were five of them, a stag and three hinds and a half-grown fawn, walking in the evening shadow just below the crest of the ridge. The Sahara here was stony, with an occasional patch of thorn or scrub, and Zayd knew that the gazelles were looking for a wadi where they could huddle against the coming chill of the night wind. He pantomimed to Zenoba and the boys to be silent, and took the Mauser from the saddle clip of the bull camel. Then he crawled to the top of an intermediate ridge. The little animals were fully 200 yards away, and the glare of the setting sun made it difficult to pick them out against the shadow of the ridge. For a moment, heart thumping, he thought they had gone. Then, for a few seconds, they were outlined against the sky as they passed over the crest—the stag, a hind, the fawn, the other hinds. He chose the first hind because hers would be the fawn, and she might still be in milk. Squinting against the glare, he took the first pressure on the trigger. The stag had already dropped from sight down the other side of the ridge, and the hind was following when Zayd fired. In the flash from the muzzle, he was not sure whether he had hit her or not. All the gazelle had vanished, and he ran, holding the Mauser, across to the ridge where they had been. Sick with disappointment in the gathering twilight, he could not see her. And then, suddenly, there she was, huddled in a hollow, his bullet through the base of her neck, dead. No bigger than a dog, but welcome. This would be the first meat they had eaten since they had finished the joints they had been able to cut and carry from the dead cow camel, after she broke her foreleg in a stony wadi three weeks ago. He straightened and called to Zenoba. By the time she reached him, his face was set once more in its proud, hard mask.

233

"Prepare this," he said, jerking his rifle toward the dead gazelle. "And be careful of the milk: it will help the child. It is the hour of prayer."

He knelt in the sand and turned his face to the far city in the darkened east.

"In the name of God the Merciful, the Compassionate," he began . . .

CHAPTER 21

Although Bisby tried to keep the sleds moving along the blind side of the ridge, it was clear that the Chukchi had picked them up as soon as they moved. As the spur of the ridge petered out into a flat plain bisected by the almost indistinguishable line of the road, he glimpsed the Chukchi sled, running parallel with them, about a quarter of a mile out on their right. Bisby watched it as closely as he could as he drove, though the darkness of the Arctic morning made it difficult to distinguish more than the swirling snowtrail of its progress. It seemed to be drawn by the single reindeer they had seen earlier. So, he thought, it was a one-reindeer, four-man sled trying to overtake a two-reindeer, three-man sled. If it were only as simple as that, the Chukchi wouldn't have a chance. He knew that. But Valentina . . . she couldn't drive her sled, still plowing along behind him, nearly as fast as he could drive his own. He looked back and reined in slightly. Already a gap was opening up, and like wolves, the Chukchi had turned inward as though to cut between. In this darkness, they could take anything and anybody they wanted off Valentina's sled and be flying back down the road before he could get his own team as much as turned and facing in the right direction. He slowed again so that Valentina could close up. At once, the Chukchi sled turned away, running parallel once more. He knew why. While he was there, they would be cautious. They remembered the rifle. For a moment, he toyed with the idea of passing the rifle to Stovin or Diane. They might

234

get a shot at the Chukchi, maybe even a lucky hit. No, it wasn't worth the risk. There were only twelve shots in the magazine: they might need all of them. And there was Volkov to think about. The Russian didn't look the sort of man who'd turn a blind eye to a shoot-out with people he probably still regarded as Soviet citizens. And presumably there were forces of Soviet law and order at Uelen. Volkov would be making a report. He's not a bad guy, but he's KGB all the way through, thought Bisby.

Gradually, the landscape was changing, becoming less flat and featureless. They had swung east now, occasionally running only a mile inland from snow-covered heights which looked out over a grey-white expanse that Bisby knew must be the Bering Sea. Ahead of them was a mass of dark colored cliffs, soaring in jagged terraces sheer from the ocean. There were low mountains beyond—not much more than hills, thought Bisby—barely 2,500 feet high. Their tops were covered with drifting white fog. He looked behind him for the twentieth time. The Chukchi, inhibited by the cliffs on their right, had turned inland. They were following Valentina, perhaps three-quarters of a mile back. And then, looking back one more time as the light of the day reached its twilight maximum, he realized that they were no longer there. He fought back the feeling of relief. They were hunters, the Chukchi. They wouldn't give up so easily, after so much toil. So what were they doing? They might know the country, of course, whereas he could only follow the line of the road and hope for the best. Were they taking a known shortcut, by which they could intercept him and take him by surprise? He cursed his lack of an adequate map. Nevertheless, as the two sleds sped on in the now faintly glimmering light of noon, he became convinced that this was what the Chukchi must be trying. Did they have a gun? Unlikely —being Chukchi and probably trigger-happy, they would have tried a shot. So they must have something else in mind.

His own chance came a few minutes later. The road turned inward toward the cliffs, and at the same time the ground on the left, westward side began to climb up the slope of a long escarpment. A number of little defiles or corries led to the escarpment ridge, like the bones radiating from the spine of a fish. In the brief Siberian summer, they would be small streams and watercourses. He waited until he saw one where the going looked reasonably good, swung into it, and pulled the reindeer to a halt. Then he scrambled down, watched by a surprised Stovin and Diane, and ran back to tell Valentina to come beside him and stop.

"Don't dismount except for you, Grigori," he said. "I want to have a look at what those bastards are doing."

Volkov looked at him silently, his face a mask of doubt. Bisby's voice was impatient. "Well, you saw them following, didn't you?"

Almost unwillingly, Volkov nodded.

"Well, it wasn't because they wanted to pay their Party dues," said Bisby. "They've got to be stopped."

"It is not suitable . . ." began Volkov, but Bisby interrupted him.

"Let's go and see what they're doing. Then we can make up our minds."

Bisby took the rifle from the sled, and the two men climbed the twenty yards up to the ridge of the escarpment. It was as light now as it would ever be during a winter day, but the landscape, as much of it as could be distinguished, seemed bare, desolate, stretching away beyond the escarpment to a line of distant smoky hills. Nothing else moved. Bisby, searching it steadily, quarter by quarter, had almost given up when Volkov suddenly tapped his arm.

"There . . . almost below us. Three . . . four men."

"And a reindeer sled," said Bisby in satisfaction.

"What are they doing?" asked Volkov.

The men, no more than large black dots in the snow at a range of more than 400 yards, were busy on what from this height could be seen to be the line of the road, curving away just beyond the point at which they stood. They were piling rocks from the escarpment at the side of the road. While Volkov and Bisby watched, they went back, unharnessed the reindeer from the sled, and dragged the sled across to the rocks, settling it upright, like a door. Then they began to plaster it with snow. Bisby laughed.

"Clever, clever," he said. "They reckon my sled will go by, round that bend, and that in this light I won't see the sled stuck in those rocks. They're right. Probably I wouldn't have. And the moment I've passed, they'll drop that sled in the road and bring down Valentina's reindeer. It would have been a couple of minutes before I realized she wasn't still behind us, and that would have been long enough. Goodbye Volkov, goodbye Soldatov, and a longer goodbye, maybe for Valentina. Clever . . ."

He raised the rifle, steadying it on the distant group. Volkov grasped his arm.

"What are you doing? You cannot shoot Soviet citizens. I shall not allow . . ."

Bisby turned on him. "I'm not a fool. I know your position, and I know mine. I promise you, I will not hurt a Soviet citizen."

He set the sights and took careful aim. The men below had finished their task and seemed to be squatting in the rocks, waiting. The reindeer, free of its sled, stood patiently by. It seemed to have its head down in the snow. Bisby fired. Below him, before the crack of the rifle reached so far, one of the men moved sharply, as though surprised. When the sound of the shot carried to them a second later, all began to move—the nearest one scrambling back up the ridge to a better position. Bisby cursed, aimed, fired again. The reindeer staggered, bellowed once, and sank down in the snow. The four Chukchi were running now, along the escarpment, up and over, down onto the further side where they could not see Bisby nor he them. Volkov tapped Bisby's arm again.

"That was good," he said. "A reindeer, that can be . . . well, forgotten. And now they cannot follow us. That was good."

"That was not good," said Bisby. "I took two shots. Now I—we—have only ten left. We could need the shot I wasted."

"I think not," said Volkov. "In an hour, perhaps a little more, we shall be at Uelen. And then"—with a sidelong glance—"you will not want the rifle."

Viewed from the high ground which Volkov, checking his map, said was Cape Dezhneva, Uelen was no more than a huddle of small wooden cabins with two long grey concrete buildings at each side and the airfield beyond. One or two tiny figures were moving through the little complex of paths around the airfield administration area, and a large transport aircraft was parked in one of the four loading bays. Volkov gave a satisfied sigh and clapped Soldatov, beside him in the second sled, on the shoulder.

"The airfield is still working," he said. "With any luck

237

tomorrow—tonight, even—we shall be out of this accursed peninsula. And . . ."

"Yes?"

"I rely on you to help me. You will know, of course, that this is an extremely sensitive area in terms of the national defense of the Motherland. It is of the greatest importance that the man Bisby remains indoors as soon as we arrive, and that he is not permitted to see anything of Uelen or the airfield that could be of the slightest significance to a foreign power."

"To the United States, you mean?"

"Of course. When this crisis is over, in the short term at least, the facts of life will once more emerge. We live on a balance, my dear Soldatov. The strong balance the strong. We must remain strong, and nothing must be allowed to weaken us. Not even some half-remembered glimpse of forbidden matters by the man Bisby."

Soldatov turned his head, and looked at Volkov through the deep fringe of his furred hood.

"You may be right, Volkov, in the short term. I do not know. But the facts of life—the balance—of which you speak . . . these have changed. There are different facts to reckon with and a new balance, new forces."

"The facts change all the time, Dr. Soldatov. I sit at my desk in Moscow and watch them change."

"Not like this," said Soldatov.

They were moving down now onto the bumpy, narrow coast road that led into the settlement. On their right was the sea, frozen, opaque as far as the eye could reach. A long spit of shingle ran out from the rocks of the shore. It was several miles long, for its end vanished into a sea mist that shrouded the northwest horizon. It enclosed a lagoon, no doubt providing useful shelter for ships running in out of the occasional icy fury of the Bering Strait. No ship was in now. Bisby looked out into the haze above the sea, the color of dirty milk, which stretched beyond the far side of the shingle. There was a faint line of white which might indicate breakers, but the sea seemed relatively calm, and there was little wind. Over there, no more than thirty miles away, was the United States . . . Alaska and the island where he was born. There'd been an Antonov on that airfield. Well, good for Volkov. He'd been right. If Volkov could unscramble the red tape that wound around everything in this country, they'd be in Seattle tomorrow.

238

Ahead of them now was the main street—the only street, it seemed—of Uelen. It was a ragged and unpaved thoroughfare, bordered on each side by small cabins. Some of them, Bisby noticed, had carved wooden heads on their doorposts, of the kind he had sometimes seen in parts of Alaska. Of course, this was an Eskimo settlement, though no doubt it had a few technicians from all over the Soviet Union. Even as he was thinking this, they passed the first three human beings they had seen, walking in line abreast beside a red-and-white sign at the end of the street, painted in Russian characters, glorifying the achievements of the last Party Congress. The three men looked up as the sled passed, followed a minute later by Valentina's. One of them carried a rifle. It was hard to identify the features behind their furs, but they looked very like Chukchi. At the end of the street, where the road curved away beside the shore toward the airfield, a telegraph pole lay sagging across the road, its wires trailing. In the second sled, Volkov looked out. There was a chill weight in his stomach.

They drove on. Nothing seemed to have been done to clear the airfield perimeter road, behind which the long white roofs of its triangle of administration buildings could be glimpsed in the mist which was beginning to roll in from the Bering Strait. The sleds travelled over it easily enough, however, and they began to pass small parties of men and women, obviously Chukchi, walking or sledding back down the road toward the settlement. They were carrying a strange assortment of objects—piles of tin boxes that looked like filing drawers, a straight-backed wooden chair, lengths of carpet, kitchen utensils. These passersby gave them long, inquisitive looks, turning around and pointing. One or two shouted incomprehensibly, but Bisby prodded the reindeer and the sled moved on. The airport itself was deserted, except that here and there a Chukchi was wandering through its small entrance hall. They climbed stiffly from the sleds and looked around. There had been a fire at one of the two check-in desks; charred paper lay all around, and the telephones, wires trailing, were on the floor. Watched now by two silent Chukchi beside the glass doors, Bisby took the rifle from his shoulder, holding it loosely in his right hand.

"Doesn't look good," he said. "Let's just have a look at that Antonov."

"It is impossible," said Volkov, "that there is no one

239

here. There is considerable traffic, at some times of the year, with Vladivostok. There are at least sixty Russians here, quite apart from the Chukchi population."

"The population here isn't Chukchi, Grigori. It's Eskimo," said Bisby.

Volkov swung on him, stopping in his tracks. "And how do you know that?"

"Oh," said Bisby, "I had an uncle, who had a cousin, who had a wife who came from this coast, a long time ago. This is an Eskimo coast. Just like on the other side."

"You mean," said Volkov, "that your uncle married a Soviet citizen?" Soviet citizen, thought Bisby, seemed to be Volkov's favorite phrase.

"Not my uncle," he said. "My uncle's cousin. Yes, I guess she was a Soviet citizen. Probably didn't know it, though, Eskimos don't go much for frontiers—Russian or American. I guess nobody told her she was one of yours. Probably wouldn't have made much difference if they had."

"All that we have seen here are Chukchi," said Volkov. He sounded defensive, almost sullen.

"You're right," said Bisby. "The others have gone. Or been taken."

From somewhere on the other side of the airfield came two sharp cracks that were unmistakably rifle shots. Soldatov put his arm around Valentina. They went on, through a cold corridor already, in the absence of heating, damp with freezing condensation. The Antonov's bay was off to the right-hand side, reached by a tube-shaped passage leading to its open door. They went in and looked around. The whole interior of the great aircraft seemed to be wrecked. Cushions had been torn from almost every seat, and determined but unsuccessful attempts had been made to wrench out the seats themselves. The galley was stripped bare, and only a couple of broken plastic spoons remained. Stovin went forward and opened the door to the flight deck. A dead man in the blue uniform and gold wings of Aeroflot sat in the second pilot's seat. His head appeared to have been battered in, probably many hours ago, for the blood around him was congealed. The instrument, whatever it was, that killed him had also been used to smash the control panel. The splintered dials were spattered with gluey blood. Stovin took one more look around the useless controls and came out shutting the door behind him.

"There's a man in there we can't do anything for," he said. "And this is a plane we can't do anything with."

Volkov pushed past him and opened the flight deck door, while the others watched. When he came out, his face was ashen. For the first time since they had left Anadyr, he seemed close to despair.

"But there are soldiers here," he said. His voice was bewildered. "This station is used by the Air Force. Where are the soldiers? What . . . what are you doing?"

Bisby was suddenly running back up the access passage toward the main hall.

"The sleds," he shouted. "I must have been mad. We left those damned deer and the sleds without any guard."

Three Chukchi were standing around the sleds as he burst through the main doors. One was carrying away a pile of blankets and skins from Valentina's sled. The other two were busy unharnessing the reindeer from Bisby's. They looked up as Bisby shouted but went on with what they were doing, laughing. Bisby dropped to one knee, raised the rifle to his shoulder, and fired. The bullet hit the hard ice a foot from the Chukchi with the blankets and whined away into the distance. After an instant of stupefaction, the three Chukchi ran. The one who had been looting the sled dropped some of the blankets as he fled, running away through the mist which was now beginning to thicken over the whole airfield.

Volkov panted up, looking at the rifle cradled in Bisby's arms. "What happened? Surely you didn't . . ."

"No," said Bisby, "I didn't shoot a Soviet citizen."

"Is anything missing?" said Stovin. Diane came up behind him and went out to pick up the blankets the Chukchi had dropped. Bisby checked the sled.

"Nothing much," he said. "I think he got away with one or two of the skins. But we shan't miss those a great deal. It was damned lucky they didn't take the deer or the sleds. From now on, we've got to be careful. Never leave a sled without a guard—maybe two guards."

Two minutes later, thought Stovin, and they'd have been alone on this peninsula, in this mist, without any means of movement other than their legs, surrounded by a thieving, murderous race. It was going to be hard enough to decide what to do, even as things stood. It would have been quite impossible without the sleds. Around them, with deceptive speed, the mist closed in

241

until it was barely possible to see the fifteen yards across the perimeter road. Bisby was right. They had to be very careful.

They stood looking around them uncertainly until Stovin spoke to Volkov. "Where else is there in Uelen where we might find people who could help us? Or where there might be communication that doesn't depend on lines? A radio transmitter, say."

"There is an oceanographic station," said Volkov eagerly. "And a hospital—small, but a hospital."

The hospital, when they reached it, proved to be the nearer of the two long grey buildings they had seen when they arrived. It was very small, with a capacity of no more than twenty beds and a tiny operating theater. And it was completely deserted. Only one person remained inside its comprehensively looted interior. She was a very old woman in a bed near the door of the only ward—"An Eskimo woman," Bisby said—and she was dead. There were no marks of violence on her and her face was peaceful. Stovin walked over and picked up her wrinkled hand where it lay on the coverlet. It flopped back, rigid.

"Stiff," he said. "She's been dead some time—more than a day, maybe. Probably died in her sleep."

On the other side of Uelen's main street, facing out to the mist-shrouded lagoon, was the oceanographic station. It was basically one long room, with three or four offices opening from it. One of them contained the radio transmitter, which had been smashed. The long room itself was littered with charts torn from the walls. Books and papers lay in heaps on the floor. A heap of broken instruments was piled in one corner; they had been destroyed so completely that it was difficult to decide from the twisted pieces of brass and chips of broken glass exactly what they had been. There was no sign of anyone there.

Stovin looked around him, feeling a sudden despair. This room, perched up here beside a frozen sea in a bleak and menacing land, had been a little outpost of scientific civilization. Now it had fallen. But to what? The Chukchi, presumably. They were a fierce people, a Mongol people, and it was within living memory that they had finally been subdued to Soviet administration. What had got into them? Did they believe that the old order was over? It seemed unlikely, and in any case, there just

242

weren't enough of them to conduct any kind of revolt as soon as people in Moscow realized what was going on. He had asked Soldatov on the previous day what the population figures were for Chukchi on this Chukotskiy Peninsula, and the Russian had shrugged wearily.

"Sto, I do not know. Not very accurately, at any rate. But probably no more than 8,000 or 9,000."

Well, it seemed there were enough of them to cause a lot of trouble. But what, exactly, was going on in the Chukchi mind?

"Something's happening in the street."

It was Diane's voice, taut and excited. She was standing beside the long window with Valentina, and Bisby and Stovin crossed to her side. Their two sleds were drawn up at the end of the oceanographic station, with Soldatov and Volkov on guard. Past them now streamed the vanguard of an extraordinary procession—scores of people, wrapped in furs and heavy anoraks, old and young, men, women and children, some with dogsleds, some striding ponderously along in snowshoes, all heading down toward the sea. Beside them walked Chukchi, dozens of Chukchi, all armed with hunting rifles and shotguns. They looked exactly like guards marching watchfully beside prisoners of war. And there was something else . . . surely?

Bisby turned to the others, his face tight with anger. "See that? Those families out there—they're all Eskimos. The Chukchi are seeing off the Eskimos. With guns."

One of the passing Chukchi saw them in the window, and then looked down toward where the reindeer waited with the two Russians beside the sleds. He called to his companions, and at once five or six Chukchi joined him. Three remained watching the sleds, and the others came into the station. They hesitated for a moment when they saw the rifle in the crook of Bisby's arm, but after a quick chattering exchange with each other, they came on. Bisby moved the rifle easily into a waist-high firing position, but his heart sank. There were four of them, and they all had shotguns. The leader looked at Bisby and jerked his thumb toward the door. Bisby shook his head and tapped the rifle. There was another outburst of furious chatter among the four Chukchi, and then the other again indicated the door, speaking now to Bisby in a slow, loud voice.

"What do they want?" asked Stovin.

Bisby spoke over his shoulder. "They want us to get

243

out and join the people in the road, as far as I can make out."

"And then what?"

"I'm damned if I know. They want us to go along with the Eskimos, I suppose."

The Chukchi leader came closer, looking more menacing. The shotgun held by the man behind him seemed to be pointed straight at the middle of Diane's body. He shouted at Bisby again, incomprehensibly. Then he reached out his hands for Bisby's rifle. Bisby stepped back and said something in a warning tone. The Chukchi jerked his thumb at the door again.

"We'll have to go," said Stovin. "There are too many of them, both here and outside. But don't let them get that rifle."

With the Chukchi behind them, they filed out of the door. Valentina went over immediately to where Soldatov stood beside the sled.

Volkov called to Bisby, "What's happening? Where are they taking us?"

The Chukchi motioned to them to get into the sleds, and Stovin called back.

"Just do as they say. They aren't taking us anywhere. They just want us to join the people in the road. And, Valentina . . ."

She looked up from where she now sat in the driving seat of her sled. "Yes, Sto?"

"Make sure you keep right behind us. We mustn't get separated, not now."

She nodded and raised her reindeer pole in response.

"She's got a lot of bottom, that girl," said Bisby to Diane. "And I don't mean what you think I mean, either."

He prodded the reindeer into motion, and Diane stared at him. Even with her nerves taut and heart pounding, she was able to feel surprised that Bisby had chosen this moment to make one of his rare jokes. That kind of joke, anyway. It was the kind that Ed Van Gelder would have trotted out ten times a day, but that Bisby never, never made. They pulled away from the station and joined what had now become the tail end of the long procession. Gradually but steadily, moved on by shouting Chukchi, they followed the escorted Eskimos down to the sea. On the long spit of shingle running along the north side of the lagoon they could now see the most extraordinary sight of any of their lives.

The darkness of afternoon was almost complete, and it was cloudy enough to obscure most of the stars. Nevertheless, there was a glimmering refulgence of light from the surface of the strait against which a dark snake of Eskimos, sprinkled with the lights of scores of lamps and lanterns, was moving slowly east. It was a few moments before they realized that this long stream of human beings, sledges, dogs, and an occasional reindeer team, was leaving the land, heading out into the open Bering Straits.

"The Straits are frozen," said Diane. She was excited, looking out to where they had seen the line of breakers as they arrived at Uelen a couple of hours earlier. They were on the ice of the Straits themselves now, marshalled there by the watchful Chukchi, who dropped back in the darkness, satisfied, as the reindeer trotted forward. There was a lot of noise all around them—dogs barking furiously, Eskimos shouting, the occasional crack of a dogsled whip, once or twice the sound of a shot. Through it all they could hear the steady hiss of the runners of their own sleds on the ice. They had entered the Straits on the left-hand, northern side of the Eskimo exodus, and were running parallel with the white line of the breakers. But, realized Stovin suddenly, these were not breakers. Or at least, if they were breakers, they had been frozen as they broke. They were heaped, undulating hummocks of ice. Far, far beyond them glimmered something else— glittering white shapes, jagged and fantastic, towering against the night sky. They're . . . but they can't be, Stovin told himself. One of the few things I know about the Bering Straits is that there aren't any . . .

"Hold on," said Bisby. One of the reindeer stumbled and almost went down. The smooth hiss of the runners had stopped, and the sled was lurching over cracked and hummocky ice. The great column of the exodus seemed now to be far over on their right, a ribbon of moving lights rapidly drifting out of sight as a thick mist began to roll over the frozen sea.

"I can't see Valentina," said Bisby. He sounded calm, but he brought the sled to a skidding halt. They scrambled down onto the ice. It was piercingly cold, and the mist chilled them through their heavy clothing. For once, however, Stovin was too anxious to worry about his physical misery. They huddled together and shouted in unison.

245

Diane was fighting back a feeling of growing panic when, at last, a faint shout came from behind them. Two minutes later Valentina's sled appeared through the mist, its reindeer panting in clouds of ice crystals, like ghosts from some Norse saga. The Soldatovs and Volkov climbed down, and in relief and happiness they hugged each other, Volkov slapping Bisby on the back with his gloved hands, saying again and again, "This is good. This is good."

"We'll have to try a different way of keeping together," said Bisby. "It's too easy to lose each other in this mist, and we haven't any lights. There's plenty of room on the ice, so we'll travel slowly, side by side. It's not good, this surface, and we don't want to lose a reindeer."

"The older one of my two is blowing badly," said Valentina. "See . . ."

Bisby went over and looked. The beast was panting heavily, and there was a rim of frozen foam around its mouth. It seemed in distress, but Bisby shrugged.

"I'd lighten your sled if I could, Valentina," he said. "But there's no way of doing it here and now. Maybe after we stop."

"Stop where?" said Volkov. "Where are we going?"

"At the moment," said Bisby, "we're going to America. But not tonight. We won't make it tonight, not like this."

"But," said Volkov, "what of all those people? Where are they going? What's happening to them?"

"They're going to America, too, some of them," said Bisby, turning away to his own sled. Volkov stared after him in the darkness, and then slowly clambered back beside Valentina. Soldatov, watching in silence, took his place beside him. The euphoria of finding each other again after the moment of panic had evaporated. As he climbed past her to the rear of the sled, Valentina saw her husband's face and caught her breath. He looked drawn, haggard, on the point of collapse.

"Ho," cried Bisby, and his sled moved forward. Valentina prodded the fitter one of her two reindeer. Her own sled started to move. Bisby kept the reindeer at a walking pace, with Valentina only ten yards out to his right.

"Do you know where you're going?" asked Stovin. I thought, he said bitterly to himself, that I was Renaissance man, the man for all seasons. But the cold freezes my mind. I have to fight it all the time.

"I know where I'm going," said Bisby. He sounded almost exultant.

CHAPTER 22

The cliff loomed in upon them, sheer and slab sided, about two hours later. Below it, the tops of a ragged jumble of rocks thrust through the ice, and Valentina's sled began now to move in from the flank, so she could follow Bisby as he picked his way through them slowly and carefully. The mist was rolling away now, and the night was clear and starlit. Bisby picked his way along the foot of the cliff, the reindeer snorting and stamping, hungry and waiting to rest. At last, in the clear bright night, he appeared to find what he sought. It was something totally unexpected to the rest of them—a long straight pole, wrapped in an old caribou skin, projecting upward from the ice at the sheer base of the cliff. At its tip, in place by wedges of bone, was a rusting tin can.

"There it is, the marker," said Bisby in satisfaction, bringing the sled to a halt with Valentina's just behind him. Getting out from the warmth of the sled blankets into the gripping cold outside the sled was always an ordeal, for Stovin, and it was no less so this time. Yet he caught his breath with astonishment, forgetting his misery, when Bisby pointed in the starlight to the cliff behind him. A few yards away gaped the mouth of a cave, a black hole in the darkness. Bisby laughed. He sounded pleased with himself.

"There you are, Sto," he said. "That's where we spend tonight."

"But how did you know . . . ?" began Stovin. Bisby interrupted. In the starlight, his face seemed to be glowing rosy red.

"I'll tell you all when we've unpacked and got inside," he said.

From behind him came Diane's awed voice. The others turned to where she stood at the rear of the group, looking to the north. Her face, too, seemed rose pink in color. And then, from behind the bulk of the cliff, rose a sight of astonishing splendor.

"Look at it," Diane said slowly. It was now as light as a summer evening, but the light shifted across the spectrum—red, silver, yellow, blue. The whole of the northern horizon glowed as though with the light of a great forest fire, the ice flinging back the glow in a carpet of phosphorescence. The glow grew into an enormous spreading flame. From it shafts of colored light shot into the air. For a second or two, the splendor on the horizon suddenly sank, then glowed again; it seemed even brighter than before. The flame was steadily changing shape. It had now become a winding red-and-silver ribbon, coiling so brightly in the night sky that it dimmed the stars. The night was pervaded by sound. It seemed to Stovin afterward that the nearest analogy was the rustling of great sheets of silk—a crackling, sibilant hiss he had never heard before. He coughed for a moment. The air smelt faintly acrid. The drifting ribbon passed them, and from it dazzling fingers shot upward into the heavens. In its red aura, Bisby's face was rapt, almost mystical. Suddenly, from the ribbon, a single ray lanced downward, passing behind the cliff toward the unseen horizon beyond it to the east.

"The Northern Lights," said Soldatov. His voice sounded weak but determined. Valentina stood beside him, half supporting him.

"I have never seen them like that," she said. "Many times I have seen them but never like that."

Behind the black bulk of the cliff, the lights in the sky were sinking, dimming to a pulsing pink glow. But Bisby stood there still, looking up into the sky where the single shaft had struck earthward. His face was transfigured. He murmured something to himself which Stovin only half heard. It sounded, he thought, rather like "At last."

Abruptly, Bisby moved, leading the way into the cave. This was much larger than might have been imagined from outside. It consisted of a large cavern immediately behind the entrance with three smaller ones radiating off it. The air inside was cold but still. It was also, they realized, not musty. The cavern had been used fairly recently. That this was so was confirmed by a pile of skins in the corner. There were twenty or more of them— Arctic fox, wolverine, and two long grey wolf pelts.

248

Underneath them was an extraordinary collection of objects—colored plastic bowls, still in their wrapping, such as could be bought in any American hardware store; pairs of cheap jeans; nylon stockings; tins of cocktail sausages.

Diane sorted through them, squatting down in the starlight filtering through the entrance. She looked up at Bisby, her face puzzled. "What's all this stuff?"

He laughed. "Trade. You know where you are?"

She shook her head.

"This is Little Diomede. Now just over yonder"—he pointed out of the cave entrance—"is Big Diomede. Part of the year they're islands, smack in the middle of the Bering Strait. Not now, though. When the Straits are frozen, even in a normal year, there's a lot of ice with leads of open water. Any good Eskimo can get a kayak here from Siberia or from Alaska, almost any winter. That's why all that stuff is in the corner."

"I don't understand," said Stovin.

Bisby laughed again. It was extraordinary, thought Stovin, how he enjoyed creating mysteries.

"I told you before, Sto, Eskimos—any Eskimos—well, they don't go much on frontiers. But the Russians and the Americans do, especially since both sides of the Straits are full of incoming missile early warning stations. But Eskimos . . . they trade. So they bring skins over from the Soviet side where there's still a lot more fur animals than there are now in Alaska. And they trade them for . . . well, for the kind of junk you see there. The kind of things you can't get in the workers' paradise across the Strait. They can get good money for those when they're finally traded farther west. It's illegal, but you'll never stop Eskimos doing it. Nobody to chase them up here— nobody who *can* chase them, anyway. So they come and go across the frontier as they please. And this is the frontier. It runs right between Big Diomede and Little Diomede. Big's in the Soviet Union and Little's in the United States. But there are—or were—a few Russian soldiers on Big. So the Soviet Eskimos come here. They leave the skins, they take the junk. And so it goes on. All you need is a kayak. And a marker—so that you can locate the cave from the Strait."

"How did you know it was there?" asked Volkov.

"It's been common knowledge amongst Eskimos for the whole of my life," said Bisby. "It was well known on

Ihovak, where I was born, in the old time. And Ihovak's a way south of here. The only thing that bothered me was *if* I'd spot the marker, now the Straits are frozen harder than any Eskimo has ever seen them. They freeze each winter, sure, but you can't normally walk over. Too much open water, even in winter. At least, my father once told me that an Eskimo once walked, somewhere around 1912. But he was the last one—before tonight."

He shivered. "Best get unloaded now and get a lamp lit. At least there's no snow in here. We can bring the deer into this main piece of the cave and use the small caves for sleeping in. We'll have to pair off, two to a cave."

For an instant his glance travelled briefly from Stovin to Diane and back again, but he made no further comment.

Volkov spoke. He sounded troubled. "Then we"—he nodded toward the Soldatovs—"are in the United States?"

"Sure," said Bisby.

"But we have entered illegally," said Volkov. "I should have realized . . . I had not imagined . . ."

Bisby fingered his chin. "You want to go back then, Grigori . . . back to all those Chukchi Soviet citizens?"

Volkov said nothing. Bisby waited a few seconds and then led the way outside. It took almost half an hour to unload the sleds and bring in the reindeer. Valentina gave them the rest of the dried moss they had brought from the cabin. It was not much, and the beasts were clearly hungry. The sick reindeer ate nothing but lay on the rocky floor of the cave, panting. Valentina bent over it anxiously, but Bisby drew her away.

"It's dying, girl," he said. "No more use. Better go and see to Geny. He looks none too bright."

Soldatov was sitting on a blanket. It had been his task to make the seal-oil lamp, and he had done it well. The flame pulsed steadily in the bowl, shedding its gentle light and heat into every corner of the cave. Now he sat on his blanket, his head down. He had said little all day, but he murmured briefly to Valentina before lying down.

"He wishes for no food," she said. "But he must have some."

Bisby nodded. In fact, when the meal was prepared, over a fire of driftwood stacked in the corner of the cave, Soldatov ate. It was a curious mixture—a meat stew pre-

250

pared from the remains of the meat joint from the cabin and several tins of the cocktail sausages from the Eskimo cache. There was not much driftwood, and the fire soon died down, to the manifest relief of the three fit reindeer, which had backed into a shadowy corner of the cabin, eyes rolling. The fourth, lying near the entrance, showed only by an occasional whimper that it still lived.

Once more, Stovin found himself enjoying the gentle warmth and soft light of the seal-oil lamp. It was a lamp that induced talk, and now it was Bisby who was talking. He seemed much less tense and more communicative than in the last two days, as though something had happened in the last hour to change his attitude. Yet, even in the shelter of the cave, there was an echo of menace. It came from outside—a distant, titanic grinding, the sound of giant impacts, a groaning of the world.

Bisby saw Stovin listening and said one word: "Icebergs."

Stovin nodded. "I thought I saw something out to the north, on the edge of the ice, when we came out from Uelen tonight. But I couldn't believe it. There should never be icebergs in the Bering Straits. There aren't any glaciers near enough to build them in the North Pacific, and the current flows north. So there shouldn't be icebergs on the north side, anyway."

"The current flows south sometimes in winter," said Bisby. "We get a lot of wood that way. For a day or two, the currents can get mixed up. Anybody who ever takes a kayak through these waters knows that. But you're right, Sto. It's never been heard of, to get icebergs in the Bering Strait. Particularly bergs coming down from the north. Because that's what we're hearing. Big bergs, half a million tons, maybe, driving into the pack-ice at the edge of the bridge."

"Bridge?" said Diane in astonishment.

"I think so," said Bisby. "Those bergs are hitting something pretty solid. It takes a lot to stop a half-million-ton ice mountain when it's moving down at three, four miles an hour. So the reason those bergs aren't plowing down right through the channel—or what used to be the channel—between the two Diomedes is that they're bashing through an outlying pack and then hitting something they can't move. Something that grounds them and stops them dead."

"What?" said Volkov. He was listening attentively.

"Land," said Bisby. "They're hitting land. Land where there's been no land for around 15,000 years. I reckon history's repeating itself—or rather, prehistory's repeating itself. We're sitting right in the middle of the Bering Land Bridge. The neck of land that stretched between Siberia and Alaska. A hell of a long time ago, the people who eventually became the Chukchi drove the people who eventually became the Eskimo right over this bridge, from Siberia to America. Just like those damned Chukchi drove the Eskimos today. And the wolves came over the Bridge, and the mammoth, and the caribou. It was the link between the continents."

"But . . ." began Diane. Bisby was not to be stopped.

"That's what I learned at college, before I couldn't take some of the nonsense any more and dropped out. I reckon it was about the only piece of anthropology that ever meant a damn to me. It was a great idea, the Bridge. I used to dream of it, but I never dared pray I'd see it."

"But," said Diane, "the Chukchi didn't go to Cornell. You don't seriously imagine that they woke up the other day and said to themselves 'Oh, there's the Bering Land Bridge again, after all these years. Now we have to get back to driving the Eskimos across it.' A pretty simplistic bit of reasoning, I think."

Her voice was impatient, even condescending. Bisby looked at her with what, she thought in slightly shocked surprise, seemed something close to dislike.

"Your wolves"—why did he always call them "your wolves"?—"had never seen a mammoth, had they? But it didn't stop their attacking those carriers, back at Novosibirsk. It's all changing, girl. Some of the things happening now never made up any part of a course at Cornell. Or the University of Colorado."

That was another annoying habit he'd developed—calling her and Valentina "girl." She set her lips and was silent. The talk gradually became more general, incongruously so, she thought, in view of their strange situation. Volkov talked earnestly and inaudibly to Bisby in the unexpected affability that now seemed often to grow up between them. The Soldatovs dozed, though Valentina was more than half awake. Worrying about Geny, obviously. And Stovin was here beside her . . . warm and intelligent and perceptive, the best of all reminders that outside this cave, there was still another, kinder world.

Even though it was changing. She glanced across once more to Bisby. He was a very odd character, but without him they wouldn't be here, and she'd be with the Chukchi. She'd better make her peace with him.

After half an hour, they prepared for sleep. The Soldatovs took one of the three caves, and Bisby and Volkov the center one, leaving the last for her and Stovin.

Before they lay down, she went across to Bisby and said, "Paul, all that you were saying about the Land Bridge—it wasn't just what you learned at Cornell, was it? There must have been something more. You seemed to have it all so . . . so ready to say."

Slowly he nodded. For a moment, in the pulse of the seal-oil lamp, his face seemed young and vulnerable.

"Yes, Diane, there was something else. You see, it's all part of a pattern. I've known about it for a long time."

"But what pattern?"

"I don't know. I'm not stalling. I really don't. It's something that goes right back to my childhood. And I had a pretty way-out kind of childhood, by your standards. Hunting, and kayaking, and . . . wizards."

She laughed incredulously. "Wizards? Oh, come on, Paul . . ."

She wondered for a moment if she had angered him again, but he seemed unconcerned. He was smiling.

" 'There are more things in heaven and earth, Horatio, than are dreamt of in your philosophy,' " he said.

Without knowing quite why she did it, she reached out her hand and took his. Her voice was mocking, but she felt for him the first moment of genuine personal contact there had ever been between them.

"Shakespeare, too?" she said. "You're a very unexpected person, Paul. It seems to me that the most curious thing about you is not that an Eskimo became a jet pilot, but that he dropped out of Cornell."

He made no reply, and she was turning away when he stepped across the yard of space that separated them, tilted her face gently with his hand, and kissed her on the mouth. Then he turned his back and went into his own sleeping cave. Her heart was pounding, and she stared after him like a schoolgirl. She thought later that she had never been more surprised in the whole of her life. Lying beside Stovin a few minutes later, she turned to him and said, "Stovin?"

"Yes?"

"Do you feel like a bit of love?"

"They'll hear," he said sleepily. "In the other caves, I mean. Here . . . what are you doing?"

He was fully awake now. "Oh, well," he said with mock reluctance, "it's not going to be easy, in these clothes, but I suppose it can be arranged."

"Arrange it, Stovin," she said.

When it was over, she lay back, a deep tide of satisfaction sweeping over her. She was lying with her mouth close to his, so that he had only to whisper.

"What brought that on, so quickly?"

She snuggled closer. "Oh, every now and then I fancy you, Stovin," she said. She raised herself on one elbow and kissed him. I do love him, she told herself. Very, very much. But that's not why I wanted him to have me, here and now.

She was sliding into sleep, listening to the distant crash and thunder of the ice, when a new sound threaded through into her consciousness. There it was again. She nudged Stovin.

"Do you hear that? Surely it's . . ."

He put a finger on her lips and listened carefully. The thin high ululation came again. It was far away, but unmistakable. Stovin settled back.

"Yes," he said. "It's wolves. Wolves, out on the Bridge."

Seven hours later, in the dim light of morning, they saw their first wolves—racing black specks toward the middle of the Bridge. Black specks that every so often stopped and seemed to coalesce into a group. After a little, they came upon the reason—four dead Eskimos, a man, a woman, and two children. They lay frozen, already dusted by the slight snow that had fallen at dawn. Beside them was a broken sled. A mile farther on were two more corpses—both men—one old, one young. This time Bisby did not stop. The two sleds were moving only slowly since Valentina's was now drawn by a single reindeer. The other beast had been dead when they woke in the cave.

Bisby spoke over his shoulder, "I guess there'll be quite a few bodies, out there."

He pointed over to their right, to the south. "There were several hundred people crossing last night, though they're way south of here now. But already they were all

254

Eskimos—well, most Eskimos aren't what they were. A few years learning white man's ways, and they lose it. When you lose it, you don't survive. That's why the wolves are following. They're no fools, wolves. They know where there'll be pickings."

Stovin found that he felt strangely detached. Their sleds were nearing the Alaskan coast, now only a mile or so away, and they were on the northern side of the ice bridge. At least, Stovin reminded himself, it wasn't wholly an ice bridge. It was quite clear that the level of the Strait had dropped. Bisby was right. There was land where there had been sea for 15,000 years. And that argued exactly the kind of changes he, Stovin, had been preaching for most of his professional life. The growing ice sheets in the north, the increased snow . . . these sucked up water from the ocean. And the sea level fell. The Bering Land Bridge was coming back—and soon, maybe, the land bridge between England and France. Even across the Bab el-Mandeb Strait, from Arabia to Africa. Given these circumstances, of course, any first-year climatology student could work out what would happen. But the astonishing thing is, he thought . . . the really astonishing thing is the speed of it all. Not a hundred years. Not ten. Just one—and then there was enough fall in sea level here to ground those icebergs. And enough pattern of the ocean currents. In a year or two, at this rate, this won't be an ice bridge any more. It'll be a broad path of dry land, tundra maybe, joining two worlds. And look at it out there! What a birth it's having!

A mile out on their left, the immense icebergs loomed like a slowly advancing fleet. One by one, they struck the thinner ice of the outlying pack, plowing through it with a titanic roar, shivering the solid ice between pack and shore like hammers hitting glass. The noise, even from this distance, was like an artillery barrage. Moreover, Stovin knew, the icebergs themselves, when they finally plowed to a halt were helping to build the land bridge. Each berg brought down rocks, fragments, even soil from its parent glacier. These it dropped where it ended its journey.

They were passing now along a stretch of ice-covered beach about a quarter of a mile wide. It ended in steep, terraced cliffs, very like those outside Uelen, back across the Bering Strait.

Bisby slowed, pointing upward and looking back at

Diane. "This is Cape Prince of Wales, I reckon. And I think that's the best way up."

Between the cliffs flowed what in summer must have been a considerable watercourse. It was frozen now, studded with great boulders, but it led high into the cliff. The going was appallingly difficult. Bisby lightened the sleds by dismounting everyone except Soldatov, who was obviously now too sick to face the rigors of the climb. In spite of his protests, he was settled back into his sled, and Volkov and Valentina hauled on the single reindeer to help it in the ascent. Their strength was not enough, and Bisby sent Stovin back to help them. The ascent proved to be the greatest physical effort of Stovin's life. Slipping and sliding on the ice, sweating and freezing once more inside his furs, kicked once, painfully, in the side by the reindeer, he hauled at the sled. It took three-quarters of an hour of exhausting toil before at last, they reached the rim of the cliff. Bisby and Diane, with the two reindeer, had arrived there minutes before, and Bisby scrambled back the last hundred yards to help them. As soon as they once more reached level ground, they dropped onto the sleds, but Bisby roused them.

"Can't stop now," he said. "Too cold. Come on, Valentina. Drive. You can't stop now. Follow me."

The first noonday stars were already showing in the sky as they began to move inland across a glimmering grey-white plateau, rising in the east to mountains of perhaps 3,000 feet, though their height was difficult to judge since their peaks were packed in fog. At the edge of the plateau, they came across the first sign of habitation. There were a few deserted wooden cabins, almost obliterated by hard-packed ice and snow, the ridges of their roofs showing above the surface of the ground. Beside one of them a wooden sign, encrusted with ice, lay on the ground. Stovin, seated in the sled, found his breathing gradually becoming easier though he was actually uncomfortable in his icy clothes. He read the sign as they passed—"Wales Village Store." It was comforting to see the English lettering again, after weeks in Siberia with the unfamiliar Cyrillic script. But there was no American in the settlement—nothing except the scudding snow driven along the ground by the quickly rising wind. It was beginning to snow again. But he was too tired and too bruised to worry any more. He closed his eyes. When he opened them again, Diane was shaking him.

Bisby shouted something he could not hear, and pointed with his stick. Blearily, Stovin looked out.

Twenty yards away stood a man. He seemed, in that wilderness, an unbelievable apparition. He wore fine silver furs and broad snowshoes, and he carried a long spear. He raised a hand, and Bisby stopped the sled and got down. The two men shook hands in the Eskimo style Stovin had seen long ago at Anchorage—hand sideways over hand. In this wilderness, Stovin thought again, it was a bewildering sight, and then he realized it was no longer a wilderness. All around them in the starlight were houses—big round snow houses with surrounding ramparts of waist-high snow to keep out the cold knife of the wind. From these houses now poured people . . . children gaping at the newcomers, women clustered together and giggling, old men looking on inquisitively. Bisby was speaking to some of them, haltingly at first, and then with growing fluency and confidence. He beckoned to the others to join him. Stiffly they got down. Diane caught Stovin's arm as he swayed. Bisby said something quickly to the tall Eskimo with the spear, and a moment later two of the women came across and helped him into the nearest snow house. As his faintness passed, he saw that it was circular, warm, and shadowed, with three seal-oil lamps burning on a wooden tub beyond the door. Behind the lamps was a heap of skins and what looked like stacks of frozen meat. Several people crowded in after them, looking on curiously. Exhaustion began to roll over him, but he saw Diane go over to help as Soldatov was carried into the snow house. Someone brought him a bone cup, steaming. He sipped it. It was tea. He found himself saying Diane's name, and suddenly she was beside him, palefaced in the shadows, but apparently well. From behind her Bisby spoke. Stovin looked up from the pile of thick skins where he had flopped down. Bisby's face was radiant, content.

"You see?" he said. "We made it. Sto, these are the Inuit. These are the People."

With an effort, Stovin forced his mind back to the bar in Anchorage where he drank with Bisby—it seemed a thousand years ago.

"I remember," he said painfully, "you told me . . . your mother . . ."

"That's right," said Bisby happily. "The People. This is where we stay."

He looked down at Stovin's exhausted, uncomprehending face, and spoke again, "This is where Sedna pointed last night. We stay."

Wearily, Stovin closed his eyes. What in God's name was he talking about? More mystery . . . always mystery, with Bisby. But all I want is sleep.

CHAPTER 23

What happened in New York during the nightmare month of January was the most dramatic of the catastrophes that struck the cities of the northern hemisphere after the disaster of Chicago—though it did not match Chicago's 200,000 dead. Nevertheless, the death toll was very high. When the crisis came, it seemed for a week, perhaps a little more, that it might still prove to be no more than an exceptionally heavy snowfall in a very bad winter. The city froze, transformers blew, elevators and lighting and heating failed in many areas. In cold apartments, old people began to die. Yet the city, struggling, remained more or less viable as a place in which human beings could live. It waited for the thaw . . .

By the tenth day of snow, the city authorities were facing a situation completely outside their experience, and they found they could deal with it only by desperate efforts in isolated patches. By the fifteenth, even this struggle was virtually over. New York, which of all cities in the world was most architecturally vulnerable to a snow catastrophe, was on its own. All that saved its central population from annihilation was that on certain days, although the cold was intense and worse than anything known there in living memory or in any records, it did not snow. On such days the evacuation of the beleaguered population of midtown Manhattan, in circumstances of incredible difficulty, began. For it was midtown Manhattan, with its towering skyscape above relatively narrow streets, that suffered worst.

The snow came sweeping in down Long Island Sound.

The East River and the Hudson River froze, and then received upon their newly solid surfaces thousands of tons of new snow. Beneath this immense weight, the Queensboro Bridge collapsed first, followed by the Madison. The blizzard that raged over central Manhattan for several days without cease left sixty feet of snow in the narrow canyons of some streets, and buried even the broader thoroughfares of Fifth Avenue, Park Avenue, and Lexington so deep that shops and offices disappeared. Only hastily provided snowshoes made it possible for police and soldiers to patrol the white desert of midtown Manhattan, leading people to assembly areas across the Hudson. Fighting as hard as United States soldiers had ever fought, 15,000 men held the George Washington Bridge and its approaches open, so that this limited movement of population could be made. For no attempt was made—or could be made—to evacuate the entire city. The appalling example of Chicago was fresh in every mind, and it was realized that such a bid would have been doomed. In the intense cold, thousands of cars refused to move, and it was in any case possible to clear only a limited number of roads. Over all the city, in Harlem and in the Chinese and Puerto Rican sections on the Lower East Side, families in tenement buildings, first isolated and then often buried in snow, obeyed official instructions and their own basic instincts to try to sit it out and wait for at least some degree of thaw. . . . Survival under the snow proved by no means impossible, and access to sources of food in abandoned shops and restaurants, especially where effective air shafts had been made or were in some way available, kept hundreds of thousands alive.

Meanwhile in Manhattan, the great skyscrapers—the Pan Am building, the Empire State, Chrysler, and the rest—thrust up into a hostile sky, like concrete arrows embedded in the ice. Helicopter pilots who flew above the city wilderness reported a sense of total disbelief at the sights they saw. And the helicopters were busy. In many of the skyscraper buildings where elevators and power had failed, considerable groups of people still lived in the upper sections . . . people who had made their way down by stairway to street level only to find the snow wall outside towering far above their heads. Gradually, score by score, they were lifted off by helicopter, though hundreds chose to remain, confident that the supplies of food and drink which existed in the restaurants and stores of some beleaguered buildings would last them until the thaw came. But the thaw did not come. After five weeks midtown Manhattan had been abandoned by all but a few thousand people. Thousands more lay dead beneath the snow, though their numbers would not be known until spring.

New York's experience was repeated in various ways in Europe, which had also made one or two abortive attempts of evacuation and, like Chicago, had suffered disaster. Both Glasgow and Oslo had managed to call off their evacuation operations after losing some thousands of people caught by relentless blizzards while actually moving south on escape roads; in Hamburg, with 15,800 dead in a single day of attempted mass movement, the toll was highest of all. By contrast, Winnipeg in Canada, stricken as badly by snow as Chicago had been, urged its citizens to stay put. Air shafts were sunk, New York style, to buried communities. Once more, however, the success or failure of the stay-put policy could not be evaluated until the spring.

In northern Europe, the problem of northern Scandinavia was total. The new Ice Age settled there, mercilessly and firmly, from the very beginning. Fortunately, the area was relatively lightly populated, and paradoxically, its scattered communities proved easier to move to safety. Some thousands of Swedes and Norwegians were gradually brought south, especially to Denmark which, though itself under strong climatic pressure, was able to accept some refugees.

But one by one the great northern cities—Glasgow, Winnipeg, Newcastle upon Tyne, Oslo, Helsinki, Moscow, Leningrad, Boston, Minneapolis—came under siege. They waited desperately for spring, evacuating as many as possible, but in general attempting to sit out the crisis. The scale of death mounted steadily—more than 3,000 a week in Glasgow from hunger and cold alone—and thousands of others whose fate was still unknown in buried streets.

Governments drew lines of catastrophe across their national maps. Above these lines, nothing approaching normal life was possible. Below them, efforts could be made. Industrial life managed in many places below the catastrophe line to achieve some limited production after a few weeks. The fuel and energy crisis, however, was

260

crippling. North Sea oil, Siberian oil, Alaskan oil . . . these were forgotten dreams. Nowhere in the northern hemisphere, after the end of the month, could a private automobile move without government permission.

In general, the great cities proved to be more vulnerable than the surrounding countryside. In both Europe and North America, small rural communities, even when completely isolated, contrived an existence of their own with only occasional support by air from central authorities farther south. The loss of livestock, of course, was virtually total, though farmers sometimes hung onto basic stock by taking animals into their own homes, both as a basis for a hoped-for future and as an insurance against short-term starvation. No such alleviation was possible in cities where the lack of energy, as powerlines collapsed with the weight of ice, or as transformers blew without hope of repair in continual blizzards, brought gripping, lethal cold. The old died first, in thousands.

Nevertheless, technological man—though in other ways unfitted to deal with such an emergency—was intelligent. Cooperation became the international watchword. In the European Community, there was an unprecedented dismantling of frontiers. Within weeks, children from buried Scottish towns and lost Norwegian villages were encamped, in every tent that could be found, in the wet but milder areas of Bavaria and Provence and the south of Italy. In North America, the United States and Canada now regarded themselves as a single unit with a single problem. The tent cities that sprang up in British Columbia, California, New Mexico, Arizona, Texas, accepted refugees—whether Canadian or United States citizens—on an equal basis. In the Soviet Union, the Russians began the laborious transfer, where possible, of northern populations to Georgia, the Crimea, and the Ukraine.

The whole hemisphere waited for the spring in hope and desperation. Yet men like Brookman in the United States and Ledbester in Britain knew that the spring must bring new problems. Much of the snow that had fallen during this terrible winter would remain all summer long; the physical facts of temperature and surface albedo would insure that. And the temperature over crucial grain-growing areas like the Canadian prairies and the Soviet Ukraine and the American Midwest—even in areas not totally obliterated by snow—would be down.

The temperature drop in the coming summer would

not seem, in terms of human physical reaction, to be one of cosmic dimensions, though it would be a shorter and colder spring and summer than had been known since records began. But to wheat seedlings, even a small drop in average temperature and the consequent shortening of the growing season would be lethal. Brookman and his colleagues knew that great areas of the overpopulated world would be disastrously hungry by fall, and even great nations in the affluent West would be tightening their belts. And beyond that short autumn lay another winter in which many millions of people, evacuated from stricken northern areas, would still be without homes. The summer for which the hemisphere hoped could bring only a brief respite. Suddenly, even the governments of Superpowers seemed to be no more than groups of bewildered men, struggling against a gigantic, remorseless, uncontrollable, unpredictable foe. . . .

The President was desperately tired. He looked at Brookman's troubled face and then at the familiar, polite mask of the features of the Director of the Central Intelligence Agency. Does all this matter now? he asked himself. International diplomacy . . . the Cold War with its hot fringes . . . they're out of date already in just a few weeks. But we seem to have to go on pretending they're still important in their old terms.

The CIA chief was speaking. "The weather up there in northeast Siberia has been a total catastrophe, of course —maybe even worse than Alaska. You've seen the satellite pictures, Mr. President? The Soviets have got all sorts of trouble."

"Yes," said the President. He rubbed his eyes, and Brookman watched him with concern. The catastrophe of Chicago had hit him very hard. The President got to his feet and walked away from the desk, looking out from the window into the small enclosed garden behind the Palace of the Governors. There were a few old frontier wagons there, museum pieces from the old Santa Fe Trail. One of the three Secret Service men in the garden was ducking behind the nearest wagon in an effort to get out of the rain that had started again. Was I wise, wondered the President, to place the temporary White House here in Santa Fe, in New Mexico? Changed times needed new thinking, of course. And the weather in

262

Washington had been appalling and communications difficult. Nevertheless, that wasn't the reason, was it? We all need a bit less Washington. By golly, what a dead hand can clamp down from that city. I wonder . . . would it be a good thing to take the White House around the country—a spell here, say, and then one in Georgia, then Oklahoma? The Secret Service sure wouldn't like it, but the people might . . . something of a personal touch. Maybe folk wouldn't feel so cut off.

He turned back to the other two. "So now we have a land frontier with the Soviet Union?"

The Director of the CIA nodded without speaking. The President crossed to the big map fixed to the far panelled wall and looked at its new, pasted-on markings, showing where the Alaskan ice and the Siberian ice had now frozen the continents together. A few months ago, the news would have seemed momentous. There would have been endless conferences, endless papers, endless strategic analyses. Now . . . well, he'd hardly thought about it. He tapped the area of the Bering Strait, looking at the CIA man.

"Does this bother you?"

The Director shrugged. "Well, it's something we have to take into account, of course. But no, sir, it doesn't really bother me at this moment. It's really not so very different from the way it was before. The satellite pictures are poor, but they show people crossing. As far as we can make out, they're just Eskimos—and a lot of them aren't making it, anyway. There seem to be a lot of bodies. But just like anybody else in the Soviet Union, I guess they take the first chance out they get. A few Eskimos more or less in the United States—even if they survive up there, and we won't know that until the spring—well, it's not exactly a major security problem. We'll know more when we can fly a few photographic missions. But as of now, Alaska is a desert."

"Hm," said the President. He sat down heavily at his desk, and Brookman saw, more clearly than ever before, that he was really quite an old man.

"I went out to the tents this morning," said the President. "Early . . . around seven o'clock. Thought I'd take a little breakfast with those people. Way down the range, toward Roswell. They did a good job down there, Mel; they've got a real tent city. Folk seem to be managing pretty well—though the sooner we get the prefabricated units up, the better. But I reckon it's better than being frozen in Chicago. It's wet, though. By golly, it's wet. The Governor told me New Mexico hasn't had rain like this in this century."

"It's to be expected," said Brookman.

The President leaned forward, tapping his hand on the desk to emphasize his point. "When the second hemisphere conference comes, Mel—and it looks like pretty soon—we must look further ahead than this coming spring. We mustn't be hassled into endless discussion of this year like we were last time. It's next winter now that bothers me—it's going to be worse than this. But at least we'll know what to expect."

"There's a lot that can be done," said Brookman. He found himself saying the cheerful words quite unexpectedly. Whenever I come into this room, he thought, I go out feeling better.

The President rose. "We're going to need imagination, more than we've ever used before. And talking of that, I have an appointment with the Chiefs of Staff. They're bothered about the Early Warning System—up in Canada and Alaska."

"There is no Early Warning System now," said the Director of the CIA. "Not in the north, anyhow."

The President held out his hand. "Oh, we had an early warning all right," he said. "We had a genuine old-style prophet. But we didn't listen, and now the man who gave it is . . ."

He turned to the Director. "I imagine there isn't even a hint of news?"

"Of Stovin, you mean? No, Mr. President. That Antonov took off all right from Novosibirsk. It was logged on the approach to Anadyr. After that . . . nothing. And I'm sure the Soviets are giving us 100 percent on this. They had some of their own people aboard, as you know."

When they had gone, the President sat at his desk, leaning back in his chair with his eyes closed. A pity about Stovin, he thought. We can't afford to lose many like that. Next winter . . . I'd have liked to hear Stovin talk about next winter. He got to his feet and walked to the mirror by the door. Better look smart for the Chiefs, he thought, smoothing his thinning hair. I look old. I *am* old. Maybe that's why I'm still useful.

Stovin was worried. He knelt on a deerskin spread beside a hole in the ice of the little frozen lake above the settlement and watched his fishing line. Over to his left, about a quarter of a mile out on the ice, Volkov crouched with his fish spear. It was strange, thought Stovin, that Volkov, who had been the one most reluctant to stay in the settlement, had adapted to its life better than any of them—except, of course, Bisby. He had watched the Russian an hour ago use an ice chisel on the four-foot-thick ice of the lake, cutting out a round hole, ice chips flying, at a speed which Oonatuk himself would have envied. After only a few weeks of practice, no one was quicker than Volkov. There he went again, driving the spear down into the hole. Another trout. That made three. His own line quivered. He took the first pull and then snatched it up. The fish had almost swallowed the little finned bone decoy. It was a large fish, and it sailed out of the hole like a leaping salmon. It hit the ice beside him once, flapped frantically, jerked itself into the air, fell back, and lay instantly frozen, like a plaster model. A scud of driven snow stung his face through the furs, and he realized that the wind was getting up. He got painfully to his feet, running a line through the gills of his two trout. Volkov waved, picking up his own fish, and walked across.

"We go back now, I think," he said. "This wind . . . it is not good."

"I'm worried," said Stovin as they walked back together, "about Bisby. It's been three days now. He said it would be two."

"A hunting trip is not predictable," said Volkov. "And he had Oonatuk with him. And the other one—Shongli."

"Yes," said Stovin. But his heart sank again as they plodded on their snowshoes into the settlement, past the "destroying place" where the possessions of dead Eskimos were ritually smashed and broken so that no dead man's spirit would wish to return. There was no sign of Oonatuk's dog team or sled. He went into the igloo. Even now, after so many weeks, he retched slightly in initial revulsion as the stench of the snow house hit him. It was a large snow house and held two families, in addition to himself and Diane and the Soldatovs. Bisby and Volkov had their own place in another snow house across the cleared patch of the settlement. The nausea was leaving him now, and he knew that in a minute or so he would

265

not notice it any more than Diane. She sat on their bed—
a pile of caribou skins on the raised sleeping platform.
She was busy making a seal-oil lamp. She looked up as
he came in, and he caught the flash of her white teeth in
the shadows. In spite of his worry, he felt the tug of desire. Diane was dirty, he was dirty, in a way they had
never been before. Each of them, presumably, smelled,
neither of them noticed it. He had already grown a beard
as some small protection against the waxen threat of a
frozen chin. Diane's hair was scuffed and messed, and
she had seal-oil smudges on her face. She looked, he
thought, like a blonde Eskimo *kooner*—one of the wives
of this little settlement of precisely six families.

"That's good, Stovin," she said as he handed her the
fish. "You're getting really good at it."

"No news of Bisby?" he said.

She shook her head.

"It worries me," he said. "If anything happens to
Bisby, how are we going to get back?"

"Get back where?" she said.

He stared at her. "Back to the United States."

She laughed. "We're in the United States. All right, all
right, I know what you mean. Don't worry, Stovin. The
spring's coming."

"It's certainly getting lighter," he said. "There's a lot
more color in the sky. Soon we'll see the whole of the
sun."

"I know," said Diane.

"But even then," said Stovin. "I don't see how we
could do it by ourselves. The distances are immense. It's
2,000 miles from here to Seattle, even. And God knows
what we'd find in Seattle, anyway. If we're going to make
a long journey like that, we need an expert. We need
Bisby."

Diane reached out and patted his hand. "Come the
spring, Stovin, they'll be flying up planes from the south.
They're sure to want to take a long hard look at what
used to be Alaska. They'll see us."

"Maybe," he said. "It's hard enough to spot people,
even if you're looking for them."

He looked at her curiously. "You're not all that worried about going, are you?"

She smiled. "I like it here. It could be worse."

There was a momentary bustle in the entrance passage
to the snow house, and the Soldatovs entered together.

266

Neither of them, thought Stovin, had made much concession to Eskimo life. Valentina was by far the cleanest person in the settlement, frequently washing her body with some discomfort and watched in astonishment by Eskimo children. Soldatov had succeeded in retaining his spectacles. He was stronger now, almost fit again, though in the early days after their arrival Valentina's willpower had been all that stood between her husband and death. He was still not able to join in the fishing with the others, but he spent his time writing notes, in a tiny Russian script, over every inch of a tattered notebook he had produced from the bundle he had packed, long ago, in Anadyr. He listened eagerly in the long evenings when Shongli and Oonatuk—the tall Eskimo in the silver furs they had seen on the day they arrived—told their interminable stories, squatting around one of the seal-oil lamps. If Bisby was in the mood, he would translate. And what Soldatov heard, he wrote down.

"I learn," he said. Stovin, too, knew that he had learned. Yet what he had learned so worried and staggered his intellect that he, unlike Diane, longed to return. There were men whom he wanted to speak to. The hemisphere conference . . . it seemed another world. It was long over by now, of course, but there would be other vital conferences. He should be there.

Valentina went across to the communal pile in the corner and took out two stiff, frozen tom cod. The fish had probably, thought Stovin, been there for weeks. The communal pile was the most efficient freezer in the world. It was astonishing that none of them had ever had a stomach upset though they had eaten, especially at first, large amounts of the seal and walrus meat which was stacked in various stages of decomposition around the walls.

A couple of the Eskimo women wandered in, giggling and laughing when they saw Stovin sprawled on the sleeping platform beside Diane and giving both him and Soldatov sidelong glances. They, too, went to the communal pile and took out fish, sorting through them carefully, occasionally testing a fish with strong white Eskimo teeth and then throwing it back. At last, they were satisfied and went out, calling reprovingly to two children rolling in the snow. They were chattering happily.

Soldatov read Stovin's thoughts and said, "These people

267

live where men should not be able to live. Their lives are short, brutish even. Is that not so?"

Stovin nodded.

"Yet they are happy, my dear Sto. They laugh. I have never seen one of them strike a child. They have little sense of property. Like Bedouin, they are lavishly hospitable. They do not seem to experience the usual traumas of sex—infidelity, impotence. They change partners, sometimes, on impulse. But the family unit remains. It is remarkable."

"Yes," said Stovin, "but these aren't the tamed Eskimos of Anchorage or Anadyr. This is a race in decline, Geny, on the point of extinction. High Arctic Eskimos, who know almost nothing about the rest of the world. Bisby says there are no more than a few hundred left. And they count themselves as the People—the only true men."

"They do not wash," said Valentina, wrinkling her nose where she sat beside Diane on the skins.

"Perhaps we have attached too much importance to washing," said Soldatov. He turned back to Stovin.

"I do not admire the life of the noble savage," he said. "That is a myth. But I am like you, Sto. I am a man of my own time. And I am beginning to learn. For the first time in my whole life, I am beginning to learn. You, too, I think."

Stovin nodded. "Yes. There's a lot of work to be done, a lot of things to be said, when we get back. If we get back."

"We shall get back," said Valentina. "As soon as . . . what is that?"

There was a commotion outside, a sound of shouting and laughter. One of the small Eskimo boys half fell into the snow house, screaming with excitement.

"Oonatuk," he shouted. "Bisbee . . . Bisbee."

The whole settlement seemed to erupt as Bisby's sled, drawn by six dogs, their breath freezing in the scudding snow, came into the center of the four snow houses. Bisby and the two Eskimos behind him stood high on the body of a great white bear. All were laughing and shouting. The three men were covered in the blood of the big animal, brown and congealed over their faces and their furs. The women and the children pulled the bear from the sled, hopping and dancing with joy. Bisby came up to them, masked in blood and snow, and smiled. But he pushed on past the snow house without speaking and went into his own. He was alone there, for the moment; Volkov was outside with the others. Bisby drew from under his caribou skin bedding the biscuit box he had carried all his life. He took out the skull of the fox and pressed it to his forehead.

"I thank you, Sedna, for the skill to kill the bear. Is there a sign?"

There was no sign. He went back to the sled, beside which lay the body of the bear, prodded occasionally by the awed children and carefully measured by Soldatov with a fishing line. While Oonatuk stretched the bear's throat, Bisby took his long knife and cut off its head, so that its spirit could be released. Oonatuk's *kooner* placed a piece of frozen fish and a lump of ice in the dead mouth, so that the bear would not be hungry or thirsty in its new world. Then, swiftly and expertly, the women skinned the great beast, cutting haunches and wedges of meat from the flayed carcass. That night the whole settlement feasted, eating the hot boiled bear in the big snow house next to the one which Stovin and Diane and the Soldatovs shared with Shongli's family. Stovin was weary after he had eaten and went back to the igloo. At least, he thought, I am not alone. Judging from the gasping and groaning in the heap of skins in Shongli's corner, Shongli was there with his *kooner*. Or, perhaps, with Oonatuk's *kooner*. It didn't seem to matter. He slept.

In the feast house, Diane and Valentina talked for a while in low voices, until Valentina went out to join Soldatov. Diane went with her to the entrance and then looked back. Volkov had gone long ago, but Bisby and two Eskimos were still eating. They ate with a furious concentrated attention, as though this was their last meal on earth. Bisby's face shone with grease in the yellow light of the seal-oil lamp. He held a piece of bear meat in his hands. At intervals, he lowered his head and bit off a chunk. The bear fat ran down his chin, and before he had finished chewing, his hands went back to the great communal platter to find another piece. One of the others— he was Oonatuk—licked the palms of his hands and thoughtfully sucked his fingers. He looked up, saw Diane watching, and nudged Bisby, grinning. Bisby rose from the meal and came over to her. Smiling, she began to speak, but then stopped uncertainly. He took her by the wrist and pulled her out into the Arctic night. She found herself fighting him.

"What . . . what . . . have you gone mad? Let me go . . . oh, oh."

She seemed like a baby in his arms. He half pushed, half carried her into the igloo he shared with Volkov. She called Volkov's name.

"Grigori, Grigori."

There was no reply. Bisby was at her now like the bear he had killed. He was kissing her face, her neck. He smelled of seal and bear, and his beard was rough on her face. She could taste the dried bear blood on his cheeks. Frantically, he pulled at her furs, forcing her back on the pile of skins of his bed. She couldn't fight him any more. She didn't want to fight him any more. He had his hands on her breasts now—not roughly, but not tenderly either. His mouth clamped on hers again so that she could hardly breathe. His knee came up, forcing her legs apart. There was no resistance in her. He seemed enormous, obliterating. His thumbs pulled back the flesh at her groin, and then he was into her like an iron rod, pounding and panting above her. She found herself laughing, crying, pleading, groaning. Each thrust was a mixture of torture and ecstasy. At last it was over and he shouted in triumph. He lay above her for a moment or two and then, without speaking, rolled away and turned his back. After a little, she fumbled around in the dark and put on some of her clothes. Then she went back to her own igloo. There was a steady sound of snoring from Shongli's corner. She was still breathing heavily when she sat on the skin pile and tried to smooth her hair. Stovin's eyes gleamed in the darkness. He was awake.

"Where have you been?" he said. "No, don't tell me. I know."

In his own igloo, Bisby struck a match and lighted his seal-oil lamp. He opened the biscuit box, looked up, and saw Volkov watching him in the darkness from the other side of the igloo. Volkov abruptly shut his eyes and turned away from him. Bisby took from the box a black feather, a raven's feather. He balanced it on the ridged eye socket of the tiny skull and watched. Like a faintly exhaled breath, a tremor of air stirred the feather. Slowly it turned on its axis and then stopped. The air was still. The feather was pointing south. Bisby nodded. The girl had brought a sign.

Spring

CHAPTER 24

Hefting the single-bladed spear over his shoulder, Bisby plodded on behind Oonatuk and Shongli along the hummocked shore. They were on the south side of the great ice bridge, and in front of them opened the ice-strewn waters of the Norton Sound. Far out at sea, the ice seemed broken. It was already light, and every so often, through inky clouds, the pale morning sun could be glimpsed on the horizon. There were other signs of spring. Shongli, with his bow, had shot an eider duck a mile back and had missed a white-tailed ptarmigan. And out on the floes, drifting in the lee of the ice bridge, lay the herds of walrus. They were too distant yet to be stalked. The great bulls, each with its attendant cows, were hauled out on the ice of the pack, drifting on jagged pans, gorged with the shellfish from the level, sandy bottom of the Strait. His father had once told him that he could remember when the Strait was almost covered with walrus at this time of year—thousand upon thousand of the beasts. But that was on Ihovak in the old time. Where once there had been thousands, now there were only scores.

Ihovak . . . it was not so far from here. Forty miles, perhaps, down the Sound. How had they fared in the past winter? But he could not go. Not yet. He smiled inside his hood. It seemed a long time ago, another world, in Anchorage when he'd told Stovin he did not return to Ihovak because he was ashamed. That hadn't been the truth but there was no point in telling the truth to a *kablunaak*. No, he could not go back. Two shamans had warned him. The shaman Etukishuk on the day before he left to go to Cornell. And the shaman Ohoto in that camper outside Anchorage. Each had used the same words.

"When you return to Ihovak, you will not leave again."

273

So he could not return. Because there was a destiny; he had a destiny outside Ihovak. Sedna had told him in many, many signs. Sedna, who lived at the bottom of the sea and ruled all things that lived and breathed and swam. Sedna, who knew all. Sedna, who had guided him even when he flew like a gannet in the *kablunaak* Starfighter. Sedna had brought him home at least to the People. But there was still a destiny. She had promised.

There was a low shout ahead. Shongli was waving. He crouched beside an ice hummock on the beach and watched. Perhaps fifty yards away, a bull walrus and two cows lay on a drifting pan of ice, bobbing slowly as the undercurrent gradually worked it through the pack to a long lead of open sea. Bisby took his own spear from his shoulder. It had a four-foot mainshaft of wood with a fifteen-inch foreshaft made of walrus ivory. The blade of the head itself was also of ivory, razor sharp, and socketed into its place with meticulous precision. The head had to move as soon as it had plunged its destined five inches into the flesh of walrus or seal, turning sideways so that the line to which it was attached would not be pulled out as the victim hurled itself away through the sea. Shongli was stalking. Deftly, silently, he leaped from pan to pan of ice, always choosing pans where he could balance, gradually closing the distance between himself and the walrus. He was almost near enough to throw when it raised its massive tusked head, bellowed once, and slid from the pan, followed instantly by its two cows. Shongli pantomined frustration and made his way back ashore. Well spaced out the three hunters went on along the beach.

We could do with a walrus, thought Bisby. Walrus meat was easy to cut, and it kept well. Good travelling meat. Tomorrow they would be travelling . . . south. Sedna had made that clear. Well, it would please the old man, Stovin. And the girl, perhaps. For a moment he remembered her panting in his arms, and his body stirred. His mind was now so far from their world that they seemed to him like creatures from another planet, but perhaps they were part of his destiny. At any rate, he would take them south, as far as that destiny allowed. And only Sedna could tell him that.

Out on his right, a great bearded, tusked head broke from the water. A moment later a big walrus embedded its three-foot tusks into the ice of a floating pan and hauled itself from the sea. The pan was drifting quite fast, perhaps three knots, in the undercurrent through the pack. It was large, perhaps fifty yards in diameter. The walrus lay to one side. Quickly, he tested the line on his harpoon. It hung free of the sharp blade, running through his gloved hands. There were more than two hundred yards of broken ice between him and the walrus. He went from floe to floe, steadying himself, balancing, the harpoon ready in his right hand. The great beast lay inert occasionally shaking its fringed, whiskered mouth in a shower of ice droplets. It was very large, fully a ton in weight. When he was ten yards away, he decided to wait no longer. He drew back his hand behind his shoulder, checked the line once more, and hurled the spear. He had never thrown better. The spear struck the walrus under its right shoulder, embedding itself deeply in the blubbery flesh. With a shattering roar and a soaring spout of blood, the walrus slid from the pan, diving deep beneath it, while the line went skittering through Bisby's gloves. He bent and with a swift movement flicked the line . . . one turn, two, three around the massive hummock of ice he had chosen as anchor. For a moment the beast broke surface again, looking back at him with its fierce fringed jaws gaping. Then it plunged and the line went slack. The whole pan trembled as the walrus came up beneath and crashed its head against the underside. The line tightened once more as the walrus changed tactics, heading out to sea, its strength still so great that it seemed actually to move the pan, for a moment, in the ice. Then it came back. Once, twice, three times it battered on the underside of the floe. Bisby drew the whalebone knife from his belt. A walrus had been known to smash its head through six inches of ice in order to get at the man who was killing it. Even as the thought came into his mind the pan split and the tusked mouth burst from the ice two yards from his feet. He stepped forward, knife poised, for the *coup de grâce*. The walrus sank from the hole it had created, and the line caught for a moment around his foot. He slashed swiftly at the line with the knife, but he was a second too late. With a ton of muscled flesh on the end, the line shot out tautly. It cut into his foot like a wire cutting cheese, leaving it hanging, almost severed, a fraction of a second before his knife cut the line. He stared unbelievingly at his leg. There was little pain—already the exposed stump was freezing. But the pressure of the warm blood in the severed arteries forced it through, though it solidified instantly in red-brown stains on the ice. He raised himself on his elbow and looked desperately for Shongli or Oonatuk. A mist was beginning to come up between him and the shore, and they were not to be seen. With a crack and a roar, the ice pan, weakened by the battering it had received from the walrus broke into three pieces. Bisby was lying on the smallest, and the undercurrent bore him, nosing through the heavier pack, steadily out to sea.

He had lost so much blood now that his mind was beginning to leave him. Was this, then, his destiny? No, no, this was no destiny . . . no destiny worth waiting for. Was this some trick, some irony of the gods? Sedna had promised . . . But now I must die, he thought. It is the time of breaking. Using all his remaining strength, he broke his whalebone knife into two pieces and placed them beside his body. The last thing Bisby felt was the motion of the current and the occasional rasping thumps of small collisions with loose ice.

He had been dead for more than a day before the island loomed out of the mist, topped with purplish-black clouds in the fading light. The pack absorbed the floating pan as it drove slowly into the jumble of ice along the shore. Bisby was back on Ihovak.

They waited for a long time, even after Oonatuk had told them there was no hope. And then at last, they packed for the journey south. The weather was kinder, a little, and the light was growing every day. Shongli took them with his own dog teams and sleds. Stovin promised him the rifle which Bisby had left in his igloo. There were still some shots left, for Bisby had not touched the rifle from the moment he returned to the People.

Each of them, for private reasons, was subdued as they left the little settlement, the dog whips cracking and the children running alongside for the first few hundred yards. South lay their old world, but it was a world at whose condition they could now only guess. Stovin was bitter; Diane was experiencing a turmoil of emotion she had never known before. Volkov was worried once more, uncertain of how his return would be judged by authority. The nearest to being contented were the Soldatovs, though

Valentina was anxious for her husband, and he himself privately wondered if his strength would stand up to the journey. But they all had reasons to go. They swung around the end of the cliff, and turned south. . . .

CHAPTER 25

Mission Report: U.S. Navy Search-and-Rescue Mission: April 18 Mission commenced from USS icebreaker Morley 0900 hrs.

Flying time: 92 minutes.   *Aircraft: U.S. Navy Helicopter Serial No. AH 1890*

Early Warning Stations at Nome and at Tin City north of Cape Prince of Wales were inspected in flight, from a height of 500 feet. EW Station at Nome appeared to be completely covered, as was the town. EW site at Tin City showed part of dish-radar system above snow, but all administration buildings were covered. No Eskimo or other human activity was observed at either site. Large group of wolves, approx. 200 strong, was observed near Nome.

South of Nome, on last leg of mission, a group of people with two dog sleds was observed signalling from the ground. Conditions were suitable for landing. Group included two United States and three Soviet nationals (see attached report). These were taken on board helicopter to USS Morley.

Signed:
James T. Davies, Lt. Cmdr. U.S.N.

Raoul Mangin, the French agronomist who was in charge of the tiny experimental station south of Ouargla on the northern edge of the Algerian Sahara, straightened in his canvas chair and looked out in surprise from the shaded verandah. A completely unexpected sight had appeared below the ridge which lay a little south of the small oasis he had created here in a desert world. A single camel, on which sat a swaying woman holding a small boy . . . two larger boys walking, and in front of them a man. He was a veiled Tuareg from much farther south. Most surprising of all, almost unbelievable, he was carrying what appeared to be the woman's bundle. I have never in my life seen that before, thought Mangin. He walked off the verandah and down through the flowers to the end of his little patch of green. Ouargla was where the new rains of the northern Sahara had ended. South from here was another world—a desert world.

"God be with you," he said to the Tuareg.

"And with you also," said the Tuareg.

The Frenchman hesitated. "You have come far?"

"I am Zayd ag-Akrud. I have come from Tamanrasset."

From Tamanrasset? He must be lying. Mangin looked again, now that the veil was drawn back for speech, at the emaciated face, the hooked nose, the deep-set, burning eyes. No, he was not lying. He was a Tuareg. The man was starving but would not make the slightest concession to that appalling fact. Mangin glanced at the woman and the boys. The two older boys were dreadfully thin but would survive. The youngest boy was in good condition. The woman . . . well, perhaps. With care. He spoke again to Zayd.

"How long ago were you in Tamanrasset?"

"Many weeks. And before that in Lissa."

God in heaven, that was more than 700 miles. And they must have lived off that old rifle all the way. It was astounding, fantastic. One of the greatest desert journeys ever made, given the circumstances, the woman, the children.

He hesitated. "You are hungry?"

Zayd did not reply but motioned toward the woman and the boys. The Frenchman now, with the quick tears coming to his eyes, knew what he must do. He spoke swiftly to his gaping Algerian servant.

"See that they are fed, at once. Milk and bread for the children, to begin with. Too much will make them ill. And for the woman, *couscous*. And oat porridge. Quickly."

He turned again to Zayd. He must behave properly.

"It is the hour of coffee."

Zayd inclined his head.

"Let us take some together," said Mangin. "And I myself am hungry. So we will take a little fruit, a little bread."

"I am in your debt," said Zayd politely, indicating the staggering bull camel, the worn blankets, the old, carefully greased rifle. "All that I have is yours."

The Frenchman had been ten years in the desert and knew what to say.

"What is mine is yours," he said. "I am honored by your visit. Perhaps you will consent to stay a little. I should value your help with my . . . my horses."

Zayd nodded. He watched Zenoba and his sons disappear with the servant. He ached with longing for the coffee, the bread, the fruit.

"It is as God wills," he said.

Diane felt the child stir within her for a moment as she bent over her desk in her room in Albuquerque. She was now in her fourth month—and that was the fourth movement this week. It seems a little early for kicking, she thought wryly. Absently, she rearranged the loose folders of her report on the changed behavior patterns of wolves. For a moment, her mind flicked back to the night in the cave on the Bering Strait when she had lain, content and satisfied, beside Stovin and listened to that thin high howling out on the ice.

Would sex between her and Stovin ever be the same again? At the moment, it seemed different—not for her, but for him. Oh, yes, they were making love again, but something had changed. He was still hurt, of course, although he pretended he wasn't. Yet what had happened between her and Bisby seemed to her now like a night of fever, of delirium, an unreal dream, almost a sexual fantasy of the kind she'd had when she was a teenager. And for Bisby himself, for the memory of him, she now felt nothing except a sort of awed puzzlement. She was certain, too, that he had felt nothing for her. Except . . . perhaps . . . there had been that moment of sudden tenderness when he'd kissed her in the cave on Diomede. Maybe there *had* been something, though it certainly wasn't anything you could call love. Nevertheless, to her surprise, she found that she hugged the memory of that kiss as though it was something she might regret losing.

Well, she'd lived for a month or two in the Stone Age, and she'd been mated by Stone Age man. Because surely,

279

in the last analysis, that was who Bisby was. A Stone Age hunter who'd been to Cornell and who'd learned to fly a jet. No one who'd watched him in that little Eskimo settlement up on the ice cap could have seen him any other way. He and Stovin were 200 centuries apart— thank goodness. Because nobody, she reminded herself, can go back. We have to live where we are, and now. We have to change, but we can't go back. Maybe even Bisby had known that. He'd always behaved mysteriously, like a man who was going forward, who knew he had a destination but hadn't yet been told what that destination was.

She crossed the room. The small pile of possessions, which had been loaded from the sleds onto the Navy helicopter when it had picked them up so many weeks ago, had at last made its way through official channels and had been delivered that morning. There they were —the parka she had worn, the gloves, even the long spiked stick Valentina had used to prod the reindeer through the land of the Chukchi. One day, she thought, I'll go back to the Soviet Union and give that stick to Valentina—wherever she is by then. I really like her. She's good through and through. I hope to Heaven that she and Geny can settle down again somewhere over there and do some more good work.

She went on rummaging through the pile. There, under the fur-lined parka, lay Bisby's battered old biscuit tin. Thoughtfully, she picked it up. It had always been so much an intensely private part of Bisby's life, guarded by him with an almost religious zeal, that even now she felt guilty at opening it, as though she were peeking into a private diary. The lid came off easily. With an eerie feeling, she sorted through the contents.

A fox's skull . . . a birdskin . . . some shiny black feathers . . . an airplane switch. And a brown-covered book. It was titled *The Old Red Sandstone*, by Hugh Miller. She'd heard of Hugh Miller, of course. Most zoologists and geologists had. He'd been a self-taught geologist of the nineteenth century, originally a stonemason by trade. In his day, he'd had influence, opened a lot of doors in a lot of minds. She opened the book. Written across the flyleaf, in a firm yellowed hand, were the words: "To Arthur Inglis Bisby, with the affectionate esteem of his friend H.M. December 11, 1841." Bisby's great-grandfather, probably. It was strangely moving. This was the book which Bisby's own father, alone with his half-Eskimo son among an alien race, had perhaps read to the small boy. Part of what he had taught him. She riffled through the pages. They fell open, as though from long habit, at a page marked with a raven's feather. It was pencilled in the margin as if to emphasize its importance. Wondering, she read the passage.

As all the species of the past have died, so it is destined for all the species of the present to die . . . We now absolutely know, as geologists, not only that a beginning there was, but that the beginning was a comparatively recent event; and further, founding on the unvarying experience of the past, that the race, at least in its existing character and condition, is to have an end . . .

If only she'd known it, perhaps Bisby and she had spoken the same language, after all. This book had been important to him, very important. But why? Was this the destination he'd always seemed to be travelling to— a change in the "existing character and condition" of the human race? And what sort of vague destination was that, anyway? Because he hadn't made it, poor Bisby. He was out there now, somewhere under the Bering Strait. There were changes coming—new geography, new men, new leaders. But Bisby would never know of them. He hadn't reached his destination.

Inside her the child stirred again, and she caught her breath at the vigor of the movement. Be patient, she said, smiling. And whose child are you, my little love? You could be Stovin's. Or you could be Bisby's. She put the book back in the tin and closed the lid. Whether Bisby or Stovin was the father, the child now would be theirs—hers and Stovin's. But she'd keep the tin. Either way, one day, she thought, I'll give it to the child.

"I miss the *taiga*," said Valentina Soldatova, looking out from the window of the new bungalow to where three bulldozers were turning the raw red earth of Akademgorodok Dva, outside Simferopol, in the Crimea.

"There is no *taiga* left—not as we knew it," said Yevgeny Soldatov absently. He was sorting through a clip of computer printouts, occasionally making an entry by hand in an old-fashioned ledger on the table in front of him. Valentina looked back from the window. Geny looked a little better, she thought, though still very pale. Of course, he had lost a lot of weight, and in present conditions he was unlikely to regain it. He glanced up at her and smiled.

"There is no *taiga*, dear," he said again. "Just the ice cap. It's a new Siberia."

She walked across to him and put a hand on his shoulder. "I know, I know. There'll be *taiga* again, one day, but it will be not far north of here, where there's never been *taiga* before. And it will take a hundred years before it's developed in the way we knew it. I shall not see it."

He turned his head sideways and kissed her hand where it lay on his shoulder.

"We are lucky to see . . . what we see now," he said soberly, nodding toward the toiling bulldozers outside the window.

"Akademgorodok Two—who would have dreamed, a year ago, that we would be rebuilding our science city in the Crimea? We have food here. It's not lavish, but it's better than millions get elsewhere in the Soviet Union. We have shelter. Above all, my dear, we have work to do. We are the most fortunate people in our country."

She nodded. How Bisby—the old Bisby, at any rate—would have disapproved of the national priority given to Akademgorodok Two, she thought, remembering the brief clash they had had over scientific elitism—long, long ago, it seemed—in the old *dacha* outside Novosibirsk. She shuddered. Poor Novosibirsk! Poor people! What a struggle they had made. And what a defeat they had eventually suffered, even worse than the disasters that had progressively overwhelmed Moscow and the urban centers of the north.

"What are those printouts?" she asked, more to get the lost cities out of her mind than for any other reason.

"Volcanic activity, actual and projected," he said. "It's increasing; virtually the whole of the Kamchatka peninsula is in eruption. And the same in Alaska, in the Aleutians. The Americans say that the Katmai eruption is nearly twice as powerful as the one of 1912. I checked the records. In 1912 Katmai ejected seven cubic miles of pulverized rock into the atmosphere. That sort of interference with sunlight . . . well, its effects are unquantifiable in the present state of our knowledge. And climate is a balance, no more. I believe Stovin is right—that it is some underlying volcanic factor that has finally tipped the balance against us in an unstable climatic situation. If that is so, we could make computer models that will give us a picture—perhaps even a time scale. But we shall need more high-altitude sampling, and it's so difficult to get Rostov to give us the planes."

"Rostov knows how important we are, just as Moscow did," she said soothingly. "They're the same people, after all. In a year, maybe less, Akademgorodok Dva will be working fully. They know that science is vital."

"They know it, of course, but they're so obsessed with the 'how' to deal with the situation that they take no interest in the 'why,'" said Soldatov.

She smiled at him without speaking. That was hardly surprising, she thought. Maybe it was too late for the "why." Maybe it was just the "how" that mattered now, and for a long, long time to come. But that was the negation of the scientific spirit—Geny would never accept that. Bisby would have accepted it. Bisby . . . his bones were up there somewhere in that wilderness of ice. Bisby had been a great man for the "how." They were alive here, in Dva, because of Bisby. People who learned "how" were going to be important, especially in a country that had already suffered more than a million dead.

Geny was speaking again, "I know they try to help," he said. "But I shall never really understand the official mind—Volkov's, for instance."

"Have you seen him recently?"

Soldatov nodded. "He's working at the new Foreign Ministry building in Rostov, in Engels Street, right by the Temernitsky Bridge. He hasn't changed. The government is now in Rostov-on-Don instead of in Moscow, and everything's standing on its head, but that doesn't seem to affect Grigori Volkov. He lives by his rule book."

"He's a resilient man," said Valentina.

Soldatov laughed. "He's good with a fish spear, at any rate. I suppose KGB men make good hunters."

She looked at him in astonishment. "You knew that he was KGB?"

"Of course, it was obvious. And in any case, Bisby did

not neglect to tell me. But Grigori is not a bad fellow. A trifle naive, perhaps."

"I think that's what he thought about you," she said.

Soldatov began to file the printouts in an orange folder. "I shall need these for the hemisphere conference next week. What an irony . . . that we shall be going to the United States now, after all that has happened to us."

"Not simply to us," she said soberly.

"I shall be glad to see Stovin again," said Soldatov. "I have missed him—he was a friend. And his mind was like a springboard to me. Each time I touched it, I myself sprang higher. . . ."

"Geny Soldatov's coming, of course," said Brookman. With Stovin beside him, he was walking through the complex of the State Capitol at Sante Fe, which was being used as the temporary Congress of the United States. Here the second hemisphere conference was to be mounted in the following week. Electricians were still working both inside and outside, connecting wires for the temporary plastic booths where the telephone translators would sit, installing microphones and amplifiers. The whole area was alive with activity as security men from many nations made their own special arrangements, and reporters from hundreds of newspapers established communication lines.

It was raining again—part of the changed pattern of this late New Mexican spring, Stovin thought absently. He watched the toiling technicians.

"They've still got plenty to do, Mel."

The big man nodded. "Yes, it's going to be one hell of a rush. But I reckon the President's right—this is the best available place in the United States. And from his standpoint, nice and handy in Santa Fe. It'll be crowded but there'll be enough space—just. Mind, this'll be a pretty restricted conference compared with the last one—the one you didn't get to, Sto. Last time we had 700 delegates. We all talked a lot and decided damned little. But the situation's moved on a piece since then. This time, as we're the hosts again, the President's laid down some real ground rules—about thirty nations as principals. Any others who want to come will have observer status only. Principals can have a speaking delegation of five each, and that includes the head of state, if he or she is the principal delegate. Observer nations can send three each, and they can't speak unless invited by the chairman. And he's the United Nations Secretary-General."

Stovin did not reply. He seemed hardly to be listening. Brookman stole a glance at him as they walked across a perimeter road where three or four military Jeeps were the only traffic. Stovin looked gaunt . . . of course, it hadn't been so very long since that helicopter picked him up in Alaska. He, Brookman, had never been more surprised in his life when he got the news. Or more relieved. He put his hand on the younger man's shoulder.

"It's your moment, next week," he said. "It's you who speaks to the assembly first—the keynote speech. The President has insisted and Ledbester and the Canadians backed him. It's really something for you, Sto . . . a vindication of everything you've ever said. Not many of us get a chance like that."

"I suppose not," Stovin said. "But I keep thinking of what they're finding now they're digging out some of those northern cities. Did you see the figures for Chicago this morning? And Winnipeg? It's hard to take much pleasure in an intellectual self-justification."

Brookman nodded soberly, but his voice was cheerful and determined. "It's awful, I agree. But life's going to go on. Some people are going to be right about things, and some are going to be wrong. Now as ever. It's still damned important to get things right—more important than it's ever been, maybe."

Brookman looked up the wet, shining boulevard outside the Capitol complex. "Here's your bus—it looks mighty full." He held out his hand. "Listen . . . take care of yourself. You seem to have lost a lot of weight up there in the north."

Stovin smiled. "I was thinking the same about you."

Brookman patted his stomach. "It's those chemical meals. My waistline's never had this kind of treatment. Give it another month, and I'll be like a boy again. And then, men, guard your women."

"I will," promised Stovin, climbing up onto the step of the bus. But I didn't, did I? he said to himself as Brookman's figure receded down the boulevard. I didn't . . .

The thought of Bisby and Diane still hurt. And soon there would be the child. He would have to come to terms with that. But he loved Diane, and he believed that she loved him. That was a start—the only possible start. It would be Bisby's child, of course. Deep in his heart, he was sure of it. And Bisby's child, for both their sakes, would have to become his.

CHAPTER 26

One by one, they shuffled into their places in the Capitol's assembly chamber. There were more than 600 men and women present, and that represented barely a fifth of the applications made. Only 150 of those in the hall were speaking delegates; the bulk of the others who crowded into hastily erected communication booths or onto open benches were television, radio, and newspaper correspondents from all over the world, and the observers from certain states outside the immediate area of crisis.

The delegates of the thirty principals sat in a four-deep crescent-shaped formation that resembled a mini-United Nations. The President of the United States, as host, was at the center of the crescent, with his Secretaries of State and of the Interior on his right, and Stovin and Brookman on his left. Near him sat the Prime Minister of Great Britain, with Ledbester, the Foreign Secretary, and two others; the French President, grave and austere; the bespectacled Chairman of the Council of Ministers of the Soviet Union, ashen faced, assisted into his seat by Soldatov and the others of the Soviet delegation. Behind these front positions, the parties from East and West Germany were positioned side by side. Around them sat the representatives of Canada and Mexico, Italy, Austria, Switzerland, the Netherlands; Belgium, Spain, Poland, Czechoslovakia, and Hungary; Turkey and Yugoslavia; the Scandinavian countries of Sweden, Norway, Finland, and Denmark; Israel, Egypt, Saudi Arabia, and Iran. The delegation from India, notable for a lady in a purple sari, sat beside a sober-suited party from Japan. And, unexpected until the morning of the conference itself, on the extreme left-hand tip of the crescent was a last-minute group from the People's Republic of China, headed by a Deputy Premier and containing four scientists. Behind this mass of delegates were the observers from the southern hemisphere—already under climatic threat as they moved into their own winter.

It was an emergency conference, with none of the comfortable trimmings that professional conference delegates had been used to in more gracious days. There was a feeling of desperate urgency, and often of despair. One of those present, an elderly Englishman who had fought with the Royal Air Force during the Second World War, remembered it later as being rather like a briefing before a big night-bombing operation—full of people being told facts they had to know, but were disturbing and frightening to hear.

Many of the delegates—and this applied most of all to the Scandinavians—were tired to the point of exhaustion. The more elderly politicians and Government leaders showed the effects of weeks of scanty sleep and the strain of continuous decision and redecision. The scientists present were, in general, younger and were frequently engaged in animated discussions with their fellows, crossing easily the boundaries of nationality and the old alliance groupings. Thus Soldatov, before the delegations took their seats, was deep in conversation with Britain's Ledbester, while Stovin talked earnestly to a tall, thin Swedish scientist who had an international reputation for his work on volcanoes.

As soon as possible, the Secretary-General rose in his seat and called the President of the United States. The Soviet Chairman put on his translation earphones as the President began his short speech of welcome. It was polite, predictable stuff, and after a little the Russian carefully lifted one earphone and spoke to Soldatov, who sat on his right.

"The tall man, next to the President . . . that will be Dr. Stovin?"

"Yes, Comrade Chairman. And next to him is Dr. Brookman, the President's chief scientific adviser."

"Ah."

Soldatov looked down the crescent to where Stovin sat. He felt a stab of concern for the American, who looked isolated and suddenly vulnerable. What an ordeal . . . to make this first keynote address to such a meeting. He watched as the President finished and Stovin rose.

Soldatov was the only one of the Soviet delegation who spoke enough English to have listened to Stovin unaided, and of necessity he had been plugged into the translation circuit used by the others in his delegation. He fiddled for a moment with the volume control on his set. At last the voice of the woman translating Stovin's speech into Russian came through clearly.

". . . should emphasize that the conclusions I am about to outline have been reached in equal partnership with Dr. Yevgeny Soldatov, of the Soviet Institute of Climatology. . . ."

The Chairman turned briefly to Soldatov and nodded. Soldatov, his whole attention concentrated on Stovin, seemed hardly to notice.

". . . will wish to hear first about the extent of the advance of the snow during the winter we have just passed, and its projected extent in the winter that lies ahead.

"I . . . we . . . believe that there is no reason to expect the snow to move appreciably farther south in the northern hemisphere. The situation has stabilized, a fact well illustrated by the disappearance in recent weeks of the jet-stream aberrations popularly christened 'Dancers.' These phenomena were of a typical transitional kind, marking our entrance into a new Ice Age, and it is unlikely that they will occur again. Because the Ice Age is here. The snow will not go away. That is an appalling thing to have to say, but its implications must be faced. You can look at the snow map now and assume that those are approximately its new frontiers.

"What we can expect is that the snow will consolidate over winters to come in its present position, building glaciers from the ground up on the areas it has already seized. Where it has seized cities, for instance, they will quite rapidly, over the next few years, disappear totally beneath the ice.

"Thus the snow changes the maps which show the populations and the dwelling places of man. And eventually, of course, the physical maps of the earth's crust will have to be redrawn because the formation of glaciers and the immense weight of the snow upon the land will change river courses and create new landscapes . . . valleys and mountains. But those changes will not be a problem for the first generations of Ice Age Man. . . ."

A little shudder of whispered comment ran through the assembly at Stovin's first use of those three words.

Behind Brookman, the thin Scandinavian tightened his lips. If he's right, he thought, then quite soon, there will be no more Sweden, no more Norway, no more Finland. Maybe a Denmark, clinging to the edge of the snowline. Even the areas around Uppsala and Stockholm where we're still holding out—even those will go sometime in the next few winters. Maybe next winter. It seems unbelievable that I can sit here and hear a man say this. Countries cannot be rubbed out in such a way. Or can they? He thought of the sunlight and albedo reflectivity figures he had been given before he left Uppsala four days ago. They can, they can.

". . . the question arises, For how long? That is a question to which it is now possible to give a surprisingly precise answer. The prospect before us is, of a long-term decline in the sun's activity, which has been continuing for many years. This decline began some time ago to tip the narrow climatic balance on which we have lived for many thousands of years. The extent of this distortion was heightened both by newly active volcanoes producing sunlight-masking dust in the upper atmosphere, and by even the reduced sunlight that reaches the earth's surface being bounced back by the albedo—the reflectivity—of the new snows. In addition, over the coming centuries, the weight of snow of which I have spoken will set off further strain on the earth's crust and further volcanic activity, cutting off yet more sunlight. Thus even if solar activity begins to increase again in 100 or 200 years' time, the new Ice Age will stay. The new volcanoes will again hold down the balance.

"We believe that now the natural state of the Earth is that of an Ice Age. We only come out of an Ice Age when we get tiny changes in orbit so that we receive the maximum benefit from the summer sun. This happened last about 15,000 years ago, pulling us out of the Last Ice Age. But all it needed, as the orbital parameters changed over the past few centuries, was a series of little climatic and atmospheric nudges to push us back again. We've had those nudges, and the next time we shall get orbital conditions likely to be effective in nudging us back toward global warmth is a very long way away indeed. In a report which Dr. Soldatov and I made only a few weeks ago, we estimated 40,000 years. On our latest calculations, we were wrong. It is easy to start an Ice Age, but hard to stop it. We can expect this one to persist for a thousand centuries—100,000 years."

That's mind-stunning, but it's meaningless to most of us, thought Ledbester. I'm looking at a Britain that's going to be ice cap north of Birmingham, and it's a situation we have to deal with in the next year or two. And what's it going to be like *south* of Birmingham? Shall we be able to run industry, maintain large populations, so near the ice line? Or even above it? The Russians managed it, in the old Siberia. . . .

". . . So much for the theory, and the projection of the future. What of the present? It is a dreadful but not wholly hopeless picture.

"First, there are the unpredictable pockets above the snow line in many parts of the hemisphere where life has been able to go on, even though the surrounding snow has reached catastrophe proportions: Boston in the United States, Stockholm in Sweden, Cheshire in England, and a great deal, at present, of the Danish peninsula, for instance. These pockets may remain for some years, but I should anticipate that the one around Stockholm is unlikely to survive next winter. We have no idea of the exact timetable, year by year, of an Ice Age, though it should be possible, as we gather the right information, to make detailed local forecasts quite soon. But these pockets will give us some chance of reorganization. Such reorganization can only be limited in scope. The present population of the hemisphere cannot be maintained. It will, whatever we do, reduce itself in its own way. . . ."

He means death, thought the French President. There has been much death already, but there will be more. Yet in France, we are fortunate. We shall be cold, but viable —not under the ice. We are a large country, and our agriculture will suffer. We shall have room for refugees, but no food. But we shall be asked to take them . . . Swedes, Norwegians. Something will have to be done. Soon the horse trading will begin . . .

". . . as regards the Soviet Union, the immediate prospects are terrible. Only southern Russia, the Crimea, parts of the Caucasus, will be free of ice. Yet Russian technology has in the past shown that it can construct artificial environments in which men and women can live, work, and produce under the most difficult climatic conditions. Many of the rest of us will have much to learn from the Soviet Union.

"My country, the United States, may appear to be rather better off in the long term though—like Britain, Scandinavia, and the Soviet Union—we have suffered heavy casualties and disastrous dislocation in the short term. To our north, only British Columbia of the whole of Canada will remain sufficiently ice-free to allow large populations to live. Our own north, with its great cities, has either already vanished or will do so within a few years. And the climatic belt immediately below our new ice cap will be . . . well, something like much of Soviet Siberia used to be. Yet we have oil in Texas and other sources of oil in Mexico, for which we can trade . . ."

That's pretty well what Mel Brookman told me yesterday, thought the President. That we could still stay on top and dominate rebuilding in the Ice Age. Mexico, though . . . Mexico would be vital. Would Mexico be willing to join the United States? If we get short enough of oil, by golly, they're going to *have* to join.

" . . . in the southern hemisphere, where winter is now at hand, New Zealand faces a snow disaster like those we have already seen, while Australia will have to deal with a paradoxical situation of drought in some areas and snow in others. But it is in the southern hemisphere, and especially in South America, that a new focus of human civilization may appear. Brazil, for example, may well continue climatically much as before. Over the coming century, the world will develop a belt of equatorial civilized states, with fringe areas as far north as it is possible to maintain industrial life.

"I am not a politician, but that is perhaps not a disadvantage, since in the years to come, politicians are going to have to become scientists, and scientists must learn to understand politics. There will be great areas of the world where the two are inextricably mixed.

"Africa, for instance. The African states, such as Angola, Uganda, Tanzania, Zimbabwe, will have much to offer to the world. Yet without the help of their various sponsors of the past—the Soviet Union, America, and Europe—they are all too likely to fall into economic and political ruin, written off as efficient contributors to human civilization for many years. This is a danger that none of us here dare contemplate. There is not so much left, today, of our planet that we can afford ourselves the luxury of waste.

"Could it be, too, that the Great Powers of the recent past, still equipped with weapons of awesome destructive capability, could become embroiled in fighting in South America, or face blackmail from equatorial states?

"Could it be that Communist China"—he looked across at the delegation from the People's Republic—"at whose predicament, in the absence of adequate information we can only guess . . . could it be that the climatic pressures on eight hundred millions of Chinese will force them outward to a warmer part of the world? These are questions we shall face very, very soon, and they are vital for the future of man. And it is with the future of man that I am going to conclude . . ."

Here it comes, thought Brookman. Only Stovin could have proposed it, at this moment. And only Stovin's reputation, after today, may be strong enough to push it through. Because God knows what some of them are going to make of it in relation to what they face back in their own countries.

". . . some of you may know"—the President, looking up at Stovin's face, saw his mouth twist for a moment with a strangely bitter smile—"that I have had a unique opportunity, in recent weeks, of studying the abilities of men to live on the ice cap itself. I lived, briefly, with an Eskimo community, and the experience made me reexamine knowledge that is common currency among scientists all over the world. I saw things differently.

"Man was a child of the Ice Age. In evolutionary terms, survival of the fittest meant that in very bad weather conditions he had to learn speech, communication, architecture. These Ice Age men—of whom a handful of high-Arctic Eskimos are the lineal descendants —evolved the most magnificent hunting culture in human history, given the odds stacked against them. Even today, a high-Arctic Eskimo covers between 3,000 and 4,000 miles a year, on foot and with his dogs, over terrain where the rest of us would find it hard to move at all.

"Ice Age Man produced snowhouses—circular buildings made of snow blocks cut in spiral tiers, each supporting the exact weight of its neighbor. And that was thousands of years before the Romans built the Colosseum. And he developed his powers of memory and deduction—an Ice Age hunter had to know as much about

292

his territory as a modern university professor about his subject. Everything was set for human evolution, *on the ice cap,* to take its course. And what happened?

"The Interglacial came—an unexpected nudge that gave us 15,000 warm years. It got warm. We developed agriculture, permanent settlements, cities, states, possessions, armies and navies to defend them, international politics to maintain them. We got Paris and London and Moscow and Los Angeles. Eventually we got the H-bomb.

"And we developed a certain kind of civilization—what I might call a Roman kind. Baths, central heating, fossil fuels, labor-saving devices. We plundered the planet to heat our homes, pulp our paper, drive our vehicles. We looked back on the Stone Age and congratulated ourselves that we'd advanced from there.

"We *had* advanced, of course. But down a blind alley. We evolved a human being and a system of living for an interglacial situation. And now the Interglacial is ended, and we're stuck down our blind alley.

"If the old Ice Age had lasted, more than 15,000 years ago, we would have evolved a different type of man by now. His base starting point would have been the modern, Stone Age desert dweller. And as the Ice Age persisted, he would have become a super-Eskimo, or a super-desert-dweller, comfortable in conditions in which modern civilized man would die. And, of course, he would not have been in trouble today.

"Think of what he might have developed, as his Ice Age culture became more and more advanced—especially since it was a hunting culture. Telepathy, for sure. And almost certainly, the ability to communicate with animals. A mass of extrasensory perceptions—even teleporting, the power to move objects without machinery, but with the mind alone. Evolution would have operated on Ice Age Man just as it did inexorably on Interglacial Man.

"It was the Interglacial that betrayed us. It betrayed other animals, too—those of you who are scientists and have read the Hilder Report will know that I am speaking of wolves. Wolves themselves changed their patterns of behavior in the Interglacial, to prey on smaller animals and to meet the competition of men. So they developed smaller, more mobile, less vulnerable groups, changed their organization, went up a blind alley. Now, as the Hilder Report makes clear, they're beginning to change back, faster than we are. Bigger packs, a different social order. Who knows what will happen to wolves in 100,000 years?"

Brookman watched Stovin carefully. He had never seen him so excited. Everyone in the assembly was listening with concentrated attention. Stovin paused for a moment and sipped some water before he went on.

"We cannot simply live around the equator, fighting for space. That will be the end of *Homo sapiens*. We need a new *Homo sapiens* . . . one who can live in the ice, build civilization, an undreamed-of civilization, in the ice. We might call him *Homo sapiens Hibernus*. Winter Man. We can begin to build Winter Man . . . now."

Again that sudden little shiver of simultaneously whispered comment ran through the assembly. Stovin was plunging on.

"We need to work on the long-term future of the human race. I realize that to all of you, facing death and hunger and physical misery in stricken countries, what I am saying will seem too distant a prospect to occupy your minds now. *But we must not be caught again.* Whatever our religion, or the lack of it, whatever we believe or do not believe, every one of us in this assembly knows that without a long-term future for our children and our children's children and their children after them, human existence is pointless.

"I propose that a considerable and growing proportion of scientific resources should be devoted to the possibilities of accelerating the development of *Homo sapiens Hibernus*. I have the permission of the President of the United States"—he looked down at the man beside him—"to tell you that we in this country are establishing, as of now, an Institute of Winter Man, to be funded from Federal monies, and to be established in Connecticut above the snow line, administered by my friend Dr. Melvin Brookman, head of the former Connecticut Institute of Technology. I shall work there myself for the rest of my life.

"The Institute will be open to all; its work and its conclusions will be international property. But, of course, it cannot work alone. We fervently hope that other countries will establish similar centers of study, research, and action. The Soviet Union, with its unequalled experience of some of the problems we shall face, would be a vital partner. And speaking purely personally, I can think of no one beside whom I would rather work than my friend Yevgeny

Soldatov, to whom I—all of us—owe so much. There is a titanic amount of work ahead of us all. We should begin immediately, in spite of our seemingly overwhelming short-term problems. And it is a curious thing about science . . . however abstruse or remote research may seem to be, it has a habit of rubbing off, eventually, somewhere remarkably close to the factory bench and the kitchen sink, and the farmer's field.

"You have heard me for one hour of this crucial year. In the months ahead, as you have seen, I can see nought for your comfort. But in the long years to come, there is still hope. . . ."

They stood and applauded him for three minutes. Brookman shook him by the hand. Well, it was Stovin's hour, and he'd earned it. Those men and women out there . . . they were in despair and they'd needed a prophet. But how long, thought Brookman, before the brief emotion subsides and the squabbling begins again? Not everybody thinks like Stovin.

In his room at the Santa Fe White House, the President got tiredly into bed and opened, as he always did, his Bible. That was a fine speech by Stovin. First speech he'd ever made, no doubt, to an audience of that size. But passionate conviction always showed through. Look at Winston Churchill. *Homo sapiens Hibernus* . . . well, I shan't live to see him. If he ever arrives. There are a lot of "ifs" . . . but there've always been a lot of "ifs" in the history of man. As long as he struggles, there's still a chance. Nevertheless, he's still only a little animal in a limitless universe. The President looked down at his Bible. It was open at the Book of Job. He put on his spectacles and began to read what God had said, long ago, to man.

Where wast thou when I laid the foundations
of the earth?

Epilogue

The leader of the wolf pack stood beside the wreck of the lone tower, where it thrust in a jumble of ice-encased masonry forty feet above the snow plateau. His forelegs were braced against the downward pull of the slope along the ridge. Below him, in the last glimmers of daylight, six black dots were moving in the lee of the high ground. Men . . .

The wolf's yellow eyes absorbed the party and its numbers. He turned and padded silently back down the reverse side of the slope to where his small pack, about forty strong, lay waiting in the snow. He held his tail out straight, horizontal with the ground, as he trotted past them to the end of the escarpment. The men were nearer now, and the wolf could distinguish individuals. But he made no new move, gave no signal, as he continued to trot forward.

Behind him, the forty wolves now stretched in line, single file, over more than a quarter of a mile. At intervals they stopped obediently as the leader made his way up to some higher piece of ground to watch. But each time he came down with his tail in the same position. The wolves kept their distance, 500 yards out on the flank of the men . . .

The leader of the men put back his binoculars into the special pocket at his chest. He turned and beckoned to the other five. Like him, they were clad in furs. He and the three women carried rifles; the other two men hauled a light sled.

"Are they hunting?" asked the girl beside him.

He shook his head. "No, they're watching," he said. "They'll not try anything. They've learned what happens when they do."

Her gloved hand grasped his arm. She tapped her rifle.

"Shouldn't we . . . well, give them something to think about?"

"No, that's against Institute instructions, unless they attack. And they won't. We're an Alpha party, and we'd drop thirty of them in the first hundred yards. Wolves know that a party of six is always an Alpha party, and they know what happens when they tackle one. They'll watch, but they'll leave us alone."

"Maybe we should make camp," said one of the men with the sled. "Easier to keep an eye on them from camp."

"No," said the leader again. "We've got ten more miles on today's program. A little pack of wolves won't stop us."

The six moved on north as Sears Tower receded into the darkness. Fourteen hundred feet below them, Chicago—already buried for almost thirty years—lay in a tomb that could not be opened for a thousand centuries.

I hope I'm right, thought the leader, looking out to the flank where the distant line of wolves kept shadowy, cautious station. I think it's what my father would have done.

Bestsellers from BALLANTINE

No one who buys it,
survives it.

THE HOUSE NEXT DOOR

A terrifying novel
by
Anne Rivers Siddons

29330 $2.50

10   **BALLANTINE BOOKS**   G-1c